The Widows' Adventures

The Widows' Adventures

CHARLES DICKINSON

AVON BOOKS ◆ NEW YORK

AVON BOOKS
A division of
The Hearst Corporation
105 Madison Avenue
New York, New York 10016

Copyright © 1989 by Charles Dickinson
Front cover art by David Shannon
Inside cover author photograph by Miriam Berkley
Published by arrangement with the author
Library of Congress Catalog Card Number: 89-30626
ISBN: 0-380-70847-7

Published in hardcover by William Morrow and Company, Inc.; for information address Permissions Department, William Morrow and Company, Inc., 105 Madison Avenue, New York, New York 10016.

First Avon Books Trade Printing: September 1990

AVON TRADEMARK REG. U.S. PAT. OFF. AND IN OTHER COUNTRIES, MARCA REGISTRADA, HECHO EN U.S.A.

Printed in the U.S.A.

OPM 10 9 8 7 6 5 4 3 2

For Donna and Casey and Peter Venkman

In memory
Katherine Larson Forrester
    and
Ethel Forrester Minshall

Considerable gratitude is owed to the following people for their assistance in the writing of this novel: Maria Guarnaschelli, Robin Straus, Arlene Lee, Tom McNamee, F. Scott Hayner, Rosalind Rossi, Derek Ragona, and Burt Constable.

CONTENTS

PROLOGUE

◆ ─────────────────────────────

Helene

INA asks me what I see and I have to be honest: I see nothing. She asks me what color my blindness takes and I find that a curious question. I am simply blind.

I tell her the color I miss most is that vivid crimson cloud of blood filling my eyeballs. That gorgeous phenomenon was the first serious indication that I would one day be blind as a bat. Proliferative retinopathy. Deterioration of the blood vessels in my retinas caused by diabetes. The blood gushed in; I imagined I could hear it filling my eyes like buckets. But it was fluid into fluid, blood into vitreous humor, silent as an injection of dye.

I was speaking to Rudy at the time, and I remember he waited several minutes after I stopped speaking in midsentence before he asked me to continue. He was a trifle peeved by my announcement that all I could see was a scarlet cloud, that yet another trip to the hospital was required.

Ina asks me to tell her about the last thing I saw. That is difficult to say, because my eyesight did not go like a light being snapped off, but leaked away a smidgen at a time. Long ago, my doctor looked deep into my eyes and reported seeing tiny red dots in there. A bad sign, in his opinion. Capillary microaneurysms, they were called. Foreshadowing. Then came that first beautiful, terrifying cloud of blood. The clouds went away, and returned, and went away again. But they always returned, and finally they remained.

When Ina asks what was the last thing I saw, I tell her it was Rudy. It is Rudy who takes up the most space in my memory. He never forgave me my diabetes, all the planning, the expense (most of all, he never forgave the expense), and the sheer inconvenience it entailed. In granting my requests to prepare my morning and evening shots or to help test my urine, his manner was brusque and faintly disgusted. He slammed doors when I was trying to rest. He pestered my sleep with questions about the locations of household items. He had no interest in me if I was not healthy.

I talked him through the steps of preparing dinner because the stove frightened me now that I was blind. Even when it wasn't turned on I felt its presence like a patient enemy, just as I feared candles, matches, cigarettes (I'd asked Rudy to smoke only at work; imagine his chagrin). Carving knives, peelers, meat forks, they terrified me with images of gashes and punctures. Proliferative hemorrhaging; death by leaking.

Rudy proved to be an able cook. He helped me keep track of my diet, counting calories, carbohydrates, scouting for the deadly sugar that seemed an element of everything that went in my mouth, coming in so many unexpected forms. He waited outside the bathroom while I urinated in a cup, then accepted the warm offering, dipped the TesTape, and reported the color. He did all this with an impassive air of disgust, a nonjudgmental loathing.

I would try to draw Rudy into conversation, but Rudy was not a conversationalist. I would work back through my memories of the time since he had left for work that morning. I sought a funny story or an interesting scrap of news from the TV. Something to throw into the quiet. But I rarely found anything to say. The only people I talked to were Ina (and, through her, Vincent) and Amanda. Ina's amusements were tainted in Rudy's eyes by her drinking. Amanda, then nearing forty, without a husband, was a sore point with her father. Vincent, who had money, was another constant irritant to my husband.

So we sat without saying much.

"Tell me what happened at work today," I said.

"What happened at work today? Once again, I didn't make enough money."

"We're doing all right," I said gently. A small pain of helplessness took root in my stomach; the nervous, helpless ache of being a burden. "No kids to raise. The house in good shape. And paid for," I said, running through the list I kept in my head. "We aren't begging."

"I'd like to get to a point a little more comfortable than 'not begging,' " he said. "At least before I die."

"You'll outlive all of us," I said, desperate to cheer him up. "Then you can live the carefree bachelor life. A room to yourself. You can smoke. Eat bad food, whatever you want. You won't have to test someone's pee every day."

He made the same financial complaint every day that we were together. He might have griped about the cost of the room on our wedding night, but I don't remember. We had bought our house from Vincent. The transaction was awkward in that Rudy was ashamed to be getting the money from his lifelong friend and brother-in-law; and he was outraged that Vincent possessed that amount of money to lend.

The purchase price of our house, which we had been renting for four years at $37.50 per month, was $15,500. My diabetes had been diagnosed our first summer there; I used glass syringes then. But my eyesight was crystalline. Amanda was just walking. I remember her cautious scaling of the steps up to Vincent and Ina's house on the day we signed the papers. Annie was Amanda's age, a source of competition between the moms. Ina was pregnant with Ray. When she came to the door she looked robust and lovely.

Rudy wore a tie, though I assured him it wasn't necessary. But Vincent also was wearing a tie and I was proud of my husband for having correctly read the ceremonial gravity of the event. Speaking primarily to Rudy, with an infrequent shift of his eyes toward me, Vincent explained that he had completed the purchase of our house earlier that day, and we would buy it from him over a period of time yet to be determined.

"I think we agreed on five hundred for your down payment," said Vincent.

Rudy took a folded green check from his wallet. He had written it, complaining, just before we left the house.

Vincent took the check without a glance and slid it under a paperweight, a balanced droplet of glass.

"How much would you be comfortable paying each month?" Vincent asked, his tone implying that the amount was none of his business, but he had to ask.

"I'm not sure," Rudy said.

"Would you be comfortable with seventy-five dollars per month?"

"Seventy-five," Rudy repeated.

"Yes," Vincent continued. He swiveled a sheet of paper toward Rudy that contained a precise column of typed numbers. "Seventy-five dollars per month . . . see? . . . for twelve months. That's nine hundred dollars per year for thirty years. Standard mortgage length. You'd borrow fifteen thousand dollars and pay back twenty-seven thousand dollars."

"Twelve thousand more than I'm borrowing?" Rudy said incredulously.

"Interest, Rudy," Vincent said. "Scandalously low, too, I might add. No bank would ever write a mortgage on these terms."

On our way home, Rudy said, "It is beyond me how Vincent sleeps at night knowing he is charging twelve thousand dollars interest on a loan he made to his own family. His oldest friend! The woman he might have married!"

"It's only three in the afternoon, dear," I said. "Maybe he'll have trouble sleeping tonight."

"Why does he have to make money on everything?"

"He sells real estate. It's his business," I said, though I too had been put off by the cool calculation of the deal, the way Vincent had all the figures typed and ready.

Rudy did not speak to Vincent for more than a year. This made our frequent social calls almost impossible to bear. At first, Rudy used our visits to the Lockwood home to present—with great ostentation and embarrassment for everyone but himself—the month's mortgage payment. Rudy took longer to write that check than he took to earn the money to cover it. When I complained about this petty ritual he began mailing the money to Vincent. But for a year he would not respond to any of Vincent's questions, would not counter any of Vincent's opinions, would not even pass the pepper if Vincent asked for it. Rudy let his silence sit over our gatherings like a condemnation. Inevitably Vincent stopped including Rudy in his sphere of conversation; he was not one to pursue a cold lead, someone in no mood to buy.

Rudy was listening carefully to Vincent, however, and memorizing his responses, which he revealed to me as we walked home at evening's end.

"What the hell does he mean, 'How's every little thing at work?'? He's just afraid he won't get his seventy-five bucks every month if my job goes bust. He's got an opinion about everything: Truman, Korea, the Cubs, the Sox, all the kids being born, the new cars. Nobody with any brains has so many goddamned opinions. He's got to have them, though. It's good for business. An opinion for every occasion. As many opinions as he needs to make a sale. And where does he get off turning his chair so his back's to me? What a rude ass. Next time, you go alone. You want to visit your sister—do it when I'm at work. I'm tired of listening to that guy flap his jaws."

"If anyone is rude, it's you," I said. "As for going by myself—fine. You embarrass me. Stay home. It will save on a sitter."

I struck off smartly, leaving him behind. It was the end of us, I realized much later. My words had transported our marriage to a strange level it would not survive.

Rudy did not move until I was a half-block ahead. Then he closed the gap between us almost at a run. His rage was something new, almost intriguing; an interesting twist in our life together. When he was upon me I ducked to the side to avoid the blow I sensed more than saw coming out of the darkness. His open hand caught me on the shoulder. I fell to one knee, cracking my other shoulder painfully against a white slat fence. Someone on the porch of the house stood up and shouted, "Hey! Stop that!"

But Rudy didn't hear and he slapped me rather ludicrously on the top of my head. Some of the blow was absorbed by my hair, but the weight of his wedding ring bore through this cushion and cracked against my skull. My eyes teared with pain. A door slammed. A light went on behind me. "We're calling the police, you animal!" screamed a woman.

I was prepared to sit there on the sidewalk, my back against the fence, until the police arrived. Rudy had moved into the shadows. It occurred to me then that I probably knew the woman on the porch. I got to my feet and moved sideways to keep my face hidden from my witness. "Don't go with him, honey," the woman called. "You can do better!"

But I didn't think I could. Or I didn't have the energy to find out. I followed my husband home.

The two blows remained our secret, a source of embarrassment and disbelief. Rudy was sweet for a long period of time. At Christmas he gave me a full-length lavender velvet robe lined with white silk; the luxurious feel of it against my skin was staggering. We made love in the afternoon while Amanda napped and I rode eagerly on him wearing only my robe, keeping both of us warm with his gift to me.

Ina and Vincent visited in the evening, and after my dinner had been eaten I excused myself, then returned wearing the new robe over my clothes. The children, exhausted from the day's expectations and realities, ignored me, but Ina and Vincent were enthusiastic in their appreciation.

"It's beautiful," Vincent assured me.

"Breathtaking," Ina added.

And Rudy, from his chair by the tree, a strand of fallen tinsel twinkling in his hair, said, "Vince, that robe cost me seventy-eight dollars. Seventy-eight dollars!"

I was stunned by the price. (Vincent whistled appreciatively; Ina murmured, "My.") Where had the money come from? What would we do without down the line to pay for my robe?

And something else: Rudy had spoken to Vincent.

I excused myself again and hung the robe in my closet. The mystery of its richness was gone, and with that a part of its allure. I owned a seventy-eight-dollar robe. The expense was ludicrous, wasteful.

At eleven o'clock I helped Amanda to bed and spent longer than necessary tucking her in, so that when I emerged from her

dark bedroom into the hall light and from there into the shadowy
hushed light of the front room, I recognized the sleepy silence
that signaled the death of a party. Vincent and Ina left soon after,
Annie draped over her father's shoulder like an extra coat, baby
Ray wrapped like a parcel of laundry against the cold.

I hurried to gather up the plates, cups, and forks we'd used
that night. I got down on my knees to work at a stain ground
into the carpet. When Rudy appeared out of the corner of my
vision, I got up and moved away. I was so tired, so anxious to
sleep, but my brain was driven by a nervous desire to keep clear
of my husband.

"When I told them the price, you looked like you were disappointed," Rudy said. "Seventy-eight bucks for a bathrobe isn't
enough for you?"

"It's too much," I said. "And how much it costs isn't any of
their business, either."

"Vince tells me the price of everything he buys," Rudy said.
"His car. His clothes. His grocery bills. The beer Ina drinks.
Only the best for the Lockwoods."

He would hit me soon, I understood; the realization came
clearly to me, almost like a voice from the next room, the voice
of one who could see into the future.

I scraped the plates into a bag of garbage, and when I was
finished I carried the bag outside. I felt certain Rudy was watching
me cross the yard to the garage. But he was not in the window
or the door when I turned back. I knew he was waiting for an
answer, but I refused to say anything. Though I easily could have
said: Vincent never mentions money. (Yet what if there was a
secret vulgar side to Vincent, a way he had with vulgar men,
anything for a sale?)

My one concern was to keep moving. I bumped the back
door locked with my hip, and passed him nearly at a run, saying,
"Get the light, please." Ducking clear of him, hurrying down
the hall, I tried to move and listen for him at the same time. I
unplugged the Christmas tree lights and when they were off I
felt better, less inclined to think everything was bound to turn
out badly.

He was waiting for me in the hall. The kitchen light was still on. He now stood at the bottom of the stairs, one foot on the floor, the other on the second step, blocking my escape.

"I thought the robe would make you happy," he said.

"It did."

"But not for long."

"I put it on to show them—without you asking me to," I said. "I was proud of it. I was proud of you. And then you had to go and shout out the price."

"It was important that they knew."

"No it wasn't."

"To me, it was," he said, poking his chest.

"Then you bought it for the wrong reason," I said, and I tried to dart past him, catch him unawares. I went up two steps, nearly to the landing, and then I saw Amanda standing at the top of the stairs just as Rudy's hand rang down against the side of my head.

A fierce light accompanied the blow, like a flare in my skull. I was most concerned about getting to Amanda and explaining to her that this was not her father hitting me, but rather a stranger within her father whom with practice and careful maneuvering we could avoid encountering again.

He hit me a second time, open-handed, across the back of my head and I rocked forward into the scratchy carpet covering the stairs. Amanda screamed above me. I heard Rudy suck in his breath and I knew he hadn't seen her there.

"Mandy," he whispered.

She screamed again. Blood ran from my nose in a watery thread. Only four blows over a span of months, and now blood had been drawn. "It's all right, sweetheart," I said to her. "I'll be up to tuck you back in."

But Amanda didn't budge. She was crying, but she also seemed to understand that her witnessing presence was in my best interests. I loved her so much then. In later years when I was a blind burden and her father was gone, when we were no longer close, I forgave Amanda for many small insensitivities out of gratitude for that saving moment on the stairs.

♦ ♦ ♦

WERE I listening to a woman tell a story such as mine, I would have two questions for her: How often did he hit you, and did he hit you when you were blind?

Rudy struck me many times, but the Christmas nosebleed was the only outwardly apparent wound I ever sustained. He was scrupulous in his use of the open hand, swinging it like a wide board. And his violence had a quick release, venting itself after only two or three blows. For all of these reasons I might have considered myself fortunate.

I had been blind for nearly two months before he hit me when I was blind. The argument was of course about money, and we were alone in the kitchen on a summer evening. We had watched the news on TV and then come into the kitchen to make supper. Ina and Vincent were expected later and Rudy began to complain that we had had them over to our house three times in a row without our being invited there.

"They're our family," I said. "You don't keep track of that sort of thing with your family."

"I do," he said. "It's not cheap having them over. Your sister drinks our beer like it's tap water."

"It's easier for me here," I said. "I know my way around."

"If you'd get out some, you'd be more confident in finding your way," he said.

"Little by little I'm getting out," I said, wondering if I was looking directly at him, if my words were striking him in the face. "And no more remarks about my sister."

I moved my face to catch a breeze coming in over the kitchen sink. He won't hit me when I'm blind, I thought. But I listened to the room at my back. I could picture every inch of the space, the high-ceilinged airiness, the pockets of appliance heat, and Rudy's glowering presence at the table.

"What can I say? She drinks beer to a serious extent. I love her," Rudy said, "but facts are facts."

"Just leave her alone."

"If she'd leave a little to help pay her tab, I would."

I heard his chair scrape against the floor, heard him step close to me. I decided later that he must have for quite some time been weighing the question of hitting me now that I was blind. Perhaps he didn't understand to what level he would sink if he beat his blind wife; was it a manageable level, a level that would allow him to view at least certain aspects of his life with some self-respect?

"Leave her alone," I said, nearly in a whisper, curious myself.

He let me have it, tentatively the first time, then with increasing gusto on the two succeeding blows, so that the colorless room of my blindness began to spin, and Rudy helped me to my feet like a perfect gentleman.

He was dead within a year.

PART ONE

◆ ————————————————————————————

Dangerous Boys

INA awoke for the second time that morning with a slip of a headache and a certain scandalous fatigue. She had been up late the night before drinking Old Style and reading magazines, the papers, a book, maps, junk mail. Helene had telephoned at her customary early hour. The morning call required that Ina set her alarm so that she was awake and somewhat alert to whatever her sister wanted. Usually it was nothing. After Rudy died, Ina spent time helping Helene overcome her fear of cooking and taught her all over again how to use the stove. She turned on the burners and held her sister's hand above them so she could feel the waves of heat pushing up at her. She put Helene's fingers on all the knobs, and Helene informed her testily that she remembered quite clearly, thank you, the function of each control. She could give herself her shot and put together her meals. She knew what foods to avoid, how much she could eat of something she wasn't supposed to eat. She could take care of herself but preferred not to. So she telephoned Ina every morning to reestablish her connection with her sister, as if Ina might have taken some offense overnight and decided never to speak to her again. She wanted to be sure she wasn't alone. Her sister's sleepy voice placed her firmly back in the world. Helene thus reassured, they made a date for later in the day, to go to the Jewel.

And having done what was required of her Ina was free for a time. So she went back to sleep for an hour. And when she awoke again she felt the desire to go fishing. This was Vincent prodding her memory. She had been aware lately of a tempering of her mourning. The intervals between moments of grieving had expanded so that she sometimes found herself in the morning being unable to recall the last time she had thought about him. She took this as a healthy sign, but a lonely one as well, for even after his death Vincent remained a companion of wrenching complexity and dimension. She consulted him as often as she had when he was alive: about matters of life, how to manage Helene, what to do with the time left to her. His answers came as clearly as if he were standing behind her, whispering in her ear.

But awakening that morning with no recollection of thinking about him fresher than a half-day old, she felt too successful at putting him behind her, as if a certain forgetful loneliness were preferable to constant, memorable grieving.

So she would go fishing.

They lived across the street from the north branch of the Chicago River, and fishing was the only activity to interest Vincent that could be classified as a sport. And only then, Rudy claimed, because fishing produced something Vincent could sell.

To reach the river she would have to go down concrete stairs built in the year she was born. These steps were rounded with wear, stones falling out of the mix, the pipe bannisters rusting where declarations of love had been gouged in the paint. She had run down the steps, tripped down them, paused on them to be kissed: by Vincent, by others. She was now almost seventy years old, with lovely blue eyes in a sagging face, and she could afford to lose a pound or two, but a long time ago she had been a beautiful girl. At the foot of the stairway was a small cement landing with a deliciously fragile privacy. The boldest lovers used the space to clutch at each other while listening for footsteps. Ina and Vincent had kissed there, and Vincent had pleaded to do more, and touched her breast as incentive. But she had refused, an absence of courage she now regretted.

The water was the color of packed shadows. Some days it did not seem like water so much as thick brown silk, a river of ladies' nylons. The bait Vincent used was a shred of bacon or a pinched ball of store bread. Catfish and carp, and the occasional gar, were all he ever caught. Vincent called carp crap, the big, silvery sluggards who ate the hook and whatever was aboard, and then were dragged without a hint of resistance to the foot of the landing. Vincent employed a wicked gaff Rudy had made to haul the fish from the water. He sold the carp to those less fortunate. Ina sampled a bite once, and even before the toxins injected into that water by industry and humanity were common knowledge, something in the taste of the fish struck her as evil.

Gar were just too strange; needle-nosed, spine-thin, they radiated an aura of bad luck and were cut loose immediately, the hook sacrificed.

Catfish she loved. They were blandly delicious, and went perfectly with buttered corn on the cob, fruit balls in juice, and cold beer. Catfish had a spirit when hooked that promised a fight. The whiskers that rimmed their struggling mouths were like the eyes of potatoes gone wild in the dark. But their appearances at the end of the line grew more infrequent until catching one was an event, and the last one Ina remembered landing was a fat grandfather cat hooked by Ray when he was on the edge of adolescence, and he had hated that his father had had to come to the rescue to get the creature out of the water and onto the landing.

The river was a place to go. A place where things were out of sight, where there was the possibility of being alone when life at the top of the stairs pressed in. Vincent took Ray there to tell him about sex. Ina had given Annie the same news at the kitchen table.

Vincent often went to the river alone, taking only a pole and a piece of bread, returning in an hour or so without the bread. They went there as a family, with Helene and Rudy and Amanda, because on the hottest nights it felt a degree cooler down there shooing bugs in the dark, the lines falling out of sight before they entered the water.

But then the river landing became inhabited by people of vague repute, nonfishermen, drinkers of hard liquor, individuals who seemed to appear without benefit of the stairs, by-products of what was going bad in the water. Finally she had to forbid her children to play on the stairs or to go down to the landing. She suspected Annie obeyed her, but she knew Ray had a taste for unsanctioned excitement and she saw him come up from the stairs in the dark with the other boys and race across the street until attaining the safety of his yard, while his friends dispersed like bugs caught in the light. She asked Vincent to speak to Ray, and perhaps he did, but Vincent possessed a faith in his son that was unswerving, and doubted that a few illicit trips to the river would significantly warp the basic perfection of Ray's nature.

Vincent's tackle box was in the front closet. Ina lugged it to the kitchen table. The box was constructed of khaki-colored steel and secured with a lock of considerable resolve, a lock to which Ina had no key.

She climbed the stairs to the bedroom and lay down on her bed. She brought the phone from the night table and put it on her stomach. She liked to call Ray and Annie in the morning. With the time difference, she could usually reach them before they left home for the day.

Ray's number rang. He was her baby. An inch shorter than Vincent, with a little weight problem. He had never married.

"Ray here."

"It's me."

"I was thinking about you," he said brightly.

"You were not."

"I was! I had a premonition you'd call."

"You did not!"

"I did! Why won't you ever believe me when I tell you something?"

"What am I calling about, then?" she asked.

"It wasn't that detailed a premonition, sweetheart," Ray said, and Ina felt the little *ting* of disappointment that was a mother's companion.

"Why aren't you at work?"

"It's only seven forty-five here," Ray said. "The sun is barely up. The freeways are barely jammed."

"Don's been at work for an hour."

"Don's a fast-tracker," Ray said. "I'm merely a laundry czar."

"Where did Daddy keep the key to his tackle box?" Ina asked.

"Oh—I had a premonition you were going to ask me that!"

"Smarty. You did not."

"I did. A dream: fish, key, lures, Mom."

"You're a mean son. Do you remember?"

"Why do you want to know?"

"I thought I might go fishing," Ina said.

Ray said nothing.

"I'm not senile. You're thinking that, but I'm not."

"That river is pure carcinogens, Mom."

"I'll be long gone by the time the cancer grows."

"Please don't. For me?"

A faint stain, still damp, lay to her right in the bedding, remnants of a spilled glass of beer from the night before. She shifted her leg and felt the coolness bleed through her nightgown to touch her thigh.

"Besides, that is no place for you to go. It's full of perverts," Ray said vehemently.

"It's not so bad. The sun is out."

"It doesn't reach down there," Ray said. "Please don't."

"Without that key, I won't be able to."

"Good. Then I won't tell you."

"Do you know?"

"I won't tell you," Ray said.

"This is your mother—"

"I'm opening another store," he said.

Ina hesitated, proud of her son, but irritated at being patronized. "Tell me where the key is, then I'll take an interest in your business," she said.

She heard Ray sigh. "I really don't know, Mom."

"All right. How many is that now?"

"Eleven, in all. Nine here, one in Boulder, one there."

"My cleaning giant," she said fondly.

"Everyone's clothes get dirty."

"Where's the new one?"

"Right by UCLA," Ray said. "It could do more business than the other ten combined."

"That's my boy."

"Thanks, dear," he said. "But now I've got to get out in it."

"No key?"

"Try the board in the garage. Remember it? That's where I'd look, anyway," he said. "But if you find it, promise me you won't use it."

She put the phone down, folded her hands over it, then lifted it and dialed Annie, who lived within miles of Ray but never saw him. Annie's housekeeper answered.

"Bixler residence, to whom do you wish to speak?"

"Annie, please."

"Momento."

Her daughter came on the line, sounding out of breath.

"It's me," Ina said.

"Mom. Jesus. What a surprise," Annie said. "But I can't talk now. I've got tennis—and I overslept."

"Just one thing. Where did Daddy keep the key to his tackle box?"

"His tackle box? I don't know. You aren't going fishing."

"I was getting blue. I thought a little fishing might cheer me up."

"At the river?"

"Of course, dear."

"It's not safe there. You told me so yourself ages ago. It can only have gotten worse. It's not safe anywhere around there anymore."

"Annie, that's an absurd California prejudice," Ina said. "My neighborhood is fine. Where Helene lives—that frightens me a little. But this part of town is still quite nice."

"I've got to run," Annie said.

"Let me talk to Meg."

"Not home. School."

"Has she discovered boys?"

"She won't tell me," Annie said. "She's almost fifteen, after all. That disinterest in the opposite sex is feigned."

"What's she doing tonight?" Ina asked. She wanted something she could hold in her memory; the occasional school picture that arrived in the mail seemed dated even as it fell from the envelope.

"Nothing specific. She's very studious. She has a friend she goes down to see," Annie said. "Her name is Katy. They're very tight. Jesus, Mom, I'm late."

"Invite me out. I miss my girl."

"You're always invited," her daughter said with an abrupt enthusiasm that Ina did not trust. "A standing invitation."

"Have Don invite me."

"Don? Don loves you. He's too busy to show it, that's all. Come out anytime. Gotta go. Love. Bye."

She put the phone down, abruptly sad. Her children in a rush out in Los Angeles, Vincent slipping from her memory. Her heart was in pieces for just the few moments she took to doze off.

When she awoke she wanted to go to the river more than ever; to prove that her children were wrong in their estimation of her helplessness. She sat on the side of the bed through a brief spell of dizziness. She went to the bathroom, then patted cold water on her face as she bent over the sink. Dots of dried soap speckled the mirror and faucet and struck her as slovenly. With a piece of toilet paper she wiped them away. She was starting to feel better; the little nap had refreshed her. In the bedroom she changed into blue jeans, a yellow cotton blouse, and her Nikes, feeling girlish and anxious to be on her way. She tied a scarf around her abundant white hair.

She went out the back door and down the walk to the garage. It was hot and still in there. The tackle box key was not hanging on the board above Vincent's tool bench, and she muttered, "Damn." The garage had been Vincent's province. He did the driving, shoveled the snow, mowed the lawn, and the garage was his base. He preferred being at work, or inside reading or talking to her, but he drew satisfaction from completing mundane jobs that had to be done. Ina could find him in the garage after she had looked everywhere else.

Within a month of Vincent's death, Ray had sold his father's LTD and left a hole in the garage that always startled Ina. The space between the smudged, busy walls—with their precarious organization of tools, bikes, and junk, and years of license plates numbered LC5885—yawned at her, reminding her that she was old and bound to be tired. Reminding her that her Vincent was gone.

One Saturday morning—the LTD sparkling in the driveway after its weekly wash—Vincent had pointed out to her how the oil stains on the garage floor were always changing. He examined them like clouds. Abe Lincoln's profile. A lion. A woman bent over a dog. A tree. Two men reading one newspaper. The car leaked oil like an artist, but Vincent never did anything to fix the problem. He enjoyed the pictures.

But Ray sold the car because Ina could not drive. With the car gone, the pictures on the floor were thus frozen. She looked at the floor from different angles, in different light. The pictures soon were gone. So carefully detailed by Vincent, they were invisible to her now.

Back in the kitchen she patted cool water on her face again and took a minute to compose herself. It had been a mistake going to the garage, to venture where memories of Vincent were so thick.

When she felt able she went to the front of the house to check for the mail, knowing there was nothing, but always hoping it would come early that day. So much of what was delivered was junk, and much of it still addressed to Vincent; everyone having a sale, everyone needing money. Nevertheless, she cherished the expectancy.

The mail had not arrived. She left the front door open, storm door on the latch. She took two slices of raisin bread and dropped them in the toaster slots. She noticed the cord needed wrapping. At Helene's not long ago, Ina had seen the cord of her sister's toaster burst into flames. It was not a traditional fire, but a fast white flame around the plug, nearly painful to look at.

"What's that horrid smell?" Helene asked, her voice curling at the end with a trace of burgeoning panic. Ina stood at her sister's side to keep her away from the flame. The tiny white storm of electric fire lasted just long enough to sear through the cord and smudge the outlet with a greasy black residue.

"It's a fire in the toaster," Ina said, carefully pinching the plug and yanking it from the socket. Helene sniffed, turning her nose frantic as a hound. "It's under control."

"Will this delay my toast being done?" Helene had asked.

Ina put her raisin toast on a plate and took it to the table. She got a knife from the drainboard and margarine, jelly, and beer from the icebox. She buttered the toast, then spread on jam. She popped the Old Style and poured it headless into her blue glass. She took a swallow. The beer was so cold that it made her real teeth ache. She found a catalog to read while she ate. It was full of impossibly slim and beautiful young women dressed in clothes that reminded Ina of fashions in vogue during the Second World War.

She took a bite of toast, chewing carefully. The ache from the beer had not entirely diminished. With her mouth full of bread, she took another swallow. It felt lost in there. She closed her eyes, sighed, and chewed.

"I was beautiful once," she said out loud, flipping the pages of the catalog.

There had been a time when she and Helene were considered quite a pair of beauties. "A toothsome twosome," Vincent had called them, even when it was no longer specifically true. But there had been a time when they were vied for.

She pushed away from the table, having finished her toast and most of her glass of beer. She carried the glass down the hall to the front door. She flipped the latch and leaned outside to check the mail, although barely a quarter-hour had passed since she had last looked. She went on through the front door and sat down on the top porch step. She swallowed what remained of her beer. Po Strode would look over and see Ina drinking at ten in the morning. A cool breeze chased around her ankles. The street was empty of traffic. After a minute, a maroon car went past.

She wanted another Old Style, and to use the bathroom, but having found a comfortable seat she felt rooted to the spot for the time being. Her headache was starting again; she felt like taking another quick nap. The street was still. It was paved and amply shaded, but still gave off a summer haze as though the ghost of the original dirt hovered over it. Before they got old, Ina and Po Strode nearly made a living running a stand out at the curb. Po sold the sweet corn, tomatoes, and melons she grew in the gardens that flourished on the quarter-acre of land between the Strode house and the Lockwood house. Ina sold preserves Helene had put up, strawberries packed thick as marbles in glass jars, and the fish—mostly carp—she and Vincent pulled from the river.

Vincent would park his car by the stand and pretend to be a customer when business was slow.

"It gives the impression you've got a buyer," he said. "Nobody likes to be the first to part with their money."

A young man came up the stairs from the river. He stood on the top step and peered up and down the street. Ina could tell only that he was tall and thin, wearing jeans, a T-shirt, and a fringed leather vest. He stood in sunlight while Ina sat in shadow. She felt invisible. She felt cool, abuzz, mysterious. Vincent would have warned her to get inside, but she felt her safety lay in remaining absolutely still. She sensed the young man wanted no witnesses. He was only thirty yards away; Ina doubted she could get inside and lock the door before he was upon her.

He lit a cigarette. He possessed a callow beauty; he had muscles and youth, that vanity of stance and movement people of a certain age acquire and inevitably lose. He smoked and looked up and down the street.

In another time, if he had stayed where he was and she stepped back fifty years, Ina would have called his attention to her. She had known how to walk, how to meet an eye; she could rattle her beads. Young girls always seemed more aware of what they were doing; the dance of youth had a rhythm for them, and consequently the end of that dance was harder on them. She had once been quite a romantic, sometimes in secret. She had been a wild lover. She had ridden horses. Now she sat with her empty glass hoping the young man did not look her way. He was raptly smoking, giving the impression of performing an act terribly urbane.

Abruptly the young man looked directly at her and she felt a bolt of fear, but then his line of vision swiveled past. His hair was very long, and tied in a tail down his back. The maroon car she had seen earlier returned. It carried young men, and one of them looked directly at her, of this she was certain. The boy by the river stairs threw away his cigarette and climbed in. Gears shifted, she heard a lively raising of voices, a laugh, and the car sped away.

Ina surmised that he had been dropped by his friends at the head of the stairs to conduct some business down at the river. She pulled herself to her feet on the porch railing and went inside. Her front room was cool and dim. She supposed she should dust. Her blind sister kept a tidier home. Ina made two transits of the room, touching objects, realigning them. Most of all she wanted to go down to the river to learn what those boys were up to.

She went into the hallway and before turning right to go to the kitchen she quickly checked the mail. Helene answered the phone on the first ring.

"It's me," Ina said. "I saw a boy on the river stairs. He's up to no good."

"He was probably fishing," Helene said.

"He wasn't carrying a pole."

"What were you doing on the river stairs?"

"I wasn't on them. I was on my porch. I saw this boy come up the stairs. He had a cigarette going like he was the king bee. A minute later a car full of kids came and picked him up."

"They're playing hooky," Helene said.

"He was doing something by the river."

"Did the phone company call you?"

"No. Why?"

"I told them you might be interested in a quiet-phone rate."

"My phone rings," Ina said huffily. "I use my phone quite often, thank you."

"It's not a sin to pay a quiet-phone rate," Helene said. "It's an economy feature."

"I made two long-distance calls this morning, as a matter of fact," Ina said. "Annie and Ray."

"And who called whom?"

"When did you last speak to Amanda?"

"Yesterday," Helene said, and hung up.

Ina poured a fresh beer into her blue glass and carried it down the hall to the front door. The beer was so cold and heavy; a sense of bounty. She swallowed a mouthful while snaking her hand out the door and into the mailbox. The phone rang and she let it. Helene would be calling back. She was afraid to remain on poor terms with her sister. Blind, she needed Ina for too many things.

She allowed it to ring, and then judged her delay sufficient.

"I wasn't trying to offend you."

"I'm sorry about the Amanda remark. Neither of us have model kids."

Ina could see the head of the river stairs through her front window and she wondered what was at the bottom of them. Her sister, sitting beside the phone with nothing else to do, was silent.

"I have to be going," Ina said.

"When are you coming over, dear?"

"Don't worry. Soon."

"I'm not worried."

Ina heard a rattle at the front door and went for the mail, but there was nothing. Had she imagined the noise? She carried her glass out onto the front porch. If Po Strode was watching there was no way she could tell what Ina was drinking, or that she had refilled her glass.

Ina lowered herself onto the top step. A car went past and her heart sped up for an instant until she reminded herself it wasn't the young men in their maroon car. Having hidden something, they would surely return for it.

A landing had been built halfway down the river stairs, a pla-teau to break the monotony of ascent and descent. Rudy had challenged Vincent to jump from the stairs to this landing, but Vincent had refused to compete. Rudy, starting six steps above the landing, hurtled leisurely through space and touched down lightly on the balls of his feet, fingers grazing the concrete for balance. Helene and Ina applauded. Rudy beamed at the girls; it was a time when they were beautiful, all four of them, and though Vincent would not jump stairs, he was willing to compete for the sisters.

"I've always been a better athlete than you," Rudy teased.

"Go to ten," Vincent said.

"Only if you'll go to eleven."

Rudy scampered ten steps above where they stood, their faces turned up to him, the sisters scared and adoring. Rudy took off and seemed to stay in the air for an afternoon. His shoes didn't slap the cement in landing so much as pat it; he rocked forward, his crouched momentum nearly taking him over the side.

"Now, Vin. Eleven," he said.

Vincent was wearing dark trousers and a crisp white shirt going soft in the heat, the sleeves rolled up. Ina could not set the year in her memory. They all were young. It was summertime and everything was green and hot. Vincent lifted one foot to look at the sole of his shoe, as if to gauge whether the leather would withstand the impact of his landing. He checked one shoe, then the other.

Rudy counted off the steps as he climbed them. At eleven, he turned with a slow pirouette of great fanfare and self-importance.

"Right here, Vincentiamo," he called. He seemed very far away, impossibly high above them. He knelt and slapped the concrete. "Here is your step, Vin."

Helene rescued Vincent. "If he doesn't wish to take part in your childish tests of manhood, he doesn't have to," she said. Ina remained silent; she wanted to see someone jump from the eleventh step.

Rudy made a noise that conveyed utter contempt for Helene's opinion, and with outstretched arms and a small yelp of effort, he flew into the air. It was so sudden Vincent had to jump aside. He gave Ina a shove, clearing a small spot for the landing, but Rudy's momentum and his surprise flight caught Helene unawares and he hit her solidly. The two of them crashed like a ball of arms and legs down the stairs to the river. Ina remembered that in the course of the fall she could not tell them apart. They went down leaving shavings of skin and scalp on the stairs' sharp edges, raising welts, tearing muscles.

Vincent rushed down, Ina a step behind. Rudy was bowed like a Moslem, his butt in the air, his head buried in his hands. He was crying, but trying to hide the fact. Helene was not crying, but sat dazed, shocked, and bleeding, bits of grit impressed in her skin.

"There are six of you," she said.

Rudy's nose was bleeding. A front tooth was chipped in the shape of Nevada. He would never get the tooth repaired, and would come to believe it lent an endearing boyishness to his smile. He cupped Helene's cheek and said, "I'm so sorry."

Prior to the fall they had been simply a quartet of close friends with a tension of possibilities flowing among them. Ina believed with the sincerity of youth that she was as much in love with Rudy as with Vincent; she pictured herself at times with either one. But the fall changed that. It was as if in knocking Helene down the long stairs to the river Rudy had been making a decision, choosing her for himself in a way that seemed oddly touching after the pain and swelling were gone.

Rudy, who had kissed Ina dozens of times as if comparison shopping, held Helene's hand while a doctor looked into her eyes and pronounced nothing of consequence dislodged. He never really let go. He never kissed Ina again, except for holiday pecks on the cheek.

Vincent waited in another room during the doctor's exam. Ina took a paper cup of water to him.

"If you had jumped," Ina said, "I don't think you'd have hit anyone."

"I'm pretty clumsy. I might've taken all four of us down." He finished the water and spun the cup like a thimble on his fingertip. Ina sat beside him. She wanted him to take her hand or put his arm around her. He went on spinning the cup, and when she glanced at him she saw that he was smiling, but trying to hide the fact.

"What?" she demanded.

"I've had my eye on you all along."

Ina finished her second glass of beer. If she wasn't careful the beer would get the best of her. She could walk, but she would be courting the danger of falling down. She stretched out her legs.

She understood that to fall down the river stairs at her age would probably be fatal.

She folded her hands in her lap and took a deep breath to settle herself. Her throat had a ragged, liquidy feel, as if she had been sobbing. She cleared her throat and looked both ways before spitting into the bushes to her left.

She had started drinking too early, too fast, this morning. It required a different set of calculations to see her through to bedtime without being overwhelmed by the beer and without losing the benefits of what she drank. She needed to be patient; let some time pass.

She had lived in her neighborhood longer than anyone she knew of. First her family—mother, father, Helene, herself—then Helene marrying Rudy Bolton and moving just blocks away, then Ina marrying Vincent Lockwood. But rather than taking a house together, she and Vincent lived in three rooms upstairs at the invitation of her parents. They were getting old and her father was sick, and they wanted the comfort of having them nearby in exchange for the house when they died.

Ina looked to her right, at the Strodes' house, with its lush gardens and rose-laden trellises and the striped awnings over the windows, through which Ina sometimes glimpsed Po Strode regarding her with a glare of disapproval. On the lot to her left, across a street perpendicular to the river, was an odd sight: an empty plot of ground, grass trimmed, enclosed in a chain-link fence. The lot was a quarter-acre, the shape of a keystone. The gate in the fence was fastened shut with a burly lock, though kids routinely hopped the fence to sit in the corner farthest from the street and have their little parties.

It was a shrine to a dog. A house had stood on the lot until one damp autumn night when a gas explosion effectively obliterated it. Ina had been asleep; Vincent was downstairs reading. The furnace was running for the first time since summer. Ina was awakened not so much by the noise of the explosion as the shaking of their house and the powder of glass that was blown onto her bed. Po Strode reported later that the concussion had knocked her to the floor while she was returning from the bathroom.

Vincent ran upstairs, still holding his book. He cut his feet on the glass and cried out. He kissed his wife at finding her safe. He put socks and shoes on over his bloody feet. Wind swung the curtains into the room, wind full of a rain already heated by the burning house.

The street crowded with running figures and figures merely standing in amazement. Cold rain made every speck of hot debris hiss and smoke. A man who lived two blocks away told of hearing the explosion, then moments later a hammer's sizzling head came through his bedroom window.

Wind-fed, the fire sucked the house under. Sparks swirled in great typhoons above the trees. The rain kept the neighborhood safe. There was no hope, no responsibility to do anything, and it became like a block party. Ina put on a heavy coat and took her glass and an umbrella into the street to stand with Vincent and the other men. The house burned like a candle gone wild, melting down into itself, the spectacle diminishing as the fuel was consumed.

Ina returned to their bedroom and shook the glass from their bed, then swept up. Vincent's blood was dried on the wood. She snuggled deep into the covers and polished off her beer. She fell asleep, but awoke a short time later confused by Vincent's absence. For a moment she was petrified. She thought she had dreamed the fire, dreamed Vincent's very existence. But she went to the window and saw him standing under her umbrella talking to Hector Strode. The fire had burned down to a thick bed of coals on the basement floor.

The house belonged to Stu and Becky Crabb. They were believed to have been incinerated in the explosion with their Doberman pinscher, Jupiter. But in fact the Crabbs had gone out for dinner and dancing that night. Only Jupiter was at home when the house lifted off. The sun was coming up when the Crabbs returned from their night on the town. They might have had every intention of capping the night with sex, then sleeping until noon.

Two firemen stood in the street smoking cigarettes and watching over the cooling remains. Stu Crabb, coming upon a smoking hole in the neighborhood where he had left his house, screamed, "Jupiter!"

The front half of the Crabbs' lot was visible from where Ina sat. A dump truck had brought topsoil to fill the hole, and a bulldozer planed the dirt smooth as a grave. Stu put up the fence and then snow fell. In the spring he planted grass.

Ina went inside her house and opted for a very, very brief nap on the front-room divan. She was annoyed with herself for falling out of step so early. On her best days she never lost touch, or else maintained it until she was under the covers with her glass and her reading materials, and to lose touch then was almost as fulfilling as love.

She stretched out on the divan and groaned, it felt so luxurious, embracing and nonjudgmental. She toed off her shoes and let them fall. She lay for a minute with her hands folded on her abdomen, and it occurred to her that she was missing something; there was something she should be doing.

Like that, she was asleep. In sleep her movements, her twitches and shifts, lost their aged determination and became numerous and quick, almost girlish. Her breathing turned smooth and light. She dreamed of younger days, of lovers arching over her, of Vincent, and phantoms she never got a clear look at.

Helene's worried call awoke her. The light in the room was turned down considerably, as if someone had stolen in and pulled the shades halfway. The phone was ringing on the table at her feet. She sat up and composed herself. She licked her teeth. She was angry with herself not so much for being caught stuporous by her sister, but for taking two naps in the span of hours. All the extra sleep would keep her awake that night.

Ina stuck out her tongue and picked a pill of fur off it, only to have the pill come to life and leap off the tip of her finger. She stepped on the tiny spider when it landed and scraped disgustedly along her tongue with her teeth, lest it had laid eggs.

Knowing only that she was late, Ina picked up the phone.

"I really need to get to the store today," Helene said with great forbearance.

"What time is it?" Pressed to her ear, warmed, the phone felt almost like a human touch. Like a bit of dream left behind, she was assailed by an instant's memory of Vincent sliding his tongue into her ear.

"It's about half past two," Helene said. "I called the time number before I called you. To see how late you really were."

"I'll be over within the hour," Ina said, and hung up.

She checked the mail and the box was full. She carried the bundle without inspecting it down the hall and into the bathroom. She balanced the mail on the rim of the sink and brought it to her lap when she was seated. The day's delivery felt substantial; she saw stamps in the pile, indications of some trouble taken.

All she really wanted was something from her children. A letter or a card was so much nicer than a phone call. A call left nothing to savor. Her children had moved so far away, as if caught in a wind they did not bother to fight against.

The top envelope was obviously computer-mailed, her name printed in a futuristic typeface whose time had come, the letters hard black, squared off, cold. She cut the envelope open with her nail and read the contents (a pitch for hospitalization insurance featuring the blandishments of a former TV actor) as carefully as a love letter.

Next was her gas bill, with a brief thank you for paying her account promptly. Then a bulk leaflet from an electronics wholesaler, a pushy outfit that mailed her notices of sales every other week, a picture of a missing child on each card.

The first stamped envelope she reached was from a mom-and-pop candle company, the stamp like a stab at warmth in a metered age. The only other stamp was on a request to sample a revolutionary truss for thirty days. It was addressed to Vincent. She dropped everything but the gas bill and catalogs into the wastebasket. The catalogs she put in the alcove cut in the bathroom wall by the old milkbox.

Standing at the mirror with a vain watchfulness, Ina scooped two fingers through a jar of Noxzema (the jar was her favorite blue, the blue of her glass) and spread the goo over her face. She worked in the pattern she had learned from her mother: from the forehead down, ending with one white finger poised at the point of her chin.

Her eyes, in the white glare she applied, were not the perfect blue of the jar. But the cream made her young. Its smooth application (and she worked it like sculptor's mud with her fingers) shielded the lines, the shadows and sags in a coat of white, like ground fog, and left only her eyes, which had so far refused to yield.

Her mother had stood at her side and instructed Ina in the proper method of washing a lady's face. Helene might have been there; Ina couldn't remember. The only phrase she could recall clearly—she could hear it spoken in her mother's voice—was "circular strokes." Wash the skin with circular strokes. They raised the dirt like a wind.

Ina wondered if her own daughter had a memory filled with just those sorts of elementary instructions. Ina clearly remembered explaining menstruation to Annie, feeling confident and rooted in the biological specifics of that process. With the topics of men and sex she had felt less confident; emotion was such a difficult concept to put into words. Annie had never mentioned those things again, except in a way that implied politeness, a sense of duty to include her mother in a decision she had already made.

Three years before Vincent's death they had flown west to visit Annie and Ray and Meg. While at Annie's, Ina had gone to the desk to collect something her daughter had requested. The desk was cluttered. Out of the stacks of bills, receipts, notes, and open address books slipped a piece of pink paper labeled THINGS TO TALK ABOUT W/MOM. Weather. Meg. Don. Money. Aunt H. Health. Ray.

It was the script of a recent telephone conversation; it could have served for any of their calls. She returned to Annie having forgotten why she had gone to the desk.

Ina ran water in the sink and bowed her head over it. She brought the water to her face in the cups of her hands, a cool splashing that refreshed her. She patted her skin dry with the thickest towel she could find. Old again. She went downstairs to the kitchen and checked the burners on the stove for stray gas.

She made sure the toaster was unplugged. She started down the hall to check the mail, and halfway there remembered with a surge of disappointment that it had already come that day.

The phone rang and it was Helene.

"You haven't left yet?"

"I answered the phone, didn't I?"

"I was worried about you."

"You were worried you wouldn't get to the store today," Ina said. Her sister would also have worried that Ina had paused for a beer, and having paused, been snared by another brief nap.

"I'm on my way," Ina said.

"Don't forget your key."

"Yes, Mother."

Purely for spite and excitement, Ina took her bag and left by the front door and crossed the street to the head of the river stairs. She imagined her sister caught in the delicious agony of waiting. She was out of the house now, out of Helene's reach.

Po Strode was cutting flowers in her sideyard. She wore a sunhat wide-brimmed as a bicycle tire, a flat basket hooked over her arm. Ina waved and Po raised her snips, then snicked them twice in further greeting.

The stairs plummeted into shadow. Ina could see the first landing and beyond it more stairs, but everything seemed to get swallowed up down there; it was like looking down the long throat of a dangerous animal. The girlish excitement of the place was long gone.

She inspected the street for cars bearing young men. She did not dare look again at Po Strode; she was too embarrassed. If she turned back now she would become the woman who wandered to the head of the river stairs, in addition to being the woman who drank in the morning and the woman who enticed other women's husbands.

She took one step down and then another. She kept one hand on the iron railing, which hummed against her palm, and one hand on her shoulder bag. More steps down and she looked back; she was out of sight.

Vincent had kissed her for the first time on the landing by the river. He was not especially shy, but very gentlemanly, and he had asked her permission, where Rudy had taken his first kiss from her almost as his right. Rudy had made her feel like property to be possessed. Vincent treated her like something that might chip.

Ina rested on the landing halfway down. She wasn't tired, only terribly excited. She felt she was on an edge; moving too fast. At the top of the stairs was a rectangle of fading sky. Her phone might be ringing, Helene calling to gauge her sister's progress. She would be heartened that Ina had left the house.

Continuing on down, she could hear the river. It was thick as slush even on the hottest days. The railing was cooler in the deepening shadows. She stepped onto the landing. Having arrived, she immediately made plans to depart. She would touch the landing as proof she had been there, then start back up. Helene would never know she had been missing.

But she was struck by how little the scene had changed over time. Even the trees had ceased to grow. The hearts drawn with chalk on the landing by her friends had only been made permanent with the spray paint of modern lovers. The opposite bank had the same look of muddy slickness, the same flakes of debris and used condoms caught in the roots of the trees. It made her feel at home.

She forced herself to remain a minute, a quick minute spent regarding her beating heart, her arms folded over her chest like sensitive monitors. She walked in a wary shuffle around the edge of the landing, looking for a clue as to why the boy had come down there. Perhaps it was an innocent errand; no bathroom handy. But at the corner farthest from the stairs she saw a dark line tied to an old boat-mooring hook. The line vanished in the water. A good hiding place, the hook was imbedded in a small cavity in the side of the landing; the line wasn't visible unless you made a point of looking for it.

Kneeling creakily on the landing, she pulled in the line, wetting her hands. The catch at the end had the weight of an excellent day of fishing, but after she had pulled in enough line the mystery came to her eye as something golden, thick-legged, almost crustaceous in its unwillingness to be retrieved.

Then she had to laugh.

She was pulling in a six-pack of Coors.

Now she had to hurry. She had come upon something of value; the beer would be priceless to someone not legally allowed to possess it.

The cans dripped down the front of her clothes and onto her shoes. The six-pack was fastened to the line with a simple knot. She picked the knot open with fingers that barely functioned and pulled the cans out of the plastic rings so she could fit them in her bag. The cans were heavy; they would slow her ascent. The boys would discover her stealing their beer and throw her in the river. Helene would never get to the store. She would call and call, and when she got no answer she would chalk up Ina's disappearance to an intemperate life.

Ina paused to rest at the landing and heard her name being called. The doorway of blue sky had reappeared at the head of the stairs, and Po Strode stepped into this space with her wide hat. She held her snips like a sword, and seemed prepared to hoist her basket of flowers as a shield.

"Hello, Po," Ina said when she was six stairs from the top.

"Ina," Po replied with a nod. Her look was a little embarrassed at being concerned about Ina, then finding her safe.

"Can you do me a favor?" Ina asked.

"What is that?"

"Is the street clear?"

"Clear?"

"Are there any cars approaching? Any maroon cars, in particular?"

Po Strode wheeled her hat to the left and to the right, taking in the neighborhood with a fresh suspicion.

"Everything appears to be in order, Ina," Po said. "The street is very quiet at the moment. No one lurking, as far as I can tell. I think it's safe for you to come up."

Ina, clothes damp, completed her ascension. The street looked wide and airy after the dark constriction of the stairs and the river landing. Po Strode was regarding her queerly.

"I saw you go down the stairs," she explained. She was a retired elementary school teacher, childless, and she wielded her snips like a pointer. "I wasn't sure if you were in some sort of trouble. I'm relieved to see you're not."

Ina stepped closer. "Can I trust you with a secret, Po?"

Po shifted to keep the basket between them. "How you spend your time is none of my business, Ina."

"Let's go into your yard," Ina said. She hurried in her Nikes across the street. She knelt and placed her bag behind one of Po's flowerbeds, and in standing up she felt safe and elated. She was once again an old lady killing time in a neighbor's yard. But against all odds and expectations she had gone to the river and returned with treasure.

She worried a damp spot on her blouse. Po Strode caught up with her. She had dropped a rose in the road and gone back for it.

"Let me catch my breath," Ina said.

A car cruised past driven by a man both old and handsome. Po, whose Hector was still alive, turned in her sunhat to regard the driver. She had always had an eye for men, Po. Her keenest watch was kept on Hector, both in appreciation and surveillance.

"You mentioned a secret," Po Strode prompted.

"I did. But I'm wondering if I ought not keep it to myself," Ina said with delicious reluctance. "I don't want to expose you to any danger."

"Who'd harm an old biddy like me?"

"Don't you read the papers?"

"I get my news from TV. Or Hector."

"Clair Berkey? Three blocks over on Alcott? Somebody beat her within an inch of her life for seven dollars. They used one of her good mixing spoons."

Po Strode made a noise of distaste with her lips. The action produced a tiny bubble of spit that inadvertently floated away. The women watched it, amazed.

"I'm aware those things go on," Po said. "I lock my doors.

But I don't need to know the details of every person's misfortune."

"It keeps me on my toes," Ina said. She heard, across Po's gardens, the phone ringing in her house; Helene already gearing her life to being alone.

"Are you in danger?" Po asked.

"I don't honestly know." She glanced at the bag at her feet, felt a thrill. She would have to be careful to wash the cans before pouring the contents into her glass.

"I was on my front stoop this morning," Ina said. "A young man appeared at the head of the river stairs. He was rather good-looking—in an unkempt fashion. I sat very still and he didn't see me. I'm *positive* he didn't see me. He waited there and then a maroon car full of other young men arrived and picked him up. Naturally I was curious about what he had been doing down by the river. I went to look and discovered this beer." She pulled the bag open for Po to see inside.

"You must go home," Po exclaimed, giving Ina a slight push. "Those boys will be back for their beer. Better yet, why don't you put it back where you found it?"

Ina looked at the mouth of the stairway. No, she would never go down there again.

"They won't be back until dark," Ina said. "Maybe not even tonight. If they were old enough to have the beer, why did they hide it in the river?"

Po waved her away. "I can't promise anything if they come for me."

"Why would they come for you?"

"I just can't make any promises. I wish you hadn't told me."

"I asked if you could keep a secret."

"I didn't ask you to put me—and Hector—in danger."

"They'll never suspect us, Po," Ina said. "We are old. Our impression of helplessness gives us all sorts of freedom."

Po Strode backed away, holding up a hand as if to deflect a blow. She checked the street for a maroon car. Some years ago, kids had decapitated the Strodes' lawn jockey, and the little headless man stood there for a winter in his natty, fading outfit, hold-

ing out a small black lamp. Hector expected to find the head in
the spring, but the snow pulled back without a sign of it.

Ina carried the stolen beer into her house by the back door.
Two boys witnessed her; they were sharing a cigarette inside the
Crabbs' fenced lot. They scared Ina with their sudden presence,
evidence of witnesses at every turn. She scared them, too, though;
they clunked against each other in their haste to hide their illicit
smoke. She estimated they were younger than the boys in the
maroon car. But why were they present at just that moment?
Were they sentries? Scouts?

She opened her icebox. Her Old Style was there, neat rows of
cold cans. She counted her stock: eight. Enough for the night and
into the next day. But rather than hide the stolen beer there, she
carried it down into the basement. An old icebox stood there,
unplugged, beneath the stairs. Vincent had bought her a new one
several years before his death. The machine in the basement was
perfectly good, merely old. Vincent had come home one afternoon followed within minutes by a department-store delivery
truck. He told her he liked the way the new one made ice. A
soft whirring in the door preceded the muffled rattle of perfect
ice pieces (shaped not like cubes, but quarter-moons) being deposited in the bin. He paid the delivery men fifty dollars cash to
lug the old icebox into the basement. He told Ina they might sell
it one day.

She opened the door and was startled when no light came on.
She put the beer on an empty shelf, changed her mind, and
transferred it to the freezer compartment. Closing, the door
snapped with a solid *chunk!* and bit the very tip of her trailing
finger. She thrust it into her mouth. Vincent, who on occasion
professed a belief in the humanity of inanimate objects, would
have told her the old icebox had waited patiently to take its
revenge for being jilted; it would have preferred a taste of Vincent,
but settled for his widow.

Before returning upstairs, Ina checked the lock on the door
leading from the basement up a short flight of stairs to the backyard. She had not used the door in ages, but when she turned
the knob the door opened easily. She tried the knob from the

outside and it turned. For the duration of her widowhood she had been living with her basement door unlocked. Each night before she took her glass to bed she painstakingly checked the locks on every door and window, and every night she had fallen into her beery slumber feeling locked up tight and safe, and the basement door had been wide open. She felt as if she had just discovered she'd been walking around for years with the seat of her pants missing.

Her phone began to ring again. She took it in the kitchen.

"I'm on my way. I've been sidetracked, but I'm on my way. Please don't criticize me."

"I'd never do that, dear. I was only worried about you. It must be dark by now."

Ina checked the light. In fact, everything appeared brightly defined after the gloom of the cellar.

"We still have time," Ina said. She told her sister, with a lilt of breathless daring in her voice, "I would've been over to get you by now, but I got involved in a little escapade."

"What do you mean?"

"I'll tell you when I see you. I may be in danger. My phone may be tapped."

"Ina, dear—"

But Ina hung up. Her sister would assume the escapade consisted of drinking more beer.

Ina went to a window that looked on the Crabbs' lot. The two boys were still there. They were sharing another cigarette. She left by the back door, checking the front door first, checking the backdoor lock twice, checking for the coinish weight of her keys in the moist depths of her bag. A thick old oak grew in her yard near the sidewalk. She went to it, waited to catch her breath, then peeked around the tree at the boys across the street. They had not seen her; therefore she was still in the house, and safe.

Ina carried her shopping cart to the end of the block so its squealing axle would not betray her. At the corner she turned right, feeling wonderful to be out and on the move. She walked beneath the cool canopy of tall oaks planted two years before her birth and now grown majestic and bothersome in the way their roots buckled the old sidewalks and their leaves and acorns produced a debris of persistent aggravation. Two blocks on and she turned left, and then in another block she turned right onto Helene's street.

Vincent's initials were there somewhere. She walked with her head bowed, looking for the letters her husband had cut with a bit of stick in wet cement. She always thought she remembered the exact location of the initials, but she never did. In the moments before finding them she always feared they had been eradicated, had grown faint over the long years of no one looking for them.

Even Vincent had forgotten they were there, then one evening on a visit to Rudy and Helene's he stood up and led them on an expedition into the darkness. Helene refused to go along, claiming she had dishes to do, and her disapproving look betrayed her hope that Rudy would stay put, too. Ina, seeing her sister discomfited, turned vivacious and enthusiastic about the idea. They filled their pockets with kitchen matches to aid in the search; Vincent said they were more romantic than a flashlight. Ina topped off her glass and they departed.

Ina could see the moon sectioned haphazardly through the trees overhead. Two houses down, Vincent stopped and struck a match against the sidewalk. Rudy, who believed he had etched his own initials in the same wet cement, said they had not gone far enough down the block. But Vincent was on his knees and an elbow, holding the match up, looking drunk, which he was not. He read like a blind man, with his fingertips, everything he touched a blur of punctuating stones and grit. He put out the match with a snap of his wrist.

The party moved on. Now Rudy felt the search was warming.

"We're in front of the Griffins' house—and we put the initials in their cement because they were such pricks." Rudy fell to his knees and struck a match.

"But this isn't where the Griffins lived," Vincent said.

That set off a second argument. They could not agree on the location of the initials, and then the composition of the neighborhood changed even as they tried to fix it in their memories.

The match burned Rudy's fingers, and with a little yelp he disappeared.

Ina found the faint letters where they had always been, where Vincent finally had come upon them with a woof of triumph that night. They had been pretty old even then, the children grown and gone, their lives constricted back to the four of them again after the brief expansion of having families. They found the letters in front of Rudy's boyhood home, which was only six houses down from where he and Helene had moved after they were married. They remembered the circumstances then, too; Rudy's father mixing the cement to fix a crumbling panel in the walk, his stern warning not to mark his work, and then Rudy and Vincent sneaking back with the stick.

Rudy knelt with a match, rubbing his fingers over the letters. VL RB.

"I don't know if he ever saw what we did," he said.

Ina arrived at Helene's house. The neighborhood lots were deep and narrow, with walks leading between the houses to niggardly back yards, then unconnected garages facing a common alley. On the front gate was a small silver sign: RUDY & HELEN WELCOME YOU. The sign was custom ordered, then Helene's name botched. Rudy had made a stink until the company refunded his money, but he never corrected the sign.

Ina went around to the back door. There was a strip of lawn along the walk, an old flowerbed next to the fence on the lot line. A young family lived in the house next door. They were strangers in the impersonal age. But years back, what had their name been? Joost? One hot night the four of them had sat in the parlor with their cold drinks, playing canasta and listening to Mr. and Mrs. Joost make love next door. Rudy tugged at his collar as Mrs. Joost's orgasmic shouts trumpeted through the screens. Vincent said in a fake British accent, "Seems a bit warm for that, what?" But he could not wait to get her home that night, could not wait to get her undressed and his hands on her.

"Is that you, dear?" Helene called.

She was sitting by the telephone in the kitchen. As if she had perfect vision, her eyes went immediately to Ina as she opened

the back door with the key Helene had had cut for her and which
Ina kept safety-pinned to the lining of her bag. She went to Helene and kissed her cheek.

"If it wasn't, would I have said so?"

"I'd know you anywhere—your tread, your scent, your aura."

"Poo," Ina said. "Did you know," she continued with a trace
of amazement, "that I've been living with the cellar door unlocked since Vincent died?"

"Why on earth would you want to do that?"

"I *didn't* want to," Ina said. "That's my point. I was checking
the locks on the cellar door and I discovered it's been unlocked
all this time. Years!"

"Why were you checking the lock, dear?"

"I was nervous."

"Why?"

"I'll explain later. Do you have a list?"

"Up here," Helene said, with a tap on her skull.

"You had your hair done."

"What do you think?"

"It's lovely," Ina said, and touched her sister's hair as further
proof.

Helene persisted in tinting her hair at a small salon run out of
a woman's home down the block. Helene favored unflattering
metallic colors—hard silvers, silver-blues, racy coppers—perhaps
falling for the seductive names, having no idea how the colors
actually looked. They were at an age when their few peers did
not dare offer honest critiques of their appearance, knowing they
themselves were vulnerable. A blind woman with hair the color
of a saucepan was routinely assured she looked radiant. Ina did
not feel she was one to argue. Vincent had cut her hair and
become quite good at it. His gentle, busy fingers in her hair never
failed to arouse her. Now she cut her own hair, sitting on a high
stool before the mirror, but rarely consulting it. She cut her hair
by touch; she was deft.

Helene asked if she had brought any coupons.

"No," Ina said. "I don't pay any attention to them."

"They can save you money."

"They clutter up the drawer," Ina said. "You have to keep track of the expiration dates. I don't want anything to do with things that expire."

Helene huffed to register disapproval at her sister's little joke, with its overtones of spendthriftiness. Ina had never had to worry about money. She just bought what she needed. Vincent had taught her that. He made money in a way that seemed almost effortless; not in amounts that could be considered lavish, but much more than enough to satisfy the needs and desires of his family. Helene resented this ability of Vincent's, for her own husband had brought money in wrenchingly, a dollar at a time, each dollar logged and squeezed in place on the budget.

Helene snapped open a change purse and felt down inside its little cloth mouth for the money she had there: bills folded to the dimensions of small candy bars, a selection of coins. Ina would write a check.

The widows linked arms and set out. Helene took a seat on the bench in the backyard while Ina went to the garage for her sister's cart. Helene had had two carts just like it stolen, malicious thefts of the rickety contraptions with their collapsible sides and cheap red wheels. No reason to take them other than pure meanness, a simple desire to inconvenience.

In the garage, Ina put her hand on Rudy's car, an Olds Omega. Its blue steel coat was dusty and so warm the engine might have just been run. A man's hat was on the front seat, resting alongside a pair of ladies' gloves. She remembered the rides they had taken, the four of them, the way Vincent pressed ever so slightly against her on the seat, even after they had been married for years, even after she had been stretched far from her original form by two babies. He never lost that attentiveness. Up they would ride into hills Rudy found. He discovered the finest in elevated locations, where a breeze was sure to rise on the hottest evening. He amazed them. He gloated over this rare ability. The horizon was a line drawn with violet ink and straight-edge, but Rudy would have them soon enough in hills where they lost their stomachs flying over the crests. Helene would take her turn driving, Rudy close beside her. She was an excellent driver. She steered with both hands and Rudy poked like a kid at the side of her breast, or in the gap between her legs, as if he wanted her to flinch in self-protection and kill them all.

"Whose hat is that in your car?" Ina asked.

"Hat?"

"A brown hat and a pair of light gray gloves."

"The hat is Rudy's. The gloves are mine. I can't picture Rudy in a hat."

"When did you drive the car last?"

"Before I went blind—obviously."

"You should turn the engine over occasionally," Ina said. "It's not good to just sit."

"You've let me sit all day."

"Oh, poo." Helene took her sister's arm and they went down the walk and through the gate. Each woman pulled a cart. Helene remarked on the chill of the shade. Her toe caught on a snag of raised concrete and for an instant her balance was gone. Then it wasn't.

"Are you all right, dear?" Ina asked.

"Yes," Helene said. She had paused to reassemble her courage to travel. "We're at the corner."

"Exactly."

Ina warned Helene to step down for the curb and she did. The street had a much different feel than the sidewalk. It seemed to hum, and Helene felt endangered as she never did on the sidewalk or in her house. She hurried a bit against Ina's lead and tripped jarringly on the opposite curb, again nearly falling.

"Easy, dear," Ina said. "I looked both ways."

They moved into the next block. Helene counted steps. The block was precise in her memory. The houses were either crisp or uncaring in their appearance. Each fence had a tilt of its own. The yards declared dog, no dog, yard mowed. All the time she had had her eyesight she thought she hadn't been paying attention. But there it was like a movie, down to the shapes, sequences, and locations of the house-number plates.

"Here we are at Jansen and Edison," Helene announced.

"No fair. You're counting steps."

"Tell me about your adventure," Helene said.

Ina hushed her with that taste for the dramatic Helene found so annoying.

"It's scary," Ina said. "I let Po Strode in on it and now she fears for her safety—and wishes I'd never said a word."

Helene, stung, said, "You told Po, but you won't tell me?"

"Po was there, dear. She insinuated herself into my adventure," Ina said. She mused, "Why do you suppose Po was blessed with a husband with longevity?"

"I don't know," Helene said, "that it's such a blessing."

"Bite your tongue," Ina scolded, laughing. "Rudy is just crushed at this moment."

"I was referring to Hector Strode," Helene said. "Do you remember what a grim young man he was? Serious to a fault."

"The serious ones last forever," Ina said.

Helene, in talking to her sister, had lost count of their journey. But the rhythm of being blind ticked reliably within her and she began to count from 44. At 201, the number of steps in the block, they were at Jansen and Flamingo. She told Ina so.

"You are amazing."

"I am. Now tell me what happened."

"I was sitting on my front porch—thinking about Vincent, waiting for the mail," Ina said. "I saw a boy come up the stairs from the river. His very appearance radiated a suspicious presence. He was menace personified. I hoped he would walk away, but he just stood there. I sat stone still. He didn't see me. In time a car full of boys his age arrived and took him away."

Helene, counting steps, turned left on Wilson. Preoccupied by her story, Ina followed.

"Do you remember that look boys got when they wanted to kiss you?" Ina asked.

"Only Rudy ever looked at me that way," Helene said, somewhat stiffly.

"What about George Bigelow? And Heywood Harms?"

"They never kissed me," Helene blurted, as if fearing a whiff of scandal fifty years after the fact.

"Never?"

"Rudy is the only man who ever touched me."

"Well, you misremember, but I won't press the issue," Ina said judiciously. They had come to the outer rim of the supermarket parking lot. Helene stood, arms akimbo, glaring at the space she estimated her sister to occupy.

"Rudy is the only man who ever touched me."

"I believe you."

"No, you don't."

"I know for a fact that Vincent kissed you. Often."

"He was like a brother."

"Not before we paired off. I could've ended up with Rudy and you with Vincent. You can't deny it."

"I can and I will," Helene said. "Rudy only had eyes for me."

"Dear, I'm not saying that he didn't. But we could've switched husbands in the beginning and we'd still be standing today just like this—two old fools arguing in a parking lot."

"That's not the same. We're sisters," Helene said.

"Maybe if you'd married Vincent and I'd married Rudy, they'd be alive today," Ina speculated. "Maybe we wouldn't have worn the other out quite so fast."

"You don't know that," Helene said.

As they walked on, Ina said. "I just remember my youth as a girlish series of brief flirtations. A kiss was the ultimate in vanity and self-expression. It meant nothing. But they surely made my blood gallop. We were together so much, I assumed your experiences were the same. You taught me everything."

Men were at work in front of the store's entrance. They shimmered in a cloud of dust and excruciating noise, cracking into the concrete with picks and a jackhammer. Helene made a sound, almost a peep of pain, that Ina barely heard. She saw a drop of blood on her sister's leg where a shard of concrete had hit and cut through the skin of her nylons. Ina drew her into the store, where the air was cool, with music in the background.

"Wait, dear," Ina said to her sister. "You've been cut."

She guided Helene to a chair by the window. Other old birds perched there, catching their breath, fluttering their coupons. Ina knelt and dabbed with a tissue at the blood. It was the merest drop, a gay bright red that seemed more festive than dangerous. Blood had spread behind the nylons, darkened, and begun to dry.

"Does it hurt?"

"A little sting," Helene said bravely. "Such a racket out there."

"Men working."

A cashier in a brown smock calling a greeting to Helene, who replied unerringly, "What are they doing out there, Margarine?"

She waved a hand, an instant's hitch in the flow of her work. "Putting up barriers," she said. "You won't be able to take your groceries to your car anymore."

"We don't drive," Helene said.

"It's just a symptom," Margie said. "The neighborhood is shot." She smiled innocently at her customer, a petite woman with huge, dewy black eyes and a matching bead in her nose. "They lose carts, so they fence us in," Margie said.

"My food it will be stealing," the customer chimed in with shy indignation.

"You've got that right, honey," Margie said. "You leave your cart to go get your car and someone'll take your groceries before you get back. We're playing into their hands. We're giving them a specific location to prey on us."

She hit a final button and read the figure that appeared in angular crimson numbers in the register window. "Sixty-six twenty-nine, please."

While the customer pulled her money from what appeared to be a satin pouch, Margie smiled wearily at the widows.

"So how you doing, Hellion?"

"I'm fine," Helene said.

"You want a Band-Aid for that? We've got them back in the lounge."

"She'll be okay," Ina said.

"Check out with me, when you're done," Margie said.

They went into the aisles.

"Why did she call you Hellion?" Ina asked.

"Don't get me started," Helene warned.

"Hellion is the nickname of a woman who kissed one man in her lifetime?"

"I worked here a long time," Helene said. "Everyone had nick-names. Margie we called Margarine because men went through her like knives."

Ina's laugh drew the looks of other shoppers.

"And furthermore," Helene continued, "you say I taught you everything—but I never taught you to be promiscuous."

"You're awfully touchy today," Ina said. "And what does it matter now if I was promiscuous and you were chaste?"

Helene's eyes snapped to, as if they worked perfectly. Ina set something she needed in the cart and directed her sister onward. People were listening and she felt exposed.

"It will always matter," Helene declared.

"Do you think Mama knows about us now?" Ina asked. "Or Daddy? And say they do—do you think they smile more fondly on you than me?"

"I don't care to discuss it," Helene said. "You're too strange today."

Ina understood perfectly what her sister meant. She was pent up with something approaching sexual desire. She didn't know if it was the fizz of the beer in her system or the exertion of going to the river, or the memories that journey had tapped, but she was itching for sensation in a way that was nearly adolescent in intensity.

"It was my adventure," Ina said.

"Pish tosh," Helene said. She walked with one hand on the cart. They followed the same route through the store every time; Helene had the steps down and could almost put her hand on each item that she needed. She said, "You saw a boy who looked suspicious. He didn't see you. He drove away in a car. What a grand escapade." She paused. "Do you need salt?"

"I need a block for the water softener," Ina said. "Although last time, Hector seemed reluctant to carry it downstairs for me." He had come over, old and skinny in his stained T-shirt and gardening pants, and Po watched so avidly for him to return you would think her husband was God's antidote to widowhood. But he did have a pleasant stink to him; Ina had forgotten how good old men could smell.

"I went to the bottom of the stairs and stole those boy's beer out of the river," Ina said. "It's in my cellar right now. That's how I discovered the door has been unlocked all this time."

"Ina Lockwood! Are you an idiot? Or a liar?"

"Neither," Ina said. She loved to see her sister stew. It was new to Ina, the ability to shock her older sister. Blindness had made Helene innocent all over again.

"What if they come for their beer?" Helene asked in a whisper.

"Why would they come to me?"

"You live across the street from the stairs. Who else is likely to have seen them?"

"Po Strode. Or that young couple on the other side of Po and Hector."

"They'll go to Po and she'll hold out for half a second—then she will point a finger directly at your house," Helene said.

"They'll think the line broke, or the knot came undone," Ina said. "They'll assume their beer is at the bottom of the river. There is nothing to tie the event to me."

"Except their beer in your cellar—which they will find in the course of tearing your house to shreds," Helene said. "The things young men do to old ladies these days. It's not a pretty sight."

"How do you know?"

"Don't be cruel, dear. It gives you wrinkles." Helene turned the corner at the end of the aisle just as Ina was about to tell her to do so.

"Roxanne Dalrymple, poor soul," Helene said. "They found her inside her icebox. Nobody to hear her scream. She suffocated."

"I don't know Roxanne Dalrymple," Ina said.

"She was a year ahead of me in school? A vivacious little thing," Helene said. "She was in chorus? And on the paper? And she ends up in her own icebox."

"How did she get there?"

"She was shoved. Crammed. By a gang of young thugs—perhaps the very young men whose beer you stole. They were never caught. It was convenient to be rid of her. So in she went."

"And she couldn't even turn on the light," Ina said.

Helene laughed in spite of herself. "Don't make fun," she scolded.

As the two sisters traveled the aisles they ran into people they had known all their lives; mostly women, widows like themselves. These friends stopped the slow progress of their shopping carts and rested against them to talk, keeping one eye on their handbags. They talked in loud voices, as though the stories about Helene had gotten her affliction wrong, passing the word that she was deaf, not blind. Their conversations were universally about the difficulty of things: of maintaining health, of getting money, of living and staying safe, of moving out, to Florida or Arkansas or a welcoming child.

"Who was that?" Helene asked after another woman had left them.

"Georgina Hoskins."

"How does she look?"

"Like you and me, roughly."

"Do I sound that whiney and self-absorbed?"

Ina patted her sister's arm. "At times, dear. But nobody blames you."

At Margie's station she pulled each item over a square of dark glass beside the cash register, and the price appeared in the little rectangular window at the same time a woman's electronic voice announced it.

"I'm exhausted, ladies," Margie reported. She arched her back and Ina could hear things softly popping and snapping in her spine.

"Add a block of salt to that," Ina said.

"Salt. Who'll carry it for you?"

"Hector Strode," Helene said with an eerie wink into space. "It's Ina's method of seduction—get him in the cellar with a fifty-pound block of salt, he has a stroke, no one knows she has him—voilá."

Margie laughed. She hit a big red key and the total came into the window: $74.27.

"I'll write a check," Ina said. "We can settle up later."

Helene, standing beside the cart, nodded.

"When are you coming back to work?" Margie asked. It was a question she always asked. Helene usually answered in such a way as to sound noncommittal and cheerfully positive, so Ina was startled to hear her sister say, "I'm never coming back, Margie. I'm blind—and I wish you'd stop reminding me of that fact."

The cashier, head bowed, mortified, snapped open a bag. When she raised her eyes, Ina threw her a consoling wink.

"I'm sorry, Hellion," Margie said. "We just miss you."

"I miss you, too, dear."

"Can you get someone to put the salt in my cart?" Ina asked.

"Hey—I can do better than that," Margie said. "My grandson is picking me up tonight. We can run your salt over to you. Curb service. He can carry it in for you, put it in the softener. What do you say?"

"That would certainly save me a lot of trouble," Ina said, made bashful by the woman's enthusiasm and need to atone for her remark to Helene.

"Consider it done, then." Margie stepped clumsily forward and kissed Helene, who, surprised by the turbulence of an approaching object, flinched so that the kiss missed her cheek and landed on her left eye.

Passing through the workers sinking poles in concrete, Ina was startled when one of the men, the oldest of the crew, soft in the eyes, but nonetheless handsome, tipped his hardhat to her. She smiled back, her day somewhat made.

Weighted by their purchases, they went at an almost laborious pace back through the streets. Helene was quiet. She could feel the day darkening down, manifested in a coolness on her skin, a new moisture in the air.

"Let me stay with you tonight," Helene said.

"What on earth for?"

"I don't want to be alone," Helene said. "Margie made me give too much thought to my condition. Damn her. Besides, you'll need my help when those boys break into your house."

"That won't happen."

"Why not stay with me then? It will save you the walk home."

"It's no trouble," Ina said. At Helene's there would be no Old

Style to drink and nothing to read. The salt would be delivered to an empty house, foiling that plan. The dangerous boys would come to the river and she would not be there to witness their rampage of anger and betrayal.

"The boy is coming with the salt," Ina said. "I have to be home for that."

Helene had been counting steps again and felt that her advancement home now had the precision of a very limited science. She heard the manic barking of Pepper, the mongrel three doors from her, and wondered if she could hit the dog with a stone thrown into the center of the racket it created.

Ina guided her sister to the gate.

"Let's unload your things," she said.

They went through the gate and down the walk. Without hesitation Helene got her key into the lock and the back door open.

"Stay here tonight," she coaxed. "Margie's grandson can leave the salt on the step. Hector will lug it down the basement for you. You know he's been in love with you for years—decades."

"Eons."

"Don't brag."

"I think it's best if I go home," Ina said. If she dallied now she might be caught out in the dark.

While Helene sat at the kitchen table fussing in her purse, Ina unpacked her sister's groceries and put them away. As she worked she called out where everything was being placed.

"I think I'll stay in my own house tonight," Helene announced. She already had her shoes off; she scratched one toe against the other.

"That's fine, dear. A sensible decision. But I must hurry."

"What is my share of the bill?" Helene asked.

"I'll pay for this one," Ina said. "I want to get home before it gets dark."

"I can pay," Helene said. "You only let me pay five dollars last time. And the time before that I contributed nothing. I'm not a penniless wretch. How much do I owe you?"

"If you insist, I'll take this twenty." Ina plucked a bill from the table.

Helene slapped at her sister and missed. "What did you take? A one? I don't have a twenty-dollar bill!"

"I took a five," Ina said. "Now we're even."

"Money. Money. Money!" Helene shrieked. "It's always money. Must you embarrass me at every turn with your money? I'm not destitute! Rudy was a good provider. If he got a free house—maybe he'd have left behind some mad money. Thirty years of mortgage payments would have taken some of the carefree spring out of Vincent's steps."

"I'm leaving now," Ina said, backing to the door, feeling as if she were actually shrinking. "I'm sorry, dear. I didn't mean to embarrass you."

"Phone when you get home," Helene said.

Once she was out on the street and traveling alone Ina wondered if she had made a mistake. She pulled her squeaking cart along the darkening walk and her imagination ran panicky ahead of her. The rounded heads of mums became clubs poised to bash her. Low branches were stranglers' arms. Dogs rushed howling at the fences. Her breath seemed to leak from her with maddening inefficiency; her lungs felt perforated. More than any other phenomenon of getting old, she was most dismayed by her body's inability to *hurry*.

She paused to catch her breath at an intersection. Out from under the trees there was an abundance of light in the sky. A car glided past before she stepped down off the curb, a car full of heads bobbing to loud music that spilled out the windows like litter.

She came to the edge of her lot and was excited to see a package awaiting her at the foot of the back stairs. Her birthday was in a month; perhaps it was an early present.

But it was her block of salt. She sighed. For those moments of thinking the salt was a package, she had actually seemed to hurry. Anticipation made her young again. She touched the block with her toe. The salt felt marblelike in its density.

She looked across the Strodes' gardens to the lights in their windows. She was watching for Hector. He possessed the strength required to get the salt inside her house, Had he really loved her for *decades?* She was upset that Margie and her grandson had come before they had promised they would, had come when Ina was not home and able to open the door so the kid could complete his journey to the basement. And why leave it on the walk? Why not on the porch? And why had she put so much stock in an idle promise made in a supermarket checkout line?

She took out her key. The locks turned over in their order and she worked the cart inside and shut the door, pressing with her hip against it until she heard the tongue click home. She locked the locks and connected the chain that unrolled from a brass disk fastened to the door frame.

While she put her groceries away, she washed out her blue glass, dried it, and filled it with an Old Style. The taste was glorious, and she stood by the kitchen window so Po Strode could look over and see her drinking and feel superior.

The water heater clicked on, and its faint whir reminded her of other things in the basement and she snatched shut the blinds. Her clumsy haste upended a paper cup on the windowsill where she had been growing a potato. Tepid water wet her hands and arms and she let fly a curse. The potato, suspended in the water with pastel toothpicks, fell like a satellite into the sink.

The street was quiet in front. She stood watch for a quarter-hour until her tired eyes began to ache. Cars went past, each in its own way suspicious, but none stopped. Voices came from the Crabbs' enclosure. They were the young voices of kids thrilled to be out and engaged in something forbidden. Their presence made her feel endangered; she suspected they had already relayed word that she was home.

She got on the phone to her sister.

"Are you all right?"

"You're the one who went home to a house full of stolen beer," Helene said.

"I'm a little nervous. There are kids in the Crabbs' lot."

"Did you check your rooms?"

"Yes."

"Upstairs? Basement?"

"I called down the basement and nobody answered," Ina said. "Upstairs too. I assume they're unoccupied."

"I'm only trying to help," Helene said.

"Your friend Margie dropped my salt on the back walk," Ina said. "Now I have to call Hector over."

"Do it tonight. They expect rain."

"Oh, blast!" Ina said. She closed her eyes. Rushed, having to rely on Hector and Po, she felt the day's strongest surge of loneliness whistle through her.

"Amanda's here," Helene revealed in a voice that seemed to be parting with a secret.

"How is she?"

"She's in the bathroom at the moment. She came over quite by surprise. I don't know why. She's wearing this hideous blue and green and purple *gook* on her eyes."

"That sort of makeup is very popular now," Ina said.

"It's sluttish. I told her so."

"How did you know what she was wearing?"

"I *smelled* it on her," Helene said. "She kissed me and she smelled like an oil refinery. I asked her what she was wearing. She described it to me and in my mind's eye I saw a slut. I touched her eyes and they were greasy."

"You're awfully hard on her," Ina said.

"She's forty-two years old," Helene said. "It's too late for her to get a husband with sex. It's time she came up with another strategy."

Her venom made Ina sad and she spared a warm thought for her children, both miraculously free of her.

"Maybe cooking," Helene mused.

Ina was exhausted. She made a quick excuse and hung up. The phone rang almost immediately.

"You must get out of that house," Po Strode warned. "I saw young men over there earlier. They were very brazen."

Ina stretched the phone cord to the window looking across the Strodes' gardens. She pulled up the blinds. A thin-faced, tired old woman stared back: herself.

"Where are you?" Ina asked.

"I'm *here*. Next door. You're in danger, Ina. You should never have stolen that beer."

"The house is fine," Ina reported.

"There were boys knocking at your door. They tried your knob. They looked in your windows."

"How many?" Ina asked. Po Strode's agitation was infectious.

"I couldn't tell. Their movements seemed *deliberate.*"

"There was a boy here earlier dropping off a block of salt I'd bought at the grocery," Ina said. "I wanted to ask if Hector could come over and carry it down to the basement for me."

"Now?"

"Rain's expected. The salt's on the walk now. It will wash into the grass and kill it if I leave it where it is," Ina said.

"I don't think any of us should go outside until morning," Po said.

"Send Hector alone. He can take care of himself," Ina said, grinning faintly at the woman in the glass, the troublemaker, the widow who would set her snares for another woman's husband.

"They prey on old men as much as they do old women," Po said.

"Can I borrow him if I walk over and get him? Then walk him home?"

"Hold the phone, please," Po said, cool as a long-distance operator.

The Strodes had thrown a party in their gardens one summer and Ina was asked by Hector to dance. His mustache as he drew her close was already turning white and his movements as he guided her among the other couples were slightly mushy with uncertainty. He had not spoken a word to her and the breath he expelled against her neck came in time with the music. Toward the end of the song he propelled her twirling into a dark hallway formed by a blushing rose arbor, and before he sent her spinning back out to the party he placed a kiss that tasted of barbecued ribs and gin on her mouth. She never told Vincent about that kiss. He was sitting with friends on a bench licking sauce from his fingers and hadn't noticed her brief disappearance. Hector never mentioned the kiss, either. His wife laughed along with the guests who witnessed the sudden maneuver, and she doubtlessly wondered what had transpired during that string of moments when Ina and Hector were out of sight.

"We'll be over shortly," Po said into the phone. "Hector's gallant streak knows no age, apparently."

Ina sat by a window in the darkened front room hoping the dangerous boys would not return for their beer while Po and Hector crossed the yard. The phone rang again and she carried her glass into the kitchen to answer it. The connection was fraught with the exotic hollowness of long distance.

"It's Annie, Mom. How are you?"

"I'm splendid, sweetheart," Ina replied, slipping into that voice of ultimate satisfaction she used in the early stages of her conversations with her children. "I'm in the middle of a small crisis— but I can talk for a minute."

"What sort of crisis?"

"It's a long story. Two conversations in one day—to what do I owe this?"

"Your call this morning was so—*uncharacteristic,*" Annie said. "I called to be sure you were all right."

"I'm fine. Honestly."

"You didn't go fishing in that horrid river."

"I didn't go fishing," Ina said. "How's Meg? And Don?"

"Don's at work. Meg's down at Katy's."

Ina heard her daughter sigh, heard a swirl of liquid. Annie favored candy drinks with deceptive, almost timed-release impacts.

"Is it dark there?" Ina asked, her attention on the Strodes' imminent arrival.

"Oh, no. Another beautiful day."

Ina chewed her lip over the inanities they were exchanging. She was amazed as always as how they held to the unimportant subjects in their conversations, cherishing the surfaces, shaping them into a nearly limitless source of material. She wondered if Annie had a list of topics on a sheet of paper in front of her.

"How's Helene?"

"We went shopping today. They're erecting barricades so people won't walk off with their precious shopping carts."

"I don't know why you stay there. There are a million nicer places," Annie said.

"It's home," Ina said. "It's paid for."

"You can make a home in another, nicer place. You and Helene could buy a condo and live like queens," Annie said.

"Queens in our dotage? I've heard about those places."

"They can be very nice," Annie said. "When people get older it's only natural to pull in a little. To keep only those things most precious to them. It's less work. Less worry."

"Have you gone into real estate, dear?"

Ina waited for her daughter to laugh, but Annie uttered only a terse "Nonsense," and Ina felt the call begin to go bad.

Noises came from out back, scrapings and thumps against the stairs.

"Can you hang on, sweetheart?" Ina asked. "I've got visitors. You remember the Strodes—I've asked Hector to carry a block of salt downstairs for me. His wife thinks I'm trying to steal him from her."

"Are you?" Annie asked, intrigued.

"Goodness, no. But it's fun to have her think I am."

"I can hold for a second," Annie said. "But *only* a second."

Ina put down the phone and went to the back door. Hector had carried the salt block up the porch steps and now squatted ingloriously upon it, knees by his ears, arms hugging his shins. He was nearly gasping, and light from Ina's kitchen glistened on his face. Po Strode stood on the first step down, poised to catch her husband when he toppled backward.

"I told him to wait and have you open the milkbox," she said. "But no—he had to show off and *muscle* it up those stairs."

The milkbox was built in the wall to the right of the stairs. It was six feet off the ground, with an outer door the milkman could open and a bolted inner door that opened into Ina's powder room. She kept things to read on the toilet there in the summer, and stuffed it with old towels and paper to insulate against the cold in the winter.

"That's a straight lift," Ina said. "Hector was right going up a step at a time." She felt uneasy with Hector's softly panting face at the level of her waist.

"My daughter's on the phone," she said. "Long distance. Could you just carry it to the cellar? You can leave it on the floor. I'll get it into the softener."

"How, for instance?" Po challenged.

"I'm here, Ina," Hector said. "You might as well make good use of me." He clapped salt dust from his hands.

"You be careful," his wife cautioned.

Hector faced the block, positioning his hands in the indentations molded for just that purpose. With a grunt Hector lifted the block off the porch. Swinging the door open for him, Ina listened attentively for the blowout of his heart. He shuffled into the house and Ina went ahead to open the basement door and turn on the light.

The basement steps were narrow and made treacherous with an encroaching collection of junk; on every step Ina saw things she would never use again, the bottles, sacks, brushes, and cartons of old shoes she could discard to squeeze into a new condo, to *pull in*. The path down was barely eighteen inches wide and Hector Strode, teetering with his burden at the head of the stairs, seemed nearly to lose his will.

"Take a rest," Po said.

Ina went down to the foot of the stairs. Silently she implored Hector to keep coming; time was passing in the precisely calibrated units of the phone company. She could imagine clearly the growth and tenor of Annie's impatience, it being exactly like her own.

"Just a little farther," Ina encouraged.

"Do you want to kill him?" Po snarled.

Ina went to the water softener and removed the lid from the brine tank. The top of the stairs was out of sight. She would let Hector decide.

There followed a crash and a violent biting of wood. The salt block came into view in its descent, bouncing over one step to gouge a notch out of the next, shards and splinters of itself disengaging from the main body as it fell. Ina wondered if Hector Strode would follow, wondered if in falling he would be reduced like a star plunging through the atmosphere to land as the salt block landed, a mere nub of itself, a scattering of such nubs that she would have to sweep into a dustpan.

But Hector didn't fall.

"I'm just awfully goddamn sorry, Ina," he said, coming down the stairs, kicking salt ahead of him. "I was taking a breather—or getting ready to—and my hands took a breather about a half second before the rest of me did. *Shit.*"

"Hector Strode!" Po scolded.

Hector turned to look up at his wife. Something in the exertion, perhaps in the mischievous excitement of the calamity he had caused, and which he enjoyed as it unfolded, something filled him with himself, for he repeated distinctly, "I said shit, and I meant shit. Now grab that broom."

"Grab your own broom," Po Strode said, and they heard her thumped steps departing, then the bang of the door.

"She'll be back shortly," Hector predicted. "She doesn't like me to be alone with women. Especially widows. Especially *you.*"

"What an imagination, Hector," Ina said. She climbed past him, and at the top of the stairs slid the broom down to him. "Put it all in the brine tank," she said.

She snatched up the phone but Annie was gone. Ina had been granted one second, then she had abused that prize greatly. Her finger rested on the button that would send her voice back to L.A. But she removed it. Annie would be eager for reaction to the rebuke of hanging up on her mother and Ina felt too strong at the moment to provide that satisfaction. The exploding salt had filled her life like a mild spice that lingered briefly and left an aftertaste of experience. Something out of the ordinary had taken place. The day had been like that.

She heard the plunk of the salt going into the water and it was like a signal of Hector's location providing moments of privacy. She opened an Old Style and called an invitation down the stairs; he stood at the bottom with the broom, a mound of pulverized salt at his feet.

"Thank you, Ina," he replied breathlessly, himself made temporarily wild by the tumbling salt and his presence without his wife in the home of a widow of mystery. "A cold beer would be wonderful."

She awaited him at her kitchen table. She had set out a glass and noticed the inner sleeve of dust the glass contained. It had been such a long time between guests. She wiped out the glass with her fingers.

Hector took the seat not across from her, where she had placed the beer and glass like a namecard for him to heed, but at her right hand. She leaned back an inch. He was perspiring. He poured beer into the glass and chuckled. He drank, laughed, and smacked his lips.

"Po will be back within the minute," he said, "so I'd best speak frankly and right now. It's so rare for me to have the opportunity to speak privately with a woman other than my wife."

"What is Po's real name?" Ina asked, viewing her question as a chock thrown under a wheel that had begun to careen.

"What? Po? Why it's short for Polly—which is short for Penelope," Hector said. He drank beer, his place lost momentarily. Ina readied another deflective question.

"I'm surprised she's stayed away this long," he said, half rising from his chair to look out the window at his house. Ina doubted that he saw much. He said nothing for a time and Ina wondered what his point was in remaining; a hair to irritate his wife?

"I've watched you over here all my life, it seems," he suddenly declared, a little sweat and beer on his upper lip.

"Hector—"

"Wait. What's the point in keeping secrets now? I'm not going to embarrass all concerned by running off and abandoning dear Penelope. But I wanted it stated for someone other than myself to hear that I long considered Vincent the luckiest man on Earth."

"And look what it got him," Ina said, fending off mortification.

"Ina, Ina," Hector murmured, eyes averted. "I just had to tell you. Not to prompt any sort of response from you—but just to have it in the public domain."

"I'm flattered. Truly. Now let's get it back out of the public domain," Ina said.

"Surely you must have known," he said. "A hundred times you must have caught me staring over here. I can't remember all the false pretexts I used to have a word with Vincent."

"I knew you liked me," Ina said, thinking of the kiss at the end of the dance. "I've always had a way with men."

"You put us at our ease," Hector said. "Other men have mentioned the same thing to me. Po resents that in you because it's a quality she doesn't possess."

"I won't have you sit here and speak ill of your wife," Ina said. "That's unfaithfulness as clear as two people in bed together."

Hector blushed and gulped beer; a little spilled on his shirt. Ina was warmed by the Old Style and the circumstances; she felt flirtatious and in command, putting a man at ease by shocking him, telling him a little of what he wanted to hear.

The remark about a man and a woman in bed had just come to her; the picture in her mind as she said it was of her and Vincent, two pale bodies, much younger, lost in a jumble of striped sheets. She could not remember ever being attracted to Hector beyond the cool friendship of neighbors. There had only been Vincent. She raised her eyes to Hector and ached for her husband. The longing stunned her and she had to stifle a groan too private for anyone ever to hear. She blinked and drank, caught off balance. She thought she had moved past such honed moments of grief.

It was Ina, then, who rose from her seat to see if Po Strode was on her way back. Hector concentrated on his beer. He was chagrined, because despite his protestations to the contrary, he *had* hoped his declaration would lead to something. He thought he might dislodge from Ina's heart an emotion that he could use. She had merely shushed him.

"I'm glad I told you," he lumbered.

"If it was important for you to tell me—then I'm glad you told me, too."

"Then we're *both* glad."

"I suspect," she said, distracted.

He brightened and leaned closer. He rested his hand cupped like a trap on the tabletop, preparing to spring should her own hand stray near.

"I want to thank you for getting my salt in, Hector," she said. "But I've had a long day and I think it's time for you to go."

He stood and looked again out the window. "It was my pleasure," he declared. "I know what Po says about you, but when the opportunity presented itself, to come help you, I couldn't refuse."

"You're too kind. What does Po say about me?"

"Women things. They carry no weight with me, and I'm the only person she ever talks to. She told me she found you on the river stairs."

"Women things," Ina mused.

"Some women—Po, for instance—can't abide anyone different, anyone the least out of the ordinary. An old woman, she sees another old woman climbing the river stairs, it gets her to thinking that maybe she isn't living her life to the fullest. She stays home all day worrying and she sees another old woman—"

"An *older* woman than herself," Ina said.

"Don't brag," Hector said, and winked. "She sees a woman older than herself out and about, she begins to think maybe she is wasting time. But that is terrible to contemplate, an old woman wasting time when time is short. Such an admission would require great courage and great insight—which my Po, bless her heart, doesn't have. So she makes you out not to be free-spirited or daring, but mad. A drunk. A walker in your sleep."

"Let her," Ina said.

They heard a commotion out back and then the crisp steps of Po Strode's return. She came through the door in such a whirl of indignation that Ina almost did not notice that she had, in her absence, tied a ribbon in her hair. Ina smiled and offered Po something to drink, which was refused. Po touched the ribbon. Hector had not risen, turned around, moved at all.

"Is he twisting your ear?" Po asked nervously. "He's become full of words and philosophies in his old age. Years he never said three sentences in a line, and now when I'd appreciate a little peace and quiet I can't shut him up."

Hector worked his hands as if squaring up a phantom deck of cards. Po came up shyly behind him and rested her left hand lightly on his shoulder. She wore no ring, bracelet, or polish, nothing to make pretty the hewn, toughened hand resting there. Her face was plain and unpainted. There was only the ribbon she had put in her hair, while her husband was declaring his love to her neighbor.

"Let's go home, Strode."

"Thank you for bringing in my salt," Ina said.

"Fool dropped it down the stairs," Po derided, hand still in place.

Hector caught Ina's glance. Then he rose to his feet.

"He got it downstairs," Ina said. "That's all I was concerned with. One piece or a thousand makes no difference to me."

"Will you be all right here alone?" Hector asked.

"I'll be fine," Ina said jovially, pushing her guests gently toward the door. "Go home. Both of you. And thanks again."

She threw the bolts after the Strodes were safe in the shadows of their gardens, then fastened the door chain. She swept the basement stars and finished with a little mound of salt and dirt that she transferred to a dustpan and threw away. She double-checked the lock on the cellar door. She looked in on her cache of stolen beer.

There were reading materials on the table next to her bed; the newspaper, junk mail she had not gotten to earlier, she would read every word. There was a water-stained spy novel of incomprehensible plotting, and a thick novel about a good woman in love with a rotten man. She set her fresh glass on the table, then turned out the light while she undressed.

The Crabbs' shrine was without movement and she stood at the window for a long time picking at her buttons; just studying the darkness. But no one was there, or they saw her watching and sat motionless with hands cupped over the lights of their cigarettes. Her clothes came off with an efficiency that saddened her. Vincent was not present to appreciate her slow disrobing, once one of their favorite things. She was out of her clothes and into her nightgown so quickly she could not recall being naked. Nor could she remember if she had eaten dinner that evening.

Then a dark car full of boys parked on the street beneath her window. A tall boy emerged. As she watched, he pointed at her house, pointed almost directly at her.

Ina tied the bow of her nightgown in a double knot. Her hands shook a bit. She stepped back into her shoes, still moist and warm from the day's activities. They returned to her the illusion of readiness, if not of speed.

Other boys were emerging from the car. She prayed they would cross to the Crabbs' lot to have their secret party, but for a long time they just stood by the car. The boy who had pointed at her house had disappeared. His friends were lighting cigarettes, playfully punching each other, their laughter rising to her.

Ina felt like a wraith descending, all insubstantial cloth and old air. A light still burned in the kitchen. The phone when she lifted it to her ear buzzed reassuringly and she set it back quickly lest the boys outside hear. She saw the car (was it maroon?) from a downstairs window, saw the boys with their insouciant poses against the fenders, hot buttons of ash suspended before their faces.

And there seemed to be fewer of them. She thought she had counted five boys waiting for the first, and now there were only four. They had been able to slip a second boy through the net of invisibility that existed everywhere she could not see.

Ina went to the front window. The street had a certain depth of shadows, but no motion, no boys clustered at the head of the river stairs.

A boy walked beneath her window and Ina gasped. He looked her way, but moved on. He was a curly-haired head and a pair of broad shoulders, the rest of him obscured by shrubs, bobbing along as if on a quick current. She decided he had not seen her. When she returned to the window facing the car only three boys remained, and, as she watched, another boldly broke away and walked out of sight into her backyard.

She dropped the phone once trying to dial. The numbers she

punched at with her fingers broke up unfinished and became worthless hailings. She awakened strangers in her first two attempts at reaching Helene, and then she decided that was just as well, for her blind sister would only be submerged in a panic of helplessness.

She would call Hector. Earlier that evening he had all but said that he loved her; now she would see to what depth his devotion ran.

The beep of dialing in her ear could not hide an insistent rapping at her back door. The door had a window that looked into the kitchen and on down the hall that ran through the center of the house. Ina could not remember if she had drawn the shade on that window.

The phone rang and was almost immediately answered by Po Strode. In the background Ina heard the upbeat din of the TV and wondered again at the hour.

"This is Ina. Could I talk to Hector real quick?"

"What about, hon?" Po asked, her voice with a ribbon in it.

"It's an emergency. Please put him on."

"Salt giving you a problem?"

"Po!" Ina cried, holding down the volume on her desperation. "It's an *emergency.* I'm not trying to steal your husband."

"Fuff," Po said, and went for Hector.

"Ina? Po says it's an emergency?"

"Yes," Ina whispered. "Those boys you heard about? The ones I took the beer from? They're outside. I think there are six of them. They're knocking on my back door."

"I don't see anybody over there," Hector said. "But it's pretty dark."

"Could you come over?"

"Six, you say? Toughs, are they?"

"I think six. Tough—I don't know. Call the police, then come over. I'd call—I wouldn't bother you at all—but you're so close."

"No bother, Ina," Hector said. "Sit tight. Don't answer the door. I'll come to the front and knock. Three rapid knocks, then two with space between. Got that? They'll think I'm your husband."

She looked around the corner and down the hall to the back door and saw that she had pulled the shade. She felt safe with Hector on the way and the police alerted. She felt the warmth of an adventure safely negotiated and wished that she had her glass handy to sit in the dark and savor. The knocking had ceased.

She looked and there were no boys by the car. She began to worry again. The knocking resumed at the front door. No rhythm to it, no hint of the code that Hector had established and Ina had forgotten. She heard only young voices and confident laughter. They reminded her of the way Vincent and Rudy would congregate on Ina and Helene's stoop and plot innocent trouble to win the girls' love. They would be anything they thought would do some good: acrobats, jesters, raconteurs, braggarts, jugglers, fools. Helene and Ina sat on the flower boxes or against the base of a tree and awaited their enthrallment. The boys were sometimes intimidated by the sisters' willingness to be fought over. Rudy was always the most daring. He broke a foot one summer walking on his hands down the stairs, and for a time he added mild obscenities to his speech until he saw himself losing ground with the girls. Vincent allowed Rudy these forms of physical daring and was content to sit and talk and comment on Rudy's displays. Vincent was all deflection, insinuation, subtlety.

Boys were now peering boldly into her dark rooms. One scratched at the screen. Ina sat motionless in a chair, listening to her heartbeat. Vincent, whose heart had proved fallible, slept on his stomach because she once complained that the drumming in his chest kept her awake. She on occasion draped a hand across his rib cage as they lay like spoons and the pounding of his heart nearly bounced her hand away. Now her own heart was tearing loose in her chest. It might have echoed Hector's code, but she would never have known. Boys were at the door, at the windows, talking and laughing, an infestation of boys. Would they leave her alone if she lobbed the six cans of stolen beer out a second-floor window?

She heard a boy say, "I see someone right there. It's an old lady sitting in the dark. Right *there.*"

She had been discovered, but she dared not move. There was

a chance she might be mistaken for shadows resembling an old lady sitting in a chair.

Other boys came to the window to look at her. They packed their curious faces into the rectangular dimensions of the frame as if she were a museum display, a peep show. Ina did not move, though her heart seemed to set her nightgown ashiver.

"I don't see nothing," said another boy.

"She's right *there.* I could fucking touch her if the window wasn't in the way."

"Is that her head there?"

"Where?"

"I *see* her. There's her hand. Her hands are folded in her lap. She's looking the other way."

"Hey lady?" They tapped on the window. "Lady?"

"Maybe she's dead."

"Lady?"

She heard a solid pounding at the back door and it matched perfectly Hector's code that came to her memory at the moment of its use. With a quick movement she began to get out of the chair, and at her back the boys in the window shrieked.

Hector was at the back door with Po and one of the boys and a chubby policeman garbed in blue, a checkerboard band around his hat.

The boy was saying nervously, "I'm Margie Blaines's grandson. I brung the block of salt home today for you? You weren't home, so she told me to come back tonight and carry it inside for you. I forgot, until now. Sorry if I scared you."

"You didn't scare me," Ina said.

The boy glanced apprehensively at the cop and at the Strodes. Po carried a skillet. Hector was armed with a tapered length of pine dowel, a gleaming spike pounded through the wide business end. Boys drifted around the corner of the house. Ina counted them as they came into sight.

"You should've rung the buzzer and stated your intentions," the policeman said.

"We knocked. We knocked *plenty.*"

"The salt's not out here," the policeman said. "Why didn't you assume it had been carried indoors and just leave?"

"My grandma would want to know *exactly* what happened to the salt," said the boy.

"Thank you for your concern," Ina said. "All of you. The salt was transported down to the basement earlier. Thank you for coming back to help. Tell your grandma I said thank you. Thank you, Po. Hector. Officer. I've caused such a stir tonight. Such a *bother.*"

She stepped without hesitation back into the comforting darkness of her house and shut the door. Everyone else would have to find their own way home. She threw the bolts and fastened the chain. Engines turned over outside, car doors slammed. She was quite proud of her exit; it had been gracious, dignified, but with a quality of dismissiveness, as if they were all present at her behest and then she was finished with them.

Before climbing to her bedroom she turned on an extra light here and there. She was extremely tired. No one could convince her that the hour was not late, perhaps getting on toward midnight. She missed the late nights with Vincent, all the free time after the children had gone.

But she did not pass a clock on her way to bed. She took a sip from her blue glass, testing to determine if the beer had warmed beyond its level of effectiveness, but it was cold enough, and delicious. She slipped between her sheets, then wriggled down deep until she was comfortable; another long drink, then a yawn. A slurp of beer dribbled free from the corner of her mouth and she caught some of it in the slow cup of her hand. She was able to laugh at herself. Vincent was laughing with her. She closed her eyes and thought: In a minute I will get up and take out my teeth.

PART TWO

♦ ───────────────────────────

The Man
in the Milkbox

Ina's birthday fell on a murderously hot day in August. The newspaper that morning carried a picture of a man and woman celebrating their seventieth wedding anniversary. They looked decrepit even to Ina, the wife eighty-seven, the husband eighty-six. Fanning herself with the newspaper, Ina was too hot to be more than mildly amazed. She imagined the couple's parents seething with disapproval, claiming they were too young to understand love, to make a marriage work. And then, as if out of spite, as if to prove their parents wrong, they had stayed together for seventy years. They had been married the day before Ina was born.

She was going to Helene's early because it was her habit on her birthday to get out of the house before her children phoned. Each call lasted about fifteen minutes. Each was in retrospect a jumble of inanities; they struck her as small storms of impatience in her ear. Spontaneity, surprise, delight, all were missing, replaced by duty. She hadn't heard from Ray or Annie since the day she went down to the river.

She dabbed at her face with a cool cloth. She had been ready to go for ten minutes but she lingered over unnecessary tasks, and she couldn't fool herself; she hoped to be snagged unwillingly by one of her children before she got away. She missed talking at length with them. In the middle of phone conversations they would abruptly express concern at the passage of valuable time and cut her off, upsetting her, though she never felt herself working toward a great truth or disclosure. Her children had been so far away for so long that she had lost the ability to read their voices for nuance.

So she left the house. She was wearing a light dress without a slip and her Nikes. Wrapped in a towel and weighting her bag were a frosty can of Coors, the last of the bounty she had found in the river, and three cold Old Styles. She expected to be detained on the street and questioned about the heft of her bag and the optimism in her step. But she took the chance because the times in general were perilous and she refused to stop living because of them. Ina understood, also, that Helene would not have any beer for her, birthday girl or no.

The frames on her sunglasses were red, the lenses a soothing, familiar blue. She thought they projected an attitude of well-to-do frivolity, which was precisely the case. It wasn't every day a girl turned seventy. The sidewalk gleamed like nickel. At the first corner she paused to catch a hot breath of air and to dab with a hankie at the loose skin beneath her throat. The neighborhood was sagging in the heat. Children played in the dusty yards, shirtless, diaperless, their motions sluggish and their cries whiny and impatient, bees drawn to the ice cream on their chins; their mothers sat spread-legged on the stoops, stunned by the heat and their responsibility. Ina raised a hand to them; some waved back.

She found the initials in the sidewalk as she came up on Helene's house. She paused and traced them with her toe. VL. Her third birthday without Vincent. He had always bought her several little gifts and then something expensive he saved for last. He presented each gift with the same touching expression of fear that she would not like what he had to give. She loved the fact that after all their years together he still could not read her absolutely clearly. A delicious little edge of uncertainty was cultivated.

She turned in at Helene's squawking gate. Helene would hear, then make her way to the back door to let her sister in.

But Helene did not answer Ina's trill of greeting coming down the walk, and she was not at the door, and she did not answer when Ina rang the bell, then knocked on the door. Everything was hot and absolutely still. In front, Ina opened her sister's mailbox and there was a water bill, a catalog, and a card from a dress shop announcing a sale on maternity smocks.

"Helene?" she called through a window to the left of the door.

She looked through the sheers and saw nothing; most comfortingly she saw no body on the floor awaiting discovery.

Ina carried her bag down the stairs and followed the walk around to the back again. The flowerbeds were choked with browned weeds and perennials. The earth had the cracked look of dry skin examined under a sharp glass. A sprinkler's arc fanned beyond the neighbors' fence of lush ivy and sunflowers. She shifted her bag. She was dying for a beer.

She knocked on the door, waited to a count of twenty, then rang the buzzer long and loud. She entertained for the first time the serious possibility that some harm had come to her sister: death, diabetic coma, a broken hip, a wrong turn into a closet whose door locked behind her. There was no chance Helene had gone off by herself. She lacked the courage to do that. It in fact was a sore point between the sisters, Ina frequently haranguing Helene to get out on her own more often. Ina feared her own death would plunge Helene into a state of helplessness that could have been prevented.

She felt in her bag for the key Helene had given to her. It was safety-pinned to the bag's blue lining but Ina's damp fingers could not work the pin clasp. It kept slipping from her grasp, and when she looked for a place to dry her fingers none existed; everything was moist, slick, and hot to the touch. She was on her knees on the back stoop cursing her sister's memory. The pin would not come undone.

She propped open the screen door with her hip and set the bundle of beer aside to lighten the purse. By stretching, then slightly tearing the bag's lining, she was able to get Helene's key in the lock without unpinning it. The door swung effortlessly in on a dim mud room of old winter coats and a jumble of Rudy's work boots. Ina dropped the purse in her haste and worry, and it hung there by the key in the lock. As she hurried up the stairs to the kitchen she heard the lining tear away.

The kitchen was untouched. The dishes were done. The air smelled scoured and rinsed. Mere blindness would never be an excuse for Helene not to clean her house. Her affliction might have made her even more fastidious; she could not count on her keen eye to spy grains of filth, therefore she took painstaking care to get them all the first time.

Ina looked in every downstairs room and found no trace of her sister. She called out her name in a clear, frightened voice, though by now Ina was certain Helene was dead and lying in the last place Ina would look.

She went down the cellar stairs, descending into darkness because Rudy had not repaired the switch at the top, believing it a simple matter to get across to the light cord in the nearest corner. Ina made this passage shuffling. She found the cord and snapped it on, but nothing happened. Perhaps Rudy saw no point in replacing dead bulbs; perhaps the light had burned out and Helene was not aware.

The cellar was actually quite nice, cool and dank. She touched a finger to her brow and flicked away silvery sweat. She decided Helene would never have ventured into the cellar. Such a trip was too blatantly dangerous.

So Ina went up to the first floor, then quickly to the second, feeling all the way that she was rising through thickening layers of heat. The upstairs rooms were solid with a sense of suffocation. Ina checked them as rapidly as possible, tearing open closet doors, getting down to look under the beds, examining the screens for the rip Helene would have left behind falling through.

But though the rooms bore her sister's scrubbed, humorless stamp, there was no sign of Helene.

On the downstairs phone (after freshening her hankie at the kitchen tap), Ina called Amanda.

"Is your mother there?"

"She's at home. I talked to her a half-hour ago," Amanda said.

"I'm at her house. I can't find her."

"She has to be there. She was complaining about the heat and making fun of Daddy for being too cheap to put in air-conditioning."

"Would she go anywhere?" Ina asked.

"Mother? No. When she had her eyesight we would go to a movie or to the library when it got this hot. Now I ask her to

come over here and she won't even do that. The discomfort of
being with me outweighs the comfort of my air-conditioner."

"Well, I'm worried," Ina said.

"Oh—happy birthday, Ina."

"Thank you, dear."

"Seventy?"

"Yes, seventy."

"You don't seem that old. You're very sharp. *With it.*"

"Hell, I could be president."

"Ha!" laughed Amanda.

"What does this have to do with finding your mother?"

"Nothing. I'm sorry. I'm just sure she's all right," Amanda said.
Ina heard a bell tone on the other end of the line. "I've got
company, Ina. Call me when you find her. But I'm *absolutely*
certain she is fine. Bye."

She took her key from the lock, the key's pin trailing a little
ragged blue flag. She noticed for the first time that outside the
dim cave of the purse the lining was patterned with small, faint
gold initials, a complicatedly fancy interlocking of V's or E's, S's
or Z's, she could not tell for sure.

Coins had scattered on the doorstep. She scraped them back
into her purse, along with an amber bottle of pills, a ballpoint
pen pressed into her hand by a handsome, insistent Gray Panther,
and a packet of plastic syringes, extras she carried for Helene. She
felt sweaty and undignified squatting there over her torn purse,
her sister missing, her sister's only child unconcerned.

She made her way to the backyard bench and sat down in the
birch tree's shade. She dabbed at her face, waited for her heart to
slow. The bench was wide enough for Helene and Ina to sit side
by side on summer nights, Vincent and Rudy had sprawled at
their feet, fireflies going off like distant flashbulbs. Vincent made
a whistle from a blade of crabgrass, the honking noise he produced sounding like something in pain. Rudy, even in the summer
before he died, did handstands on the grass, his glasses, change,
keys raining out of his pockets.

The steaming air that closed around Ina was suffused with a
ticking that grew insistent when she gave it her full attention:

insects, birds, distant traffic. It was relaxing just to sit still and listen, as if the blood beating in her ears had cooled and drained away. And as she looked around at her sister's backyard she sensed there was a clue in front of her that she was missing.

She swung her eyes from the backdoor across the browned grass, the ragged shrubs and the fence that marked the property line, a small garden that Rudy had put in and Helene abandoned, a stack of flagstones against the back wall of the garage, two trash cans, the walkway passing alongside the garage and then up three steps to the gate in the alley fence, a flowerbed gone to weeds except for nearly immortal sunflowers, and then the fence that ran behind the tree and the bench where she was sitting.

The air ticked and she watched.

Set high in the garage's back wall was a small four-pane window turned so it was a diamond shape. The window had always been dark because the garage door was always closed. But now there was light in that window, a dusty, hot light that drew Ina up off the bench and across the yard to the garage's back door. As she approached she heard the hum of a motor. The side door was locked, though the dark blue knob vibrated in her grasp with the rhythm of an engine. She hurried around to the front of the garage. Her heart was beating furiously again and her face was blistering hot, though dry to the touch.

The garage door was open. She smelled gasoline, a smell she had always liked. Helene was in Rudy's Omega with the windows shut and the engine running. Ina heard the radio playing through all that glass, which was cool to the touch when Ina tapped on it.

Helene turned her head to her sister, but her eyes did not come around quite far enough. Her hand stretched gracefully out to touch unerringly on the radio volume knob. The music fell away. The window by Helene's head lowered an inch.

"Yes?"

"It's me."

"Why—happy birthday, dear."

"Thank you. What are you doing in there?"

"Isn't it obvious? I'm keeping warm."

Ina laughed with relief and anticipation. She went around the car and her sister had the door unlocked by the time she got there. Ina sank into the seat next to Helene, whose cool, smiling face was turned to her sister in welcome. Ina pulled the door shut, and the day suddenly was near perfect, among her best birthdays ever.

"Isn't this heat beastly?" Ina asked.

"Isn't *this* divine?"

"Yes," Ina agreed. That air was cold on the moistest parts of her body.

"You sound overheated," Helene said. "I can almost hear your heart over all the machinery."

"I was *worried* about you," Ina complained. "I come to your house and there's no sign of you. No note. No *word.*"

"Sorry," Helene said without contrition.

"And only by chance do I find you out here. With the motor running. Sitting alone."

"Did you think I'd killed myself?" Helene asked, a dark fascination lighting her voice.

"I thought—no, I didn't. But you could have made a miscalculation."

"I'm careful to open the door. I do this quite often," Helene said.

Ina plucked her dress away from her bosom, letting the cold at her.

"It *is* heavenly," she allowed. Her head drifted back against the seat. "I remember Mother complaining how hot it was being pregnant with me in the summer. I can't remember a cool birthday in my entire life. That does something to a girl."

"Mine is always ice and snow," Helene said. "How much gas is left, by the way?" She tapped a dial in front of her. "This one is the fuel gauge."

Ina leaned across the seat to look. "Between a quarter tank and a half tank," she said.

Helene nodded. Her hands gripped the wheel.

"I spoke to Amanda," Ina said.

"Did she call?"

"I called her from your house—to see if you had gone over there. She has air-conditioning."

"I know," Helene said. "So do I."

"But what if you want a cold drink or to use the bathroom?"

"Why—I go use it," Helene said. She looked straight ahead through the windshield's blue glass. To the rear, the glass was colored with the alley's scorched glare.

"She had a caller," Ina said.

"Oh?" Helene said, her voice going low and excited with curiosity, such a strange and abrupt transformation that they both laughed.

"I heard her bell when I was talking to her," Ina said. "She was immediately anxious to be rid of me."

"Do you suppose it was a man? At this time of day?"

"Perhaps a friend just trying to cool off," Ina said. She had memories of Vincent coming to her in the afternoon; work put aside, the children in school, the bedroom light perfect.

"Perhaps," Helene murmured, preoccupied.

"She told me your love of air-conditioning was not strong enough to overcome your dislike for her."

Helene looked toward Ina. "Are you trying to start a fight? Or ruin my afternoon?"

"I'm sorry, dear. No."

"I love Amanda."

"I know you do."

"I'm certainly closer to her than someone I know is to her children."

"Meany," Ina said, accepting the blow because she had started the little tiff. "*Cruel.* My kids are two thousand miles away."

"For a reason."

Ina took a deep breath. The air felt warmer, closer, the hot light from the alley beginning to worm through the car.

"I said I was sorry," Ina replied.

"You're right, dear. I'm sorry, too. Who could be at Amanda'a at this time of day?"

"Go inside and call her," Ina said.

"She wouldn't admit to anything. She could be panting to beat the band and she'd play dumb. I know that girl."

"It's no crime having company. She's forty-two years old."

"Forty-two. Living in an apartment. No husband, let alone kids. A tedious life," Helene said.

"No wonder she entertains men in the afternoon," Ina said lightly, and laughed when her sister faced her to judge the intent in the remark. "We all have to have something to look forward to."

"Did you look forward to *that?*" Helene asked, almost in a whisper.

"Of course," Ina said.

"Well don't sound so proud!"

"I'm not—I didn't. I loved Vincent."

"Are you saying I didn't love Rudy?"

"I didn't say anything of the sort. Let's just drop it."

Helene gripped the wheel at ten o'clock and two o'clock. She turned up the air-conditioner. The car had been Rudy's last major purchase, his way of celebrating when they owned their house free and clear. Even then, it took him almost a year to work up the courage to part with the money.

"You really know where things are in this car," Ina said, grateful for the opportunity to praise.

"I've driven it enough. I always thought I was a better driver than he was."

"You were," Ina said. "He scared me. He went too fast."

"He was in control, though," Helene said. "Rudy never put anyone in danger."

"*Helene.*"

"Yes, dear?"

"I was agreeing with you. I wasn't belittling Rudy," Ina said. "Make it go backward."

Helene turned her eyes on Ina. "What?"

"Back it up. Then put it back in. It'll be fun."

"You are *crazy.*"

"I'll guide you," Ina said.

"I'm blind," Helene said, nearly wailing. "You are so cruel."

"No. *No.*"

"You think I don't miss being able to drive? You think I've forgotten how I used to be?"

"No. I didn't mean that," Ina said. "I just thought it would be fun. What harm can it do? You said yourself you used to be a good driver. Well, you're *still* a good driver—only with a slight disadvantage."

Helene laughed, a giggle of intrigue.

"You'll guide me?"

"I'll be your eyes. It will be fun."

Helene found the seat belt and fastened it across her insubstantial frame. Ina grew nervous; she might have underestimated the power they were about to tap. Helene reached beneath the dashboard and with a metallic grinding released the parking brake.

"First time it's been off since Rudy died," Helene said.

"Does the engine sound fast to you?" Ina asked.

"It sounds rocky."

"You don't have to do this."

"Scared?" Helene asked, looking over mischievously.

"A little, yes."

"I want to do it now." Helene placed her right foot on the brake and then by touch and memory moved the shift lever to Reverse. There was a hesitation as the gears took a moment to engage, then a twitch of readiness toward the rear.

"We caught them sleeping," Helene said with a smile. "They never expected to have to work again."

Ina turned in her seat to look out the rear window. Everything back there was hot and bright. The engine roared in her ear, a blind woman was at the wheel.

"Is it safe to proceed?"

"Maybe I should get out and look."

"I'd run you down," Helene said jovially. "If someone is coming they'll see my rear end and honk." She suddenly let loose with a mad laugh. "This was a *splendid* idea, dear. I feel so *alive*. Here goes."

She lifted her foot from the brake. The car did not retreat gradually but lunged half its length into the alley before Helene slammed down her foot. The women were rocked in their seats.

The car's interior was filling up with sunlight, a substance that seemed malevolent. Ina, only recently cool, had begun to perspire all over again.

"Guidance, please," Helene said.

"We've moved about halfway into the alley. The car is stationary. Feel free to terminate the experiment."

"It's idling like a damn jet," Helene said. She tapped the accelerator with the car in Neutral, but the rev did not diminish. She put it in Reverse again and eased off the brake.

Helene in control, the car rolled back. A gleaming corridor of sun and shadow opened to Ina's eyes. To her right was the quiet street the alley emptied into. She saw cars parked at the curb, a cat asleep on a garbage can, a trio of boys standing in the alley mouth.

"If this is going to work," Helene said in a scolding tone, "I'm going to need more help from you. I know this alley—but I could have mashed a toddler for all the directions you gave me."

"Forgive me."

Ina looked beyond her sister's reproachful face to the other end of the alley, where a police car had just turned in.

"Pull it back into the garage," Ina said. "The police are here."

"Where?" Helene asked, unruffled. She smoothly put the car in Drive and they glided into the garage's shadows.

"Easy," Ina said. "Three feet. Two. Eighteen inches."

Helene stopped the car. "Is my ass out of the alley?" It was the question Rudy had always asked.

Ina watched the police car pass. "You're fine," she reported.

Helene took a deep breath and wiped her hands on her dress. "Let's drive over to Amanda's," she suggested.

"I think that might not be wise."

"It's only a couple blocks. It's the middle of a hot day. No one will be on the streets."

"It's *dangerous*," Ina said. "There are children at the end of the alley. You couldn't react quickly enough to my instructions."

"Nonsense, dear," Helene replied. "We'll go so slow anything in our path will have *minutes* to get out of the way."

"Should we call first?"

"And spoil the surprise?"

"She's allowed to have a life of her own," Ina said.

"You just navigate," Helene said testily. "Leave my daughter's life to me. How much room between the car and the edge of the garage door on my side?"

"A foot, a bit more than a foot," Ina said.

"This damn car is just so *big,*" Helene complained. "I remember it was like steering a barge in a closet getting it out of here. But it *can* be done." She smiled at where she thought her sister waited, and felt with her hand until it lay on Ina's thigh. "I'll need you outside for this part of the trip, dear."

Ina opened her door and stepped back into the heat. Helene's window came down.

"Over to my side," she called.

Ina passed warily in front of the roaring engine. The car had taken on a dangerous element. It was no longer simply a cool pod of comfort on a steaming day. Helene had given it life, set it in motion.

"How do the tires look?"

"Maybe a tad low."

"We should stop at a service station. Fill 'er up. Check the oil. Inflate the tires to regulation pressure. Rudy was a stickler for that sort of thing. I have a credit card."

"Do you have a license?"

"Of course, dear."

"Is it valid?"

"Do you think I'd drive if it wasn't?" Helene asked. She put the car into Reverse, her foot on the brake. "Here's my plan," she said. "When the car is almost halfway out of the garage I'll start to turn the wheel to the left. You have to watch the wall on my side *and* the right front corner of the car. Shall we try it?"

The car began to roll backward and Ina wanted only to call to her sister to end the escapade.

"You're not helping," Helene chided. "I'm blind, remember. I need distances, positioning."

"Park it, Helene. This won't work."

"I'm driving to Amanda's today. With or without your help."

"You wouldn't get one hundred feet."

"But what a hundred feet! Imagine the carnage. The *scandal*. Are you going to allow that?"

Ina looked down the flank of the car. She saw herself elongated there, her torso like a ballerina's in a summer dress.

"Must I?" she asked.

"It would mean the world to me if you would help me do this one thing," Helene said.

"You've got about eight inches between the car and the wall," Ina said.

Helene let the car back up approximately half its length, then she began to turn the wheel to the left, letting the car nudge back inches at a time. She stopped at Ina's word.

"You're within an inch of the wall."

"Thank you, dear." Helene brought the wheel back to the right. The car slid forward. Space like stacked slivers appeared between the car and the left-side wall.

"How's my right front corner?" Helene asked. She was very hot, perspiring, with the window open, and from throwing the bg steering wheel.

"It will be tight," Ina assessed.

She had taken up a position in the alley. Helene sat for several moments without speaking or moving.

"Are you all right?" Ina asked.

"I'm replaying something in my mind. Do you ever do that?"

"Yes."

"I'm trying to see how Rudy got this car out so easily. He had such a touch."

"We still have time to park it," Ina said. "I'll treat you to a cab ride to Amanda's, then I'll take you both to lunch someplace nice."

"You and your money," her sister said with a sneer. "You think you can run my life because you have a little more money then I do."

"That's not true," Ina said.

"It's very much a fact, dear. And the answer is no."

The car was moving again, and Ina allowed it to shave paint from the garage-door frame, producing a shriek of friction.

"You *let* that happen," Helene accused.

"I want no part of this," Ina said calmly.

"I'm going to Amanda's!"

So go. *Go!*" Ina saw sweat fly with her words; what a hot and miserable day it had become. Helene began to cry. The car wedged against the door frame, she eased her forehead down on the wheel and wept. A moment later she had the presence of mind to put the car in Park and close the window. Ina stood in the alley, in the sun, in her damp clothes. The jutting tail of the car would block any traffic that happened along. She squinted her blue lenses and tapped one foot. In time, Helene lifted her head. She found a hanky in her purse and soaked up the tears that had mussed her face, then dabbed at the wetness behind her ears and at the base of her throat. Waiting in the heat, becoming less than amused, Ina nevertheless had to marvel at how much alike they were: the same gestures, mannerisms, and speech, their mother's same carefully structured feminine style designed to imply competence and effortless grace.

The window dropped again.

"Have you abandoned me, dear?" Helene asked.

"Never."

"Standing there in the hot sun?"

"We've been out here so long the sun has practically set. It's almost *chilly.*"

Helene laughed and touched her nose with the hanky. "This little trip is something I very much want to do," she said. "I'm asking for your help."

"Turn the wheel to the right and go forward."

Helene smiled and obeyed. Space appeared alongside the car. There was a dark, minor gouge in the garage-door frame, as if it had been pressed by an insistent hand. The surface of the car was unharmed.

"Straighten the wheel and come back until I say when, then turn hard to the left," Ina said.

She felt young—sixty-five, tops—moving from point to point to wriggle the car out. Light on her feet, she called out commands to her sister, a hand shading her eyes to see into the shadows, the other hand on her hip. A sensation in her joints and muscles of looseness, of lubrication, reminded Ina of her youth.

"Now hard to the left," she ordered, and like the difficult birth of a monstrous child the car was free.

Ina got in beside Helene.

"Bring the wheel around to the right to straighten out," Ina said. "And close that damn window."

Helene giggled, her head of metallic hair swirling in a half-arc of disbelief and an ache to see.

"We're out?"

"We're out."

"*Oo.* This is scary, dear."

"It's not too late to go back," Ina said, although now that they were out of the garage they could not go back; they had pushed into a current that carried them now. They could not return without traveling through the circle.

"No. I want this," Helene said with a firm nod.

Ina drew a deep breath of cooled air.

"Three boys are standing at the end of the alley," she said. "We'll give them the chance to move of their own accord."

The alley was straight and lined with urban artifacts so common they were invisible. In the distance Ina could see where things came to a point.

Helene was driving at a pace Ina could have beat walking, creeping up on the three boys. These boys were dressed in cut-off jeans, patchy bermuda shorts, Bulls T-shirts. Their hair was very short. They tossed a baseball back and forth. They appeared not to be aware of the car, though bits of glass, pebbles, and even a-beer cup popped and crunched beneath the slow roll of the tires.

"Stop here," Ina said. She licked salt from her upper lip; Vincent used to do that to her as a way of lengthening their kisses.

"Have the boys moved?"

"No. They don't seem to see us."

"They see us."

"Why won't they move then?"

"Because they're arrogant punks," Helene said, and punched the horn with her little fist, but no sound came forth. She covered the wheel with a frustrated slapping and groping for the magic button that produced the sound that would clear their path. But there was nothing.

"Our horn seems to be broken," Ina observed.

"Thank you, dear."

"Go forward again," Ina said. "Perhaps the momentum of the car will convince them we mean to pass."

The car ticked and crunched to within a yard of the boys and still they did not move. Ina told Helene to stop. They were nearly out of the alley, far enough for Ina to see up and down the street. Cool shade, no traffic. A perfect day for driving blind.

The three boys were intimidating. Up close, they looked very young and supple, their muscles aerodynamic and sheathed in skins three distinctly different shades of brown. One boy had a gold cross dangling from an earlobe. Another had a think gold chain looped through the upper rim of his left ear. The adornment made Ina wince, imagining the pain of the chain's insertion. The chain shook and the cross danced when the boys laughed, and they laughed frequently. They were where they were and they would not move, and every word or gesture, every passing moment, was a source of amusement to them.

"Wait here," Ina said. "Put it in Park."

She opened her door. Helene, frantic, clawed for his sister's arm.

"Where do you think you're going? Are you mad?"

"Wait." Ina stood up in the heat and hooked one arm over the door frame. She held out a hand that faintly shivered.

"Excuse me, gentlemen," she said. "We wish to pass, please."

Two of the boys did not look at her. The baseball passed back and forth between them. The third, the one with the cross, deigned to study her. His eyes were quite attractive, Ina thought, heavy-lashed, but he had switched them off perfectly dead and cold in the instant it took to shift his gaze from his friends to the car in the alley.

"We's here," he said.

"What did he say?" Helene asked. Ina hushed her.

"There's sidewalk galore for you to play on that is not in the path of our car," Ina said.

"Galore?" one asked derisively, getting big laughs from the other two. "Did she say *galore?*"

"Indeed," said another, and the trio hooted appreciatively, then went quickly through a round of slapped palms. To Ina, the boys seemed to tinkle and gleam there in the heat. She thought them absolutely beautiful and snakelike.

"What did they say? Can I go?"

"I've asked politely," Ina told the three.

"You can just politely wait," said the boy with the cross. "We is here first." They turned away from the widows.

Ina leaned down the spoke in a quiet voice to her sister.

"We're in Park, aren't we, dear?"

"Yes. May I go?"

"Leave it in Park, but floor it."

Helene grinned. "Really?"

"Really."

"Now?"

"Now."

Ina stood again. In a moment the engine roared with such force that a squall of dust and exhaust blew up around the car. Ina coughed and waved. One of the boys had dropped the baseball and run into the street after it. The other two seemed not the least impressed, nor even curious.

"My sister doesn't see too well," Ina said, "and in a moment I'm going to tell her the way is clear and we may proceed—even if it isn't."

"What you sayin'?"

"Please move. I won't ask again."

Ina sat back down and shut the door. She locked it, then locked Helene's door, then made certain the two back doors were locked.

"They're moved," she said. "You may proceed, dear. You'll have to start a right turn soon. I'll tell you when."

Helene put the car in Drive and they resumed their journey.

"The neighborhood's gone to hell," Helene said.

The three kids had begun to retreat a step at a time, but they refused to move to the side, and they regarded the car's inexorable progress with outrage and disbelief. The kid with the cross snatched the baseball from his friend and threw it hard at the windshield. Ina held her scream, afraid Helene would be startled and send the car hurtling forward. But the ball, released too soon, traveled high and merely skipped off the roof of the car and shot down the alley.

"What was that?" Helene asked.

"I didn't hear anything. Are you okay?"

"I am in utter control."

The kids teetered on the rim of the street. Only two remained, the baseball's owner having deserted the cause in pursuit of his possession. The kid with the cross folded his arms.

"Stop a moment, please," Ina said. Helene braked with more force than necessary, and when the car rocked the boys flinched.

Ina did not want to alarm Helene by opening the car door and speaking again. Helene considered their path clear.

"May I proceed, dear?"

"Wait. There's traffic." She raised her hands in final supplication to the boy with the cross. He gave her the finger.

"You may proceed," Ina said. "Slowly. Begin a turn to the right."

"I'm certain I heard something back there," Helene said. "A very audible thump."

"Maybe it was a snowflake hitting the roof."

The car advanced on the two kids until only their torsos were visible over the cliff of the hood. Ina was willing to run them down, but then one kid jumped clear with a smile, and the kid with the cross hopped deftly onto the car's front bumper.

Helene braked and he nearly toppled back off.

"What was that?"

"A pothole. Turn sharper. You're overshooting the street."

"When you can't see, sensations just assault you," Helene said, bringing the car around. "You don't have the sense of a noise about to surprise or something frightening about to jump out at you."

"You're doing fine," Ina said, watching the kid. He had slithered up the hood until he could spread his long hands across the windshield, as though he planned to suction the glass from its frame and get at the two old women. He was grinning, his tongue flicking wet and pink at them. He appeared absolutely delighted to be embarked on such mischief and pressed his mouth to the glass.

"Where are the wipers, dear? A bit of rain has fallen."

"I didn't hear it," Helene said. "It will only intensify the humidity." She touched a button and the wipers made a pass across the windshield toward the kid's mashed lips. The blade hit his hand first, snagging in its arc, and giving him the time to pull his mouth away. He sucked on his finger, pushing it slowly in and out of his mouth, wrapping his tongue around it, rolling his eyes in mock ecstasy at Ina. His friends were back, too.

"A hair to your left, dear. You're veering."

"This has made my day," Helene said. "This has made my golden years."

The kid sat, legs and arms folded, directly in Helene's line of sight. He talked with his friends in a laughing, musical chatter as they ran alongside the car. Everyone was having the time of his life.

Ina instructed Helene to brake at a stop sign. The kid on the hood, when the car paused, turned to look warily at his conveyors. The car proceeded through the intersection and into the next block. Ina had a headache from concentrating on the scene before her, waiting for the first child to run under the tires. The next intersection was Amanda's block and Ina had her sister turn left.

"We're almost there," Ina said. "I can't believe we're doing this."

"Shouldn't we get gas? Check the oil?"

"Let's not push our luck."

"Protect the machinery. Rudy's motto. We should do that first thing."

The kid was stretched out along the hood now, his fingers laced into a pillow on the windshield, his long legs crossed at the ankles. A car turned into the street at the end of the block and came toward them.

"Get to your right," Ina ordered. "A car's coming."

Helene, jumpy, brought the car over too sharply and with cold aplomb nearly crushed one of the kids.

"Too far!" Ina shouted. "Stop!"

"Oh," Helene said. Her tongue made a bulb of her lower lip as she awaited the next command. "Don't yell at me," she said. "We must avoid panic."

"There are parked cars to the right. A half-foot at the most," Ina said. "I didn't make that clear and I apologize. Bring the wheel left just a smidge."

The approaching car was upon them. The driver was a young man with a splintered windshield on the passenger's side. He went past easily, never taking his eyes from the kid on the hood.

"You may proceed," Ina said.

One of the kids had come to Helene's window, his hands spread like frogs' pads, his features smeared across the glass.

"Are we going to sit here all afternoon?" Ina asked.

"I'm letting my heart decelerate, dear. No call for sarcasm."

"We're on a public thoroughfare," Ina said pointedly. "Even a nondriver such as myself knows we can't just sit in the middle of it."

Helene brought the wheel around without a word and they went on. The three boys seemed relieved by the resumption of their odd parade. The car arrived at a stop sign at North Avenue. Ina prayed a police car would pass and see the burden they carried, then swoop back to save the old ladies, sending their young tormentors to vanish into the warren of alleys and gangways that held the neighborhood together. But although drivers looked curiously at the reclining figure, no one stopped, and they even jerked their gaze away at the first hint of meeting the boy's eyes.

Traffic cleared on the perpendicular byway. Ina told Helene to proceed.

"Left turn, dear. We're going on North Avenue."

Helene flinched an instant in her turn.

"Left! Hard left!" Ina cried.

"But North Avenue? Why North Avenue?"

"You wanted to find a gas station. Ease out of your turn now. You're doing splendidly."

They traveled so cautiously that traffic began to collect behind them. Ina looked and the impatience of the driver immediately to the rear was like a raw rage that intimidated her. The two kids had broken off their pursuit. They waved good-bye to their friend on the hood.

"North Avenue is so busy," Helene said.

"Let's try going a tad faster."

"What's my speed?"

Ina looked over at the speedometer. She didn't need to put a number on their pace; she knew they were going too slow.

"About eight," she said. "Let's try fifteen."

"I wanted to stay on the side streets."

"No gas stations on the side streets."

A car went around them, the driver so enraged at being delayed that he gave the finger to two women his grandmother's age.

"Bear right a smidge. Perfect."

"I'm sweating again. You've made me so nervous," Helene complained.

"Hush. I see a station in the next block."

"I hope you know where you are," Helene said. "I can't find Amanda's from here."

"You'd think we'd driven off the end of the earth."

"I'm just saying I'm lost."

They rolled through a green light, and halfway into the next block Ina guided Helene to the right, then up a slight incline into an Amoco station. The kid on the hood rolled deftly off, then stretched as if after a nap. Before vanishing into the shadows he spat pointedly on the glass shielding Ina's face.

"Left, dear," she said. "Full service is to your left."

They rolled over a black wire and the bell that sounded summoned a man in oily jeans and a soiled blue shirt.

"Lower your window," Ina said. "The attendant's coming."

"Fill it with ethyl, please," she said to the man. "And check under the hood and the tires, please."

"Have him do the windows, too."

"He will. It's full service, dear." She closed the window. She was pleased with herself for reaching that brief sanctuary. "We're on North Avenue?" she said. "What cross street?"

"Fennimore."

Helene thought for a moment. "Amanda's isn't far away. We can take Fennimore in to Cistern, then Cistern over to her block."

"Shouldn't we call?"

"And tip her off?"

Ina shut her eyes and sat back, off duty for the moment. She had been to Amanda's several times, twice on surprise visits with Helene, and both those trips had been like primers on embarrassment.

The attendant had the hood up, blocking the scalding wash of sunlight. The boy's deposit of sputum had run down her window and spread out along the bottom of the frame. With the engine off, the interior of the car had begun to slowly cook.

"Open your window," Ina said. "He wants to show you the thing for the oil."

"You're dangerously low," the attendant announced, displaying the thin dry dipstick against a blackened rag. Helene, with a theatrical touch for her sister's benefit, asked the man to hold it closer for her to inspect, shading her dead eyes with her hand.

"Put in what's needed of your very best grade," Helene said. "And check the radiator, battery, and transmission fluid, too."

"And the windows," Ina prompted.

"And the windows," Helene called out, though the attendant had not moved. "And the tire pressure." She shut the window.

"He's muttering, 'Old bats!' " Ina said.

Helene laughed nervously. "Is he? He sounds conscientious and sincere. Eager to serve."

"My foot. To these guys, full service means someone to hold the nozzle.

When the attendant was finished and came for the money, Ina was ready with the credit card she had found in Helene's billfold. She had been thrilled to go through her sister's possessions, to be given permission to descend into a place where her presence years ago would have elicited accusations of deceit and threats of bloody reprisal, and as girls would have meant a punch to the arm and vows of furious retribution. Now she was needed there.

In searching for the credit card Ina pretended to be lost long after she had pulled the card from its slot and placed it on the dashboard.

"I don't see it," she said, her fingers picking rapidly through a lifetime of folded notes, cards, phone numbers, and photos.

"It's right there," Helene said impatiently, jabbing her finger at the very slot Ina had removed the card from.

"Maybe Rudy used it last," Ina said. She did not know what she expected to find in the wallet. Most of the photos she'd seen before: a young Rudy, Amanda's high school graduation picture, Ina's kids at school age, when they were photographed annually like hardened criminals, then Ina's granddaughter Meaghan, then at the back of the pack a young Ina and Vincent standing arm in arm at the base of the stairs leading up to the church where Helene and Rudy were married. Vincent's face burned from his morning shave. That day had been a scorcher, too.

The attendant tapped on the window with the credit card.

"This card expired two years ago, ma'am," he said. Ina reached past her sister and took the card.

"I couldn't believe it when I looked at it," the attendant said. He seemed very nice. He looked from one woman to the other, as if trying to guess where the money to pay the bill would come from.

Ina opened her purse. The torn lining startled her. She had never expected to go for an automobile ride when she visited her sister that day.

"What was the total?" she asked.

"Twenty-three fifty."

Blushing furiously, Helene kept her eyes turned away from the attendant. He smelled of fried chicken and licorice, and this odor poured into the car with the heat. He was standing altogether too close.

Ina handed over a twenty and a five. "Keep the change for all your help," she said, and was saluted with the money.

"He's gone."

"Aren't we the big tipper?"

"He did a lot for us."

"It's his job," Helene said.

"Forward, then a gradual left."

Helene started the engine, revved up the air-conditioner, put the car in gear. The damp bloom of her hanky fluttered from the neckline of her dress. She followed directions out onto North, then left into the overarching shadows of Fennimore. The car moved with a regal slowness that was annoying in the context it traveled in, but not unsafe. Helene had a touch.

"It's not safe to carry cash in this city," Helene pouted.

"You're right," Ina said. "Thieves never take any interest in expired credit cards. They're the perfect answer to those pesky muggers."

"Where am I going?"

"Nudge it left a hair."

"We must be almost there."

"Nearly," Ina said. They reached Aspidistra and Ina had Helene turn left. The street was narrow, ending in a cul-de-sac, beyond which was a shady little park where small-time drug dealers and deviates congregated. Ina directed Helene down the street and around the dead-end loop in search of a place to park. They came back to the mouth of the street. Ina looked up at Amanda's second-floor windows and saw drawn blinds and fogged glass. The place looked inviting, private. She was tired of the stale cold of the car.

"Park in the alley?" she asked her sister.

"If that's all that's available."

Helene cut the turn into the alley too sharply and sent a trash barrel toppling. Newspapers, smut magazines, melon leavings, peels and skins, and a noxious black brew spilled onto the ground. Helene sat motionless. She seemed to await some repercussion of the mishap, like the recoil of a rifle.

"It was only a trash can," Ina said. "Those things spend more of their life upended than upright."

"That doesn't alter the fact I struck it," Helene said. "It might have been a child."

"If it was a child standing there I'd have warned you to be careful."

"Where am I?"

"Go forward a count, then turn the wheel left," Ina said. She had Helene stop behind Amanda's building; strenuous jockeying was required to get the car enough to one side for traffic to pass.

"You'll have to slide over to get out," Ina said.

"Maybe we should leave her be."

"That's my advice. I know you won't heed it, however."

"We've come this far," Helene said, shrugging.

Ina popped the heavy door and slid out into the heat. The damp portions of her dress stuck to her. She pulled the fabric free of her skin, then shook, then laughed. It felt good to get out, to stand up. Helene followed, keeping one hand on the car's hot paneling. She had found a pair of sunglasses somewhere; they looked like Rudy's, with tear-drop lenses covering much of her face, the lenses providing golden mirrors for Ina's smile of loving derision.

"Where did you get those?"

"They're Rudy's. Do I look ridiculous?" Helene asked.

"Yes."

"I think my eyes should be covered if I'm driving," Helene said. "They make the fact that I'm blind less obvious."

"Good thinking."

"Should I lock it?" Helene asked.

"If you want to drive home, yes," Ina said. The hood was marked with swirls in the dust and tennis shoe prints. One hand-print was so perfect it might have been placed by a proud child for his mother to frame and hang.

Helene took Ina's arm. Helene was trembling. Out from behind the wheel, about to butt in on her daughter, she was afraid of blundering, but unable to halt her progress toward the event.

They went through a gate and down a gangway marked with a chalk hopscotch course and emerged into a tiny square of yard. The day's paper waited on the seat of a lawn chair.

Down a cool brick tunnel, they went around to the front of the building and stood finally before the buzzer to Amanda's apartment.

"Last chance," Ina said.

"Don't you ever just have to *know* something?"

"Yes. Usually I regret afterward finding out."

"Call me stubborn," Helene said. She had taken a small envelope from her purse and a key from the envelope.

"She's forty-two years old," Ina reminded her. "If she was half her age you'd still have lost the right to pass judgment on her life."

"Pish tosh. If she's sixty and unmarried I'll still judge her," Helene said. She stabbed at the door with her key, furtive clickings against the nicked, varnished wood. Ina took her sister's hand and guided it to the lock.

Arm in arm they took the stairs to the second floor, where Ina pressed Amanda's bell; she thought at that moment that she and her niece needed a code of warning: two longs, two shorts. Beware! I am out here with your mother!

"She may not answer," Ina said, voicing her final hope.

But from within they heard the rustle of footsteps, a hesitation while they were inspected through the door's peephole, then the brief urban ritual of unfastening chains and opening locks. Cool air rushed to embrace them when Amanda pulled back the door and for a moment Ina was glad they had come.

Amanda did not bother to hide her disappointment at the appearance of the two old women. In fact, Ina thought at first that Amanda would deny them entry. She swiveled her head to the left, craning a look back down the hall, seeking something, or perhaps sending a warning with her gaze, a code of her own.

"I should've guessed," Amanda said. She stepped forward and kissed Helene on the mouth because she knew her mother considered such kisses unsanitary. She pecked Ina on the cheek. Ina shrugged when Amanda caught her eye with an imploring look. She wanted to pass the message: Your secrets are safe with me.

Amanda wore a man's white shirt that hung down to the middle of her thighs.

"We came over to get cool," Helene said.

"I'm glad you did. It's beastly out."

"Beastly?"

"Beastly," Amanda repeated. She hurried ahead of them down the hallway that split the apartment and ended in the kitchen. Amanda ducked her head into one room, then popped back out at once, confused at evidently not finding what she was looking for.

"How hot is it?" she asked over her shoulder, looking into the next room.

"Beastly," Ina said.

Slat blinds were drawn in the first room Amanda had looked into. The room had a cool, tropical flavor. Books and papers covered a desk in one corner. The bed was a mess; the upper right corner of the fitted sheet had come off, exposing the worn flower print of the mattress and tantalizing Ina: What force or exertion had torn the sheet loose?

A man's summer-weight suit jacket hung over the back of the desk chair. Ina hurried Helene past, forgetting for a moment that she would take her clues from other sources.

Amanda had flown on ahead, searching in every room but finding nothing that she sought. Her voice came to them from the kitchen.

"Would you like something cold to drink?"

"Why is she running away from us?" Helene whispered.

"Something cold would be nice," Ina said.

"I smell a man," Helene said.

They came into the kitchen and the man was there, crouched on the counter and smiling like a gargoyle. He wore tan trousers, a V-neck T-shirt, and black socks. He curled wide, hairy hands around the counter edge for balance. Ina thought he was quite handsome. She led Helene past him to a seat at the table, where a bowl of yellow apples sat. Helene's head turned an inch toward the man as they went past.

"I smell cologne . . . and something else," Helene said. "That *stink* they give off when life is too easy."

"What on earth are you talking about, Mother?"

"A man. I smell one."

"Maybe you smell Daddy," Amanda suggested, with a wink for her guest.

A tall woman, Amanda was slightly heavy through the hips and legs, but with a waist unstretched by children, and ample breasts lost in the billows of the man's shirt. She had a physical ease about her, a shameless acceptance of herself. Ina always had assumed Amanda had had many lovers. Her hair was cut short, then curled as it grew out, and for the time being Amanda was letting the gray in it remain. No rings or wristwatch adorned her hands. Ina was always a bit startled by how much she enjoyed Amanda's company when they finally did meet after weeks of hearing about Amanda's life filtered through the loving malevolence of Helene.

The man on the counter shifted his weight just a bit, and Helene's head turned toward him again with a wary, listening air.

"Would you have a cold beer, Amanda?"

"I sure would."

Helene gave her sister a scolding look.

"Did you two walk all the way over here?"

"Yes, the heat was beastly," Helene said, and with a grand flourish that made everyone nearly laugh at her she plucked her hanky from its mottled nook between her breasts.

"I'd have picked you up if you were set on visiting."

"Ina called you to report I was missing," Helene said.

"I knew you'd turn up, and I was right." Amanda smiled at the man on the counter.

"Did you have company this afternoon?"

"A friend *did* visit," Amanda said. She set Ina's beer on the table, centering the can on a pink party napkin.

"No names?"

Amanda took an ice cube tray from the freezer and with a practiced and measured blow cracked it on the edge of the counter, an inch from the hand of the man perched there. She fed him a chip of ice.

"His name is Gordon. I've known him almost a year. Forty-two of which I've been on this planet—giving me the right to tell you to mind your own business . . . Ina," she said, and laughed.

"This Gordon. What does he do?"

"He beats his wife," Amanda said caustically.

Ina laughed. The man on the counter—was he Gordon?—had shifted again. He seemed to be losing patience with the ruse and less willing to remain in his peculiar state of hiding. His attention wandered. He absently picked at something caught in his teeth. Ina feared he might fall off the counter, or begin to hum.

"Is he married?" Helene asked; Ina's next question, too.

"None of your business," Amanda said.

"Do you see marriage in the future, Mandy?" Helene asked. "Any grandchildren in my future?"

Amanda's eyes glistened. She ran a fingertip around their edges.

"I'm sorry. I can see I won't get any straight answers here today," Helene said. Her daughter set a glass of ice water beside her, then touched her stringy neck with a wet, cool hand.

"Where were you, that you had Ina so worried?" Amanda asked.

"She was in the car—running the air-conditioner," Ina said.

"I hope you had the garage door open."

Something occurred to Helene and she turned toward Ina. "Did you close the garage door before we left?"

"You didn't say to."

"Oh dear. Oh."

"It will be all right," Ina said.

"The people in my neighborhood prey on any sign of weakness. They'll see that door open and that—"

"But the car is there," Ina said. "They'll think you're home, and watching from the window, armed to the teeth."

"Yes. *Yes,* the car is there," Helene said.

"It's a shame we have to think like that," Amanda remarked. She positioned herself so the man on the counter could rub her shoulders. She seemed inclined to fall against him, and his thorough hands caught bunches of cloth and lifted the tail of the shirt up over Amanda's thick legs and white underpants.

Ina concentrated on her beer and the coolness of her surroundings.

"What are you saying?" Helene asked.

Amanda's eyes fluttered open. She had been drifting away. For an instant, she locked eyes with Ina, communicating a fervent desire that the two women depart.

"I think about how dangerous it's getting around here," Amanda said. "The family three doors down? They come home the other night and there is a stranger asleep on their kitchen floor. He wakes up and robs them with one of their own knives, then runs out the back door."

"Where was this?" Ina asked, alarmed.

"Down the street."

"Amanda!" Helene said. "Is that true?"

"I heard it was true." The man leaned forward and pressed his mouth to Amanda's neck. Her head fell forward to open a space for him. Ina wondered if the man thought she was blind, too. Would he just go ahead and unbutton the shirt Amanda wore, slide his hand inside?

Ina shifted her attention away from them, but not before noticing a thinness at the heels of his socks. She guessed that Helene would not want to leave soon; the air-conditioning felt wonderful and she had not yet begun to nag.

"Do you ever hear from Dennis Frisch?"

Amanda rolled her eyes at Ina.

"All the time. I haven't seen him since high school, but he calls every night just to say hello," Amanda said. She had one hand on the man's knee, the other behind her back, playing with something there.

"Daddy was always afraid he'd get you pregnant."

"I know. But Dennis had no future. And now you wish he had gotten me pregnant, don't you?" Amanda challenged. She looked at Ina and Ina was smiling; this was like a play she had seen before.

"I'd never wish that," Helene said.

"Imagine . . . that baby would be twenty-four or twenty-five now," Amanda said. "He or she would be through with college, probably married. I'd be a grandmother, in all likelihood."

"Sure, you're a grandmother," Helene said. "What about me?"

"I'm going to deny you that," Amanda taunted. "I'm all alone, no husband, no kids, just to spite you." She had drawn away from the man on the counter, as though by putting a tag on her life she had reminded herself that he was of no help to her.

Helene got to her feet. "I need to use the bathroom," she announced. "Have you rearranged the plumbing again?"

"Yes. And I've put the toilet paper where you will never find it."

"Good. When did you scrub this kitchen last? It stinks." She followed a series of memorized handholds to a small powder room off the rear of the kitchen. They heard her slam home the bolt on the door.

Amanda stepped to Ina's side.

"Get her out of here," she pleaded in a whisper. "Today's the one day I can see Gordon—and I don't want to waste it listening to her carp at me."

"Why are you hiding him?"

"What's all that muttering?" Helene called.

"It's just your imagination," Amanda sang. "Because she has me tyrannized," she hissed to Ina. "Because he's married."

"Oh, Mandy—"

Gordon slid off the counter, helped himself to a sip of Ina's beer, kissed Amanda on the neck, and sauntered out of the kitchen. Amanda went after him.

Ina sat enjoying the solitude. She did not want to go back out in the heat. Neither did she want to press on Amanda's time. She would get Helene out of there. Take their chances on the open road.

Ina heard water running in the bathroom sink. A moment later the toilet flushed, a piped roar in the walls, and then Helene began to fight with the bolt on the door.

Amanda returned, looking mussed.

"Are you all right in there?" she asked at the bathroom door.

"I'm *trapped*," Helene said.

"Relax, dear," Ina counseled. "Wait."

She took the doorknob and pulled it toward her, hoping to ease the tension on the bolt. Helene fought with it, breathing harder, getting panicky.

"Helene? Dear?"

"What?"

"You're not relaxing."

"The pipes are backing up. It smells in here."

"Honey," Ina said, "put your left hand just beneath the bolt on the door. Push there at the same time you slide open the bolt."

"Don't you think I've been doing that?" Helene asked derisively.

Ina led Amanda a distance from the door. "Is there a window in there?"

"A tiny one. But it's painted shut."

"What about the milkbox? Would Gordon go through the milkbox for you?"

Amanda's look was bewildered. "The milkbox? There are no milkboxes anymore."

Ina covered her eyes. She was stunned with embarrassment, having become a cliché of her age. A milkbox set in the wall would be of scant use in a second-floor apartment.

"You're absolutely right," she admitted, touching Amanda's arm.

"Where did you two go?" Helene asked.

"We're right here," Ina said at the door.

Then like the easiest thing in the world Helene slipped the bolt and opened the door, releasing a warm puff of sewery air, and the old woman.

Gordon returned with a shuffling silence and resumed his place on the counter, as reliable as an appliance. Ina studied his physique and decided he would be a tight fit going through the milkbox. His shoulders would be a problem; he would have to point his arms straight together and go into the opening like a diver. Later in the entry he might get snagged on his erection.

"I think it's time we headed home," Ina said.

"Why, we only just arrived."

"Catch your breath," Ina said. "Then we'll be on our way."

"What's the rush?" Amanda asked without enthusiasm.

"My stomach is bothering me."

"Beer is *good* for that," Helene chided.

"It soothes," Ina said. "But I'd really like to just get home and lie down."

"Lie down here," Helene suggested with a magnanimity that made her daughter wince.

"I feel more comfortable on my own couch." Ina stood, and like an alibi witness her stomach growled, so low and booming it nearly echoed on the tile, and all three women laughed. Gordon, stone-faced, waited.

"Good-bye, Mandy," Ina said, kissing her on the cheek. She looked girlish up close, standing with one foot resting atop the other, in a shirt too large for her, her face smeared by the man who silently waited for her guests to leave. Maybe it was love that rooted the man there during this strange charade. Ina hoped so, but she doubted it. He would have Amanda out of her clothes before the two old women were out of the building, be inside her before they reached the car, and be finished and dressed long before they reached home. Ina did not think Amanda would surprise her mother late in life with a husband.

Helene kissed her daughter good-bye on the landing outside the apartment door. The hallway was quite warm, like a processing area preparatory to entering the serious heat.

"I'll call you," Amanda promised, and shut the door before her mother could respond.

Arms linked, the women went down the stairs and outside. It felt, perhaps, a degree warmer. Ina could not get her mind off what had to be going on upstairs in those cool rooms. It made her weak in the knees with desire for an earlier time, for Vincent.

"We must walk to the end of the block and circle back to the alley," Helene said. "In case she's watching us from the windows."

"She's not. I checked," Ina said, depressed by the thought of unnecessary travel in the heat.

"Very well, then. If you're sure."

They went back through the tunnel and across the pinched yard. Someone had put out a line of wash; two bedsheets, a girdle, a brassiere, three pairs of men's boxer shorts, all varying shades of white, all the clothes motionless as wallpaper.

The car was still in the alley. Ina held the door while Helene slid across the hot vinyl and put the key into the ignition. The engine turned over and the air-conditioner roared to life, blowing hot first, then tepid, then cool, then blessed cold.

Helene said, "I smelled a man back there. I smelled a man who was at one time eager to please—but now is less concerned about doing so."

"Sherlock!"

"Am I right? Did you smell him?"

"My senses aren't as keen as yours, dear."

"It was a man," Helene said with a nod. "He was everywhere and nowhere. Like a flu bug."

AFTER nearly a half-hour of laborious and acrimonious jockeying of the car, they got the thing put away in the garage, then went across the yard to Helene's backdoor. Glass sparkled on the walk and in the grass. The inside door was pushed open, revealing shadows both mundane and sinister.

"There's been some trouble," Ina whispered. She pulled her sister away. "Someone has broken your door."

"It was those punks in the alley," Helene said. "I knew I'd rue the fact you forgot to close the garage door."

"We have to call the police," Ina said. "They might still be in the house."

"Let's go in. Let's confront the bastards."

"Don't be ridiculous," Ina said. She pulled Helene back across the lawn and into the alley. She remembered the casual menace of the kid with the cross and the vicious way he had thrown the baseball at them. Of course he would follow the trail back to the source, to the garage it had taken Helene twenty minutes to exit from, to the open garage door, to the old lady's empty house.

"Do you know your neighbors?" Ina asked.

"Young couples who keep to themselves. Like everyone, they're quiet."

"Surely they'll let us use the phone."

"Or shoot us as trespassers."

They went around the garage and down a short walk to a gate bearing a sign warning of the presence of a vicious dog.

Ina read the sign to her sister. "Do you believe it?" Ina asked.

"In this neighborhood, I'd believe anything," Helene said.

"I mean—do you believe they have an attack dog on the property? Have you heard it?"

"I hear dogs all the time," Helene said. "In the alley. In the street. I don't bother to pinpoint them."

"A dog that merits a warning sign would have a pretty loud bark, wouldn't it?" Ina said.

"Rattle the gate," Helene suggested. "See what happens."

The latch was unlocked. Ina dropped her sister's hand and stepped into the yard. The grass needed cutting. A sprinkler was turned on along the fence, watering tomatoes, corn, sunflowers, ivy. Another garden had been planted in the small lee alongside the garage. Ina could see tomatoes, watermelons, and pumpkins hidden in a tangle of vines, bees almost staggering under the workload of their good fortune.

"You there, dear?" Helene whispered.

"Yes."

"It was an urban ruse, then. Don't invest in the alarm, invest in the sign warning of the alarm," Helene said.

"It's too soon to say."

"I smell fertility," Helene sniffed.

"They have two gardens. The grass is long."

"Are there toys in the grass?"

Ina, willing to be in no hurry if Helene was in no hurry, inspected the yard and on the back stoop saw an orange ball and a miniature basketball hoop, a doll carriage with a missing sunshade, and a wooden box so stuffed with toys it resembled a machine that had sprung its innards of colored plastic and fat rubber gears.

"There are toys," Ina reported.

"Fertility. I smell it. I hear children yelling and laughing all the time, too," Helene said. "They're as hard to pinpoint as dogs. There are children *here*."

The stairs up to the back porch were made treacherous by a pair of roller skates. Potted flowers were arranged on each step; their dropped petals had been crushed underfoot, leaving behind flat samples like pressed corsages.

Only four steps, they seemed to tower over Ina, she was getting so tired. It might be an hour before the police arrived, hours after that before she got home to a beer and her bed. Depressed by this, she lowered her gaze to rub her eyes and saw a dog's stool roughly the circumference of her last Christmas tree's trunk.

"We've got to get out of here," Ina said, tugging at her sister's arm.

"No, we're safe here. It's a feeling a mother gets."

"I'm a mother. And I've seen proof of the existence of a very large dog."

"What do you want?" someone called. A woman's voice came from a window above them and to the left. Ina saw a small face regarding them dubiously.

"We need to borrow your phone. My sister is your neighbor. Someone broke into her house," Ina said.

They heard her say, "Oh, dear." In a minute she was at the back door, a young woman with black hair in a French braid, and a loose, light blue smock to accommodate her pregnancy.

"Oh, dear," she said again. "You know—I *thought* I heard something earlier. I was napping with my kids and I heard glass break. I swore I heard it. But my husband is a fireman—he just started his shift at noon today—and I get nervous when he's away. He tells me I hear things." She held her door open for the women to enter. "Please come in. Use our phone."

"Is your dog chained?"

"We don't have a dog. That sign is just a sign."

"And that?" Ina said, pointing to the feces.

"Rubber. Like inflatable snakes to keep birds away."

"I told you," Helene said. "An urban ruse."

She showed them into the kitchen. Corn peelings lay in a green silken pile on the table. The air bubbled with heat. A small fan pivoted on the counter. Ina went to the phone and dialed 911. As she explained their predicament, the woman scraped the peelings into a paper bag, then turned on water in the sink. A little girl, holding a scrap of blanket and wearing a tutu, appeared at the hall doorway. She regarded the strangers suspiciously, then hurried to her mother.

"This is Mickey," the woman said, kissing her daughter's ear. "How old are you?"

Mickey wouldn't say.

Ina hung up. "They're sending someone over. They doubt anyone's still inside."

"We moved here because we could afford the house," the woman said. "We've put thousands of dollars into it—and my husband is afraid we won't get it back. He has to live in the city—but I don't think this is a place for kids. I don't know why I ever did."

"It used to be," Ina said.

"How many do you have?"

"Two," Ina said.

"Just one," said Helene.

"I'm Katherine Grunwald. Mickey here is three. Cale, he's still asleep upstairs, is five. Boy and girl." She drew a breath of that cooked, fragrant air, as if winded by the length of her introduction.

"I'm Ina Lockwood. This is my sister, Helene Bolton."

Katherine smiled enormously, pleased by something rare transpiring. Ina listened for sirens. Helene patted her face with her hanky.

"It is hot, isn't it?" Katherine said. "I always look forward to summertime, then when it arrives I can't wait for it to cool off."

"When are you due?" Ina asked.

"November fifteenth." She massaged her belly with her hands. "My first two were big—this one shows every indication of being big."

"I knew it," Helene said.

Ina tipped her head toward Helene, for Katherine's benefit, and said, "Helene claimed she smelled fertility here."

The young woman laughed and swept Mickey up into her arms. "That's a joke with my husband and me. I can get pregnant almost at will, he says. We were going to wait to have another one, until after we decided what to do with the house. But then we came home from a party one Saturday night and started necking, kissing in the car, and we decided to risk it once without him using anything, because he didn't have anything with him. And boom, I got pregnant that time."

She rose suddenly on her tiptoes to look through a window facing Helene's house.

"The police are here," she announced.

They thanked her for her time and the use of her phone. She invited them back.

"She was nice," Ina said on the walk to Helene's.

"Nothing will come of that little meeting," Helene said. "The young, they're all talk. Haven't you noticed?"

"Such a gloom-monger."

"Pay attention sometime. Everything is a gesture of what they think they should be feeling."

"The young—do you keep in touch?" Ina asked.

"You're heartlessly cruel, dear."

A police officer waited by the backdoor.

Ina made introductions. Helene was oddly quiet for being the owner of the house. She clung to Ina's arm with an air of near-helplessness.

"The house is empty," said a second cop, coming through the backdoor. "There's been some vandalism. You'll have to let us know what's been stolen."

"It's my house," Ina said. "And my sister is blind."

The cop rubbed his chin. "It's a dilemma under any circumstances. Burglary is a violation of one's sense of privacy." He turned to Helene. "I was burgled once. It took me a year to get over it. Like a death in the family. Regardless, your house is safe now. If you can come up with an inventory of what's been taken and a description of those items—in the next few days—we'll get on it. Your insurance company will ask for the same thing. I've got to be honest: the chance of making an arrest or recovering your possessions is extremely thin. *Nil,* in fact."

After the police departed, Helene refused to go into her house. She and Ina sat on the bench in the backyard, holding hands.

"You can stay with me tonight," Ina said. "After a good meal and a good night's sleep we'll come back and take care of this. I'm just exhausted right now."

"Some birthday for you," Helene said.

"Now that you mention it, this has been one of my more memorable birthdays. Chauffeured around town by a blind woman. A burglary."

"Should I drive us to your house?"

"Let's walk. It's cooled off a smidge. It's not far and there's plenty of light."

"Go look inside," Helene said. "Give me a damage report."

"Will you be all right?" Ina asked. She was reluctant to enter the house. Who knew what the police might have overlooked?

"Don't be gone long," Helene said.

Ina paused at the door into the house. One of the cops had swept glass into a pile, then leaned the broom against the wall. The interior shadows were creepy and enlivened by the history of what had taken place there.

It occurred to Ina to remain motionless there on the threshold for five minutes, then make a show of returning to Helene's side. She could easily fabricate a report of the home's damage. But she was curious herself about what had been done; ultimately she would be responsible for setting it right.

Reaching in through the doorway and hooking a strand of spider-web, she found the light switch and turned it on. Helene faced her with an eerie attentiveness. The entryway was untouched beyond the gash in the frame where the door had been cracked open.

She took the stairs to the kitchen. For just an instant she thought the intruders had ripped the tile up off the floor; then she realized she was looking at a topography of spilled sugar, salt, and flour. Her approach sent tiny windstorms whirling over this landscape. Across the kitchen and down the hall she saw clues to more harm done: sparkling glass, torn cloth, flipped chairs, the crushed base of a lamp. A line of black ants already moved across the sugar dunes, a scouting party dazed to incredulity by a bounty of sweetness.

Ina went back down the stairs. She pulled the door shut and like a bad joke the lock clicked home as if nothing had happened. Helene's gaze had drifted away but swung back toward the noise her sister made.

"Is it bad?" she asked.

"It looks worse than it is. They spilled some things. Just being mean," Ina said. She would telephone Amanda and tell her what had happened. She would need help cleaning the place.

"Let's burn it down," Helene suggested, mock-cheerfully. She had stood up. Tears ran down her face.

"Don't go hysterical on me, dear," Ina reprimanded. "This is your home. Tomorrow we'll start putting things back in order."

INA'S house was dim with twilight and stuffy with the day's accumulation of heat. She sat Helene at the kitchen table while she went to open windows. She had done all the talking as they walked back arm in arm through the light tunneled out of the old trees. Helene seemed to be in a mildly shocked state.

"Would you like a beer?" Ina asked brightly, returning to the kitchen. Helene had found her way to the rear screen door, where a breeze blew.

"No, thank you," she replied, but without her customary prim edge of condemnation.

Ina was relieved—*delighted*—to be in her own house. Only mere blocks from Helene's house, she nevertheless felt safe and removed. The Strodes were next door and Vincent could better watch over her. She opened a beer and took a big swallow, then poured what remained into her blue glass, another touchstone of her reality.

"Why do we live apart at our age?" Helene asked, her back to Ina.

"Because we *can*," Ina said. "Because we would strangle each other after a day in the same house."

"I don't think we would."

"Vincent was the last person I'm going to live with," Ina said. Helene sniffed. "It was just a thought."

"When we get your house back in order you won't want to live with me, either," Ina said. "I drink beer. I keep late hours and I sleep late. Everything you disapprove of."

"You've explained your side of things quite nicely," Helene snapped.

"Are you hungry?"

"My stomach is a mess of nervous juices," Helene said. "But I should eat something. And it's time for my second shot."

Though she was reluctant to stir up the heat, Ina cooked them a meal of spaghetti, carrots, a cucumber salad, and plums for dessert. She drank beer throughout, and when the meal was over she offered Helene a glass of wine.

"It will help you relax," Ina said. "Perhaps you could nap."

"Would you lie down with me?"

"I can't," Ina recalled. "I won't sleep tonight if I do. I'll keep watch over you, though."

Helene brushed imaginary hair from her eyes. Ina slid a chair next to the refrigerator and climbed onto it to retrieve a bottle of wine from the cupboard. She never touched the stuff, she couldn't remember how the bottle had come into the house.

The dark cork came out in pieces, crumbling under the drilling of the bone-handled corkscrew Ina found at the back of the drawer. Bits floated in the pale gold wine. She pushed these around with her finger, trying to pin them to the side of the glass. She tasted the wine; it was horrid. But she could not tell whether the wine had gone bad, or merely was not to her liking. She put the glass in her sister's hand."

"Drink this," Ina coaxed.

Helene sniffed it, then wrinkled her nose in prissy distaste. "Gasoline," she said. "I could run the car on it."

"It's a very mild Rhine wine. It will relax you."

"Why this desire to relax me?" Helene asked. "Am I already

such a burden that you have to sedate me? I can go to a hotel, dear, if it's a matter of that."

"Hush. Drink."

Helen moved the glass of wine in her hand, on the table, in the air in front of her mouth. She appeared to be afraid of losing something in submitting to the drink.

"You don't *have* to drink it," Ina said.

"Rudy disapproved of liquor."

"I know," Ina said. She listened to the hush of the room, a click from the cooling stove. "Do you ever think they're watching?"

"Rudy and Vincent? Of course," Helene said. She held the glass like a ball, the bowl cupped in her hand.

"Disapprovingly?"

"Rudy *disapproved*," Helene said. "It was his way."

"I knew Rudy. He wasn't like that."

"I was married to him. I know." She put the glass to her lips and sipped.

Ina watched carefully. Her sister's eyes were closed. A wash of color like light through a page swept across Helene's face.

"My!" she gasped. "That's quite nice, isn't it?"

"Is it? I couldn't tell."

"Well—I have to say . . ." But then Helene's thought deserted her and she was quiet for a time. She took another sip and closed her eyes. In a moment she took out a hanky and dabbed at her face, as if plunged back into the hot center of the afternoon.

"I think I *will* sleep a bit," she announced, setting the glass down on the table without opening her eyes.

She selected for her nap the divan in the front room.

"Don't let me sleep more than an hour."

"I'm going to let you sleep until you awaken on your own," Ina said, as if issuing a threat.

"Rudy is watching right now," Helene said dreamily. "He is monitoring this episode of innocent fun."

"Where was he when your house was being broken into?"

"Oh, he blames you for that," Helene said casually. "He says you should have closed the garage door."

"He's right," Ina said. Helene stretched out on the divan. Ina removed her sister's shoes, then helped her on a whim to struggle out of her dress.

"Do hang that," Helene said.

Ina thought that if her luck improved, Helene would sleep through the night and she could enjoy in peace and solitude the final hours of her birthday. Helene would awaken early, blind in a strange house. She would awaken Ina with her demands to be shown to the bathroom, test her urine, give herself a shot. But those were future considerations Ina was willing to put off at present.

Her sister was nearly gone.

"I'm driving," Helene said. "We're on a highway. We're going very fast and you're telling me exactly what to do."

"Go to sleep," Ina said.

"Don't take a bath. Rudy will watch you."

"Go to sleep, knucklehead."

"You never knew Rudy watched you bathe, did you?" Helene asked, her voice adrift.

"No, I didn't."

"He said he wanted to compare you to me. I stopped him, of course, before he reported the results of his comparisons."

"Go to sleep."

"I'm warm and I'm flying."

"Go to sleep."

"Just this one time, dear, I'll do as you say."

Ina hung Helene's dress from the doorframe where the night breeze would get at the dampness, the fear of being on the move, of visiting Amanda, everything soaked into that thin cloth.

She brought in the mail and relocked the front door. Helene was snoring. Ina left the front porch light on, believing it gave a sense of movement, of watchfulness, to the house. The kids in the Crabbs' shrine would see the light and pass the word that she was at home and on her toes. She thought: What if the vermin who ransacked Helene's house stole her address book? But wouldn't Helene have Ina's address and phone number memorized, and have no need to enter it with her more distant acquaintances? And what good would it do her committed to paper?

She dropped the mail on the kitchen table. She washed dishes in hot water without filling the sink and without soap. Scalding water just cool enough to dart her fingers through laid waste to enough bacteria to satisfy her. Glasses, plates, pans, a knife greased with low-salt margarine. The chore went too quickly.

She dried her hands and looked in on Helene. The breeze through the room was cool and Ina spread a light blanket over her sister. Helene's lips fluttered with each breath, like two slips of bluish paper. Was Rudy watching? What did he think of the wife he had left behind?

She checked all the windows and the locks one more time, then carried her beer and the mail upstairs to her bedroom. The bulb in her night-table lamp went dead when she snapped the switch. She put the mail down. The bulb was warm to the touch, the white glass dome heated just that fraction by the little explosion it had contained. She shook the bulb next to her ear; a shred of filament hissed inside.

New bulbs were downstairs, off the kitchen, in a drawer in the pantry. Sitting there on the bed with her feet aching, the mail squashed under her thin rump, the beer making her see dots of exhaustion in the dark, the lightbulbs seemed miles away.

She went through the dark hall, down the stairs, and at the bottom looked in on Helene. She breathed in soft little gasps, like a child crying in her dreams. A late summer light was stuck high in the trees. The news would be on soon, broadcasting nothing of interest to her. Morning seemed imminent, a pearlish threat approaching from the east, and she was still awake.

In the dim hall leading to the kitchen, Ina was stopped mid-stride by the cracking of wood. The sound had the finality of a snapped pencil. She took a deep breath and waited, eager to believe the sound was harmless, a mere shifting of the house. A coolness rushed around her legs. She rubbed one ankle against the other. Sounds to Vincent were little mysteries that left him dissatisfied until he tracked them down and named them. He had a fearlessness, a willingness to seek out the thing that troubled him most at the moment.

A crack again; a sustained, frightful screaming of wood under stress, the sound coming from the dark end of the hall, from the kitchen or beyond. Ina turned in a circle, a helpless orbiting of the space she occupied. She thought to awaken Helene but could see no point. She thought to call the police but knew no reason to as yet.

Something made of glass shattered in the darkness ahead. Helene whimpered, turned her thin bones on the divan, and as Ina watched helplessly she threw off the cover and sat up. Ina wasn't quick enough to Helene's side to prevent her high-pitched, worried cry, "Ina?"

"Here, dear. Lie back now. You've only been asleep a minute."

"I heard something." She looked in the correct direction.

"I did, too. But everything's locked up tight. No cause for alarm," Ina said.

"Your voice is shaking."

"What a thing to say. I'm a rock."

Helene stood up despite Ina's pleas that she remain on the divan. If she moved around, and the crisis passed uneventfully (as it always had when Vincent was on the case), then Ina would have trouble getting her sister back to sleep. The night might become interminable.

"I'm awake," Helene said stubbornly. "Two are better than one. Nobody has to know I'm blind."

They went carefully down the hall to the kitchen; Ina was glad she had Helene along.

A voice came from the bathroom, a desperate, hushed, muttering voice trying to remain calm.

"I'm calling the police," Ina loudly announced.

No response was immediately forthcoming, then the voice responded, "Call the cops and I'll kill you." The bathroom door was half closed. The light was off.

The silence that followed that threat was palpably expectant, everyone involved listening for the next development. Ina left Helene stranded in her blindness to go to the cupboard and get a rolling pin, a heavy, hollow glass truncheon with a white flour sleeve that she slipped off so it would not get blood-stained in what was to follow.

"This will do," she whispered to Helene, touching her sister's fingers with the weapon's cool weight, to reassure her.

Some manner of struggle was taking place in the bathroom. Ina sensed her house fractionally shaking, as if a huge animal was scratching its back on an outside wall. Someone cursed. More glass broke.

"My husband has a gun," Ina yelled. "Come out where we can see you."

"Stay back! I'll kill you! I swear I will!"

Ina sat Helene at the kitchen table.

The person in the bathroom heard Ina begin to dial the phone.

"Put that phone down! I've got a bomb! I'll blow us all up!"

Ina slammed down the phone.

"Come out. We have a gun," she said.

"Don't you dare come in here. I'll kill you!"

The threats had an eerie singularity to each, as if neither party were listening to the other.

"Call the police," Helene whispered.

Grunting came from the bathroom and under cover of this racket, rolling pin poised to swing, Ina went to the bathroom door and pushed it open.

For an instant she was about to scream, for there in the dimness was a stranger—a chubby man in a striped T-shirt with short dirty hair, a flustered look, a little bug of a mustache—growing out of her bathroom wall. His arms hung down to the floor, and he held a knife. Angrily he slashed at her and hissed vile imprecations and threats of death.

"My milkbox," Ina said, crestfallen. Splinters of wood and glass from a shattered jar of flowered soaps and spewed sachet messed the floor.

She disappeared from the man's sight long enough to call the police. Out the back door window she saw a second stranger, fatter than the first, straining to free his lodged partner. He wore no shirt at all. His look was porcine. A bag presumably full of loot lay at his feet.

Ina went and stood in the doorway to the bathroom. The man had stopped struggling. He was holding himself up with his arms like a man condemned to an eternal push-up.

"Let me go and I won't kill you," he offered.

"I'm not holding you here. Look at my bathroom. Look at what you've done," she said.

He threw his knife at her then, a quick flip rising from the floor, and the blade chipped the doorframe near her hand and clattered away.

Ina shouted to Helene, "He threw a knife at me!"

"Did he hit you?"

"No." She picked the knife up off the floor and set it on the counter.

"Then you'll be okay," Helene said. She sat folding and unfolding her hands. "Have you any more of that wine?" she asked in a timid voice.

"In a minute," Ina said. "I'm kind of busy right now."

"Who's in there?" Helene said.

"A fat burglar."

"How did he get in?"

"He tried to crawl through my milkbox and he got stuck."

"There's no chance he'll wriggle out?"

Ina sighed. "I'm afraid not."

In fact, she was worried about what further damage her house would have to sustain in order to free the man from his predicament.

"Thank your stars he got stuck coming in," Helene said.

"Ever the optimist," Ina said. "That's what I love about you."

"Why, thank you, dear."

Ina felt she was living the night over again; her hope once more was to rush this mess to a conclusion so she would have some free time to herself.

The burglar called Ina to him. His demeanor was resigned, imploring.

"Would you perhaps have an ottoman or a chair and pillow I could rest on?" he asked. "I'm in pain holding myself up. And if I hang down, it cuts off my oxygen."

Ina brought a chair from the kitchen, but refused to provide a pillow. She was thanked profusely. She looked out the back door window. The other man was nowhere in sight, but the bag of loot remained.

"Your fat partner isn't the heroic type, is he?" Ina asked. She was uneasy with the other burglar out of sight; he might have run away, or he might be seeking a weakness in the front door lock.

"He's a savage," hissed the man. "No telling what he'll do to save me."

"Stop talking that way or I'll take back my chair," Ina threatened.

Laughter in the backyard announced the arrival of the police. Ina opened the door to them and they tried to stop, but their stern professionalism kept cracking and sliding away, and when they thought they were alone whoops of hilarity rolled across her backyard. More police cars arrived, then still more, until the street was clogged and festive with the law. Each car's pair of policemen would take a look, laugh, share a snide remark, then wander back to their beats.

Through it all the fat burglar remained silent in his entrapment. He did not beg to be released, or demand a lawyer. Resting with his arms folded on Ina's chair, he appeared primed for a nap.

Police efforts to free the man failed and a call went out to the fire department. The plan, to cut into the milkbox frame and enlarge the hole, elicited no response from the burglar.

A fire engine arrived. The bathroom was emptied of all police. Ina was in the kitchen, sneaking a sip of beer. As she passed the bathroom door the burglar made a vulgar slurping noise and she paused. That hesitation, that moment without the hovering presence of the police, drew the burglar from his taciturn shell to whisper, "I *am* going to kill you."

Then the police lieutenant in charge of the scene came in the back door and a drill began to bore into the wall of her beloved house. With all the activity and the sudden noise she couldn't be certain of what she had heard.

Po and Hector Strode came over. They surveyed the scene dressed as if for a summer outing, a hat for her, a bow tie for him, their hands clasped, their air nonchalant. They regarded the fat legs and plump butt protruding from Ina's house with polite disapproval, as if their neighbor had painted her house an obnoxious shade.

Ina went to them with some relief.

"You attract excitement," Hector said.

"Is it male or female?" Po Strode asked.

"Male."

"What does the other half look like?"

"This is his better side," Ina replied.

They watched in silence as a thin-bladed saw was used to cut downward from the drill hole. The work was slow, the wood old and hard. Sawdust powdered on the scrawny weeds that struggled in the abandoned beds around Ina's house.

"Who will pay for this?" she asked Hector.

"Your insurance, certainly," he said.

"He threatened to kill me."

"Who did?"

"Who do you think?" Po said to her husband.

"Just a minute ago—when I was alone with him for a moment," Ina said. "Even after I brought him a chair to rest on—after I was *nice* to him—he threatened to kill me. As if it were my fault."

"Build a bigger milkbox," Hector said. "Or a smaller one."

"Or none at all." She knew the milkbox would not be repaired, but would be closed over like a wound. She saw it now as a weakness, as risky as living all that time with the basement door unlocked.

A piece of her house the height of the milkbox and four inches wider was cut, and with this extra space the man in the milkbox was able to be slid out backwards. Three policemen helped. He was lowered to the ground and from there he sat heavily, like a boneless man. He tenderly probed the pinched skin at his waist. Sometime between the threat to Ina and his release, his hands had been cuffed together. The police soon took him away.

"He threatened to kill me," Ina told the lieutenant.

"Don't believe him. He's trying to intimidate you. We know this guy," he said confidently.

"There was another one who ran away."

"Even fatter?"

"As fat."

"They're brothers. But don't worry, they aren't killers."

A pinkish square of plywood was brought to Ina for her inspection.

"This will cover that hole," said the cop. "It will do until you find someone to repair the damage."

"Who's going to pay for this?"

The cop shrugged. "Ultimately, you."

They nailed the board over the hole. Po and Hector wished Ina good night and floated back through their garden toward home. Watching them go arm in arm to whatever awaited them (would they make love, aroused by the excitement she attracted?), Ina was nearly brought to her knees by longing for Vincent. Throughout this latest episode she realized she had operated in the faith that he was watching over her, or waiting for her, with the bemused look he always got when she was involved in something that took her attention away from him. She decided she had done well.

Helene, in all the excitement, had found her way back to the divan. She was reclining with her eyes closed and the blanket tucked expertly around her.

"Helene? Are you asleep, dear?"

"Are they gone?"

"Yes," Ina said. "Everyone has gone home. We're locked up safe and sound again."

"I think I'll try to sleep now."

"Me, too," Ina said. She squeezed her sister's leg. "Helene?"

"Yes, dear?"

"I'm getting out of here," Ina declared.

"Now?" Helene asked, eyes opening, worried at being left alone.

"No. *Now* I want to sleep," Ina said. "When we wake up we'll talk about it."

"I'm sorry this had to happen on your birthday," Helene said. "It will be a brighter world in the morning."

"I'm sure you're right."

"I always am," Helene said.

PART THREE

◆ ──────────────────────────────

How They
Will Get There

Ina's children had not gone to the West Coast immediately upon leaving home, but in time had both taken up lives in California, as if they had finally arrived at the edge of what they were looking for.

Annie, the elder, was first to go, marrying Don Bixler, who got along with Vincent better than any of the men she had ever dated. Don was a tad dour, Vincent said, but he had his father-in-law's eerie capacity for accumulating wealth and he took a determined delight in all manner of responsibility.

For a year following their wedding, Annie and Don lived in the city and the two families swapped Sunday dinners. Meaghan was born in a snowstorm while Don was on the road in Phoenix, not due back for four days. Vincent drove his daughter to the hospital. Annie lay in the backseat with her head in Ina's lap, her feet elevated against the window glass. Of that ride, Annie remembered her mother's helpless entwining fingers in her hair, the agony that seized her periodically, and the soothing slap of her father's wipers that would nearly put her to sleep in those blessed moments between contractions.

Annie, Don, and little Meg needed more room. They bought a spacious, four-bedroom house in Wheaton, west of the city, so far away that Vincent complained he would never see his grand-daughter again. But Don was traveling more and more. Sometimes he was gone two weeks at a time, and out of sheer loneliness Annie often brought the baby back into the city to spend the night, and occasionally two or three nights. Don resented this. Annie phoned him on the road to tell him where she was staying each time, and from the strained lowering of her daughter's voice Ina and Vincent were free to fill in the other half of the conversation.

More and more Don's presence was required in Phoenix and inevitably that city became their home. He bought a house in the desert and then flew Annie out to see it. Meg stayed behind; she was walking, getting into things, and she whooped delightedly whenever Ray or Vincent galloped her around on his shoulders. Ina was dismayed watching her grow up so fast, and then she was gone with her mother and father into the desert. Meg visited in the summer, staying for a month if Ina could wheedle the time from Meg's parents, and each year she seemed like a different girl. It was inconceivable that a girl could grow so much in one year. Ina had forgotten the rapidity of her own children growing. She had to study photographs to remember them as babies, but had arrived full-blown, lurking and secretive in the house to fashion their silent privacies and eat the food until it was time to move out.

Meg, at the age of nine, was the person to break the news to her grandparents that the Bixler family was going still farther west, to California. Meg's father, in his inevitable rise through the firm, had begun to travel frequently to L.A., and Ina pictured him as his company's trailblazer, the trusted hand who pressed ever westward, making the way safe for those to follow. They sold the house in the desert and moved to California, where Meg reported ecstatically in her first phone call from there that she could smell the ocean from the new house, that she could walk to the beach. Her summer visit that year was held to a week, Meg impatient the whole time to be back with her friends, to be on the beach, to be out of Chicago's sodden summer air. They took her to the North Avenue beach, but she wasn't interested beyond a curt assessment that Lake Michigan paled in comparison with the Pacific Ocean.

She was extremely unpleasant that week, with a preadolescent intolerance for any experience not a part of the life she had left in L.A. Ina, cringing, looked forward to her departure. She also feared her granddaughter would never return.

Ray had purchased a small, twenty-machine laundromat during the time his sister's family was in Arizona. His laundromat was in a Puerto Rican neighborhood and Ray lived in the back room to watch over his investment. Three times in the first month of his ownership the plate-glass windows were shattered by bricks tossed as casually as chewing gum wrappers.

But the location was ideal, on a busy corner in a neighborhood of apartment buildings occupied by people with too many children and not enough money for their own washers and dryers. He kept his prices low and stayed open around the clock. He lost weight and sleep and made what he considered a staggering amount of money, a fortune accruing to him like a persistent river of quarters and dimes.

Ina and Vincent were proud of Ray's success, but feared for his safety in that neighborhood. Vince paid a visit near midnight and found his son barricaded in his little room. He had cut a horizontal slot at eye-level in the door and covered the slot with a sliding metal panel. Over the back of the door was bolted a plate of quarter-inch steel and it was a fight for Ray to open the door after suspiciously peering through the slot to see his father blinking in the laundromat's protective brightness. The back room air was stale, smelling unpleasantly of tomato sauce, onions, and Ray. He had a cot, a desk, a chair, and a lamp squeezed in there. Leaning against a squat black safe in the corner were a shotgun and a baseball bat. Vincent helped his son count the change that blanketed his cot. Vincent called out numbers and Ray tapped the figures into a calculator. Vincent enjoyed himself.

Bells over the laundromat door rang as customers came and went, the jingling like soothing words to Ray over an intercom he had wired into the room. At 2:00 A.M. every machine was in use. Then over the intercom, like a bulletin of war, came an explosion of glass. Ray sighed. He stood up, brushed his hands on his pants, and removed the iron bar from behind the door. He took up the shotgun.

The customers made no sound; they stared at the floor, or the backs of their children's heads. Both windows had been broken. Ray walked out onto the sidewalk. No one was around, though a cluster of young Hispanics lounged against a car at the distant end of the block. None looked Ray's way.

He picked up the brick and carried it inside.

"They have a competition," he told his father, "where they try to throw the brick so hard it breaks one window going in and the other window going out. It's quite a feat. Strength. Angle of approach. Very *scientific.*"

In time a man named Alonzo, a father of four, a regular customer, offered to manage the laundromat for Ray in exchange for a small salary and use of the back room as a place to live. He promised the breaking of windows would cease once Ray was no longer on the premises. Ray's Anglo features, his stockade in the back, the shotgun that he toted while he emptied the coin boxes, all those things enraged the young men of the neighborhood, who were without resources beyond destruction to counter him.

Ray hired Alonzo and the breaking of the windows stopped. Ray still owned the laundromat, but over the years he had sold shares of it to Alonzo, who had overseen the laundromat's expansion into the stores to either side of it, who had put his wife and children on the payroll, and who now lived in a three-flat two blocks away, renting the other apartments to his parents and his brother's family. Ray received each month from Alonzo a statement and a check for his share of the laundromat's proceeds.

Ray moved back in with his parents for a few months after Alonzo began to run the business. Ray was required only to appear at 4:00 A.M., the slowest period of the day, to pick up the money and close the day's books. Alonzo met him cheerfully at the front door. Ray never went in the back room again; that was now another man's home.

But Ray's time was no longer filled with anything of interest. He hung around the house, read, slept, joined his mother in an Old Style, dropped in on his father at the office, made a pest of himself. At some point he decided to travel a little, packed his things, and departed. He lived first in Boulder, Colorado, and after a year there bought a failing laundromat two blocks from the university campus. He installed new machines, painted, laid all-weather carpet, rolled a jukebox into the corner, and then for three weeks let everything run for nothing: free music, free snacks, free washers and dryers.

He still owned that store, and received a monthly check and statements, but when he headed west again after two years he had learned never to give anything away. Once the prices went back on the machines, the kids stopped coming. They had places on campus to do their laundry. His return on the Boulder store was twenty-five percent of what he made from his Chicago location, and it took nearly a year to make back what he had spent in that three weeks of something for nothing.

Ray owned five laundromats in Southern California when he returned to Chicago for his father's funeral. He took a flight that was intended to be nonstop to O'Hare, but which was forced down in Denver with mechanical problems. During the three hours it was expected to take to find a new plane, Ray rented a car and drove to Boulder. He planned to drop in on his laundromat; his surprise would startle the manager with his omnipresence. He sat for several minutes across the street from the store, fully intending to turn off the engine and go inside. He could see the manager through the window filling a detergent vending machine and speaking to a young woman doing her wash.

The sun was warm on Ray's legs; the rental car was too small for him, a tall man, overweight. And as he sat there he could not think of one good reason to go inside. The thought of springing himself on his employee now seemed the idea of an untrusting owner. It was enough that the man was busy during the few minutes Ray had happened to witness him in secret.

An older man came down the street carrying a basket of wash and as he put his back to the door to push inside, the manager stepped quickly and opened the door for him. The old man interested Ray because he reminded him of his father. He had been seeing such men everywhere. In the airport, sitting in coffee shops, renting cars; dozens of men who startled Ray for the instant he required to convince himself that he was not seeing his father.

He had not yet begun to miss his father. The death was still a novelty, something so strange it was not quite to be believed. His mother had called with the news and after he hung up the phone he thought he might cry. But he hadn't. It was just a feeling that passed, a hollowness at the back of his eyes. A genuine curiosity descended. For the next several hours he packed, made arrangements for his businesses to operate in his absence, canceled appointments, each task accomplished against a backdrop of detachment. Friends offered condolences when he told them why he had to go out of town and he accepted these uncomfortably, as if he hadn't earned them. His father was dead; Ray didn't know how he felt.

Years had passed since he and Vincent had spoken of anything of importance. His father had lost some requisite dimension when Ray moved out. Perhaps sooner than that, when Ray bought his first laundromat. The advice his father might give him on any specific subject would only echo what Ray had already decided to do.

So the father whose death would sadden him would be a much younger man, a memory. He would be the thin, quiet man in sparkling clothes who loved to play games with his children; catch, tag, hide-and-seek. He once took a game of hide-and-seek to such an extreme that when the children could not find him during a bedtime game and grew bored with the search he remained hidden all night (he claimed, though Ray's mother would never submit to sleeping alone) in the dusty little cave under the basement stairs. He would be the man who winked at Ray when he went to get his mother a beer. The man who went off in the morning to sell real estate, though not every morning, and on the mornings he did choose to visit his office the choice never seemed to have any urgency behind it. Ray accompanied him once and his only memory of that day was of a large, paneled room with maps on the walls, his father on the telephone interminably. He was tossed candy bribes to curb his boredom and fidgeting.

That man was gone now. Gone also was the old man, the flat voice on the phone asking about the machinations of the laundry business, as if that were the most fascinating topic imaginable. The questions and answers would be repeated during each phone call dialed east or west, and that was one reason he didn't call much anymore.

Now his father was gone and his mother would be lost. The depth of her grief was something he did not want to witness. He feared being unable to help her, or absorb her pain, or match it. Vincent Lockwood had thinned away to a memory for Ray. That was something of a luxury, a gift bestowed in part by his father, who taught his children to move on to their own lives.

But there would be no such thinning out for his mother. Ray feared his father's death would leave her helpless, an unimaginable state. Or she might deflect her grief deeper inside her, to hide it from her children behind a shield of false enthusiasm, or more beer.

He carried beer for her from the west, in fact. The six warm cans lay wrapped in a towel at the bottom of his suitcase. During a conversation more than a year previously she had mentioned a curiosity about a brand brewed in San Francisco. He would surprise her; he would cheer her a little with the prospect of something exotic when the wake and funeral were over.

She always drank her beer out of a tall blue glass, and she filled the glass only three-quarters full so that the foamy scum could not be seen unless some boorish individual tipped his nose to look down into her cool well of comfort. Usually that individual was Ray. He always asked, "Tea, Mother?" The blue glass and her careful monitoring of the liquid's level kept the beer a secret from all but her most trusted acquaintances; or so she believed.

She had never embarrassed anyone with her drinking, least of all herself. However, Ray had always suspected that she had hurt Vincent. Vincent brought her beer when she requested it, and bought it for her at the store, but drank little himself. He would be caught by Ray examining her as she sipped from her blue glass, and his look was blatantly perplexed, as if trying yet again to understand what it was he did not provide that she required beer to fill that space inside her.

Ray could never be sure. So much of what they meant to each other was a mystery to him. They had know each other for so long, their love went so far back in time, that it was beyond explanation or understanding to anyone but themselves. They told their children stories of their romance, but these were set pieces, with roles like little plays that skimmed the surface. They were meant to reassure Annie and Ray that love was never a question with them; a way to make their children feel safe in that love. The rest was nobody's business but their own.

That his father died first had been a huge relief to Ray. His father being left behind by his mother had been a fear of Ray's for several years, growing more insistent the farther he moved away. His father—light-hearted, smiling, holding his mother's hand or touching her cheek at every opportunity (once squeezing her breast in a secret movement secretly observed)—loomed helplessly in Ray's imagination without the presence of his mother. And what must he have thought, relying so exclusively on, loving so devotedly, a woman who drank beer with such relish? Did he ever think it should be the other way around? Did he ever fear she would fail him?

She never had. Not that Ray knew of. And now that his mother had seen his father safely off, Ray wondered what would become of her.

HELENE, standing at the bottom of the stairs, woke Ina with her patient cries for assistance. Ina was wrapped in damp sheets, her room in the morning sunshine already breathless with heat. An extended moment was required to place herself in time, location, and circumstance, and when all was in order she discovered herself to be excited.

"Such a life you lead," Helene said when she heard the scratch of her sister's step descending the stairs. Helene's dress was crumpled in that fractional way only a fastidious person would notice. Ina said nothing about it, knowing Helene would not cease talking about her appearance until she got home and changed.

Ina went into the bathroom to inspect the damage to her house, to reassure herself that the previous night had taken place. The room smelled of heated air and pine disinfectant; and an underlying stink of the man trapped so long in her wall, as if in lodging there he had seeped into the wood like a resin, a coating of him shaved off and remaining behind as he was pulled free.

"Did you go yet?" she asked Helene.

"Once."

"Are you ready again?"

"I think so. Could you get my shot ready?"

"Of course, dear."

While Helene used the bathroom, Ina poured an Old Style into her blue glass, then set it aside where she could nibble at it while caring for her sister.

Helene double-voided in the morning, the second sample providing a truer measure of her blood sugar, and this sample she presented warm in a five-ounce cup to Ina. Ina set the cup on the counter and after waiting a moment dipped the TesTape in. The yellow paper turned dark blue.

"It's high this morning," Ina reported.

"That cheap wine you forced on me," Helene said. "I had terrible sugar dreams."

"Poo. It was all the excitement," Ina said. "Where do you want it today?"

Helene kept in her memory a map of her body, using it to track the rotation of shot sites in order that no part of her skin would be punctured too frequently.

"Thigh. Left," Helene said, and with a demure extending of her leg pulled her dress up above her hip. Her skin was quite slack and pale, with a blue undertone like a second skin pulled taut beneath the first.

Ina, adept at the dosage monitor developed for blind diabetics, filled a syringe, swabbed alcohol over her sister's skin (Helene sucked in her breath at the cold), and then pushed in the needle.

Helene did not tense up; she hardly moved. She had learned long ago to disengage her mind from the event so that she operated on a form of autopilot for the half-minute it took to get her shot. Ina spoke only in generalities during these moments; Helene never remembered anything she said.

They ate a meal almost monumental in its lack of excitement: bran cereal, muffins, milk, and apricots. Ina sneaked cinnamon onto her muffin, and beer with her milk. The sky was hazy with pollutants, dust, pollen, and dirt that the heat would not let go. She saw Po Strode working, her head protected by a wide wheat hat, doing something inconspicuous to her gardens. She did not water or trim, but took full blooms in her hands as if in inspection, and then spoke a few words. Now and then her gaze would drift to Ina's house, and Ina chose to believe her friend was simply keeping watch.

She said to Helene, "I want to go see my children."

Helene calmly nodded. Her blank eyes remained steadfast in their patience to learn whether she would be left behind.

"And I want you to take me," Ina finished.

"Take you?"

"Yes. I want you to drive us to California."

To her credit, Helene laughed. A short laugh that perhaps was painful, for tears came to Helene's eyes.

"I thought this through last night—this morning," Ina said. "After all the excitement, I couldn't sleep. I honestly believe such a trip can be made. I covered every detail—"

"In your humble opinion," Helene said.

"*You* convinced me," Ina said. "If I hadn't seen you drive us to Amanda's I wouldn't have believed it possible. But you did it. In *daylight*. In a gargantuan and complex metropolis. Places like Missouri, Texas, the desert—no place would present more of a challenge than where you've already driven."

"Thank you, dear," said Helene. "Let's just fly. Have Ray meet us at the airport. He'll chauffeur us around. He'd do anything for you."

"Anyone can fly," Ina said. "We can travel on back roads in the dead of night. From midnight to four A.M., nobody is out and about. During the day we'll sleep and lounge by the pool. I'll take you places and describe them to you. It will be a trip of a lifetime."

Helene sipped her milk, Ina her Old Style. It surprised Ina, in describing the journey, how much it meant to her. For the first time since Vincent had died the time ahead of her had some shape and meaning beyond caring for Helene. She was in an anxious, anticipatory state.

"If it was later in the day I'd swear you were drunk," Helene said then in a frightened and hateful voice.

"I'm not drunk," Ina said. "Furthermore, I don't *get* drunk."

"I'm sorry, dear. That was cruel of me."

"Yes, it was."

"But it's such a . . . crazy idea."

"It can be done," Ina said. "With care, it *can* be done. Ask me a detail. I have the answer."

"Who will watch the house?"

"Yours, Amanda. Mine, Po and Hector. In fact, I may sell mine."

"You *are* drunk. Or mad."

"It doesn't feel the same," Ina said. "That thief ruined it for me. I've been threatened with death in my own house."

"Where will you live?" Helene asked worriedly.

"I don't know. Maybe with Ray? Maybe you'll like driving me around so much we'll buy a camper and cruise the night away," Ina said.

Helene laughed again and Ina warmed to her, that she was being a good sport; the possibility remained.

"Why don't you learn to drive?" Helene asked. "Then you can drive us to California."

"So you admit the destination appeals to you," Ina said, anxious to get that fact on record.

Helene nodded. "I'd like to visit California."

"I *should* have learned to drive when I was young," Ina said. "But Vincent convinced me it was unnecessary. I had him." Ina took a sip; a familiar ache had opened within her. "Time has proved him—me—wrong. Now I haven't the patience to learn to drive. I have you."

"Who will take the blame when we run down a child?" Helene asked.

"We won't."

"We might. We could," Helene said determinedly.

"What child will be on the road from midnight to dawn?" Ina asked, though the prospect haunted her. The plans she had made, all the answers she had provided to her sleepless queries, could not remove her fear of the unexpected. It was both what she desired and feared most from the trip.

"But if we do?" Helene pressed.

"I will take the blame," Ina said.

They haggled on through the day, leaving the kitchen for short errands of necessity—to fill a glass, use the toilet, lower the windows against a breezy downpour. And although Helene never said the word, Ina was content in her belief that the journey would be made, indeed was already under way.

Helene was anxious for darkness to fall and asked Ina frequently for a report on the state of the evening. Darkness, Ina understood, would free Helene from the responsibility of returning to her house that day. She was happy to be locked in safe at Ina's for another night.

"First thing," Ina said. "We must concoct a credible story. We are going on a trip to California. We are taking your car. A friend of ours is driving. That will explain our extended absence and the absence of the car. Can you leave in a week?"

"A week?" Helene said. "Of course not."

"Just tell Amanda to watch the house. Then pack. We're off."

"What about the car? It needs work," Helene said. "I've got to buy travelers' checks. We should plan a route. Do we carry food? What about my medical supplies? And what about money? This will be expensive. A week isn't nearly time enough."

"Those are all technicalities," Ina said. "It's important that we don't let small obstacles stand in our way."

THEY walked to Helene's house the next day. While her sister sat, fretted, and gave orders, Ina cleaned up the mess. The house already had a stink to it; they should have come back as soon as possible. The sugary floor was alive with ants—and one wide roach who didn't budge as Ina's toe descended crackling through him.

She swept everything into a small mountain by the back stairs, scooped the mountain into bags, and carried the bags outside. The Omega was there in the garage. Wide, dusty, with an undertone of perfect patience, the car was the key to everything. She put a hand on the cool shell. She left a mark; fingertips like petals, a crescent of her palm.

Back in the house, the stink remained.

"Something foul," Ina said.

"I traced it while you were outside," Helene said. "It's coming from my and Rudy's room."

Ina found it easily enough: a neat deposit of shit in Helene and Rudy's bed, the covers smoothed carefully over it. A stain, barely damp now, was also on the rug.

Ina stripped the bed in one enraged snap of the sheets and blankets and hurried the bundle outside. On the stain she poured vinegar and rubbed it nearly into a froth, though she suspected the rug was a lost cause. She brought a fan into the room. She directed its fresh wind into her face for a minute before positioning it on the floor.

In a wall toward the front of the house she found a hole as round and smooth as if it had been made with a paper-punch. The edge of the hole was powdery to the touch, of indeterminate depth, and something in the hole bit her fingertip and held on when she yanked back her finger.

A small mousetrap had hold of her. The bait plate was empty. She freed her finger; a blue slash throbbed on her knuckle. She frankly marveled at the evil of the people who had broken into Helene's house.

She stood breathing, not daring to move. The small trap made her wonder about the presence of others. The mess in the bed: another trap, more difficult to conceal. What else? How long had they been in the house? And how much time had they needed to prime the house like a bomb to await the old women's blundering fingers?

She found two more holes, each with a trap that she tripped with the tip of a pencil. She threw the traps in the wastebasket in the kitchen, where Helene sat watch with a mournful look.

"Is it bad?" she asked.

"More sad," Ina said. "That people like this exist in the world. I guess I knew they were around, but didn't want to admit it."

"It's a great relief to me," Helene said, "that you're here."

"Where would I go?"

"It doesn't smell so terribly. You must be making progress."

"Yes, progress."

"I called to tell Amanda and she wasn't concerned," Helene said. "She told me it happens all the time. It's happened to her. No offer of help. No offer of a place to stay."

Ina was stealing a swallow of beer from a can she had smuggled in. Someone rapped on the backdoor. Helene's gaze swung that way. The day was getting on, and still very hot.

Katherine smiled through the gap the door-chain permitted. She carried with both hands a tub of potato salad, a pitcher of lemonade balanced atop the lid.

"I was worried about you both," she said. Mickey, nervous as Ina, hid behind the woman. When the chain came off and the door opened they made a little parade up to the kitchen—Ina, Katherine, and Mickey, who made soft toodling sounds with her mouth as they marched into Helene's presence.

"It isn't much," Katherine said. She touched Helene's arm. "I'm sorry this had to happen."

She did not mention the stink or the grinding remnants of sugar underfoot, or Helene's shocked look. Katherine stroked her daughter's hair. When the visit had reached its conclusion she touched Helene again and said good-bye, then motioned Ina to follow. At the backdoor, Katherine asked in a low voice, "Were you here last night?"

"No."

"Someone was. I saw them moving around. They kept the lights off," Katherine said, her eyes very wide. Her daughter had gone outside and now stood patiently on one foot, waiting for her mother.

"It's worth knowing," Ina said.

"I don't like that she's here alone."

"We're going on a trip. That will be some relief."

"Wonderful. Where?"

"To California. To visit my children and grandchild," Ina said. "A friend of ours is driving us."

"I was born in Berkeley," Katherine said. "I miss it sometimes."

"Do you go back?"

"Not for years. My family is here now," Katherine said. Something made her laugh. "My mom and dad sold phallus candles to the tourists on Telegraph. He was also a recruiter for the Marines in Oakland."

Her daughter had gone to the end of the walk, standing one-legged again, and made soft whoopy music with her mouth.

"Be careful," Katherine said. "Have a safe trip."

Ina stood in the warm shadows inside the backdoor after the woman and child departed. She finished her beer in two long swallows.

"Let's drive the car to my house," Ina said to Helene.

"Now? In daylight?"

"You've done it before."

"I don't know."

She took Helene by the hand and led her upstairs into the hot crown of the house, where the rooms felt dead and buried. Curtains had been ripped from their rods and fashioned into a noose to hang one of Amanda's old dolls from the light fixture at the top of the stairs. Ina untied the doll, its frilly pink dress sticky and bunched together in back. Ina brought the damp fabric to her nose and caught a nostalgic whiff of semen.

"Let's get your clothes," Ina said, desperate to be moving. She wanted to get her sister out of that house; get her on the road and safe.

"We can come back for them," Helene said. "I need a rest. This heat is making me woozy."

"Don't go woozy on me," Ina said. "We need to get your clothes. You need makeup. Toiletries. What about any keepsakes? If you weren't coming back, what would you take?"

The question startled Helene. "What do you mean, not coming back?" she asked.

"Just pretend. A game. What knickknacks would you keep if you knew you would never set foot in this house again?" Ina said.

"But I am. I don't want to play that game," Helene said.

"Here. Sit."

Helene waited on the edge of the bed while Ina snatched dresses out of the stuffy closets, folded them in half, and shoved them into plastic garbage bags. She filled another bag with shoes, yet another with undergarments. A small ceramic boy on the dresser top caught her eye; he was standing with his arms outstretched, his smile beatific, and Helene had been using his arms to hold her rings. Ina poured the rings into a shoebox and put the boy in Helene's hand.

"What about him?" Ina said. "Would you keep him?"

Helene rolled the boy around in her fingers. She wiped dust off his head and off the lapels of his short-waisted dove gray jacket.

"Of course," Helene said, handing him back.

The rest of the contents of Helene's house she did not mention. Dusk was coming on. Predators would be making their way up from daylight sleep to slink over and see what was happening with their friends.

Ina positioned Helene at the kitchen table while she made several trips upstairs to collect the bags of her sister's belongings. She went on outside to pack it all away in the car.

Getting out of the garage was not as complicated as before. The streets were busy but Ina and Helene traveled as if they were unduly afraid of children running from between cars. The speed they generated did not cause comment from other motorists. Ina had Helene park at the curb a half-block from her house. They walked from there. Ina was afraid of Po Strode seeing Helene pull into the driveway. After dark, they went back out and drove the car the rest of the way home, into the garage where Vincent had seen pictures in the oil on the floor.

INA announced that they must begin to live at night, to accustom their biological clocks to the disciplines of the trip. Toward that end the widows fought against sleep until nearly 2:00 A.M., when Helene's head toppled onto the back of the couch.

Ina took her sister by the shoulders and turned her out along the divan, positioning her legs, removing her shoes, covering her with a blanket.

"We just went into a ravine," she whispered at Helene's ear. "We're burning now because you fell asleep at the wheel."

The night was so quiet. The emptiness of the street was reassuring. Even at midnight Ina had counted fourteen cars in a half-hour; some were moving quite fast. She heard the buzz of tires, horns, a siren; all of it in the distance, but nevertheless quite real, a warning din.

But at ten past two the desired solitude had been achieved. For two hours the city would be theirs. They would have the opening required to get out of town, find a place to stay before dawn, and then they would be on their way.

She sat at her bedroom window with her blue glass, determined to see her way through the dark time before 4:00 A.M. The light at that hour was of interest to her, the feel of the air and the pace of the street; she was on a reconnaissance mission of sorts. She wanted to be able to report to Helene that the 4:00 A.M. world was a safe place to travel. They would not be in peril if their night's journey extended a few minutes past that hour, for whatever reason.

But why did Helene even have to know the time? And would she be able to tell the difference? Four A.M. was in all probability little different in tone and light from four-thirty or quarter to five, thus creating for Ina an extra half-hour to forty-five minutes of travel. There was no real need for her sister to know the precise time every moment of the day.

But at a little past three o'clock Ina retreated from her stand at the window, backpedaling with a luxurious sigh into the cool sheets of her bed. She lay there for a time almost too brief to mention, and then she was gone.

SHE phoned Annie in the morning to tell her about the trip. She needed to firm the plan in her mind, and by telling her children a sense of commitment would be attached.

It was a Sunday. Don answered, his voice crisp and impassive, a voice that gave nothing away. He surprised Ina with news that Annie was in church.

"Annie doesn't go to church," Ina said.

"She does now. Or she has for the past six or seven weeks. She goes to an eight o'clock service, then plays tennis at ten."

"I wonder why church."

"One morning she just *went*," Don said. "She calls it time to herself. On the one morning I'm home."

"Is she well?" Ina asked.

"As far as I know."

"Does Meg go?"

"Lord, no. Ann didn't ask her. She didn't ask me, for that matter." Don paused. "Can I help you, Ina?"

"I just called to chat," Ina said.

"How are things in Chicago?"

"Hot."

"The fires have begun here," Don reported. "You can see the glow at night. It's beautiful. We've hooked up a pump and hose by the pool, just in case."

"Could you stand visitors, Don?"

"Who? You?"

"Helene and me," Ina said. "We're coming west later this month—or early next."

"Wonderful," he said with a salesman's enthusiasm. "You're always welcome. Both of you. How long will you stay?"

"We don't know yet," Ina said. "It's my trip. My idea. Of course we'll also stay with Ray. You won't have *complete* responsibility for us while we're there."

"Ina. Hey. Stay a week. A month," Don said. *"Mi casa, su casa."*

"Thanks," Ina said, nearly a murmur. She wished she liked Don better, or made headway in knowing him during those brief times they spoke to each other.

She was intrigued by her daughter attending church. Annie had been in the choir as a little girl, her mouth a perfect O, her head tipped back and glistening. But she went only because she loved to sing.

"Will you fly into LAX?"

"We aren't going to fly, Don. We're driving," she said, adding quickly, "Being driven."

"Are you sure? That's a long way."

"I don't want to fly. I'm looking forward to the drive tremendously."

"Who's driving?" he asked. She listened for suspicion in his voice but there was nothing. In truth, she assumed, he probably wasn't even interested; let the old bats drive, walk, crawl, my house is your house as long as they are at their house. He was drawing out the final moments of their conversation on the fumes of politeness.

"A young neighbor of Helene's. Her name is Katherine. She's from out there. Berkeley," Ina said. "She wanted to visit and offered to drive us."

"Her car?"

"No, Helene's."

"What kind of mileage does it get?"

"I couldn't tell you."

"Gas prices are all over the map. Make sure this gal chips in."

"She will," Ina said.

"How long do you plan on taking?"

"I don't know," Ina said. She hadn't thought even once about time; everything about the trip as she pictured it was open-ended.

"You can make LA in four days, easy," Don said. "This country's system of interstate highways is a marvel. Just steer and go. Four days, easy. If you want to travel hard, three."

"I think we'll take a little longer than that."

"Sure," Don said. "I don't blame you."

"We'll give you reports along the way."

"Can I have Annie call you?"

"Sure, Don. Thanks."

THEY ate dinner late and watched the news from behind TV trays.

"We should try to stay up again," Ina said when the news had ended.

"Can I nap before? You could wake me at midnight."

"You can shut your eyes," Ina said. "I think that would be a splendid idea."

"You should, too," Helene said. "It's almost more important that you be alert."

"I'll try—but I'm not sleepy."

"On the road, in the dark, with those hypnotic white lines, you will be."

Ina cleared the trays just to have something to do; making extra trips for herself to the kitchen so the time would seem full. She was just so jumpy since the trip had come into her head. Keeping busy was a problem. She had packed her bags the first morning and now they lay at the foot of her bed. On more than one occasion she had thought to go to the bank to withdraw money (she wasn't sure if ten thousand dollars was too much, or enough, or ostentatious; but who knew how long she would be gone?) and then postponed the errand. She understood why: Helene was living with her.

The rootedness, the immobility of blindness that Helene complained about had begun to afflict Ina, as if her own eyesight were going bad. It was one reason Ina was in a hurry to be traveling. On the road, Ina would be in charge again; at present, Helene held her fast with her innocent, small, cumulative demands, and with her helplessness.

She drank an Old Style while Helene was in the bathroom washing her face. The sounds Helene made were all watery clickings, a carefree humming of a song Ina could not place.

An hour and a half remained until midnight. There seemed little purpose in Helene going to sleep for such a brief period of time. She would awaken cranky and then complain during the hours they would be awake to travel.

"Why not just stay up?" Ina asked, when Helene came out of the bedroom. "It's nearly eleven."

"Because I'm exhausted," Helene said.

"We haven't *done* anything all day. How can you be exhausted?"

"Don't pick a fight, beer breath."

Her sister felt her way down the hall. She was getting to know the house. Earlier that day Ina had watched Helene at the last instant avoid walking into the dining-room table, escaping with a neat, quick change of direction when a collision appeared unavoidable.

"We have to turn our systems around," Ina said, following her.

"When the time comes, I'll be awake," Helene said. "Right now—I'm sorry to say—I don't see the point in just sitting up from midnight to four A.M. There's nothing on the radio. Nothing on TV. We just bicker. Is that how this trip is going to be? You and me bickering across America?"

"I'm trying to get us ready," said Ina.

"I know, dear."

"Should I get you up at midnight?"

Helene, on the divan, rubbed her eyes. "No," she said. "I want to sleep."

"Then sleep, damn it."

INA thought she also would sleep through the early hours. She was drained by the hot day and the lassitude of making no progress. But something about the hour of midnight pulled her off her bed and down the stairs. She felt magnetized. Everything about the hour was familiar—the air, the shade of darkness, the movement outside the house and in the street, the breathlessness as she soaked it all in.

She ventured out onto her back stoop. A coolness that had not found its way into her house suffused the air. It was air she would gratefully have slept in when she was a girl. The room that Vincent had converted into his office was long ago an enclosed screen porch at the corner of the house, with a glider and wicker furniture and two cots the girls unfolded on hot nights only slightly quieter than this one. They were ordered by their mother to wear socks and flannel nightgowns and to sleep under blankets. But when their parents were asleep, Ina and Helene, after much giggling and accumulated dares, hopped on the cool, groaning boards of the floor and shed their gowns and socks, dancing naked in the air for longer than was necessary. A moth hit the screen. One of the girls screamed, their parents stirred like the beginnings of a storm, and Ina and Helen sprang to their cots, pulling their nightclothes in after them.

Vincent and Rudy came stealthily to the porch, never knowing if the sisters would be there. Ina and Helene teased them with hints of what they were wearing under the covers. Helene's cot was closest to the screen. Ina could lie on her side, her head in her hand, and see the boys across the languid plane of her sister. She felt unobserved. She was set back in darkness, mystery, and privacy. Her free hand in its hidden place fanned gently, insistently, until she was ready to dissolve. She wanted the boys to leave (and Helene to sleep) so she could finish.

A car went past, a dark figure at the wheel, moving slowly enough to attract attention. Her uneasiness made her angry; no longer could she stand in the comfortable night air without being on her guard. Yet she didn't want to go inside; the air was stale there and she wouldn't be able to sleep.

But the car returned, firmer in its destination, and turned into Ina's driveway. The lights went off. The driver uncurled from the seat. A tall woman dressed in something pale, carrying a large purse, coming toward Ina with a secretive, tiptoe motion: Amanda.

"What brings you here?" Ina said too loudly, afraid Amanda didn't see her. She did not want her niece to scream, or to think she was not observed.

"I'm looking for Mom," she said, her face angled to one side, as though Helene watched from the corner of the house.

"She's here. She's staying with me for a time."

"Her house is a shambles."

"The break-in," said Ina. "Kids being malicious."

"There's graffiti all over the wall."

"Graffiti?"

"Words and symbols—gobbledygook."

"She's here and she's fine," Ina said. "Come on in." And the question: Why not just call?

The kitchen light seemed to affect Amanda adversely; she held back, sniffed wetly behind her hand, and muttered something.

"Pardon?" Ina said.

"Nothing."

Amanda stood with her face half turned from Ina, the far half sheltered by her hand. She pretended to be interested in a little poem about herbs lettered on a shellacked piece of walnut hung on the kitchen wall. Ina gently pulled Amanda's hand away. Her eyes were wet. Blood was dried in the corner of her mouth, and there was swelling.

Amanda turned, coming apart, into Ina's embrace. She patted the woman's broad back (in her arms, Ina felt Amanda loom, a monument to unhappiness) and fed tissues into Amanda's clutching hand as though to staunch a gash. Each time Amanda tried to speak, she failed. Ina counseled patience and relaxation. Her cooing filled the room. She did not want to wake up Helene.

When Amanda's crying had subsided, Ina felt safe to ease her grip on the woman. Amanda stood up straight, rolled her shoulders, sighed. Ina put a beer in her hand and showed her to a chair.

"I was scared," Amanda said. She sucked air, fighting her tears, as if this were the hard part and once past this segment of her story the rest would flow.

"I went to Mom's for help—and no one was there. The house looked so *dejected.* Graffiti all over it, lights on, but empty," Amanda said.

"Your mother's had a rough few days," Ina said. Then she quieted, fearing she had stopped Amanda's willingness to speak.

"I thought: Where else would she be but here?"

"Of course."

"So here I am."

"You're welcome, you know," Ina said. "Did you want to spend the night?"

"Could I? I won't be any trouble."

"*Amanda.* Be trouble, if you want," Ina said. "Stay as long as you like."

"Thanks."

"Did that handsome man on the counter do that to you?" Ina asked, pointing casually at the blood and the swelling.

Amanda's look turned fearsome. "That," she said. "And this, too," unbuttoning her blouse and folding it back to reveal two sickening greenish bruises, the sizes of limes, in the soft skin above her breasts.

"And this," she went on, turning her left leg out, hiking her skirt to show off a third bruise the color of a thunderhead.

"Call the police," Ina said heatedly.

"He'd kill me."

"Lord," Ina murmured.

"He's gone now. I'm almost positive of that."

"Then why are you here?"

The fierceness had been bleeding from Amanda's eyes and now it was utterly gone.

"He scares me—I'll admit that," she said. "If I can just stay out of his way for a while everything will be okay."

"How long has this been going on?"

"The punching—only recently," Amanda said. "He's been kind of mean to me all along, now that I think about it."

"Why did you put up with him?"

"Do you have to ask?"

"We're going on a trip, your Mother and me," Ina said.

"Oh yes?" Amanda said, and Ina nearly laughed to hear Helene's ladylike false enthusiasm echoed in her daughter.

"To California," Ina said. "A friend is driving us. A young woman from there."

"California," Amanda said, rolling the word off her tongue like something exotic and delicious. "Would you have room for one more?"

Ina's error struck her as incredibly shortsighted and foolish. Of course, mention their trip to a woman already half on the run, a woman in fear for her life.

"It would be fine with me," Ina said. "But the final decision would be up to your mother. It's her trip. Her car."

"I don't know if I could get the time off," Amanda said. "How long will you take?"

"We'll go slow," Ina said. "We need a vacation. Perhaps when we get there you can fly out and meet us. Stay with Annie or Ray for a week or so."

"What appeals to me is leaving *soon*," Amanda said.

"We're still getting organized. So much to do," Ina said. "When we will finally leave is a mystery."

"Who's driving?"

"Katherine. Helene's neighbor."

"The one with the kids?"

"Do you know her?"

"We've nodded to each other," Amanda said. "She seems tied to her kids and husband."

"She wants to visit her parents in California. We offered cheap transportation in exchange for her driving," Ina said. She took a deep breath. Her fabrications seemed to grow holes and weaknesses even as she uttered them; only the most rudimentary coincidence would be required for Amanda to see Katherine in her backyard, to bring up the proposed journey, and for the lies to be discovered. Ina's hope was to get on the road before that happened; once they were on their way, they could not be stopped.

"I need to get some sleep," she said, standing. "Stay in the room at the end of the upstairs hall. It has clean linen and a bath. Your mother's asleep in the front room."

Amanda kissed Ina carefully with the unpunched corner of her mouth.

"Thank you, Ina. How will we play this in the morning?"

"Sleep as long as you wish. When you come down, I will go along with whatever story you concoct," Ina said.

"I hate when things are left up to me," Amanda said.

"I could make something up for you—but we'd only have to rehearse in the morning," Ina said. "I trust you. You can trust me."

She checked the locks on the doors, ran her fingers over the smooth board covering the milkbox hole. What would Amanda make of that? Would she feel any safer in Ina's house than in any other location under siege?

Amanda was in her slip, in the nightstand light, when Ina came by to say good night and make certain she had towels, soap, a washcloth, a toothbrush. She was delicately probing one of the bruises at her collarbone. The one on her thigh was as dark and defined as a hole in her leg.

"He just gets so enraged," Amanda said, looking evenly at Ina.

"He just smacks me because I'm handy. I don't know what to do with him but hit him back."

"This looks fresh," Ina said, touching her own mouth in the spot where Amanda was bleeding.

"He came over tonight," she said. "He wanted to apologize for being an asshole, make everything better, then—you know. I told him I never wanted to see him again, so he hit me. I ran," she said. "I shouldn't have run, but I did. He might've trashed my place. Who knows? I'm not going back for a while."

"Get some sleep," Ina said. She kissed her niece's cheek. "I'll keep your mother off you as long as I can."

INA was awakened by a stirring in the house below her. Water ran. A chair leg scraped. Ina had no interest in the hour. She knew from the weight in her legs and behind her eyes that she had not slept enough. This brought to mind a point of preparation she must address to Helene: There was no sense just one of them turning their body clocks around to the new schedule of travel. She required that commitment from her sister.

She turned so her back was to the windows, which despite their blinds and drapes admitted an abundance of unwelcome sunshine. She felt it heating the air she lay in. It lapped like a tide at her feet. She positioned her feet in a cool pocket under the sheets, and found a similar spot beneath the pillow for her hands. She had always wished Vincent would have trouble sleeping so he might come to her for those little tricks she used (in addition to beer) to send her off. But he fell asleep after a kiss from her, a pause first on one elbow while he said secret prayers, and then a brief stretching out and arranging of his long physique under the covers. He sniffed, a last sound, like a candle doused by rain; and like that he was asleep.

She had to fight for it herself now and then. Beer helped; for many nights in a row (especially the difficult darknesses following Vincent's death) it carried her away on a golden sea, full of swirling boats, not unpleasant, and devoid of dreams. It served its purpose in a manner she found enjoyable, unavoidable. On those nights the Old Style didn't work she was always disappointed; she felt deceived, led on.

Her eyes opened again. She examined a stain in the ceiling. She could discern no shape, which saddened her. Vincent would have found a shape. He would point it out and name it, and each time they made love in daylight she would see that shape like a friend as she squinted past his shoulder.

She wasn't going to fall back to sleep.

Helene was at the kitchen table, drumming her fingers. Ina kissed her good morning.

"I need to test," Helene said.

"All right," said Ina.

Helene went into the bathroom. In her absence, Ina arranged the gear for Helene's shot.

Helene returned with her cup.

"I smell Amanda's perfume," she said. "Now why is that?"

Ina regarded her sister's question. Put forth with a random innocence, it had hit a mark nonetheless.

"Because she was here. Is here," Ina said. "She's sleeping upstairs."

Helene looked up at the ceiling. Ina thought she heard movement there.

"Why?" Helene asked, her voice low and worried.

"I'll let her tell you."

"But you know," Helene challenged.

"I do, yes."

"So you'll let her tell her own lies," Helene said, "and bear the consequences of living within them."

"Yes, dear," Ina said with a laugh.

"It's a man?"

"My lips are sealed."

"It takes no clairvoyance to guess that," Helene said. "She has a home. A job. Why come here at all—if not for protection?"

Ina held her tongue, though the desire to lay a groundwork of escape for Amanda was nearly intolerable.

"Then get her down here," Helene said.

"Let her sleep. She was up very late."

"You must've been, too. And you're awake."

"Only because I couldn't fall back to sleep," Ina said. "I don't need the sleep I used to. And that reminds me: Are you with me on this journey west? And if you are, I think you should at least attempt to stay up with me so your system adjusts. You're our main cog, dear. Our most valuable player."

"And if I'm not with you?"

"Then tell me now. It will require a change of plans on my part," Ina said hastily, regretting that she had ventured into this line of conversation at this point in the day's spectrum of emotions.

"What plans?" scoffed Helene. "You have a wild—*daft*—idea. We're no closer to going to California than we were a year ago."

"I could leave today," Ina boasted. "A run to the bank for some traveling money and I'm off. I'm packed. My affairs are in order. My children expect me."

"Rubbish."

"The delay has been in dragging *you* into line," Ina said harshly. "In getting you to admit you're even going."

"Because we're not," Helene said, turning away from her sister's voice.

"I'm going," Ina said. "The question is if you're going. And if you aren't—where *are* you going?"

"Home."

"Home. Exactly," said Ina. "And I'm going with you. We'll get Hector Strode to look over the car. We'll firm up our itinerary, get some money, and slip away under cover of darkness. I must warn you," she said, lowering her voice, "that Amanda has asked to accompany us."

"Why? She has a job. Who'll watch my house?"

"I'm just telling you that. She asked me. I said it was up to you."

"I don't want her coming along," complained Helene. "She's too critical. We wouldn't have any fun."

"You dope! Of course she can't come along. How would we explain the fact you're driving?"

"Don't call me a dope," Helene said.

"Sorry. She thinks Katherine is driving. Another reason for us to hit the road soon. How long can we count on Amanda and Katherine not running into each other?"

"What should I tell her?" Helene asked.

"Not enough room, of course. But why?"

"Katherine is taking back a carload of plants?"

"No. Kids. She's taking her kids back to show off to the grandparents," Ina said. "We get a free ride. Katherine gets a couple of extra pair of hands on the trip. It's perfect. I should plan crimes."

"An extra pair of blind hands?" asked Helene.

"We're a package deal. She wanted me, but she'll put up with both of us," Ina said. "You can rock. You can change a diaper."

"Of course. I'm the most valuable player."

"You are," said Ina. "Are we straight now on the story?"

"Straight enough. And what you said about the free rides? How much money *are* you bringing?" Helene asked.

"I'm mulling that. How much do you think?"

"I was hoping you'd provide a guideline," Helene said.

Ina covered her sister's hand. She had decided early in the planning that there was no point in Helene knowing how much money they carried west. Enough to finance a new life? The amount might only make her nervous.

"I've figured it this way," Ina said. "It's your car and my gas. It's my idea and my family we're visiting—so I'll cover your room costs. You pay for your meals. Fair?"

"No," said Helene. "Don't you think I can afford this trip?"

"Why should you pay for me to see my kids?"

"They aren't strangers to me," Helene said. "I'm not just a chauffeur here. I can pay for my half of the rooms."

"If you insist," said Ina.

Helene nodded halfheartedly, as if she had won a prize she had been reluctant to fight for. They heard a heavy step descending the stairs. Helene touched her lip with a finger.

"Kids," Ina whispered in her sister's ear, and Helene nodded.

Amanda came into the kitchen dressed in her clothes from the night before. She wore no shoes and her stockinged feet hissed across the floor as she went to her mother with a soft, "Hello, Mom," and a kiss to the temple, her eyes on Ina all the way. Ina made a rolling motion with her hands, a signal for any number of things.

The wound on Amanda's mouth looked more settled, as if it had peaked in meanness and pain overnight and would now begin to heal.

"Ina says you're on the run from a man," Helene said, fishing.

"I said no such thing," countered Ina.

"Why are you here?"

"I needed a place to stay last night," Amanda said.

"What's wrong with your apartment?"

"I had an unwelcome visitor," Amanda said, with a shrug toward Ina.

"A man?"

"*Yes*, Mother. A male of the species."

"And was he violent?" Helene asked, amazing her sister.

"He's . . . hot-headed."

"Come here." Helene waved Amanda to her and Amanda obeyed. She might have expected a hug of sympathy or regret, but instead she was inspected by her mother's cool, quick hand shaping itself to Amanda's face and searching until it approached the welt on her mouth, and Amanda drew away.

"Has he hit you?" demanded Helene.

"Take me to California," Amanda pleaded. "It will be good for all of us."

"We aren't going to California," Helene declared. Ina did not say a word; the fate of her trip was out of her hands.

"Who is this man?"

"An ex-friend," Amanda said. "When we get back from California he'll have forgotten all about me."

"This is now," Helene said. "Did you know about this?" she asked coldly of Ina.

"Only since last night. I think Amanda is right. This will pass," Ina said. She needed to put her groundwork back in order, yet she was uncertain where to begin.

"You tell me," Helene said to her sister. "Is my daughter all in one piece? Is her face swollen and bruised?"

Amanda shook her head so violently Ina thought she heard the air being disturbed.

"She's fine," said Ina.

"You're my eyes. I've got to be able to trust you to be honest," said Helene.

"Trust me. You see what I see—and I see no bruises. A woman all in one piece."

"Thank you," Helene said. "Though I know you're lying. Amanda is forty-two, and old enough to run her life."

"To California then," Amanda said.

"We spoke with Katherine this morning," Ina said. "She's taking her two kids to visit her parents—before the new baby arrives. We're sort of intinerant babysitters. She just doesn't have room for you."

"We're not going to California," Helene said. "Not with my daughter in danger."

"I'm fine."

"She's fine."

"Are you sure?" Amanda said to Ina. "I need a vacation bad."

"Five people. Plus all the luggage, the kids' equipment," Ina said. "Space is at a premium."

Ina set a cup of coffee in front of Amanda. She chewed a nail, glanced at her aunt, who hovered like a mother, afraid of the power Amanda possessed.

"You can fly out," Ina suggested. "Meet us at Annie's or Ray's. Maybe you could drive us back."

"I can't afford to fly," Amanda said.

"Sure you can. Cheap fares are everywhere," Ina said. In daylight, Amanda's predicament did not seem quite so dire and now Ina was anxious to have her out of the house. Her violent lover would have gone to work, leaving the apartment to Amanda. Here, she was a hostile witness to the plan, someone to outwit, someone who might kill Helene's meager enthusiasm with the merest word, as she had nearly done moments before.

"Why not go home, take a shower, change clothes?" Ina said,

massaging Amanda's thick, tensed shoulders. Helene seemed to watch the space they occupied, her manner aggrieved, her role usurped.

"Everything will be fine," Ina said.

Amanda rose and left the kitchen willingly enough, but then signaled to Ina from the end of the hall. She hiked her thumb up, then climbed the stairs.

"She gone?" asked Helene.

"Can't you tell?"

The floorboards groaned overhead. "Her face felt fat," Helene remarked. "She could lose twenty-five pounds."

"I'm going to see if she needs anything."

"Be honest. Has he beaten her?"

"No, honestly."

"Because she pulled away from my touch."

"Next time, touch her. Don't frisk her," Ina said.

Amanda had put on her shoes. She scraped a lipstick, a hanky, a pack of cigarettes, a lighter, a beaded change purse off the bureau and into her bag.

"What if he's waiting for me?" she demanded in a frightened whisper.

"He's married?" Ina said.

Amanda nodded forlornly.

"Does his wife know?"

"No."

"Then he's been gone probably since last night," Ina said. "Why give himself away now that everything is over with you? He's at work right this minute. I guarantee it."

"Did we fool her?" Amanda asked.

"No. She knows something, but not enough for her to butt in."

"Thank you for taking me in last night."

"Let me buy your plane ticket," Ina offered, with a glance at the door.

"I can't."

"Sure you can. When we get to California I'll order it from there," Ina said.

Amanda smiled, not at Ina, but at something she had heard. "Mom warned me about you and your money."

"I have a little money," Ina said. "But not enough to be afraid of." She departed on those words; she was not going to entertain insults about her wealth when she was only trying to spread a little of it around. Let Amanda find her own way to California, if she was going to burden herself with her mother's stubborn pride in having not quite enough to live without worrying.

PART FOUR

◆ _____

Slow and Steady
in the
Dead of Night

Two o'clock in the morning, the eleventh day of September, a Monday. For the occasion, Helene wore new sunglasses with water-blue lenses and lemon frames. She sucked on a chip of ice. They were traveling toward California at twelve miles per hour.

"Los Angeles seems very far away," Helene said.

"A lifetime away," said Ina.

She kept Helene out toward the middle of the street. Their windows were open and each car they passed along the curb produced a succulent little *pop!* of turbulence that was not the first nice surprise of their trip west.

"A hair left," she said. Her fingers dipped into the cooler at her feet and came up with a dripping piece of ice. She put it in her mouth.

"Want one?"

"Please," said Helene. She held her tongue out like a tray and Ina set a shard of ice upon it.

"Light turning red. Thirty yards."

Helene's foot was a tad heavy on the brake. Ina rocked forward; ice-water sloshed.

"Fifteen feet to a full stop."

Ina felt very secure, very patient. Hector Strode had changed the oil, the plugs and points, flushed the radiator, rotated and inflated the tires, topped off the brake and transmission fluids, and charged the battery, spending a hot day in Ina's driveway with his shirt off. His skin was dark and lizardy after a summer in the garden. Ina brought him lemonade and thin cookies dusted with sugar. He asked her a question or two, usually about the trip, to which she would fashion a lie that fit in with the construction of lies she and Helene had been building. She did not stay long on each visit. Hector must not be delayed, she said to Helene.

Po Strode also came over and Ina knew it did Po's heart good to see her husband working alone. Po had agreed to watch over the house. Ina took her on a brief tour of the rooms, showing her the few plants that needed watering ("Dusting, rather," Ina joked, feeling nearly barren next to Po's fecund touch). Po promised to come over at dusk and burn some lights. She promised, also, that she and Hector would come back before bedtime to turn out the lights, leaving only the porch light on. Ina wondered if Po and Hector would make love in Ina's house; it was something she and Vincent did when they could, not mussing a bed, but finding a place and doing it quickly, sometimes standing up, sometimes with her sitting on a sink, a way of putting a stamp on their visit.

The air was cool as they traveled and Ina discovered that if she put her elbow out the window the air blew up her short-sleeved blouse and swirled around her breast in an exciting fashion.

"How far have we gone?"

"Six miles," Ina said, choosing a figure at random.

"We must have gone farther than that," Helene complained.

"We're barely making ten miles an hour," said Ina. "Remember: slow and steady in the dead of night. That's how we'll get to California in one piece. Two pieces."

Ina had delayed their departure one hour. She wanted to give the route they would be traveling that bit of extra time to calm down, for people to find their way off the road. It was a simple matter to wait. Helene was jumpy, tapping the car key on the kitchen table, threatening to call the whole thing off. She was angry because she had lied to Amanda in order that they could depart in secret. Amanda had been told that Ina and Helene and Katherine and her two children would be leaving at the crack of dawn Tuesday. Amanda had promised to come over Monday afternoon to help load the car and say good-bye.

"And we'll slip away a day early," Ina explained. "She'll come over, see we're gone, see Katherine, and that will be that. You can call her and tell her we're okay. But not where we are."

"I've never lied to her," said Helene.

"We're just effecting our escape. It's not really a lie. More like a stratagem."

They had made their way to North Avenue without seeing anyone, then turned west. Two women in the shadows of a factory loading dock stepped forward and waved, thinking the slow-moving car was on a different mission. Ina guided Helene over railroad tracks that abused the Omega's shocks, then up an incline and over a bridge that pinched the road half a lane tighter. A station wagon full of silent women traveled parallel to them for a mile. A man drove. The women had slack, tired faces, their hair done up in babushkas, three women in the rear riding backward so that when the driver finally pulled ahead of the Omega and turned onto the Kennedy, Ina got three blank looks absolutely without curiosity as they hurtled up and away. Ina did not mention them to Helene. She said a prayer to Vincent, thanking him briefly and insufficiently for keeping her away from such an existence.

A laundromat flared to life on their right, and she thought of Ray. Children, up past their bedtime, stared at her through the smudged windows. Ina wiggled her fingers at them while she waited for the light to change. They did not know how to take her and turned to their mother for help, but then Ina had to move on before they got an answer.

She enjoyed coming to red lights. They provided a little break in her duties. They freed her of the responsibility to move ahead. Better yet was a long line of rail cars bearing white stones that rumbled across their path. Ina was able to have Helene put the car in Park for nearly ten minutes. A man sitting on the back steps of the caboose waved to them and spat a colorless wad of something that blew away in the train's following wind. The gates rose and they went on. No other cars had been held up by the train and Ina felt singled out for something special, an extravaganza of light, noise, and motion staged for their benefit.

They passed through a wooded pocket where the air was cool.

Ina reported to her sister that she saw white lights in the trees; she admitted to the desire to travel faster.

"Don't tempt me," Helene said.

"We're coming out of a bend," Ina said.

Streetlights resumed ahead, and she took a breath. So slowly were they moving that Ina feared something unfortunate outrunning them from the woods.

"Soft left," she said.

And what danger were they voluntarily courting? Hector Strode had offered Ina a revolver. He had made this gesture on the sly, in one of the moments when he was working on the car and Ina came out to visit, but before Po witnessed or sensed their conversation and came over to monitor it. He pulled a cloth off a small box to reveal a gun nestled in a bed of clean blue rags.

"Pick it up," whispered Hector, looking about. "It isn't loaded."

Ina refused. She would only nudge the box with her toe, an attempt to push it back toward Hector Strode.

"I think you should take it with you," he counseled.

"Why?"

"Because of what you are planning," Hector said. "You're going to cross a country *crawling* with crooks, killers, rapists, child-molesters, con artists, pickpockets, second-story men, sex-torturers, arsonists, cat burglars, car thieves, psychopaths, peder-asts, armed robbers."

"White-collar crime is America's foremost criminal problem," Ina said with a deflecting smile. Hector Strode regarded her, aghast.

"Pray you only run into white-collar criminals," he said. "Pray you only cross paths with embezzlers and check-kiters."

"You keep the gun," said Ina. "You need it to protect Po."

Hector leaned under the car's hood to tighten something in-comprehensible to Ina.

"Thank you for worrying," she said, with a shy glance to the rear to see if Po Strode in her omniscient jealousy had sensed something touching in the air and floated over.

"That creature," Hector said, straightening up. "The one who got stuck in your wall? Shoot him in the head and no jury in the world would convict you. It was dark, you saw something coming *through* your wall. You fired once, twice, thrice."

"I'd have missed once, twice, thrice," Ina said. Never had she seen Hector in such a state. He had a grease mark the shape of a scar above his brow.

She said, "Vincent always liked to speculate on the lives of the people he passed each day. The people he talked to. Sold a house to. People on the street. How many had had sex the night before? Or at lunch? How many cheated on their taxes? How many had falsified their credentials to get a job? How many had killed someone?"

"That's beside the point," Hector said, peeved at Vincent being brought into the conversation. He knelt and put the gun in its box at the bottom of his toolcase.

"It's here," he said. "If you change your mind."

They were on the road now, unarmed. They had slipped away without a word to the Strodes, knowing Hector and Po would want to stand in the driveway and wave until the travelers were out of sight. They had disappeared in the dead of night. The idea was to travel light, yet the back seat was loaded and no room remained in the trunk. Ina had packed every piece of clothing she could possibly imagine wearing, in addition to everything salvaged from Helene's house. They were carrying five cases of Old Style, 120 cans hidden here and there, and transferred three or four cans at a time to the icy waters of the cooler.

Ina also was carrying more than twelve thousand dollars, all of it in twenties. The amount excited her; they would never need it all, but it was available if the mood or necessity struck. To lose it to the wind, to a fire, to a thief, would be a setback, but not a setback fatal to the trip. The bank clerk, when Ina withdrew the money, had the temerity to ask if she was *certain* she wanted to withdraw that amount of money. Quite certain, Ina replied, and remained stoic and patient as the clerk (a girl who looked no older than Meg, but without Meg's air of routine competence) encouraged her to take the money in traveler's checks. With nearly the passion of Hector Strode, the girl recited a litany of dangers awaiting Ina's emergence from the bank. Only then, her duty discharged, did she enter the vault and return wheeling a cart of cash—conspicuous, crisp, greenish-gray—watched over by an elderly guard in a uniform with one shirt button missing and his hand on his revolver. Ina instructed the clerk to divide the twenties into stacks of ten, and around each of these bundles Ina slipped a thin red rubber band and deposited the money in her bag. She later rolled each two hundred dollars into a cylinder to facilitate its hiding in the car. Another clerk, an older woman with a supervisor's judgmental twist to her lips, did the paperwork and slid it across the counter for Ina to sign. She'd been in the bank for nearly a half hour and only now was she getting close to her money; it had gone into the bank a little at a time over the years with a vacuumlike sucking speed that never ceased to astound her. In retraction, she felt herself fighting against that greedy suction.

As she made her preparations to leave with her sixty small bundles of cash, the clerks watched with obvious disapproval. Ina was tempted to roll her eyes maniacally, to cackle, to hobble out with her money clutched in her hands like so much mattress ticking. But she wouldn't give them that satisfaction. It was her money; she had left quite a bit behind. She walked home, aware of the weight she had taken on, mindful of tricks of fate that befell women of her age under such circumstances (run down by a car, her fortune ripped from her hands and sent in a whirlwind of cash into the sky; or selected by a purse-snatcher for no other reason except that she was old), understanding all the while that she would be portrayed on the news reports as afflicted with senile dementia for withdrawing and carrying into the world such an irresistible amount of money.

Ina could not say how much money Helene carried. Helene wouldn't tell, revealing only that every cent was in traveler's checks, and every one of those checks were snug in her purse stashed beneath the front seat on the driver's side. Ina knew only that they were a pair of passably wealthy widows out on the road together, unarmed. And that fact made Ina nervous.

For as they distanced themselves from Chicago Ina felt the city pulling at her like a planet. She already missed her house, where everything was in place, where she could always find something to read, or drink, or her welcoming bed. She knew what to expect from her unraveling neighborhood. A certain level of precaution there would see her through the remaining days of her life, of that she was certain. At home, she knew who lived on all sides of her.

But she had chosen the unknown and now it unwound all around her a little slower than she would have liked. They were traversing another dark stretch, the air a little cooler than the previous span of woods, when a 7-Eleven blazed forth on their right, so sparkling and obnoxious in the night that Ina nearly cried out. The lot was full of cars; one police car, the cop glimpsed through the front window chatting with the cashier. Ina spoke a command to correct Helene from drifting off course, and over it all she heard through the 7-Eleven's briefly open front door the machined exultation of a pinball game.

Then back into comparative darkness they slipped.

"Woo," breathed Ina.

"What was that?"

"A store. Nothing."

"*Nothing?*" Helene said, irked. "All this new territory we're discovering and what's in it for me? I'm just driving."

"It's dark, dear," Ina said. "I've discovered neon never before witnessed by civilization. And road signs. Shade to the right. Other than that, nothing."

"It occurs to me," Helene said. "Are you watching our rear?"

Ina said, "Yes."

"It might not occur to the nondriver. Most danger comes from the rear," Helene said.

"It occurred to me," said Ina. "There's nothing behind us. Dangerous or otherwise." She had positioned the rearview mirror so that she could see headlights approaching. In truth, almost nothing behind them would be of interest to her, being ground already safely traversed.

An hour slipped by. Her plan had been to reach St. Charles that first morning, then spend the day along the Fox River. She thought the proximity, the sound and aroma of the river would soothe Helene and make Ina feel somewhat at home. But the late start and the slow pace had ruined her schedule already. They were a good twenty miles from St. Charles, with less than an hour left to travel. She wanted to be off the road by 4:00 A.M., and here she was considering diverging from that strategy on the first morning out.

Ina asked, "Would you feel comfortable going a tad faster?"

"No."

"Two or three miles per hour could make a great deal of difference."

"No," Helene said adamantly, and even slowed the car a bit.

"Come right, dear. Not too far. I only suggested that because I wanted to reach St. Charles our first night on the road," Ina said. "At this rate, we won't make it before the end of our driving time."

"You planned badly," Helene said. "I can't help that."

"Just drive twenty miles per hour. It's a good, safe speed—yet it covers an impressive amount of ground."

"I feel like I'm going sixty now."

"You're going twelve," Ina told her. "There's a light ahead. Start to slow." She talked her down to a crawl, then nearly to a stop, before the light went green and she had Helene accelerate. Ina looked to her left in the intersection and saw less than fifty yards away an ambulance approaching with its crown of sparkling lights. They were well across, moving fast enough to avoid a collision. But the prospect shook Ina's confidence. She had willingly—excitedly—sent them hurtling into the darkness. Now everything was a mystery beyond the rim of light they threw.

"Faster. Faster," Ina cried. "The road is clear."

Helene did go faster. A mile per hour or two, then five, and soon they were racing along at twenty-two miles per hour. The wind in their faces was nearly icy.

"Where are we?" asked Helene.

Ina didn't respond, but guided her sister around a gentle curve in the road, past a post office, past a baseball diamond dark but for a square greenish light on the backstop, past a police car waiting to ambush speeders (and did their vehicle register so low on the radar that they were suspect for their lack of speed?), through another empty intersection, past another 7-Eleven.

Up ahead, an animal ran into their headlights. Ina saw that the creature's fate was entirely its own. The animal could move or perish, there was nothing Ina would say to risk Helene's swerving the car at her scream or locking the brakes in a panic stop. The animal possessed a lumbering, humped gait, orange eyes in the light, and a silvery coat that went dark with a thud beneath their tires.

"What was that?" Helene asked instantly.

"Opossum."

"Not a child?"

"Opossum," Ina repeated. "Not his lucky morning."

She looked carefully behind them, afraid of seeing the first glow in the east. She made course corrections, she coaxed and badgered Helene to keep the car on the road and heading west.

"I have to use the toilet," Helene said, a mile farther on.

"I do, too. We can't stop."

"I can't wait," Helene said with a regal tilt of her features.

"My bladder is weaker than yours. It's been stretched thin by a lifetime of beer. But we don't stop until St. Charles."

At a speed of twenty-six miles per hour, the right front wheel dropped off the pavement in an explosion of gravel that caused both widows to yelp. Helene removed her foot from the gas. The right rear wheel fell. The car slowed.

"Anything dead ahead?" asked Helene.

"Not yet," Ina reported. They flew within inches of a black mailbox rooted in a cement-filled bucket, Ina congratulating herself on her hair-fine calculations.

Helene brought the car to a stop. They were four miles on the wrong side of Saint Charles.

"Press on," Ina said, "We're half on the road and half off."

Helene ran her hands loosely over the steering wheel. To the right of the car was a dark lot, fringed with white scraps of cup and bag, the land separating a transmission repair shop from a twenty-four-hour diner called Little Athens. The Little Athens parking lot was empty. A stocky man with his hands in his apron pockets watched from the restaurant's front window.

"Are you hungry?" Ina asked idly.

"No. My stomach is all achurn."

Without motion, the air was sticky. Ina licked her top lip clean of salt. She opened the cooler and took out a can of Old Style. The fizz of opening got Helene's attention.

"*What* do you think you're doing?"

"We're sitting here wasting time. I'm having a beer," Ina said.

She had lost sight of the man in Little Athens. Deeper in the restaurant was a customer drinking coffee at a counter, and beyond him was the fake orange glow of warming lamps. The man in the apron came outside and fed coins into a newspaper box, then pretended to scan the paper.

"Let's get going," Ina suggested.

"If I'm driving and you're drunk—does that make me a drunken driver?" Helene asked with acid curiosity.

"I'm not drunk."

The man folded the paper under his arm and stepped toward them with grave concern to call, "Do you require assistance?"

Helene was startled. She looked wildly in the direction of the voice. Ina leaned just slightly out the window.

"No, thank you. We'll be on our way shortly."

The appearance of Ina's ancient face surprised the man into a proprietary attitude, for he came over to them so quickly that Helene could hear his footsteps over the sound of the engine.

"Do you know the hour?" he asked. "It's dangerous on the roads this time of night."

Under the apron her wore a tight pink shirt that looked like silk covered with little green Eiffel Towers. He crouched to look past Ina.

"You shouldn't wear sunglasses at night," he warned Helene.

"We're looking for St. Charles," Ina told the man.

"It's straight ahead." He pointed down the road. "You can't miss it."

"Thank you."

"How about some coffee? A sweet roll? An egg?"

"No, thank you. We must go to St. Charles without further delay."

Helene jerked the car into Drive then and accelerated with enough mustard to spin the back tires.

"Careful," Ina warned.

They bounced back up onto the highway; the man from Little Athens fell behind, disappeared.

"Who was that?" Helene asked.

"We stopped by a restaurant. He worked there. Or owned it. If we weren't running short of time I'd have liked to stop. I'm hungry," Ina said.

"I'm swimming."

"Patience."

It was twenty-five minutes to four. They passed a small airport, the runway marked like a driveway with blue lights. Another mile, and the smell of the river came through the window.

"We're entering Kane County," Ina said, reading a sign.

"Hurrah."

"We are in St. Charles."

"Hooray."

"I think it's important that we keep moving at all costs," Ina said.

"Now?"

"Not tonight. But from now on. Stopping at lights, stop signs, that's all part of the journey," Ina said. "But unplanned stops like that back there—that's where we'll encounter trouble. We were lucky tonight. Because who else is out and about at this time of night?"

"No-goodniks," teased Helene.

"I'm serious. Who chooses to be up at this hour except those who don't like to be seen in daylight?"

She was looking for a place to stop for the night. They descended a hill and crossed the river, and a block beyond the river she ordered Helene into the small parking lot of the Treehouse Motel.

They took a room on the ground floor, which made both widows nervous. Helene held Ina's arm as the night clerk, a sleepy old man whose pace in registering the women and showing them to the room made Ina feel hyperactive by comparison, opened the door with the key, turned on the lights, pointed out the bathroom with an impatient jab of his finger, and headed back to bed.

It was twenty minutes past four o'clock.

"We made it," Ina said.

"We made it to St. Charles, Illinois," Helene said. "A ways from California."

"But we're out of the city. We won't go near another city until we get to L.A.," Ina said. "We can't be stopped."

"Guide me to the facilities."

On the wall was an oil painting of a stag being disemboweled by hounds. The bedspreads didn't match, but the linen felt clean to the touch as Ina sat waiting for Helene to emerge from the bathroom. Safely off the road, Ina was numb with exhaustion. She felt wonderful, though, accomplished and capable. She drank from her can of beer. She heard the ice machine through the front wall as it turned out its bounty. She took a blue plastic bucket and filled it with ice, then scooped ice into their cooler after emptying the night's melt on the grass.

Helene was back, sitting on one of the beds, inspecting the bedspread for pills.

"The water tastes funny," she said.

"Here in the west it's all runoff from the Rockies," Ina said. "How do you feel?"

"A little lightheaded," Helene said. "I think milk and graham crackers now, then a nap, would be good before I double-void and have my shot."

The bathroom was small and filled with mirrors: a full-length mirror on the back of the door, a triptych mirror over the sink, a shaving mirror on an accordion mount, and seventeen different mirrors of various size, shape, and glass-tint hanging on the walls, as though the bathroom had once belonged to a person of immense vanity who liked to be pleasantly surprised. Ina didn't care for the effect: She kept discovering herself at startling angles, none of them flattering. The shower curtain was a New York Times crossword puzzle, some of the squares filled in with ballpoint pen or laundry marker.

She shed her clothes, used the toilet, washed her face and removed her teeth, and found Helene asleep when she came out. All the lights were on, the curtains open. Helene had fallen asleep in her traveling clothes, her legs off the bed, the upper half of her body neatly folded atop the bedspread.

"Helene?" Ina hummed, nudging her sister. She did not awaken, but did toss her arm over her eyes, as if to complain about the brightness of the room.

Ina drew the curtains, noting the tone of the light as morning progressed. She heard a radio come on somewhere, a blast of news at 5:00 A.M. She removed her sister's shoes and set them by the side of the bed. She knew Helene would scold herself for sleeping in her clothes, but Ina did not have the strength or enthusiasm to get her out of them. Instead she positioned Helene's legs on the bed and folded the blanket over her. She left a light on in the bathroom. She was nearly asleep herself when she remembered to get up out of bed and chain the door. She heard scrapings outside, sounds she couldn't explain. But the door was locked, their room was paid for, and that little bit of security freed her to go back to bed, and to sleep.

THEY stayed in St. Charles an extra day because they were tired from the novelty and requirements of travel. On Tuesday afternoon, Helene sunned herself on the lawn outside their room. Ina used the time to steal away to telephone Amanda.

A man answered.

"May I speak to Amanda?"

"Just a second." His voice was without emotion or curiosity; he sounded neither dangerous nor friendly.

"Ina?" called Helene. Ina heard the lawn chair squeak.

"I'm right here," Ina said. "Stay put."

Amanda said, "Hello?"

"It's me."

"Who?"

"Ina."

"Where are you?" Amanda asked. "What in the world is going on?"

"Are you all right?"

"Should I be worried?"

"Can you talk?"

Amanda laughed, very theatrical, utterly believable. "No," she sang.

"Do you need the police?"

"*No.* Where are you?"

"Traveling west," Ina said, glancing around the room. It was a room abundant with daylight, with a generous window framed in white curtains. The bathroom had porcelain taps, hot and cold in blue script.

"I'm sorry I missed your departure," Amanda said. "I got occupied. Are Katherine and the kids with you?"

"Of course. They're outside playing," Ina said. Through the door, down a hill between a warehouse and a restaurant, she could see a narrow slice of the river. The water was greenish-brown and looked warm to the touch. The river's smell—a mix of industrial pollutants and nature's appealing decay—filled the room and the town.

"We got as far as Omaha," Ina said carefully, concocting. "Katherine drove like a bat out of hell. Your mother and I played with the kids, or we slept. We'll be there in no time."

"Omaha," Amanda repeated, though not directly into the phone.

"You're certain you're all right?"

"Not definitely," Amanda said, lightly. "I want you to keep in touch, *Mom.*"

"We will."

"I've got to go now."

A stranger, a small man in olive shirt and pants, squatted inches from Helene and gouged dandelions from the lawn with a weeding tool. Ina wondered if Helene was aware of him; she appeared to be asleep. She had spread the neck of her dress to get as much sun as possible on her whitish skin.

"I heard voices," she said when Ina drew near.

"I called Amanda."

"So she knows?"

"Not yet," Ina said. "We have been granted an extra day of travel. She thinks we're with Katherine."

Helene said, "She's been easy to fool all her life."

"She hasn't been to your house," said Ina. "She missed the phony bon voyage party we had scheduled."

"Because of that man?"

"You'll have to ask her why," Ina said. "And if you talk to her, we're in Omaha."

"That will throw her off our trail," Helene said derisively. "If she's interested."

The gardener displayed a very fastidious little mustache, a row of whiskers each precisely hyphen-length. Ina studied him for several minutes. Each weed he extracted with its furred white root, he placed carefully in an old Folger's can. He worked with a suspicious patience, seeming to backtrack over ground already cleared. She wondered if he was eavesdropping. They had been discussing extra days of travel, fake parties, false destinations, the desire to confuse their pursuers.

"Your grass is in need of watering," Ina said to him.

He regarded her from his crouch, squinting up one-eyed, for the sun was on Ina's shoulder.

"Quite the contrary," he answered. "It's had too much water. Rain three days, then Boyd, my assistant, watered it yesterday because it was the day he usually watered."

Helene seemed frightened by the sudden exchange, drawing shut her dress with her fist, pulling her legs under the chair.

A MILE out of St. Charles at midnight, doing eighteen through a darkness that seemed more inclusive west of the river, Helene admitted to not knowing anyone had been there.

"What if I had been alone?"

"You were—for a time," Ina said.

"He could've gone through my handbag, if I'd had one nearby. Or fondled me."

"He didn't know you were blind," Ina said. "You were a guest taking the sun while he worked at your feet. You maintained the proper class distinction by refusing to acknowledge the help."

"What did he look like?"

"Fifties. Slight. Trim mustache. Dirty hands."

"He *smelled* interesting," Helene remarked with a shy laugh.

"Earthy? Fertile?" teased Ina.

"I can't place it now," Helene said, her tone regretful. "And if I didn't know he was there, why do I remember he smelled interesting?"

"Come back right. You smelled him *after* you knew he was there."

"No. My senses shut down then because I was upset I hadn't been *aware* of him."

They were traveling primarily west, but tending also slightly to the north, more north than Ina wished. She had scolded herself in the first minutes after leaving the motel for not looking farther ahead and putting them on a route that was more in the direction of their destination. Soon she would turn them south for the long leg through the heart of the state. They would take the southwest passage to her children, avoiding the snow-topped gargantuan mountain ranges, spending their nights on desert highways, then glide on into L.A.

It didn't seem so far away.

"I should've *known* he was there," Helene said.

"If people think you can see—you *can* see. You're safe," Ina said. "The impression is everything."

"Don't move. Keep my sunglasses on and my mouth shut. Betray no helplessness. Those are the keys," Helene said, with the nod of the satisfied cataloger.

"We need to make a left turn here soon," Ina said. "We're traveling northwesterly, more toward Oregon than California."

"I've never been to Oregon," Helene said agreeably.

"My children are in California."

Her map showed minor blue roads heading south, but they bore no identifying numbers. Ina hated the idea of turning down a road she couldn't name.

"Isn't there one road that goes directly to California?" asked Helene.

"Untraveled at night, dotted at convenient intervals with clean, charming motor inns?" Ina teased.

"Yes," laughed Helene. "That road."

"No."

She decided on Route 111 west of Sycamore, for no other reason than that they came to a stop sign at the highway, there was no intersecting traffic, and the turn was easy to talk Helene through. For the previous three or four miles they'd been traveling parallel to a railroad track, and upon turning south they dipped under a trestle that smelled fleetingly of creosote and rain water.

"Smell that air," said Helene.

"The bayou. Gumbo."

"No. Mexico."

"Farther. Guatemala," Ina said. "Bolivia."

"Do you remember Rudy's plan to drive to El Salvador?" Helene asked, even glancing at her sister.

"Refresh my memory."

"He met a man—I don't recall the circumstances—but the man was a native of El Salvador and in the course of their fast friendship he expressed a desire to take Rudy and me to visit his homeland. The place, it wasn't the mess it is today. And what is, señorita?"

"Nothing," said Ina. "And we're barely doing ten. Can't you talk and drive?"

"Talk and drive, yes. Talk and speed, no," Helene said.

"Go on with your story—though you're making me sleepy."

"What pressure," cried Helene. "Here, where boredom could be fatal. The exotic nature of the trip appealed to us. We'd drive our car down through Texas, across the Rio Grande, through Mexico, and spend two or three weeks at his home in paradise. He would pay for the gas, the family he'd left in El Salvador would feed us, put us up. We got our passports. Our bags were packed."

"Come right, dear. You're straying."

"Roger," replied Helene. "A day or so before we were to leave I come home and there's Enrique or whatever his name was in our garage. The hood of our car is up. He smiles at me. He's wiping his hands on a rag. Rudy's not around. He thanks me, shuts the hood, and goes away. That night I mention this to Rudy and he tells me not to worry. Maybe Enrique was inspecting the condition of the car. He doesn't want to get halfway to El Salvador and have the car break down. I can live with that explanation, but just barely."

"He was a smuggler," Ina said.

"No. Stop trying to get ahead of my story," Helene complained. "Dawns the morning of the trip and there is Enrique at the front door with a wife and three children. The woman is pregnant. Enrique introduces everyone to everyone."

"They all meant to go," said Ina.

"Just tell me the punchline," Helene shouted. "You know the story better than I do. Tell me how it ends."

"He was going to smuggle a gun through Mexico," Ina said peevishly. "He wouldn't dare travel in Mexico without a gun."

"You cruel ass, you."

Something with green eyes, low to the ground, wandered into the headlights and the car appeared to split in two its frozen emerald stare. But there was no sound, no thump. Ina rolled her shoulders, trying to relax.

"Stop sign, ninety feet. Seventy. Slow down," Ina said. "Slow down!"

But Helene had other ideas, even adding weight to the gas pedal, and they blew through the empty intersection without pause, without tripping any alarms.

"Very nice," Ina said acidly. "I ruin your silly story—so you try to kill us."

Helene drove on without another word. For nearly an hour they traveled and Helene was fastidious in her adherence to Ina's commands.

"Hector Strode offered me a gun to bring along on this trip," Ina said, finally bored with the silence.

"Did you take it?"

"Absolutely not. We have a blind driver. Why would we need a gun?"

"Why, indeed?"

"So you didn't go to El Salvador. Where did you go?"

"You remember."

"I do?"

"We went and got you and the four of us drove to the dunes," Helene said. "You got drunk, if I recall."

Ina truly did not remember, though she was of the belief that she never had been so drunk that it was taken note of by those around her.

She said, "My memory is faint, dear."

"We lolled in the sand," Helene said. "Four pink bodies turning red. You drank beer—Rudy and Vincent took turns going to the stand to get it for you."

Ina squinted, eager to remember. A darkening horizon had been visible in sections like chunky beads between the undulant hills of sand. She recalled a stinging wind kicking up; the iron smell of rain, a squall line taut out over the lake, the chiding screech of gulls blowing overhead, the beach emptying. Moms and dads sprinting ahead of the storm, with children, beach umbrellas, towels, the last of the food and drink, all gathered messily in their arms. A dash for the cars parked beyond the last tall dune, where the storm was less of a certainty and the day's humid stickiness still held.

The four of them, however, stayed put. Ina remembered Vincent's hair blown across his face; Rudy standing with his shirt unbuttoned and his chest thrust out at the glowering storm line. Ina drank, it had been reliably reported. And Helene?

"I remember it rained," Ina said.

Headlights gleamed suddenly ahead; wide, rectangular lights, a smaller pair of amber fog lamps suspended beneath.

"Approaching vehicle," Ina said. "Come right a bit."

They heard laughing as the car passed.

"It rained. It stormed. We had no shelter but the car," Helene said. "The storm had given everyone sufficient warning to get away. Only the four of us hadn't paid attention."

"We were young and daring," said Ina.

"At our age—who knew if any storm wasn't our last?"

The rain had started with a cold drop that struck Ina squarely in the throat when she looked up to inspect the sky. The water wormed its way between her breasts. Rudy tried to button his shirt but the wind kept ripping the cloth from his hands. Beer cups—they were blue with red stars, waxy at her lips—blew straight up in the air, trailing diminishing threads of golden liquid. Ina couldn't believe they all belonged to her.

Vincent cried out, "It's not too early to make a run for it," but they all knew there was no chance of getting to the car dry.

"Yes it is," judged Helene.

A harsher wind tore her words away. The temperature plunged twenty degrees in that instant, Vincent sneezed, and a beat later the rain reached them and like that they were drenched and shivering. Vincent threw his wet suit coat and thin arms around Ina and hustled her away. They paused in the valleys between the dunes, sheltered from the wind, pounded by the rain, to catch their breath before attacking the next slope. They lost their footing on the way down the last hill and took on a lacquer of wet sand where they fell. When they reached the car the doors were locked and ten minutes elapsed before Rudy and Helene appeared at the crown of the last dune. Like wet shreds blown off the cap of a wave, they hopped playfully arm in arm down to the edge of the lot and across the blacktop to the car. Ina and Vincent watched them wordlessly, lips blued, colds already sprouting in their chests.

"We got soaked," Ina said. "And sick."

"Us, too."

"Why did you take so long?"

"When?"

"Then. Why did you take so long to get to the car?"

"I wanted to hurry. But Rudy said, 'Take your time. We're already soaked. I have the keys. Let them stand in the rain.' "

"What a mean man," Ina said.

"He liked getting people's goats," Helene said. "He told me once when we were in bed how that was what he did better than any other person on earth. Got goats."

"Hardly a marketable talent," Ina said.

So they entered a second angry silence that lasted nearly an hour. The only sounds were Ina's soft commands, which Helene obeyed without question or comment.

Ina examined the silence, the source of it. She knew she had brought it on with her remark, but she had been irritated by the image of Rudy telling Helene to hang back in the rain, while Vincent's teeth chattered, his clothes sticking to him. A long cold at his age might have put a strain on his heart that robbed him— robbed her—of a few extra days at the end of his life.

A mile north of the town of Watermark, with an hour of travel remaining, Helene announced that she was losing feeling in her accelerator foot and had to stop and walk around. Ina directed her off to the side of the road. Helene brought them to a stop and shut off the engine.

The air smelled of turned earth, crushed mint, manure. In time the car's engine stopped ticking and they were certifiably alone. The sensation made Ina uneasy. She missed the drumming of the city, the way it breathed over her shoulder, reminding her any time she paid attention that it was there.

"We have an hour to travel," Ina said. "And no place to stay when that hour is up."

"I want a bed and shower," Helene declared. "Within minutes, if not sooner."

"Where would you suggest I find them?"

"I'm driving. You're in charge of logistics, navigation, and matériel. Do your job. How much closer to California are we than when we started?"

Ina, curious herself, checked the figures.

"One hundred nine miles," she said.

"It will take us two weeks just to get out of Illinois," complained Helene.

Ina sat with her arm out the window, feeling pleased. One hundred nine miles. The distance impressed her. One hundred nine miles traversed with a blind woman at the wheel, no children struck, no damage to the car, no one the wiser. She reached behind the seat, dipped into the glacial ice melt in the cooler, and extracted an Old Style.

The countryside was opening up to her, whether from her eyes' adjustment to the pitch, or the slow roll of the earth toward sunrise. Twenty yards down the highway she saw a faint amber rectangle on a post. To her right was a fence, and beyond the fence, watching them with stilled heads, were two animals of impressive dimension, either horses of cows.

"Let's get out and get your blood circulating," Ina said. She opened the door and the interior light revealed Helene in her sunglasses, her hair blown by travel into a state as close to dishevelment as she ever allowed.

In the ice chest, Ina found three apples floating in the slush. She told Helene to activate her emergency flashers and these provided a steady beat of illumination.

Helene sat with her feet on the ground, her left hand out and elevated, awaiting Ina's guiding touch.

"Where are we going?"

"Hush. Here, hold this." Ina placed a cold apple in Helene's palm.

"I can't eat this," Helene said.

"Did I say it was for you?"

They went down an incline into a damp, grassy ditch, Helene complaining all the way with little peeps of surprise and outrage. Invisible bugs rose up to bounce off their faces. The animals (horses, Ina could now see, the flashers going off like sparks in their eyes) had stepped back from the fence as a matter of routine caution; but not too far back, for they smelled the apples.

"Horses," Helene said suddenly.

"Two of them."

"Hence the apples." She held out the fruit.

"We need to get closer."

The horses, with snorts of anticipation, returned swishing through the grass. First one, then another, huge head lowered over the fence. Ina put Helene's empty hand on one horse's forehead, on a white mark the shape of a bottle. Helene squealed when his rubbery lips plucked the apple from her.

Ina fed an apple to the other horse. She set it on her palm, then put her hand forth in offering. The horse bit it with teeth like rocks cast golden in the emergency light. He chewed reflectively, wet bits dripping in the grass. The other horse, already finished, watched enviously.

"Any more?"

"I have one left."

"Two horses, three apples? Your planning is off all around to-night, dear."

She gouged into the apple with her fingers, twisting, until a ragged, juicy crack opened and she tore the apple into two rough shares. She gave one to Helene, who had it in her hand no more than an instant before the horse had snatched it, nipping skin, drawing blood, causing Helene to yelp. Ina threw her half into the grass and the other horse, after a baleful, put-out look at Ina, swiveled his head down after it.

"Let's see," Ina said.

The mark was precise, a dark place the shape of a staple in the whiteness of her hand. Ina squeezed it tenderly for blood, raising a drop or two that looked black. She wiped these away.

"There must be a doctor in Watermark," Ina mused, infuriated with herself for snagging their journey.

"You *had* to stop," Helene accused.

"You said your foot was falling asleep. It was a chance to stretch our legs."

"And get bitten by a horse. A rabid horse, in all probability," Helene said.

"No such thing," Ina said, though she wasn't sure. The two animals looked harmless; without the lure of food they had lost interest in the widows and drifted away from the fence.

Ina sat Helene in the passenger seat. The bleeding wasn't serious. The wound had a shriveled, fungal ugliness in such murky light. Ina took ten minutes finding the first aid kit in the trunk, and when she opened it a small rubber-banded packet of cash fell into the shadows under the car.

"Damn it," said Ina.

"What?"

"Nothing. I'll be right there."

She set the kit on the roof of the car. Helene had pushed her sunglasses back up into her hair, giving her an incongruous *hip* look that Ina had to fight against laughing at out of frustration and pure sisterly meanness.

"Why did you curse back there?"

"Because I dropped some money, honey."

"How much?"

"I don't know. It was in a rubber band."

"A bundle, then?"

"Yes, a bundle." She knew it was two hundred dollars, ten twenties, easy to remember, easy (in theory) to keep track of.

"Go find it before you fix me up," Helene ordered. "I can't stand the thought of a bundle of money being lost."

Ina took the flashlight to the rear of the car. She played the beam across the field, seeking the horses. She caught one and he flicked his tail as if the light were a fly. The other looked squarely at her. Golden eyes, a ruminative chewing of grass, like an old man nibbling his beard. She found the money and returned it to its hiding place in the first aid kit.

She pressed a ball of cotton saturated with alcohol to Helene's bit. She hissed in pain, but did not draw away.

"Lord," she cried when Ina was finished. Helene shook the hand out with a youthful snap to her wrist. "It stings!"

"Come on, baby. Give it here."

Ina trained the flashlight beam on the wound. Cleaned, it did not look as serious. No need for stitches, certainly. But they would have to find a doctor in Watermark. Ina squirted an oily yellow secretion of antiseptic ointment onto a small square of gauze. She held it in place over the wound with two strips of tape, then two more in the opposite direction.

"Can you drive?" asked Ina.

Helene made a loose fist around the dressing. "I think so," she said. "I'm exhausted, though."

"Me, too. This has been all my fault."

Helene grinned. "I know," she said.

Watermark, Illinois, announced its civic pride with a large billboard on 111 that declared itself the home of the 1978 Girls State Cross Country champions. Seven girls in weathered blue shorts and gold jerseys ran side by side out of the billboard. Beneath each runner was a name, and only first names (TONI, JOAN, JENNIFER, JANE, CAROL, MARYANN, BRIDGET), the girls and the fame of champions making last names unnecessary in that town.

Parked beneath the billboard was a police car, the shadowed figure behind the wheel apparently asleep. The speed limit dropped from forty-five to thirty at the billboard, then down to twenty-five farther in town. Helene was doing sixteen. The houses they passed were absolutely still at 3:45 A.M. Ina had assumed there would be early risers, stalwart, hardworking men up before the sun to fix breakfast and read the paper, then making the drive up to DeKalb to start work at seven.

But there was not a trace of movement. Not at the fire station (where Ina could see through the dark front window the red-dot lights on the dispatch board), and not at the gas station at the far end of town where a German shepherd slept out front on a blanket thrown over a stack of tires.

"A sleepy little town, Watermark," Ina said. "Pull over to your right. Slower. Good. Park it."

The road ran on ahead, funneling into the early morning, the next outpost eighteen miles away, the town of Brooks. A green state sign announced this, with the hopeful reminder on the second line, ST. LOUIS 246.

"Did you see a doctor?" Helene asked.

"I barely saw Watermark, let alone specific occupations."

"What about side roads? What about a motel? Where do visitors to Watermark stay?"

"With family," Ina yawned. She was beat. Her sister said something derisive about the tourist trade there, and Ina laughed and just kept laughing. Helene looked her way oddly, concerned, then shrugged. She began to laugh, too, pleased at being the author of the remark that touched off such hilarity.

After a minute they reined it in. Helene sighed. Ina opened a beer.

"We can drive on to Brooks," she said. "That's eighteen miles away. Roughly an hour."

"Too far," complained Helene.

"Agreed. We'll make our stand in Watermark. We can catch a nap here until the town wakes up—then get directions to a motel. Or we can explore the greater metropolitan area and hope we stumble on one."

"I'm game," said Helene.

"Let's turn around."

They toured the town, crossing 111 several times in their search. Each street perpendicular to the main drag ultimately ended at a T-intersection, beyond which were fields of corn or soybeans. Now and then, lights came on in houses as they watched, evidence of life in Watermark. The policeman, on each of their three passes, remained so immobile, upright behind the wheel, that Ina became convinced that he was an inflatable doll employed to save the cost of an actual cop to cover that dead shift.

They found Watermark High School at the southeast corner of town. The school was a one-story building with small windows set high in the red brick walls. Ina had Helene stop and turn off the engine in the parking lot alongside the football field. The day was well begun. It frightened Ina to be moving in such inviting light; anyone was likely to be on the roads. It scared her to be without a place to stay, and with her driver wounded.

Ina got out to stretch her legs and walked over to a portable latrine wheeled in for football games. The door opened with the whine of a spring. She took a seat on the cold rim. In the whitish plastic shell she felt she was relieving herself in a noxious fog. Sunshine surprised her upon reemerging. She fetched Helene and talked her through the process, right up to the point her sister said, "I can mange from here, thank you," and Ina let the door bang shut.

They were asleep when the school buses pulled in. So close together they seemed linked like a train, the buses braked, released the sleepy children, and rolled back out. Cars arrived and parked, and kids—happier, it seemed, to have their own transportation— got out and ran, some smoking, many laughing, into the school. Two boys, seeing the car with the sleeping widows, parked so close in front and back that Ina and Helene could not move. Ina, nearly awakening once, dreamed they were traveling at the speed of light in bumper-to-bumper traffic.

"How do we get out?" Helene asked after Ina described their predicament.

"We ask," said Ina. However, she was reluctant to call attention to their situation. It might create a stir, draw a crowd.

"This is a public high school," Ina said. "They know the answer to everything."

They touched up their makeup and smoothed their clothes, ran their tongues around their sour mouths (Ina drank some tepid beer, and spat it out on the windshield of the car behind them), then put on their sunglasses. Ina needed hers; every surface of the scene they traveled in looked enchromed.

Helene took Ina's arm.

"It is imperative that they don't discover you are blind," said Ina. "We're in daylight now. We're out among the enemy."

"Like vampires."

"Something like that."

A boy in a blue MONITOR sash guarded the front doors. After a long examination of the two old women as they approached the school he allowed them to enter without a challenge, without even jumping up to get the door, deciding they had grown beyond the influence of hall passes.

Ina left her sunglasses on so as not to draw attention to Helene's. Helene complained in a whisper about the speed with which they were walking.

At the principal's office they were asked to wait. They took chairs in a corner, comfortable chairs of worn green leather and tubular aluminum arms nicked surreptitiously with crude little hearts and genitals and dripping daggers. At five minutes before the hour of nine a bell went off that caused the widows to jump, then laugh self-consciously. A thick river of children flowed past the office's floor-to-ceiling windows, many peering in curiously at the two old ladies.

"There's another in about four minutes," said a woman behind the office's counter.

"Another what?" Helene asked, looking toward the voice.

"Another bell. To start the second period."

"So many children," Ina said, though the river was diminished, and those passing now nearly ran, without a glance to either side.

"Not as many as we'd like," the women lamented. "Enrollment in the last three freshmen classes has gone down twenty-two percent. There's talk of consolidation with Brooks, Teetrum, and Coalville to make one Burgundy County school. I'd hate to see it, personally. Who knows who'd have jobs?"

"Oh, dear," said Helene. Ina smiled faintly at her sister's falsified concern.

"Is there someone we can speak to—it doesn't have to be the principal," Ina said.

"Miss Grasshorn, our assistant principal, will be here soon. She patrols first period—and is sometimes late getting back. If you'd care to wait."

"We've waited long enough," said Helene. Ina turned to regard her, wondering what had become of their strategy.

Ina said, "My sister means we've had a long night of traveling and we'd like to find a place to stay, and a doctor. My sister has—"

"No doctor in Watermark," the woman said. "You'll have to go to Brooks. Why come to Watermark High looking for a doctor?"

"We got to town late last night—early this morning—and we hoped to find a motel room for the night," said Ina.

"Oh, there's no motel in Watermark."

"Well, no wonder we couldn't find one when we drove up and down the streets," Ina said cheerfully. "In time we grew sleepy. We came upon Watermark High and decided to take a nap in the parking lot. We planned to ask assistance in the morning, then continue on our way refreshed and—more importantly—enlightened."

When Ina was finished, the woman smiled. "I can see myself in your glasses," she said.

"Is there a motel in Brooks?" Helene asked irritably.

"I don't know. I don't get to Brooks much."

"The second part of our plight is something *you* might be able to help us with," Ina said. "When we awoke from our nap, students had arrived for school. Cars are parked so close in front and back of us that we can't move." Ina handed the woman a slip of paper. "These are the makes and license numbers. They have fifteen minutes to move—or we'll move them ourselves."

"Oh, dear. How?"

"Break a window. Put the car in Neutral. Push it out of the way," said Helene.

"My sister is getting testy," Ina said.

"I need authorization to use the PA," said the woman.

"Fifteen minutes," said Ina, and returned to her seat beside Helene. The woman rushed out the door.

"How's the hand?"

"Aches like a tooth."

"Can you drive eighteen miles in daylight?"

"I'd rather not."

"Soft beds and warm food await at the end."

"She—we—don't even know if there's a motel in Brooks," said Helene.

"We'll find out."

"What's beyond Brooks?"

"St. Louis," Ina said.

"Then California. Easy as pie."

"Think how we've thrown our pursuers off our trail," Ina said. "Amanda. Katherine. The forces of sanity. Who'd think to look for us in the principal's office of Watermark High School?"

"It's clever, I'll grant you that."

The woman returned, preceded into the office by a second woman; she was short, petite, with hair cut into blunt wings, and she sported dangling pineapple earrings.

"I'm Miss Grasshorn," she said politely. She did not offer to shake hands, a relief to Ina, who was angry with herself for not devising a code to tip Helene when such a common ritual was being conducted.

"Miss Wickless tells me you're trapped in our parking lot."

"Hemmed in. Front and back," said Helene.

Miss Grasshorn held the slip of paper Ina had given to Miss

Wickless. She had worried it into a small tube and held it by the ends between thumb and forefinger.

"I'll summon the owners of the cars to my office," she said.

"Is there a motel in Brooks?" Helene asked.

With a glance at Miss Wickless, Miss Grasshorn replied, "Yes, there's a motel in Brooks. The Palm, on Ordway Avenue, just off one-eleven at the south end of town."

"Is it clean?"

"Very."

"How about a doctor?"

"Dr. House," Miss Grasshorn said. "His office is right on one-eleven. Three blocks north of Ordway."

"Our lucky day," Ina said. "A Brooks expert."

"They threatened to break into one of the cars if they weren't moved in fifteen minutes," Miss Wickless said breathlessly.

"They don't strike me as the violent type," Miss Grasshorn said, looking at the widows.

"I'm just repeating."

"We *did* say that."

"It occurs to me," Ina said, "that you only have to fetch one student. Both cars needn't be moved for us to get out."

Miss Grasshorn said, "You two go out to your car—and I'll have one of the culprits out to move his car in a minute."

"His? Why not a her?"

"Want to bet? I've been here fourteen years. It's boys," Miss Grasshorn said.

Ina and Helene departed the office arm in arm. A new monitor was on duty. He possessed the manners to shut his *Studies in Physical Sciences* textbook and hold open the first door for them, then jump around them to open the outer door.

"Thank you, kind sir," Ina said.

"Sure," he replied with worldly nonchalance, as though he were routinely addressed as "kind sir."

The air had a bite to it, a windy insistence.

"A storm," Helene sniffed.

"Maybe just autumn."

"No, a storm."

"Should we bash one of the cars and run for it?" Ina asked. "How much traffic can there be between Watermark and Brooks?"

"Enough. And that's contrary to our master plan."

They had reached their car.

"Why do you think Miss Grasshorn knows so much about the Brooks motel?" Ina asked, unlocking the door, lowering Helene into her seat.

"I have no idea," Helene said. She started the engine.

"Maybe Miss Grasshorn and Miss Wickless?"

Helene laughed. "No. Miss Wickless was a functionary. She needed authorization to breathe."

"Then Miss Grasshorn and Dr. Whoozis?"

"House."

"Her gynecologist? How deliciously tawdry."

"Perhaps Miss Grasshorn and the principal," Helene speculated. "They spend long nights working together. They have things in common. They can talk. There is no need to constantly fill in the details of a story."

"Brooks doesn't seem far enough away for two prominent school officials," Ina said. "They'd be recognized."

"Do you think so? Miss Wickless hadn't been to Brooks. A town this size, three miles out of town may be farther than anyone around here ventures."

"Brooks might as well be Paris," said Ina.

A smirking young man came toward them, hands in the pockets of his jeans, hopping sideways between the cars. He looked chilled; his face was pale, sleepy, his shaggy hair whipped by the wind into an unruly snarl he tried to control with twitches of his head.

"Here comes our jailer," Ina said.

"Is he going to speak to us?"

"He's looking this way. He looks proud. This will be a good story to tell his friends."

He came to Helene's window.

"He has an announcement to make," Ina said.

Helene lowered her window an inch; he put his mouth to the

opening and said, "Our plan was to park on both sides and in front and back so you'd piss your pants before you got out. But we couldn't find two other guys to get with the program. You were lucky."

Helene shut the window. "Should I have thanked him?" she asked.

The boy unlocked the car in front of them (a rusty red Toyota with an Illinois State University sticker in the rear window and an Iron Maiden decal on the bumper) but then sat for several minutes combing his hair, checking his look in the rearview mirror, glancing at Helene.

"He's performing an extended toilet," Ina said. "God forbid he should make this easy on all of us."

"When and if he does free us," Helene said, "where will we go?"

"To Brooks. For a hot bath, a good meal, and sleep," Ina said.

"In daylight?"

Finally the kid started the car and, with a flip of a finger, opened a lane for them.

"The ass has moved," Ina said. "Forward slowly. Start a turn to the right."

She talked her sister to the mouth of the parking lot. A flatbed truck passed. A VW, a young woman chattering to the child in the backseat, went by in the opposite direction.

"It's clear. A left turn," Ina said.

"The whole atmosphere is different," Helene said nervously. "It *feels* busy."

"I'll get us there," said Ina.

The streets of Watermark, for all their simple grid design, confused Ina in daylight, and the service station she had seen in the darkness was not where she expected it to be. They circled back past a diner on 111 busy with the late breakfast trade (the police car now parked there) and waited at an intersection while a fat woman in an orange vest ferried a knot of grade-school children across.

They found the service station a block from where Ina remembered it, and this discovery placed her firmly in their setting.

"Stay here," Ina said. "If anyone asks, the car is making a terrible racket when it gets up to forty-five, and your husband in Brooks is a mechanical wizard who will fix it in no time."

"My husband's dead," said Helene. "It's immoral to pretend otherwise."

"All right, then. *My* husband."

"Your husband couldn't fix a flat."

Ina felt a twinge in her spine slamming the door. She went wide around the station's one island of three gas pumps, careful of the bell hose stretched to warn those inside of her approach. The front office was full of little items for sale on a whim: maps, soda pop, gum, mints, gas additives, beef jerky, nail clippers, cigarettes, blue windshield-washer fluid, ice scrapers, pens.

She waited an arbitrary length of time, until she saw Helene fidgit. About six minutes, Ina estimated. No one came to help her. She went outside and stepped on the bell hose, setting off a clangor in the lube bay shadows.

A man was at the cash register when Ina came back inside. His look was apologetic. Ina could not figure out from where he had appeared.

"Gas?"

"No. A tow."

He glanced past her, to Helene's car.

"What's the problem?"

"It makes a terrible noise at forty-five," Ina recounted. "My husband can fix it. But he's in Brooks."

"Brooks?"

"Yes."

"Seventy-five dollars each way," he said. "It costs me to deadhead back."

"Fine," Ina replied. She seemed to startle him, agreeing to the price, then taking cash so readily from her bag. She counted eight twenties onto the counter. "Can we go? We're in something of a hurry."

"Maybe I can take a look at it for you," he suggested. "You might harm it—something rubbing against something—if you tow it."

"My husband would kill me if I let someone else work on it," Ina said.

He gave her a ten in change; the bill was soft as cloth, filthy. Ina turned to see how Helene was doing, and when she turned back again the attendant was gone. He soon rose up from behind the counter like a prop in a play.

"Where did you go?" she asked with a startled laugh.

"I've got a little room down there," he said. "Big enough for a desk, a safe, file cabinets. Want to see?"

"No, thank you," she said, though intrigued.

"Put it in myself," he said proudly. "Got a phone. My alarm controls are down there. It's air-conditioned. Got a back entrance that comes up behind the building. Twice I've been held up, I just jump down there and pull the door shut on top of me. It locks automatically. They get what's in the register, but by then the police are here."

"Very clever," Ina said.

"I think so."

"Can we go?"

"I have to wait for my relief," he said. "I can't just up and go to Brooks and leave the place unattended."

"How long will it be?"

"Just a matter of minutes. I called Eddie, he said he'd be over pronto."

The bell went off and the man darted out the door. Ina peeked over the top of the counter. A flight of steps, outlined in fluorescent yellow tape, dropped out of sight. The wall of the stairwell that she could see was thickly papered with nudes.

The attendant returned, saw Ina's curiosity, and asked, "Sure you don't want to see? It's my little corner of the world."

"Thanks. No."

She glanced out the window, embarrassed, and saw the police car getting gas. No one was behind the wheel. Helene sat impassively, her chin in her palm, appearing to take in the day's details.

"One of the prices for quick responses to holdups in free gas," groused the attendant.

"Small price," Ina said.

"Two holdups in four years against probably forty bucks of free gas a week? I don't think so," he said.

A tall kid appeared in the door, a can of Coke in one hand, a rolled-up magazine in the other. He nodded self-consciously to Ina, then stared wordlessly at his boss, awaiting instructions.

"Eddie, I'm towing a car to Brooks," he said. "Watch the place until I get back, okay? Gas only. Take a message on anything else."

"You bet, Rod," said Eddie.

Rod took a key from a pegboard behind the cash register. Ina followed him out.

"One Sunday morning I put Eddie in charge while me and my wife and kid went to church," Rod recounted with a wary glance back. Eddie was already reading and sipping his Coke. "I was gone ninety minutes. When I get back, Eddie's doing an oil change on Ray Douglas's Camaro. Eddie'd never done an oil change in his life. Then I noticed there's oil all over the floor of the bay. I asked Eddie where it came from. He said he'd also done two other oil changes while I was in church. One of them, he must've forgotten to put back the plug."

They decided the widows would sit in the tow truck cab. Rod solicitously greeted Helene, who nodded vaguely at Ina's too-hearty introduction. Helene was miffed at being made to wait, and at Ina's talk of dead husbands being resurrected for the sake of convenience. A clean towel was found in the trunk and spread across the truck's seat.

Rod lay on his back, hidden from the waist up under their car, getting the hooks in place.

"Good rubber," he said reappearing. "No rust. Bottom of the engine looks pretty good. No obvious leaks." He winked at Helene. "A cream puff."

Helene, like a pro, said, "Thank you."

Rod helped the women into the cab, Ina first, her voice in description of the high step, the height of the seat, floating back to Helene. Helene missed the step the first time, and Ina made a joke of it.

"It's a tricky one," Ina said, trying to provide her sister something to fix her bearings on. The second attempt, Helene was aboard. They smoothed the towel, their dresses. Ina was uncomfortable having to hold her legs together and away from the gear shift. Their car dangling behind like a trophy caught in traffic, they rolled onto 111.

"What happened with the oil change?" Ina asked, after Rod had worked through the shift pattern and had the truck moving at a speed that Ina considered, in relation to the previous pace of their journey, breathtaking. Helene felt it, too. The wind messing her hair, the hurtling sounds outside the window, made her smile.

"All I could do was wait," Rod recalled. "Eddie had forgotten to write up any tickets. He didn't recognize the customers. There was nothing else I could do but wait. Somebody was out there with an engine that didn't have any oil. We found the plug on the hoist, right where Eddie had set it. But that was over a year ago—and nobody's ever come back to demand we pay for a new engine."

"Kind of spooky," Ina said.

"Eddie thinks the guy took forty-eight directly across to the interstate, got on, and punched it right up to seventy. After a minute at that speed, with a semi on his tail, the engine seized up, the car stopped dead, and the semi killed him."

"One idea," said Ina.

"I like it. The guy couldn't be so spineless that he wouldn't complain about a ruined engine," Rod said. "Would he?"

"I'd complain," said Helene.

"So who's kept this baby in such mint condition?" Rod asked, looking across to Helene.

"It's my husband," Ina said. "He has a passion for that car. He's always fiddling with it. Washing and polishing it. Changing the oil." She felt backed into this fabrication by Helene's refusal to play along; she was perfectly willing to let Helene give Rudy credit for the car, but if she wouldn't, someone had to take it.

They passed a pig farm, a grain elevator, an elementary school, and finally a small green sign, welcoming them to Brooks.

"Where should I drop you?" Rod asked.

"The Palm Motel. You know it?"

"South end of town?"

"Vincent and I own it," Ina said. "He's got a little shop in back. We try to run a family place. But someone's always checking in at eleven and checking out at noon."

The Palm Motel was constructed of bright white tile trimmed in green, flower boxes on every window, and a small playground in a chained-off square cut into the center of the parking lot. The look of the place pleased Ina. She was proud of it in a way, to have assumed ownership sight unseen, and then to find her business looking so crisp and appealing.

Ina directed Rod to unhook the car at a point far from the office. She feared someone emerging to greet her as a stranger.

"Nice place," he said.

"Thank you. We've been thinking of putting in some tractor-tire flowerbeds. Do you come across many of those?" Ina asked.

"I'll keep my eye open," he said.

They shook hands through the window of the tow truck. Then he was off and they were alone again.

"You lie so well," said Helene.

"We're here, aren't we? In daylight? Without you driving?"

Folded like a piece of thin sculpture in a lawn chair, a man watched TV behind the Palm Motel check-in counter. He held the TV on his lap with both hands.

"What?" he asked of them, without rising.

"We'd like a room, please," Ina said. "Two twin beds."

"It's just past noon. I'll have to charge you for two nights," he said, eyes on the screen.

"We only want to stay one night."

He sighed. "Our day ends at one o'clock in the afternoon," he explained. "You come on one day and want to stay over to the next day. That's two days."

"That's absurd," Helene said, her back to the man.

"Forget it," Ina said, touching her sister's arm. "We'll check in."

"Let's come back in an hour," Helene suggested.

"You could do that," the clerk nodded. "But tomorrow is all booked up."

"So after all this—you have no vacancies?" Ina asked.

"For tomorrow, no."

"I find that hard to believe."

"Believe it or not. It's the truth."

"I get it," Ina said. "We can check in now, but we have to check out before one. In forty-five minutes?"

"Oh, no," the clerk said. "Once you have a room, you have it, so long as you pay your bill. If you check in today, you'll be able to stay tomorrow."

"But you're booked up tomorrow."

"Whoever had reserved the room you get, we'll put them in another room. Trust me, it works like a charm. Do you want the room?"

"Yes," Ina said. "We better check in before one o'clock, when all the rooms fill up."

Finally he set the TV down and uncurled from his chair. He was a cadaverously thin man, extremely tall, with slim hands and bluish nails. He slid a registration card across the counter to Ina, and placed a pen atop it.

"How will you be paying for this?" he enquired, glancing as he spoke at the TV on the floor.

"Cash," Ina said.

"I'll need a major credit card."

"I don't have one," Ina said.

"I must have something to charge if you destroy the room and split. Or run up a bill from room service. Or steal all the towels."

"Young man," Helene snarled, "you amaze me at the way you run this business. Since we've come in that door"—here she waved at a wall containing only a rack of tourist brochures touting Illinois—"you've used every imaginable obstacle to our checking in and spending our money here. I demand to see the manager."

"Now, now," Ina said. "I just want to check in and go to sleep."

"You can see him," the clerk said. "At the moment he's in room eleven down at the end."

"Will a hundred-dollar security deposit do? In the absence of a credit card?" asked Ina.

"I think five hundred."

"Fine. Write up the receipt. Wait here, Helene." She went to the car for more cash. She felt trapped by circumstances, the man behind the desk, and by her exhaustion. They simply could go no farther that day. They needed food and sleep. Helene was late with her shot and she needed a doctor to look at her bitten hand.

She paid the bill for two nights, and also the five-hundred-dollar security deposit; the clerk scooped the bills toward him and into a drawer under the counter. Ina read the receipt carefully, then put it in her purse. She was presented with the key to Room 6.

"How late does room service stay open?" Ina asked.

"Oh, we don't have room service here at the Palm," he replied, almost proudly.

"Then what is the danger of our running up a tab there?"

"None at all. I was only using that as an example."

"Are there towels for us to steal?"

"There are towels. But I know *exactly* how many are in the rooms, and I count them the minute our guests leave," he said.

"Do you know—if this was my motel, I'd fire you immediately," Helene said.

"Oh? Well it's not, is it? So you can't, can you?"

"Did you win the lottery?" Ina asked. "Did you give notice and today is your last day?"

"No," said the clerk. "This is my job. Most people think I'm quite good at it."

"I bet they haven't been guests of this motel," Helene said.

"You're not the owner's son?"

"Absolutely not! I got this job without anyone's help," he said. "I work hard and I earn my money."

"You watch TV and give potential customers a hard time is what you do," Ina pointed out.

"That isn't true. I happen to be on my lunch hour. I'm taking my break—*and* working. How many employees *anywhere* can say that?"

"The TV goes off when lunch is over?" Ina asked.

"At one o'clock—start of the new day—off it goes."

"You were unpleasant just because we interrupted you?"

"Unpleasant? Define unpleasant."

"You," Ina said.

"One person's unpleasantness is another person's professionalism. I explained the motel rules," he said. "It was your decision whether you went along with them."

"And since we have," Ina said to Helene, "let's take advantage of it."

"That's what the five-hundred-dollar deposit is to guard against," he warned.

Room 6 was clean, lacking in frills, thin-walled (they could hear music somewhere, maybe all the way from Room 11), but it possessed two firm beds and easy access to the ice machine. Ina put a handful of cubes in a glass and poured warm beer over them. She swirled this foamy mess, then took a long, impatient swallow. She was suddenly happy, nearly deliriously so. Helene, too, was humming when she emerged from the bathroom. Already she had changed into her nightgown. Her face looked so clean that parts had been scrubbed indistinct, particularly her eyes and her mouth. Ina guided her to the edge of the bed.

"Safe and sound," Helene said. She gave herself a shot and ate two graham crackers.

She was asleep by the time Ina finished in the bathroom. She had taken a shower and shaved her legs (reaching periodically outside the hot, lancing water for her beer, taking a fast drink, the icy froth filling her deliciously) and in bending over with her razor dizziness assailed her and she had to snatch at the edge of the tub to keep from falling.

She sat on the bed brushing her hair. How far had they come from St. Charles? How long had they been on the road? In working out the answers, she was startled at the brevity of their journey.

PART FIVE

◆ ───────────────────────────

Motor Haven

HELENE'S horse bite had healed by the time they crossed the Mississippi River south of St. Louis.

"Could you throw a rock across it?"

"No," Ina said.

"Could we swim across it?"

"In our youth, surely."

They were an hour into the night's leg of travel and Ina carried a secret: Since their stop in Brooks, the fact of what they were doing was officially out in the open. The forces of sanity were in pursuit.

Ina had called Amanda from the Palm Motel while Helene was asleep. She had pulled the phone into the bathroom and shut the door on the cord.

"What the hell is going on with you two?" Amanda wanted to know.

"Whatever do you mean?"

"I went over to Mom's. Katherine was out watering her garden. I thought she was with you," Amanda recounted. "She had no idea *what* I was talking about."

"An urban ruse," Ina said.

"A what?"

"We needed a story to help us get away."

"Get away from what?"

A valid question, Ina decided, in reflecting afterward on the conversation. They were two comfortable widows, with a little money, nice houses, the encroachment of the criminal element only a recent phenomenon. What were they doing so far from home?

"Get out on the road. Get started," Ina had told Amanda. "You wouldn't have let us leave, ever."

"I didn't know you could drive," Amanda said.

Again, an avenue of escape was presented to Ina. How easy to create a fiction of lessons taken, tests passed, accreditation bestowed. But that was too simple. She was proud of how far they had come and in what manner they had traveled.

"I can't," Ina said.

"Then who . . . ? *No!*"

"It's gone remarkably well."

"My mother is driving? A *blind* woman is driving?"

"She's a very good driver," Ina said. "I'm very good at describing things."

"You can't travel like that," Amanda declared. "What about traffic? And pedestrians? What about the *unexpected?*"

"We have reduced that sort of risk to a manageable level," Ina said. "We travel at night on secondary roads."

"Where are you now?"

"I can't tell you, dear."

"Obviously you aren't in Omaha."

Ina laughed. "Obviously."

"I would bet you're still in Illinois," Amanda mused. "Probably quite close to Chicago. The state police could find you in no time."

"Oh, don't make threats, Amanda," Ina said, seeking a light tone, for Amanda's calculations made her feel exposed; she should have waited until they were out of the state before she called.

"The police won't bother us," she said. "I don't think you know your mother's license number, or even what her car looks like. And in the dark, traveling at fifteen miles per hour, we present the most nonthreatening motorists imaginable. We'll be in California in no time. You can come visit."

This resolute optimism exasperated Amanda. "You *can't* cross America with a blind woman at the wheel," she said.

"Just wait."

"This scares me," Amanda said. "First, just the danger of what you're doing. What if you hit someone? *My* mother will go to jail. You're just a passenger. You'll get off, maybe with a fine."

"I'd take the blame," Ina said. "I'll tell the judge I'm the brains of the outfit."

"That's my other point," Amanda said. "It scares me that you would even *consider* this. It strikes me as senile."

Ina paused to look at Helene through the crack in the door. She was turned toward the bathroom, asleep in a motionless, near-death fashion that seemed to circumvent breathing.

"Did you hear what I said?" Amanda asked, as if pressing an advantage. "Senile? Senile dementia?"

"I'm not—*we're* not—senile," Ina declared.

"Then come home. Tell me where you are and me and Gordon will pick you up."

"No," Ina said. She was within moments of ending the call.

"Prove to me you're not senile," Amanda said, nearly cooing.

"I don't have to prove a thing to you," Ina said. "We want to make this trip and we're going to make this trip. I'll stop calling if you're going to be this way."

"Don't stop calling."

"How *is* Gordon?"

"He hasn't been around for a while," she said, her voice shifting into a tone of practiced disinterest.

"I'll call again soon."

"Tell me where you are," Amanda pleaded.

"No. We'll be fine. Don't worry."

"I *will* call the police. Regardless of what you say, I'm calling the police."

"They'll laugh at you," Ina predicted.

"What about Annie and Ray? Do they know what you're doing?"

"They know," Ina said.

"I bet they don't."

"They're fully supportive of our plan," said Ina.

"Oh, Ina, don't bullshit me," Amanda said. "Well, count on this. They'll know thirty seconds after you hang up."

"Go ahead," Ina said. She supposed there was no avoiding her children learning of their plan.

Amanda drew a deep breath that sounded moist, the residue of a bad cold, or tears.

"Once more," she said. "Please let me come and get you."

"We're outside the Quad Cities. In a HoJo's there."

"You're lying," Amanda stated, and after a long hesitation, as if weighing her frustration against her desire to maintain the connection, she hung up.

Now they were parked, motor running, lights out, on the west bank of the Mississippi River. They both had wanted to stop; the river was a landmark, a signpost of a certain level of achievement, and they didn't want to just hurtle past without paying attention. They had come a ways.

Ina, studying her maps, envied Helene her lack of responsibility. All she had to do was drive; the pointing of her, the anxiety of watching for the road's hidden dangers, these fell to Ina.

Two barges passed on the river; both were going upriver at a pace that was leisurely and indomitable. Big as cities, their dimensions staked out with yellow running lights, the barges carried something heaped high against the horizon of the far shore. Figures moved in the pilot houses. From one barge, they heard music coming across the water.

"What time is it?" Helene asked, fitting the words around a song she hummed.

"Quarter of three," Ina said, though she didn't know, and didn't care. Helene punched buttons on the radio. The air was full of songs they didn't recognize, or harmonious static, or weather reports that kept the widows' attention only until they were certain the forecast did not affect them.

"Let's throw in a line."

"You know what's across that river?" Ina asked, making the discovery that instant in her perusal of the maps.

"Illinois."

"Menard Correctional Center," said Ina. "Home of the vilest of the vile."

"What does that have to do with us?" Helene asked. "We can go fishing. *They* can't. Let's not waste the opportunity."

"What if someone escapes?" Ina hypothesized. "First thing they'll try to do is get out of Illinois. They'll cross the river looking for a car."

"Fish or drive. But I just can't sit still," Helene said. "All I need is guidance."

Ina got them turned around, back on the road west, then safely off the road before sunrise.

They skipped a day of travel. Ina needed a respite from her duties. The place where they were staying—Hendricks Motor Haven—allowed them to park the car behind their cabin, where it couldn't be seen from the road. She felt temporarily unobserved and she wanted to savor that.

She did not announce to Helene her intention to stay for a while; they simply arrived at an unspoken agreement not to push westward. Helene fell asleep at midnight. Ina stayed out on the porch for another hour or so, until she had drunk enough beer to fall asleep.

Rain was falling in the morning; a whispering rain, good for sleeping. The air was sweetly warm; the trees, beginning to go red and gold at their boundaries, murmured and dripped as the widows took their lunch on the cabin's screened front porch.

Mr. Hendricks brought the food out to them on a tray, keeping it dry under a yellowed plastic dome. He stayed to talk; really more a summation of his life that sounded to the widows rehearsed, or else so familiar he had long ago stopped thinking about or examining what he was saying: He had been widowed for eight years, owned the Motor Haven forty-two years, built each of the eight cabins himself, in 1955 he put in the indoor plumbing a cabin at a time at a cost of $10.45 per, since his wife died he had taught himself to cook, saving the wages of an extra employee, but still business was slow, theirs was the only occupied cabin of the eight, he turned down business every day, people wanting a cabin for a couple hours, but he wouldn't allow that at the Motor Haven, nor could he in good faith raise rates because he wasn't providing any different or better services than he had in 1970, when last he raised them at his wife's behest. They were welcome to stay as long as they wished, he would let them eat in peace.

"Think he has children?" Ina asked, watching the man shuffle away; at the front door to the office he scraped his shoes clean on the sharpened spine of an iron dachshund.

Helene said, "I think he probably is too dense to father children. He's charging us eight dollars per person per night—and he hasn't raised his rates in seventeen years? And he turns down business? I'd have left him years ago. A man that stupid—would he even know where children came from?"

Ina removed the dome from the food. Mr. Hendricks had prepared Polish sausage, mashed potatoes, creamed corn, and hot apple mush. A basket of corn muffins was wrapped in a dishtowel. She set a plate before Helene, leaving off the apple dessert.

Then she went into the cabin for a beer; it was cooler than room temperature, but only barely. The Hendricks Motor Haven did not have an ice machine. She had requested ice and Mr. Hendricks returned in an hour with six cubes melting in a pink Tupperware bowl. She'd thanked him. Didn't use much ice himself, he admitted. She crunched it privately while Helene slept; there was no sense dropping the cubes into the cooler. The teeth she still possessed ached when she was finished.

"That's one thing I thank my stars for," Helene said when Ina was seated.

"What's that, dear?"

"That Rudy died before me," said Helene. "He'd have ended up like Mr. Hendricks."

"He taught himself to cook."

Helene waved her hand dismissively, her mouth full.

"He's lost," she said at last. "You can hear it in his voice. I'll wager from day to day he doesn't talk to anyone but who's staying in his cabins. And other than us, who's that?"

"Let's ask him to come with us," Ina teased. "He can drive. We won't spend half our life in Missouri."

"No, thanks."

Ina gave her sister a muffin.

"I think of the two of them," Helene mused, "Rudy would have done better without me than Vincent would have done without you."

"Vincent was not a helpless man," Ina said.

"You were never apart except when he was at work," Helene said. "And when you were together, you did everything for him. How do you know if he was helpless or not?"

Ina stacked the dishes on the tray when they were finished and covered it with the plastic dome. The rain had neither diminished nor intensified, but fell in an absolutely vertical downpour.

Ina made tea at the sink with the rust-tinged tap water and a jar of instant provided by Mr. Hendricks. She stirred the tea into a lukewarm froth and set the glass in front of her sister. Secretly she hoped Helene would knock it over.

"Un-iced tea. Directly in front of you."

Ina took her seat again; while inside the cabin she had put on a sweater against a chill she sensed settling.

"Are you warm enough?"

"I'm fine, dear."

Ina said, "A more pertinent question might be—which of us is getting along better without her husband?"

"I don't want a fight. We both do as well as we can," Helene said.

"Who misses her husband more?" Ina said, with a taunt in her voice.

"I don't want a fight," Helene repeated; in sipping from her glass she left a thin brown cloud of tea on her upper lip. Ina could see it breaking apart as the tiny bubbles burst.

"Do you still dream about Rudy?" Ina asked, drawing the sweater tighter around her shoulders.

"I don't recall ever dreaming about him."

"You said you did. You told me several dreams in which Rudy figured prominently," Ina said.

"Perhaps I did."

"I *still* dream."

"Hooray!" Helene burst out sarcastically. "You continue to pine. That makes you the better widow."

"I still see him in crowds," Ina said, and as she said it she wondered what the point was in examining this facet of their existence.

"Does he speak to you?" Helene asked, her voice going tender.

"In crowds? Or alone?"

Helene raised her head. "I will be sitting in the kitchen doing what have you, and after a certain period of time it will dawn on me that I have been very definite in my belief that Rudy is in the next room—and I am waiting for him to come talk to me; it is only a question of when he finishes whatever he is doing. These I called my rude awakenings . . . for obvious reasons."

Ina chuckled. "Ironically, that was our secret nickname for him. Rude. His Rudeness," she said.

Helene, hurt, charged, "He was never rude a day in his life."

"Not for a day," said Ina. "But for several moments at a time he was unabashedly rude. What about the time he folded the tip and stashed it down that waitress's blouse?"

Helene's look became faraway, as if her memory was not sufficiently oiled to focus rapidly at such a distance. Ina's sole image of that night was of a young girl in some sort of low-cut blouse and apron getup, her look mortified, Rudy's thick finger hooked in her cleavage, pushing the folded bill home.

"Oof," said Helene, blushing.

"He was a little tipsy," Ina said, sorry now that she had brought it up.

Helene slammed down her tea glass. A wave of tea rolled up into the air and returned to the glass without losing a drop. Her look was fierce, willing now to be engaged.

"How about the way dear Vince picked his scalp in public?" she wondered. "And ate what he found?"

"His only bad habit," said Ina.

"Or the way his attention drifted when he was being spoken to?"

"Only when he was bored. Never with me."

Helene paused a moment. Ina could see Helene's mind working, circling, probing for an opening.

"Just with his own children," Helene said, and Ina knew by the sting in her heart that Helene had scored.

"That time—years ago—a family gathering," said Helene. "Annie had a camera she'd got for her birthday."

"I remember," Ina said softly. She could picture only the mood of the light falling in their backyard. The people present were specifically featureless, so well did she know them. "You and Rudy. Amanda. Vincent, Ray, and Annie. Aunt Agnes. Mother and Dad," she recalled.

"Was Dad alive?"

"Oh, sure. That was way prior to sixty."

"But what I remember most—and I love Vincent, keep in mind—was the way he gave Annie no credit for any brains at all. 'Have you got film in that thing?' 'Is everyone in the picture?' 'You're going to cut off Grandpa's head.' 'Don't you think Aunt Agnes should sit down front?' Pester, pester, pester. I was so embarrassed for her."

Fat, arthritic Aunt Agnes, every movement a struggle, finally was maneuvered to a chair down front. Her dress, in the picture that was passed around the family a week later, was snagged on one arm of the chair, committing an enormous thigh and garter snaps to posterity. Their father's head made the picture with a clean quarter-inch of summer light above his white hair. Their mother sat at his side; people said Ina took after her most in looks, Helene in temperament. Ray and Amanda were on the flanks, awaiting permission to depart the frame.

Annie asked her father to move in tight ("Closer. *Closer*," she said) and then with a movement deft as an incision she cropped her father from the edge and snapped the picture. She left his shadow in. He teased her mercilessly when the picture came back.

"Nobody claimed he was the perfect father," Ina said, rising for another beer.

"*You* did," Helene countered.

Ina walked to the rear of the cabin, as far as she could go, into the tiny bathroom to open the milk-glass window. A strip of weedy ground had been cleared between the back of the cabin and the woods. The rain striking the leaves imparted a sense of motion, though there was no wind. She felt trapped by the cabin's boxy economy, the rain that held them there, and Helene's talent for the line of talk they had been following. Moreover, she resented Helene throwing an unflattering light on Vincent. In their situation, what was the point? Vincent had never disguised his preference for his son. But he loved Annie, too, and he would rescue her from problems long before he would come to Ray's aid. But even that aid would have a mocking air. He was confident Ray could solve his problems; he assumed Annie would need his help.

"Ina?" Helene called from out front.

"I'm here," said Ina, stepping out onto the porch.

"You had me worried."

"Why?"

"I was afraid I'd finally said the *perfectly* wrong thing."

"And driven me away?"

"You'd be lost without me," Helene said bravely.

"We could split up," Ina teased, "and see who gets to L.A. first."

"I wouldn't go. I'd go home."

"And what would you do there? Move back into your house? Be terrorized by those hoodlums?"

"Something could be worked out," Helene said determinedly.

Ina sipped her beer. Her third (fourth?) of the day. Staring for a long time at the rain, she wondered not for the first time if she was a drunk.

To be scandalous, to raise a storm in her sister, she proclaimed, "Once I'm in California, I'm not leaving."

"Don't be silly," said Helene.

"It's a fact. I'm not going home."

Helene folded her arms beneath her bosom and turned her face away from Ina.

"I'll stay with Ray . . . or get a place of my own," she said, leaning toward her sister to be certain she was heard. "I'll tell Hector and Po to put the house on the market—furniture and all. I've got it all planned out."

"This is very cruel," Helene said, her face remaining averted. "You might have told me this before we left."

"You wouldn't have come," said Ina.

"Of course I wouldn't."

"Which is why I didn't tell you. If you'd refused, I'd have flown," Ina said. "Either way, I was going. This way, I got you out, too."

"Out?"

"Out. In the clear. You risked death at every turn where you lived."

Helene massaged the skin beneath her eyes. She was crying, not in a dramatic fashion, but with a genuine disappointment Ina was saddened to have provoked.

"I'll never see Amanda again," Helene said.

"You will. The instant we're settled in California. Amanda will be on the next plane out. You think her future is rosy in Chicago?"

"She has a good job," Helene said. "She has friends."

"She would come in a *second,*" Ina said. "But I'd have to buy her ticket. That's how financially secure she is in Chicago."

"It's always money with you," Helene scolded. "Show me into the cabin. I want to get away from you."

Ina gladly steered her sister to a chair in front of the room's small black and white TV. The picture was clogged with snow, but otherwise perfect for Helene's needs. Ina found a soap whose plot her sister recognized, then left her there entranced by the overheated emotions of the plot.

Ina returned to the porch and took Helene's chair, for it afforded the better view of the cabins, the woods, and the road beyond the Hendricks Motor Haven sign with its patiently winking red VACANCY light.

She swallowed beer with the relish she always brought to her drinking. The history of her love of beer went back a few years. Had Vincent ever said a word against it, she would have stopped that instant. Of this she was certain. However (and endearingly of him, she now reflected), he had never once expressed the opinion that her drinking troubled him. She now and then imagined catching out of the furred corner of her eye a glance of reproach from him; and her children, especially Annie, were even more forthright in their disapproval, but never expressed themselves beyond exasperated looks they thought she missed, or by abruptly departing a room when she entered with her heavenly blue glass.

But, curiously, only Vincent's opinion mattered to her. Only he had the power to change her. She waited on his first word of disapproval and that word never came. She did not drink every day (at least while he was alive) and this ability to go two, three, even four days without a beer saved her her opinion of herself. She was *not* a drunk. But since Vincent's death the question had resurfaced. The beer she consumed now seemed more like a lubricant, an oil she poured into herself in steady but not unseemly quantities to smooth the workings of her brain, her bones, and her heart as they scraped against the abrasive loneliness she encountered every day.

Her father drank, and her mother, too, and years after their death Ina could not say why with any certainty. Her father's life was a mystery to her; the pains and disappointments (and the triumphs, too, for he was a handsome, intelligent man with a talent for business) remained secrets he chose to keep to himself. He didn't talk much, even to his wife, which was perhaps why Ina's mother drank.

Their drink of choice was not beer, but rather sweaty gin killers with cuts of lime and ice that Father chipped from the block into the glasses. Mother's face blushed at the first sip, then seemed to relax and loosen like tight strands of resolution dissolving. During the summer they went by themselves to the porch, where they sat without talking about much beyond one of father's labored anecdotes from work. In winter they repaired to the parlor at the front of the house and father would snap an icicle from the eave above the front door and shatter it into glass-sized pegs that vanished amid the gin. Limes, out of season, were missed for the green tease of health they provided.

Ina and Helene sampled this drink late at night, after their parents had gone to bed. Curiosity drove them to mix what remained in the two glasses. They first tested it with a dipped, licked finger. The flavor of their skin must have skewed the taste, for nothing could be so medicinally vile and still be voluntarily consumed. So they each sipped a burning share and spat it disgustedly into the sink. Helene, three days later, reported that the taste remained locked in her memory, she couldn't get rid of it.

Beer, however, for Ina, was a revelation. She was married, carrying Annie through a stinking hot summer, and Vincent was away in the Navy. Rumors were rampant that he would be sent overseas. She lumbered through the house feeling oafish, useless, grotesque in appearance. Her face sprouted blotches like weeds in the heat. Annie, still a month from arrival, kicked and punched at Ina from the inside, butting her head into Ina's ribs, or sitting like a stone on her spine.

Helene and Rudy stopped over. Rudy carried a tub of beer and poured a generous offering into a glass. He presented the glass to Ina. She was sitting in the front room, holding her enormous belly up off her thighs, which chafed if she wasn't careful; she took the glass of beer. She was only curious. She was ready for something different in her life; a child, a new sensation. Forever after, when Helene complained, Ina reminded her it was Rudy who introduced her to beer. She sipped.

A not unpleasant, slightly bitter taste. She held it in her mouth like something dangerous (a poison to be spat out on the sly, as she had intended the first time with Vincent's come, planning to make an excuse and hurry to the bathroom. But no excuse presented itself in the aftermath and she carefully allowed the deposit to slide thick and warm down her throat; not, it proved, regretfully), *sloshing* the beer between her cheeks, testing, and swallowing.

She sipped again. And again. Waiting with each drink for her attention to wander as her parents' did when they were drinking their gin rhapsodies, for her voice to grow loud, for her to repeat long stories whose fine points and endings seemed resolutely of scant interest.

But nothing of the sort happened. Only a rather merry heat took charge just beneath her skin so that her cheeks, the backs of her hands, the tips of her breasts, the small of her back, mois-

tened with a new sort of excitement. The sensation made her
long for Vincent.

She requested Rudy to pour her a second glass despite her
mother's protestations that the beer wasn't good for the baby. But
she had done enough for the baby, just then; fed it, cradled it,
absorbed its blows without complaint. She wanted something for
herself. Without realizing it, Ina might have been a drunk by the
time Annie was born. Kissing in the darkness of his first night
home, Vincent told her, smiling through their crushed-together
mouths, that she tasted of alcohol, and she remembered being
uncertain if he disapproved.

Now Ina's blue glass was empty. She did not want to go inside
the cabin, though she had to use the bathroom, and the rain and
her memories were perfect for her limited ambitions of simply
sitting, drinking, and remembering the day away. She doubted
they would travel that night, therefore she saw no reason to rest,
or plan the next phase of their route, or limit herself.

Music intended to imply hothouse romance played on the TV.

"Can I get you anything?"

"No, thank you," Helene replied curtly.

Ina used the bathroom, washed her hands, and dried them on
one of the thin Motor Haven towels. A spider skated up the
mirror. Another walked the edge of the water glass. A third—and
a fourth—levitated by invisible strands from the ceiling over the
tub. They were the color of the sleep she dug from her eyes in
the morning. Rudy would track them, pulverizing each in midair
with a crack of applause. Vincent, believing spiders good luck,
would leave them be.

"Are we going on tonight?" Helene asked.

Ina, surprised, said, "Are you ready?"

"I'm tired of this place. It's too damp. I feel useless just watching television."

"If the rain stops, we'll travel," Ina said, reassured in her hazy
state by the steady rattle on the cabin's thin roof.

"I can drive in the rain."

"We shouldn't. It would be safer not to."

Ina refilled her glass, but at the door she stopped when Helene said, "I'm worried about Amanda. I'd like to try to call her again."

"She'd be at work now," Ina said. "Later in the afternoon we'll try again."

Twice recently Helene had insisted on calling her daughter, and Ina volunteered to dial the number. She dialed her own each time, figuring the only people liable to answer were Po or Hector Strode, and the chance of that extremely slim. Ina was afraid Helene would tip their location, or let slip the license number of the car, thus exposing them to the full arsenal of pursuit available to the police. They would be caught within days, chastised, and then put on a bus home, two old bats whose senile plan was foiled before somebody got killed.

But primarily Ina was afraid Amanda would use her troubles at home to frighten Helene into demanding that Ina guide them back to Chicago. Once back, they would be trapped.

The angle of the rain had changed and Ina moved her chair deeper onto the porch to keep from getting wet. She had a blanket to wrap around her legs, and an apple and a knife to peel it. Vincent could skin an apple into one continuous twirl, then lower it like a snake into his tipped-back mouth. Ina simply enjoyed slicing off thin disks of skin and meat, then sectioning them with her front teeth before swallowing. Mr. Hendricks came out and got in his car, waving to her; she toasted him with the golden weight in her glass.

She took a drink.

That sound, the sound of her father chipping at the ice with his ice pick, and the clink of his catching the ice in his glass, that was the sound she hated most when she was young. It was a signal that her father's day as his true self was at an end. Mother's too, for he fixed her a drink when he made his. That ice sound would draw Mother from whatever she was doing (more than once, Ina remembered, terminating a conversation with her daughter in midsentence) into the parlor or out onto the front porch to await Father and her glass of gin and lime.

Sometimes Ina and Helene would eavesdrop on those evening privacies, and come away stupefied and saddened by the extent of the silences and the complete lack of sparkle to the few sentences that dribbled between husband and wife, like a chess game through the mail.

But what was the sound—*her sound*—that set her children's teeth on edge, sent them fleeing at her approach, touched off their anger? In California, she could ask them; *there* was a reason for the trip. Was it the little gas explosion of a popped tab or bottle cap echoing off the kitchen tiles? Was it the gulpy sound of the beer pouring into a glass? Or maybe it was simply the refrigerator opening at a certain hour; the hour she had set for herself as a goal, the hour prior to which drinking a beer was a sign of a life without control, and after which she was free to do as she most desired.

She sliced off a piece of apple and chewed it. Every day she thanked Vincent for having had the money to buy her the best in bridgework. There was no telling the hour from the light. The rain had frozen time in the gloom of a late afternoon. She might think it was dinnertime, or morning, or time for her nap, if not for the evidence of her empty beer cans, the TV prattle, and the memories she had overturned. The time was, in fact, a matter of minutes before two o'clock.

The addictions of her children were of scant interest to her. Neither had displayed an inclination to allow his or her habits to get the better of them, a trait she knew they inherited from their father, but which she also felt applied to her, as well. She drank beer every day, quite a large quantity of beer on those days that seemed to require it, but never had she felt she had relinquished control of her life to her drinking.

Vincent was notable for his lack of excesses. He would have a beer with her late at night, when she would confess to him a loneliness, and he would take part in her drinking not out of a desire for drink, but just to give Ina someone to see her through her solitude. He would listen to her talk, or cry; he might tell her stories of his own, something that had taken place in his time away from her, and she closed her eyes and rested her head back on the pillow (for even then she had learned to love drinking in bed) and let his words run over her; words aglow, caressing, honeyed. At some point whose specific moment always eluded her in the morning, he took her blue glass from her hand and set it aside. He might kiss her and tuck her in; he might kiss her, gauging the pressure of her desire in her return of the kiss, and reading something in her kiss, kiss on, kiss lower, kiss lower still, and she would squirm languidly beneath him. Nearly too numb to move, but not to feel, she left everything to him.

In her sexual memories Vincent was not a young man, but he also was not within twenty years of his death, and she never tried to get a good look at herself. Whether her breasts flopped or her stomach was pouched from children wasn't important to the impact of her memory. She was always—from the first time he put his hands on her to her final touch of his face at his funeral—a core of nerve impulses bound in electric skin, eager to be *moved*.

He had pale skin that burned in the summertime, and in three days peeled along his shoulders. She played with this burned skin as he lay on his stomach in bed. Rolling the rubbery peelings into tiny pellets, setting them on the nightstand for later disposal. The peeled area revealed his customary paleness, as if there was never to be a change in his basic element, which was what she counted on most of all. She rubbed at other patches on his back and chest, looking for skin to peel, but it held tight to him everywhere else. He did not go out in the sun often; he mowed the lawn in white trousers and shirt, with the sleeves buttoned, and a long-billed red fishing cap. Annie and Ray had made fun of him for the humiliation he drew to the family with that eccentric dress. On another occasion he had relented in her desire to go to the beach, and in falling asleep in the sun had burned the backs of his legs. Kneeling to peel away his itchy skin she lost her breath at the sight of his balls bunched under him, and she kissed him there, not for the first time, but for the first time from that angle of approach.

They traded places. She stretched out in the warm spot he had shaped while he balanced on his knees at her side. He poured a cool puddle of lotion into the small of her back. Lilac swirled with the beer smell in the pillow. His hand, heel first, then palm, then fingers, spread the lotion up her spine like a wave, fanning it out onto her ribs where it would run dry and more would be added. His slick fingers slipped off the edges of her back, gliding down the plumped-out sides of her breasts. More lotion was added to the shallow bowl at the base of her spine, and this deposit he directed down into the crevice of her butt, which rose against the pressure of his hand, and farther down where liquids lost their individuality, where she nearly lost hers. He would bring his face to her there from the same angle she had kissed his balls, elevating her slightly with his fingertips as if she were a tray of delicacies, then pushing in, his beautiful face seeming to pass through her sopping boundary and smile at her from the inside. She could not hold still and she felt him laughing down there as if she were making him work for his treat, when what she desired most was to be pinned in place with his tongue and brought off with the ease and frequency that was their secret. Her eyes opened to look at him, and at the age she gave him in her memories his stomach had slackened, the hole in his navel deepened. His penis curved up from between his legs, but the cushion of hair at its root bore spirals of silver. He kept his wedding ring on but not his watch, and in its place on his wrist was a hint of its shape on his skin.

Something crashed on the floor of the cabin, pushing Ina back from her edge. She bruised her shin on the doorway rushing inside. This pain she regarded almost as a punishment for subjecting herself to memories that served no purpose, that only left her feeling hollowed out and lonely.

Helene was on the phone. She had found her way to the edge of the bed, taking the glass of tea along, and then somehow the tea was knocked over like one of Ina's cruel wishes coming true. It spread in a puddle sparkling with glass beneath her feet, and from the tip of her slipper dripped pale liquid.

"Who is this?" Helene asked impatiently of someone on the phone. "I demand you tell me who this is."

She seemed to listen, her gaze directed at the spilled tea.

"I'm Amanda's mother. Where is Amanda?"

Ina went to her sister and touched her shoulder. Helene glanced up, startled, and raised a cautioning hand. Ina got a towel and a wastebasket from the bathroom, then knelt before Helene and picked up pieces of glass. She set them carefully in the wastebasket, lest she create a disturbance.

"Must I call the police?" Helene asked.

Ina blotted the tea with a towel. They would have to request another from Mr. Hendricks, who had only stocked the room with two, a matched pair, monogrammed HH. She listened to the silence of her sister listening; she imagined Gordon in Amanda's apartment, saw him squatting secretly on the kitchen counter, pictured him landing solid blows to Amanda's face.

"When do you expect her?" Helene asked like a receptionist. "Where is she now?"

That was the question Ina wanted answered. She carried the towel into the bathroom and dropped it in the tub. She waited at the mirror, studying the lines on her face, listening, and wondering what Vincent ever saw in her.

"Are you a friend of my daughter's?"

My eyes are still beautiful, Ina declared to herself. They were a faded blue, an unassuming color that required a sensitive nature to be recognized and appreciated within the disconcerting flaws age had pressed into her face.

"Let me give you my number. I want Amanda to call me the moment she returns. Have you a pencil handy?"

Ina ran a brush through her hair. It needed a good washing. A shower and some sleep would improve her disposition. She suspected her trip west was about to end.

"Please write it down. You might forget. Please find a pencil."

Helene covered the phone with her hand, and called to Ina. "Could you tell me the number here, please?"

Ina sat down on the bed across from her sister.

"Let me have the phone. I'll give him the number," Ina said, touching Helene's hand.

"He's getting a pencil.

Ina put the phone to her ear. The connection was full of scratches and pops, like birds landing on the line.

"Shoot," said a man's voice suddenly. He sounded not unpleasant, not brusque. He might have been napping, Amanda at work, the call an intrusion and an embarrassment he had now recovered from.

Ina read the number off the phone.

"Who's this?" he asked suspiciously.

"Ina Lockwood. Amanda's aunt."

"We've met," he said with a sly chuckle. "You remember me?"

"I think so."

"Listen—tell her mom not to worry. Amanda's a big girl. She'll call."

"I know," Ina said, wishing Helene would leave and give her room to maneuver with this man. He possessed for Ina a history far richer than Helene would ever have imagined.

"We want to continue our trip," Ina said. "We hoped to leave early tomorrow morning. It would ease my sister's mind considerably if Amanda would call this evening."

The man teased, "From what Amanda has told me, you've been avoiding her."

"We've tried to reach her. She's never home."

"You haven't tried too hard. We're real homebodies."

"I appreciate your help in this."

"You're just bullshitting your sister, aren't you?" he said gleefully. "I think you're both bats, personally." He hung up.

"Thank you again for your help," Ina said. "Yes, good-bye."

"Let me guess," Helene said. "He hung up right after you gave him the number."

"No. He was very nice."

"He was insolent. Rude," she said. "He wasn't even going to write down the number. He was going to memorize it."

"How did you call?" Ina asked.

"What a *stupid* question," Helene said. Her feet were still elevated protectively above the cool spot where the tea had fallen. "I've got to get home," she said.

"Why?" Ina asked cautiously.

"To make sure she's all right. I didn't like the tone of that gentleman's voice at all."

"Amanda will call tonight," Ina promised. "There's nothing

you can do at home. After she calls, we'll press on," she said
with a stab at enthusiasm.

"That man—when I threatened to call the police?"

"Yes?"

"He threatened *me* with the same thing."

"A blind woman driving across the country? I imagine it's
against the law."

"It's silly and foolish. We're going home."

"Let's wait until Amanda calls."

"Why can't you just do as I ask?" Helene shouted.

"Because it's not what *I* want," Ina said. "I could say, fine,
we'll go home. But I could just keep us heading toward California.
Would you know the difference? I doubt it. I could be under-
handed with you, but instead I'm being honest."

"I'd know," Helene said.

"How?"

"People along the way. Clerks. Waitresses. Accents changing.
Someone would say something. *I'd* know."

"I wouldn't let you talk to anyone. You stay in the car now
while I check in to the motels. You're a snob with waitresses.
You'd just be happy you were on your way home where thugs
have destroyed your home and your daughter is too old to be
bothered with you."

"Lies. All lies," Helene responded airily. She probed with her
toe at the floor, seeking tea and broken glass.

"I cleaned it up," Ina said.

"Thank you. In my anxiety to dial the correct number I forgot
where I'd set the glass."

"Quite all right, dear. Are you hungry?"

"A snack would be nice. Then I think I'd like to rest."

She removed her dress and handed it to Ina, who hung it in
the closet. Helene was under the covers. She took three crackers
from Ina and ate them carefully. She cupped her hand beneath
her mouth for protection. She said, "Those times we tried to call
Amanda, whose number did you dial?"

"Amanda's, of course."

"Not yours? Not mine?"

"Don't be silly."

"I'm your prisoner," said Helene.

"You're my sister. We're dependent on each other. I need you as much as you need me."

"No," Helene said, her eyes on the ceiling, a fresco of water-stains. "You've taken me prisoner."

The phone rang in the dark. Ina had been awake for twenty minutes, listening to her sister's restless sleep, wondering idly as to the hour. The rain had stopped and now a wind scratched a branch across the cabin's back wall; she thought mice were making the noise until she investigated. Returning over the cold floor she struck her shin again, the same spot as before, like applying a second coat of bruise.

She lacked the energy to travel, but nevertheless considered it imperative that they move that night. The momentum of their journey, the force of habit that edged them west day by day, had been lost. Helene's determination to go home seemed tentative. Ina sensed a willingness to be convinced otherwise. There had been an implication of relief in Helene's accusation that Ina had taken her prisoner. Helene's world now was Ina, and on a more profound level than it had been in Chicago, where Helene at least had the benefit of knowing the neighborhood, of having mapped the place in her mind, down to the number of footsteps in each block. Now they had traveled into a country Helene had never seen. The responsibility for getting them safely through was entirely Ina's. She must see that country whole, must see its details, its contours, its dangers. Helene only had to follow, and this understanding of her reliance on Ina seemed to comfort her. She was so deeply asleep that the two rings of the phone before Ina answered produced only a shifting in her posture of unconsciousness.

"So you're in Missouri," Amanda said.

"Somewhere in Missouri. What time is it?"

"Almost midnight."

"Thank you for calling. Your friend upset your mother."

"I should've answered," Amanda said. "A world of grief would have been avoided."

"You were home?"

"Yes, Aunt Ina. Do you want me to be more specific?"

"Why didn't you talk to her?"

"An idea," Amanda said. "If I took the call, I wouldn't have got your phone number. *Gordon* answered, Mom got upset, and then gave him the number so I'd be sure and call as soon as possible. So I know you're in Missouri."

"She wants to come home to be of help to you," Ina said.

"I don't want that."

"I know. I don't want her going back, either."

"So you want me to leave you alone?"

"That would be nice," Ina said. "Is he still there?"

"No."

"Has he hit you recently?" Ina said in a whisper.

"Is she listening?"

"She's asleep."

"The last time was three days ago. A small fight about money," Amanda recalled.

"And he hit you then?"

"We came out even. Punchwise. Two apiece." She laughed. "He tells me he hits his wife harder and more often than he hits me. That's his testament to his love for me."

"Maybe we *should* come home," Ina said.

"Will that get you to give up your silly trip? Tales of my domestic violence?"

"I don't like him," Ina said.

"I don't either, at times. But he's all I've got at the moment," Amanda said, sounding cheerfully resigned, relieved to have somebody.

"Should I wake her?" Ina asked. "I don't think she'd believe me if I told her you called while she was asleep."

"Then wake her up," Amanda said.

"Wait." Ina put down the phone, seeing the room clearly now, a lunar phosphorescence coating the windows. But also she was painfully alert to what she was required to do: awaken Helene and set in motion a long night's questions, recriminations, and accusations. A trip's worth of Helene wondering if she had done the right thing in leaving her daughter's side.

Ina tapped on Helene's warm shoulder. She flicked on the nightstand light, and then as quickly snapped it off, a brilliant pain lancing her eyes and a laugh of foolishness escaping her. The laughter stirred Helene. She rolled crankily into Ina's poking finger.

"What?" she muttered irritably, her voice coming from the warm, white star hanging in Ina's vision.

"It's Amanda on the phone."

"Manda?" Helene said.

Ina knew she had her. Helene moved toward the sound of her daughter's name, a hand already reaching. She licked her lips, held the phone to her breast.

"Could I have a cup of water?"

Ina went for it, getting a beer for herself and taking her time pouring it into the glass, which she didn't bother to rinse out. She dawdled, letting Helene break the ground in private; but she listened, too, and no sound came from the other room. She returned, leaving a light on behind her.

Helene had not moved.

"Talk to her," Ina said, putting the water in her sister's free hand.

"My throat is horribly dry," Helene rasped, drinking. "I don't want to sound like I've been crying." She handed back the cup. "Could you drape a sweater over my shoulders?"

Finally, she said, "Hello?"

Again, Ina had to be content with half the conversation. For a long time her sister said nothing, but leaned into the phone with a determination to hear, to understand and believe every word being spoken to her. Ina, sitting, sipping, wanted Helene to believe as much as Helene wanted to be put at ease.

"I was very *worried* about you," Helene said, nervously twisting a button on her sweater. "I call you . . . and a strange man answers." With just a hint of suspicion, she said, "Tell me again who he is."

So she had begun to have her doubts. She was sitting up a little straighter, the phone held less feverishly, no longer an icon.

"He wants children?" she asked suddenly, causing Ina to nearly choke on her mouthful of lukewarm beer.

"What does he do for a living?"

These questions seemed not to take Amanda aback, for Helene listened with genuine interest, even a softening of the skeptical set in her face, to whatever her daughter was telling her.

"Should I come home? I'd like to meet him," said Helene.

Ina filled in Amanda's reply.

"It was Ina's idea, really. A trip to see her kids. Her idea of an adventure," Helene said.

She listened again, still worrying her sweater button; her expression grew impatient, affronted.

"I'm an *excellent* driver," she said. "We travel when traffic is at a minimum. We don't go fast. And Ina tells me where to go."

Ina swirled beer in her mouth. Footsteps marched past on the gravel drive. Mr. Hendricks? A new customer?

"This is costing you a fortune," Helene said, her traditional long-distance kiss-off. "He sounds promising," she said. "I'd like to meet him when I get back."

A pause, then:

"All right, sweetheart. I love you, too. Good-bye."

Wordlessly she held the phone out, and Ina put it in its place. When Helene was certain there was no chance of Amanda's overhearing, she remarked, "He sounds nice enough. In her estimation. And I'm tempted to believe her, snot though he was to me."

"What did she tell you about him?"

"His name is *Gordon*. She met him after we left on our trip," Helene said. "He's two years younger than her, but says he still wants to try and have children. He works two jobs and lives with his sister."

"What jobs?" Ina wondered, fascinated by Amanda's creation.

"He's a teacher. And a bartender, which doesn't thrill me. But teachers aren't paid nearly enough, you know. They've talked about buying a house together. He was in her apartment when I called because he had a free period and she asked him to pick up her dress from the cleaners—they were going dancing after work."

"What a prince," said Ina.

"I only wish he'd been civil on the phone," Helene said.

"He was probably in a hurry."

"He wasn't too hurried to be rude," Helene said, and her hand grabbed for something in the air as she spoke; an instant later her sweater button bounced on the floor with a diminishing series of clicks and they were on the road again before Ina remembered she had never bothered to look for it.

PART SIX

◆ ——————————————————————

Old Bats
Out of Hell

Roads in the west were perfect for their needs, running wide and forgiving and lacking in surprises. Approaching traffic proclaimed itself from miles away as two small jewels that took on weight and luster during the long interval preceding their arrival. Ina coaxed speed from Helene, letting them slip up on forty mph, and even a little beyond. She felt there was room for error. The side of the road looked harmless, a soft bed of sand and stones worn to nubs by the incessant wind. Ina was prepared to send Helene and their car into this dark zone, confident they would have time to stop before encountering anything of substance.

In daylight, examining their surroundings from a motel window, she saw low, old, red mountains in the distance, always in the distance. The desert floor was scratchy and irritable. Lizards sunned on the warm hood of the Omega. Cacti shaped like spiny balls were uprooted by the wind and bounced off the tires. Ina went outdoors only for ice. When darkness fell she reloaded the car while a fine, burning sand scoured away at her old skin. The roads themselves had an indirectness that aggravated Ina no end. Too much land, she decided. Too much craving to see all of it. Aside from the streaking US 10, with its point-to-point commercial ambiance and battleship trucks, the other roads seemed in no hurry to get anywhere. They were full of unmarked small digressions that tempted Ina with the possibility of making more progress. She resisted, fearing the desert, the emptiness, and most of all the cold that seemed an improbable memory during the day, but that frosted the glass like an animal's breath as they traveled.

She was worried about the Omega. The car was running fine,

but at a routine gas stop on the Arkansas-Texas border the car's oil was down a quart. It was down that much again 245 miles (and four days) later, when they stopped for gas again. Without telling Helene, Ina stowed a case of high-grade oil in the trunk and topped off the crankcase each morning before setting out. Consequently she tried to maintain a route that stuck close to the interstate, now and then passing beneath it, in order that help would not be too far away should they break down.

But the roads were poorly marked and in the dark she lost her sense of direction. There were entire nights when she just guided Helene's sure touch without knowing where they were, whether they were even heading west. Time lost its meaning on those nights. They drove until sunrise, Ina praying it would rise at their backs. One morning the horizon ahead of them began to bleed away, and like a pilot reluctant to scare the passengers, Ina got Helene headed west again with a roundabout series of turns that Helene didn't notice (or didn't mention). Ina steered them toward a motel she had seen some miles back. The place was nice and they stayed an extra day. Ina needed the time. She never calculated how many miles back toward Chicago they had traveled.

No question, she was ready for the trip to end. In her planning she had not foreseen the vastness of the land they would be crossing. It had been merely maps spread before her, a distance large in theory, even imposing. But with her sister, a good car, food, beer, money, curiosity, and a little time, it seemed a nation they would be able to shape to their own use as they passed through it.

West of Dallas, she had felt herself start to slip. The land, rather than slide beneath them in their inexorable passage to L.A., started to grow, expand, an expanse growing more imposing as they attempted to cross it. In the emptiness on the fringes of Lubbock, Texas, they struck something that Ina didn't see in the road and flattened a tire. She opened a beer, making no motion toward even a hint of getting out and putting on the spare.

"Are we just going to sit here forever?" asked Helene.

"We have plenty of gas. It's warm in here. The sun will be up in a couple hours. Until then, I'm content," Ina said, imagining an oil stain flowering under the car, wondering what Vincent would see in it.

"Didn't you plan for this contingency?" Helene's question was not sarcastic, merely surprised. "Surely you knew there would be problems," she said.

In fact, Ina had imagined a trip beset by problems, but problems that fell in an orderly fashion, easily solved, with the least restraint placed on their steady progress westward. These problems would take place within a society crowded with mechanics, attendants, tow truck drivers, and good samaritans eager to accept her money in return for solving her problem. But in the cold wind west of Lubbock there was no one to take her money. She even fingered a packet of bills, as if the soft rustle of cash might attract someone.

A little snow snapped past in the wind. Then came streams of dust, paper scraps, the flickering of someone's hat. The space out in the darkness gave the impression of being utterly flat, ironed smooth with heat and wind. She wished fervently to be on their way, so that they might leave the place behind as something avoided in the dark.

Helene slept for an hour with her head against a pillow jammed into the angle of the door and the seat. Ina adopted a similar pose on her side of the car, but to study, to remember, to drink, not to sleep. Her body clock in the course of the long trip had turned itself around sufficiently for her to be most awake during the hours of actual travel. Helene could fall asleep within a half hour of checking into the morning's motel, but increasingly Ina required two or three hours of reading and beer to relax. She cherished that time alone for the absolute freedom from responsibility it presented. It was time bittersweetly reminiscent of the most hectic years of motherhood, when moments to herself were like gold coins she discovered rarely in the quiet corners of her tumultuous house. There were children who would never leave her alone, who in time pulled away from her, turned her out in her own home, and toward whom she now traveled with an undeniable impatience and anticipation.

A gust of wind shook the car so hard beer splashed on her

dress. She patted the wet spot with a paper napkin. The dress needed washing anyway. She looked forward to doing her wash in one of Ray's machines, pouring quarters into the slot to enrich her favorite child, in hopes that he would invite her to live with him. He was the obvious choice. With no wife or children, he presented the fewest obstacles to her moving in. Ray also reminded her of Vincent.

Ina reached to turn up the heater a notch. Helene's petite skull reposed atop the lumpy hill of her coat draped backward over her sleeping form. A blue sedan with an official look hurtled past, kicking pebbles off the side of their car. A hundred yards past, in answer to Ina's diminishing prayer, the brake lights flashed and the car returned to them. An airman in the U.S. Air Force offered assistance, calling to them across the buffeted road. His girlfriend or his wife sat pressed against him. Ina got out of the car. The wind tore at her hair, at her thin coat. The airman ran across the road to her. He wore mittens with slots in the palms so his fingers could emerge from the warmth to work. He urged Ina to take Helene and wait in his car. But she had forgotten all the places she had hidden her money and she didn't want wads of it blowing away, so she stood at the rear of the car while the airman dug through the luggage and removed the jack and spare.

"Go get in my car!" he shouted.

"My sister—will she be all right where she is?"

"She might knock over the jack."

"She's asleep. I don't want to disturb her."

"Okay. Go! You're making me cold."

Ina checked on Helene: to be sure she was asleep, to be sure the car was warm, to get her beer. The airman's girl slid over to make room as Ina got behind the wheel. The girl had hung an Air Force dress coat over her shoulders, her slim bare legs tucked beneath her. She had on a dark silk blouse, but no shoes or stockings, and she wore striped boxer shorts that apparently belonged to the airman as well.

"Won't that nice man buy you any clothes of your own?" Ina asked with a nervous smile.

The girl laughed and attempted to pull her disparate garments tighter around her. Her hair fell across one eye and she flicked it back with a finger. She smelled of something volatile. Ina thought she looked younger than Meaghan.

"This thing have heat?"

"It's on full blast," she said, her voice resigned, with a twang. "Government issue—don't work so hot."

"We appreciate your stopping. We might have been here for the winter if you hadn't happened along."

"Come daylight you could get help," she said.

Ina watched Helene as the car was jacked up off its punctured tire.

"Can I lend you a dress? You're shivering."

"No, thanks. We'll be home soon enough. I got clothes there."

"I've got some extra clothes in the trunk. Not your style—but you could mail them to me in California."

"You're going to California? We was almost stationed there at Edwards—but we got Reese." She chewed her fingernail; a fleck of something dark came off on her tooth. "I'm hoping for Europe next. Or maybe Japan."

"What happened to your clothes?" Ina asked.

"Lost 'em," she said. "He lost 'em playing cards. He and his buddies was playing for wives. I'll get 'em back by and by. They was just an old skirt, old civvies. Don't pay to wear any good stuff to poker night." She sat up straighter, then took a pack of cigarettes off the dash and lit one with a match from her purse.

"Lighter don't work," she explained. Ina thought she was a pretty girl; putting on a little weight under the jaw, but her eyes were large, knowing, dangerously bored.

"Dewey had to get some hot cards just to save me my shirt," she said. "I thought surely I was going home with Fred and Dot."

"Yes?"

"Fred was the big winner. Luckily he won Evelyn Sargent—and not me."

"What does that involve?" Ina asked.

"It's up to them," the girl said, smoking. "Fred and Dot live off base. Evelyn and Tom live on. They might go home, have one more drink, then go to sleep. Fred and Evelyn might do it. Would

Dot let them? I don't know—she seems like she might be the type. Tom'll go pick up Evelyn in the morning. Once the game's over, it's nobody's business what anyone else does with anyone else. I believe that truly."

"What do you do while your husbands play cards?"

She sucked in smoke, clasping the cigarette with her teeth in an unattractive fashion.

"We talk about things. Base things. Who's got a promotion. Who's expecting. Who's getting sent where," she said. "We have some drinks. Talk about the game."

"Don't you get nervous?"

"I used to get real embarrassed," she admitted.

"And each hand that your husband loses, you take off an item of clothing?"

"Why . . . yes. You're asking so many questions."

"It's so beyond anything I ever experienced—or even heard of," Ina said. "If someone had told me, I wouldn't believe them."

"It's just a way to do something a little out of the ordinary," the girl said. "The guy who wins each hand can tell the losers' wives what to take off. He also wins the right to have his wife put something back on. We've worked up some ground rules—no fair starting off with blouses or pants. Traditionally we all start with the shoes, then stockings, and so on. Some of them wives come with so many sweaters, socks, camisoles, football jerseys, T-shirts, and what have you—I wonder what all the fuss is about. The first guy who lets his wife lose all her clothes loses his wife to the winner of that hand. Tom just had no cards tonight."

"Don't you get your clothes back at the end of the night?" Ina asked.

"It's up to the winning couple. I was standing there with no undies until Dewey was *gallant* enough to give me his right in front of everybody. Fred and Dot are pricks. They'll have all the clothes in a pile at their place next week—winners host—and we'll all sort through it. Dot, at least, is nice enough to launder the stuff. But she don't iron, so you get your stuff back kind of in a mess."

Her husband had finished the job and put the bad tire in Ina's trunk. He lowered the car onto its new tire and stowed the jack. A very reluctant morning light had begun to seep up in the east.

"Did Dewey ever lose you?" Ina asked.

The girl placed her hand on Ina's arm, met her curious gaze. "He wouldn't dare," she said.

THEN, on a highway in Arizona, Helene finally struck something of consequence with the car. They were in the final hour of the night's travel, moving faster than was probably necessary through a neighborhood on the eastern edge of the Phoenix sprawl. The yards were landscaped with pastel gravel and cacti in pots. Ina had been pushing Helene ever since they entered Arizona. Having reached a state contiguous to California, the completion of the trip seemed not just possible, but inevitable, and the time and distance remaining (plus the time and distance already traveled) made Ina impatient to arrive. They had been running most nights at thirty-five to forty mph, and Ina had been keeping them on the road until 5:00 A.M., sometimes starting out an hour before midnight. The desert roads seemed uninhabited. For one night's leg in New Mexico they had covered two hundred miles without encountering a single car. Their solitude became spooky toward the end. Ina directed them into Teepee Town (where the cabins had round rooms and ceilings that came to a point) with immense relief. They had been traveling in a land that might have been entirely of her imagination; the rigors of imagining the dusty ground, the chilled darkness, the star-gorged sky, the startled, flaring eyes at the side of the highway, had drained her of the energy to imagine people to fill that world.

Coming up on Phoenix she directed Helene to stop at a stop sign. A dark old car, its left headlight out, waited at the opposite side of the intersection.

"There's a car facing us across the intersection," Ina told Helene. She waited for the other driver to proceed, but he did not. She checked left and right. "I guess he isn't going to move," Ina said. "Go ahead."

They had been on the road so long, traveling in this manner, that Ina allowed her eyes to swing to the right in an idle taking-in of the scenery illuminated by an orange highway light above the intersection. She was as shocked as Helene when they hit the other car as it tried to turn left in front of them.

Ina's head shot forward and in her recoil she felt something tear in the side of her neck. She was left with a hot pain that immediately began to subside into a cool sensation of liquid running beneath her skin.

Helene began to scream. Their car was stopped; she'd had wits enough to put the thing in Park. But she was shrieking in pain and surprise, her hands held away from the wheel as if it were scorching, and a little cut bled beneath her nose, the residue of a bounce off the steering wheel.

She screamed on and on—and her screams took form, coalescing into a tirade of condemnation against Ina for bringing them on the trip, getting them that far, and then allowing them to blunder into an accident when they were so close to California.

The driver of the other car had emerged. Ina was relieved to see that he was an old man. He was possibly older than the widows, judging by the labored manner in which he circled his car to inspect the damage. He appeared translucent in the light, with a thin white shirt buttoned to the throat, baggy pants, black socks, and open-toed sandals.

"Helene! Helene!" Ina ordered in a harsh whisper. "Shut up, Helene! Shut up!" She pinched her sister's arm. "Helene! Listen! We've only got a second now to get our story together. Are you listening?"

Helene, to her credit, went silent. She sniffed and dabbed at her nose with a hanky produced from the notch in her door's armrest.

"The other driver is an old man. Older than us. He's looking at the damage now," Ina said. "Now listen—when I say so you open your door and get out. I'm going to slide out your door, too. We have to confuse him. I'm going to tell him I was driving. We can't let on you're blind. Got that?"

Helene nodded.

"All right. Go."

Helene fought with the door, then unlocked it, then finally

stumbled out into the road. She hugged the car's flank and listened for her sister. The other driver glanced her way; he was raptly fingering the damage to his car.

Ina took the key from the ignition as she slid out and shut the door.

"You wear sunglasses at night," the man said. "Of course you can't see."

"I'm not wearing sunglasses," Ina said, dismayed that the question of who was driving would arise so soon.

"Not you. Her." He jabbed a finger at Helene.

"She wasn't driving. I was."

"*She* was driving," the man said, jabbing again. "I saw. I *watched.*"

"You're mistaken," Ina said carefully. "I was driving."

"You're lying, ma'am. That woman in the sunglasses was driving your car," the man said.

"The police will sort that out," Ina said with a dismissive air. She was cold standing there in the middle of the road, with the land beyond the orange illumination a riddle of clicks and rustles and odd cries.

"You've been drinking, ma'am," the man said, something like glee in his voice.

"My . . . you are full of accusations," Ina said.

"You're a couple of drunks who hit my car when I tried to turn," he said.

"A turn for which you didn't signal."

"I signaled."

"You used no signal, sir. Furthermore, do you intend to have some insurance company pay for your broken headlight?"

"My lights were perfect," he said. "Until you hit me."

"Your left headlight was out," Ina said.

Helene, perhaps weary of the argument, perhaps just chilly, told Ina in a low voice that she was going to wait in the car. She quite expertly found her way behind the wheel, then slid on across to Ina's seat, a touch Ina appreciated.

"And *she* was driving," the man repeated.

"Silly man," said Ina. "Get the police." She returned to the car and pulled the door shut on them. It felt strange, sitting behind the wheel, with Helene to her right. The car felt off balance and unnatural.

Helene said, "I should have a little of your beer."

"Why?"

"If you're the driver, I'll have to be the drunk."

"But what about the rest of the night? Who'll drive us to the motel?"

"I'm not going to get drunk. Just get the smell on my breath," Helene said. "We've had an accident with liquor in the car. We're in trouble regardless. Find a mint in my bag. We've got to tame your beer breath."

"I have beer breath?"

"Do you think it's a secret you drink?"

"I didn't know I stank."

"Perhaps not stank. Smelled. You've taken on the smell of beer."

They waited almost a half-hour before the police arrived. The sun began to rise, garishly beautiful violet light splashed across the desert. Twice drivers not yet awake or already asleep had to skid to avoid hitting their little accidental tableau. With a twitching of rear ends and tail lights these cars squeezed past.

But no one stopped. Ina assumed one of these motorists reported the wreck because although no one involved left the scene of the accident to summon the police, a squad car finally arrived, at an hour Ina earlier had trusted would find them safely in a motel, Helene asleep, and Ina proceeding toward that state.

Her breath cold from sugarless mints melted in the cavern of her smelly mouth, Ina stepped out of the car. Helene, contrary to Ina's wishes, followed, and they met up with the cop and the other driver at the point of impact, Ina and Helene on one side, the old man and the police officer on the other.

"Licenses, please," said the cop.

Ina handed over Helene's. The picture on the license was faded beneath cracked lamination, like looking at someone younger through a fogged window. There was a resemblance to the driver in the determined line of the mouth, and a certain wary squint.

"Mr. Gibbons and Mrs. Bolton," the cop read. He said to Helene, "And you were a passenger, ma'am?"

"She was driving," Gibbons barked.

"No, I was a passenger."

"You were *driving!*"

The police officer swiveled his blue-shaved jaw in turn from Gibbons to Ina to Helene, at each person seeking some bit of vital information.

"Who was driving," he asked.

"I was driving," Ina said. "My sister Ina is blind." She glanced at Mr. Gibbons. "Therefore, it isn't likely she was driving."

"Prove it," Gibbons said.

"Mr. Gibbons, please," said the cop. "Just relax, sir. *Are* you blind, ma'am?"

"Yes, sir," Helene said.

"One blind, the other one blind drunk," cackled Gibbons. "It's lucky I wasn't killed."

"Please join me in my car. All three of you," the cop said.

The backseat of the police car was closed off from the front by a heavy mesh fence bolted to the ceiling and to the back of the front seat. Helene sat up with the officer. Ina smelled disinfectant, vomit, and Mexican food. The car was warm, the air close. The rear doors and windows could not be opened from the inside and Ina felt a thrill of claustrophobia, glancing over at Gibbons, who dabbed at his forehead with a handkerchief.

She longed for another mint. That cold taste in her mouth was gone and now she feared the permanent stain left by a lifetime of beer was about to betray her.

The cop took a long time writing data on a form. A radio suspended under the dash popped and gurgled and on occasion uttered something intelligible.

"Mrs. Bolton—" the cop began, his eyes on Ina in the mirror. Ina saw Helene tense to answer, then remember where she was, *who* she was, and settle back into the silence required of her.

"Yes . . ." Ina said.

"Your license is expired. Long since expired, ma'am."

"A crime ring," muttered Gibbons.

"Please, Mr. Gibbons. Now, Mrs. Bolton, I have to ticket you for driving on an expired license."

"I understand," Ina nodded. She liked this cop; he was polite, he fit easily into the etiquette of officialdom. His dark blue shirt with light blue trim did wonders for his eyes.

"That's for starters," Gibbons burst forth. "Smell her! She's roaring drunk!"

"Mr. Gibbons, please."

The cop got out of the car, a gust of invigorating cold swirling in.

"Are you all right, dear?" Ina asked, curling her fingers through the mesh to probe at Helene's bony shoulder.

"I'm fine," said Helene.

"Blind, my ass," Gibbons snarled. "You're trying to pull some scam here. *She* was driving, and you both know it."

"You tell us your scam . . . we'll tell you ours," Ina said agreeably.

Mr. Gibbons folded his arms and looked haughtily away. "I have none," he said.

"You're trying to pull something. You've got that sneaky look about you," Ina said, leaning toward him in hopes he would be annoyed.

The cop returned. "Let's continue," he said. Nonchalantly he held a pack of gum out to Helene in offering, watching her for movement, some sign of seeing.

"Are you totally blind, ma'am?"

"Totally," said Helene.

"Have you been drinking, ma'am?"

"A little beer," Helene said, stiffening.

"It's illegal to have open beer in your car, ma'am. Were you aware of that?"

"Her husband died," Ina said, leaning forward. "We're on our way to California to retrieve him. She sips a little beer to pass the time, to ease her grief. Who does it hurt?"

"What's your name?"

"Ina Lockwood," said Helene. "My husband's name was Vincent. He was out west visiting our children. I drink a little to forget. But Helene—she doesn't touch the stuff."

"Open liquor. Bad license," Gibbons said. "What's next? Guns?"

"Mr. Gibbons, please."

"*She* was driving. The one up front there was driving," Gibbons persisted, punching at the screen. "I was goddamned paying attention. My senses were clear and I watched them get out of the car. *Her* first, then this one."

"She's blind, Mr. Gibbons," the cop said.

"Blind. *Schmind.* I don't care what they say. *She* was driving."

"Just relax, sir. This is taking way too much time for a minor traffic accident." He met Ina's eyes in the mirror. "And you, Mrs. Bolton, were you drinking?"

"No, sir. At night, after a hard day of traveling, I'll have a glass of something to relax. But nothing more," Ina said.

"All right. Now, Mr. Gibbons. Tell us your version of the accident," the cop said.

"Can I get some air?" asked Ina. "I'm feeling a trifle faint and nauseated."

With gallant impatience the cop swung out and opened Ina's door. She felt better just to sit there with her feet on the ground, watching the drivers who glanced curiously at her as they went past. The sun was up full now, crimson on the rim of the desert. The day had turned busy. Ina was for a moment exhilarated to be awake and present on such a glorious morning.

"Ina?" the cop said, and Ina fought the impulse to turn and answer.

"Ina, where did you get that cut on your lip?"

Helene touched the soreness. A little blood had caked darkly there like a smudge of mud or the defacing on a poster.

"Why . . . I must have hit something," Helene said. She appeared to be surprised. "I'm afraid I don't remember."

"I'll tell you," Gibbons said. "The steering wheel. I saw her crack it a good one."

The cop, for the first time, did not politely shush Mr. Gibbons, and the old man glared triumphantly at the women, as if he had begun to see the battle turning his way.

"Perhaps a beer can," Helene mused. "I was having a sip when we were hit."

"Four in the morning and she's drinking," marveled Gibbons. "Death on wheels."

"Mr. Gibbons."

Ina took deep breaths of cold desert air. She expected to be asked to turn back inside and close the door.

Gibbons gave his version of the accident:

"I was at the stop sign here. I'm ready to make a left turn. This car stops across from me. I go to make my turn when they barrel across—straight into me. They start the Chinese fire drill with the drivers, trying to confuse me. But I pay attention. I'm not easily fooled."

"Where were you going?" the cop asked.

"Home."

"Where from?"

"A card game."

"You have anything to drink there?"

"No, sir. Just coffee. I quit the other stuff thirty years ago. It killed my wife."

"You were going left—turning north," the cop said. "You were traveling east, then turning north. But you live on the west end of town. Why were you going east?"

"I was looking for a place I could buy a cigar," Mr. Gibbons said. "I wasn't sleepy and I felt like having a cigar."

"You could find a cigar back toward Phoenix," the cop said.

"Maybe," Gibbons said. "It was a nice night—I didn't know I was bound by law to go straight home."

"When did the card game break up?"

"Three. Three-thirty," Gibbons said, after taking a moment to remember.

"And your host's name?"

"You gonna call him? He'll be dead to the world until noon. *He* drinks."

"What's his name, Mr. Gibbons?"

"He's my brother. His name is Stan."

"His phone number?"

"I don't know. He may not have a phone—but if he does I guess his number is in the book."

"Is his name Gibbons, too?"

"Stan Gibbons."

The cop squared his shoulders, rolled his neck muscles, covered a yawn.

"When you turned left, Mr. Gibbons? Did you have your signal on?"

"You bet."

"No, you didn't," said Ina.

"You'll have your say, Mrs. Bolton. Now, Mr. Gibbons. You came to a full stop? And the other car came to a full stop?"

"That's correct."

"Then you proceeded to turn left?"

"It was my turn. I was there first."

"How fast would you say you were going?" the cop asked.

"Wasn't speeding. If that's your drift."

"Did you accelerate hard into the turn? Or ease into it?"

"It was a firm turn," Gibbons allowed. "I didn't burn rubber . . . but I didn't pussyfoot it, either."

"Could you have stopped?"

"If I could've, I would've, now wouldn't I?"

"The damage to your car just seems more severe than a low-speed collision would produce," the cop said. "Your headlight's bashed clean in. You've got wrinkles in the fender almost back to the front door. Mrs. Bolton's car, on the other hand, has only minor damage. Her headlight is broken, some wrinkles in the body . . . and that's about the worst of it."

"Look at that beast she was driving," Gibbons said. "It's armor-plated. My car is made of that cheap tin and plastic crap they use nowadays."

"Thank you, Mr. Gibbons. Now, Mrs. Bolton? Your version of what happened."

Ina leaned toward the mesh partition so that she might better be heard.

"I came to a stop," she said. "Mr. Gibbons was stopped opposite me. He wasn't signaling a turn. Left *or* right. Everything seemed in order, so I proceeded into the intersection, where Mr. Gibbons struck me."

"Were you hurt?" the cop asked.

"What about me?" Mr. Gibbons demanded petulantly. "You didn't ask me if I was hurt."

"I'm sorry. Were you hurt?"

"No. But you could've asked."

"You're right. I should have," the cop asked. "Were you hurt, Mrs. Bolton?"

"I felt something snap or burn in my neck," Ina said, placing a finger on the spot. "Then it turned cool. Wet-feeling. I don't think it was anything."

"I'll bet you have a lawyer, too," Gibbons said.

"I wanted to be sure to mention," said Ina, "that Mr. Gibbons' left headlight was out."

"After you hit it," Gibbons claimed.

"No. Before."

"Mr. Gibbons," said the cop, "were you in another accident earlier?"

Ina turned to look at the old man, curious herself. He had in an instant composed his face in its familiar expression of pitying disgust, but for the breadth of that instant his face had gone soft with relief and defenselessness and in that look Ina saw his scheme laid open for anyone to imagine: In the night (maybe not even *that* night, but a night of recent vintage) Gibbons had hit something with his car. Perhaps another car, or a man crossing the street, or a young woman home late from work and retrieving the mail from the box by the road, or a child running out of that pocket of invisibility that haunted the widows with its potential for tragedy. Perhaps he had been drinking and didn't know what he had hit, but only awoke in the morning to find his car scarred, his mind empty. Whatever—he had struck something. In the scrambled moments after impact he had run away. He stayed out of sight for a time (an hour, a day), thinking and plotting. And on the night in question he took his damaged car and lay in wait for someone to hit, and thus create a fresh, innocent history for the marks left by the mistake he was running from.

"This accident . . . *this* accident right here," said Gibbons, "is the only accident I've been involved in tonight or any other night."

The cop wrote in silence for several minutes, then presented Ina and Gibbons with tickets that ordered them to appear in court on a date six weeks' hence. Ina knew she would not be there; she doubted she would set foot in Arizona again. She was curious what charges Gibbons faced, but he folded his ticket into his pocket and said, "Let me out."

"One moment," said the cop. He continued to write, then said, "Mr. Gibbons. Mrs. Bolton. These are serious charges you both face. I'll have to hold your licenses until the court date. Since you are at odds over who is at fault in the accident you both may wish to hire an attorney. There are good ones around. My name is there on your ticket. I'll be at your hearing. If you have any other questions, I can be reached at that number from seven-fifteen to seven-thirty A.M., Wednesday through Sunday. Drive safely."

He set them free, then, Ina first, so that when they opened the door for Helene she would have Ina to help her. Gibbons backed his car away from the position it had assumed on impact. He turned around and disappeared to the west.

"No cigar," the cop said to Ina, with a little smile of detection.

Ina almost put Helene in the driver's seat, but she felt she was being subjected to a small test much like Mr. Gibbons had undergone when the cop noticed the old man had gone home without his cigar. She got Helene to the passenger's door and discovered it was locked. She had slid out the other door in exiting. Now they stood helpless under the curious inspection of the police. Even the location of the keys was a mystery to her.

"Wait here," she said.

"Where?"

"*Here*. Don't move."

"Is the policeman still there?"

"He's watching us." She went to the driver's side of the car.

Silvery headlight debris was flung out on the road. But the cop's assessment had been correct: Beyond the broken headlight, the car seemed barely nudged. She got in, reached over and unlocked the other door, then went back out to get her sister.

"Now we can go," said Ina. She positioned Helene clear of the door's lumbering arc, then opened it.

"Get in. You're very close. The seat back is an inch from your hand. There."

"You're driving?"

"He's watching us. Who do you suggest drive?"

Helene grimaced. "Could he tell us apart? Could we pull a switch in the car? One of the charming Mr. Gibbons' Chinese fire drills?"

"Don't be silly, dear. Pull your feet in before I cut them off with this door."

Ina was ready to move. She felt they had been stuck too long on that point in their journey. Hours ago she had looked away, exhausted by uneventfulness, and ever since then they had been trapped by that moment of inattention and Mr. Gibbons.

"Put on your seatbelt," Helene said. "The policeman will note that immediately. It labels you as a careful, conscientious driver. Me—I'll take a swig of beer."

"Don't you dare."

"Breakfast. A bath. A nice soft bed," Helene said dreamily. "That's what I'm in the mood for."

"Great. Get us out of here," Ina said.

"Which way are we pointing?"

"Straight west."

"All right," said Helene with a nod. "See the D on the steering column? You know how to put it in drive, don't you?"

"I think I do, though I never have."

"Put your foot on the brake. The pedal on the left," Helene said. "Get us out of the policeman's sight and I'll take over."

"It's daylight," said Ina.

"It is? It feels dark to me."

"Do you have the key?"

"In the ignition."

Ina fingered the slot, though she remembered taking the keys as they exited the car to confront Mr. Gibbons.

"I removed them after the accident," Ina said, feeling dazed. What she feared most was someone honking at her, drawing attention to her. She was frankly amazed at how little they impeded traffic. The cop's presence helped; people weren't inclined to complain. But cars skirted them as if they were a poorly situated historical monument grown familiar over time.

"Are they in your purse? Your pockets?" Helene asked. "I thought the engine was running all this time."

"No, dear. That's the vibration of the traffic we're sitting in the middle of," Ina said. "Did I give them to Mr. Gibbons?"

"Why on earth would you?"

Ina turned her purse over on her lap. An impressive little avalanche of tissues and cash rumbled out, propelled by the weight of at least thirty dollars in change, including a roll of quarters she had forgotten she was carrying.

"No keys," Ina said. She squinted out the window, into sunlight that was suddenly painful. The cop had not moved. Off to the side, out of the flow, he simply watched. Ina longed to spy the sparkling pile of keys somewhere between herself and the cop, fetch them, and *proceed*. Years had passed since they had arrived at that spot.

"Here," Helene held out a pair of keys to Ina. "Our spares. Lose them at your peril."

Ina found the ignition key and stuck it greedily in. The engine's power shocked her when she turned it on. The seat behind the wheel was full of a danger she had not recognized in her lifetime as a passenger.

"Caution, dear," warned Helene. "Did you adjust your mirrors?" The side mirror was fine, but the rearview mirror was skewed for the passenger's use, so Ina turned it until the land behind the car came into view. "Thank you," she said. "I hadn't."

"You must think like a driver now."

Ina put the car in Drive, her left foot crushing the brake pedal, and she felt the buried nudge of power engage somewhere beneath her. A long blue truck slid before her eyes; she read silver letters taller than herself flashing by, but they did not come together in her brain as words. Next passed a yellow sports car, then a school bus with sleepy children stuck to the windows.

"Traffic, dear?" asked Helene.

"There's so much of it."

"I used to like traffic," Helene mused. "Rudy hated it. But I liked looking at the people. People with fancy cars looking so superior. Poor people, though, never looked embarrassed about their cars."

"Quiet, dear," warned Ina. "I see a gap."

The opening was not in front of them, but was proceeding toward them from the north; a window adequate for passage by an overly cautious driver. The vehicle at the far end of the opening, still well down the highway, was an old pickup traveling at a pace that impatient drivers would consider annoying. Ina counted down the cars to the gap and then the gap arrived and she sent them forward too quickly. Helene rocked. Scenes, neighborhoods, endangered objects flashed by. Ina watched the old pickup pass across her rearview mirror. Out the side mirror she caught a last glimpse of the cop. He wasn't even watching, which was a disappointment in light of her successful transit of the intersection. When she looked back at the road she had begun to drift left, in the direction of her glance in the mirror, and she tapped the brakes and swung the wheel too far to the right, so that Helene rolled against the door and a car on their tail honked and swooped around them. Ina stopped the car.

"We there?" Helene asking brightly.

"Smartmouth," Ina replied. She was trying to catch her breath. She had been a passenger all her life and in that time she had never once paid attention to Vincent's way of handling a car. She thought she might have picked up some of his rhythm through simple observation, but she had not. She was helpless.

"See. You do need me," Helene said.

"Slide over," Ina ordered.

"Is it in Park?"

"Yes."

"Is the cop gone?"

Ina looked in the mirror. They had gone around a gentle curve and the intersection was out of sight.

"Yes. Hurry."

Ina guided Helene back behind the wheel. She was in a chipper, vinegary mood, and Ina was glad to be riding again.

"Have you seen a motel?"

"No, dear. I'm not keeping us on the road out of spite."

"I need to get off my feet. I'm losing sensation."

"I'm looking."

She had no idea where they were going, where they were; she kept them pointed west. There was no avoiding traffic. Every street seemed to be a major thoroughfare, clogged, overwrought, impatient, and the widows' painstaking car was a plug in the system. They were cursed at, tailgated, given the finger, chewed out, harangued, and Ina felt her clothes soaked through the back with nervous perspiration.

"Find a motel," Helene said. "I'm begging."

Ina did, a mile on. The Desert Flower Inn was H-shaped, the color of sand, and boasted of microwave ovens in the rooms. Ina paid in cash while Helene fidgeted in her seat. Then while Helene used the bathroom, Ina unpacked the car. The broken headlight was like an irritation so minor it was easily forgotten. Yet she felt it must be attended to before she freed herself to the bliss of beer and sleep. Now that they were off the highway the pull of exhaustion was narcotic. Her body was stiff and sore; her head ached from the concentration required of travel and deceit.

"You know someone who could fix our headlight?" Ina asked of the desk clerk, a young woman smoking a thin black cigarette in a pink holder. She looked beyond Ina to the car.

"What happened?"

"Somebody broke it. We were eating dinner and when we came out it had been bashed in," Ina said.

"You got an out-of-state plate?"

"Illinois."

"There you are," the clerk said. "People don't want outsiders in Arizona anymore. You're expanding farther and farther into the desert. You're using up all our water. Some days it's hardly a trickle comes out of the faucet. And the price! You'd think it was fine wine."

"We're just passing through," Ina said.

"The person who busted your light . . . he didn't know that. He couldn't take chances."

"Can anyone fix my light?"

"My boyfriend will be in later. I'll ask him."

Ina gave the woman a twenty-dollar bill; it retained its tubular bent after a long journey rolled up in hiding.

"Give him this. It should cover a new light—and any labor," Ina said. "If he needs more, let me know."

"Keep your money," said the woman. "Tom'll do the job—*then* you can pay him. If he gets the money up front he might be wrongly encouraged."

Ina backed out the door, nodding, practically bowing, pushing the twenty out of sight. Elated to have done something about the headlight, she hurried to their room.

"Where have you been?" asked Helene.

"At the office. Trying to get the headlight fixed."

"And did you?"

"I don't know. I might have set the process in motion," Ina said. "Do we need ice?"

"We could use some. There's no water, either. I went to wash my face and nothing came out of the taps," said Helene.

"Nothing?"

"Not *nothing*. But barely enough to work up a decent froth," Helene complained.

"The clerk said water here is dear."

"Or course. We're in the desert."

"And you got us here," Ina said like a booster. "A blind woman drove from Chicago to Phoenix, Arizona. You should be proud."

"I am," said Helene.

THEY awoke in the afternoon sunshine, Ina with a headache from too little sleep. The headlight had not been repaired. She had wanted to awaken late, in the dark, to find the day cleansed and forgotten. But they were still snared on the shards of the accident, the headlight a wound that wouldn't close.

She talked Helene into taking some sun. Helene reclined, wrapped in an afghan, her face turned to the west, her lenses aglow, giving Ina the privacy to reach Amanda, out of breath from something.

"It's me," Ina said.

"Wait," Amanda answered, dropping the phone. "Are you in L.A.?" she asked, winded, the background of her voice speckled with thumps and errant cracklings.

"No. What is that?"

"I'm putting away groceries. Where are you?"

"We're getting close."

"I'm ready to come to L.A."

"Did you really call the police on us?"

"Why?"

"Because we were stopped," Ina said. "I'm sure they checked us out. But nothing was mentioned of our escapade."

"Maybe the cops of wherever you are aren't hooked in," Amanda said.

"Everyone is hooked into everyone else," said Ina.

"Why were you stopped?"

"We hit something."

"A busload of gifted children?"

"No. An old grump," Ina said. "He hit us as much as we hit him. I became Helene—the driver. Helene became me—transporter of alcohol. The drunk."

"I bet she loved that," Amanda said.

"She was good."

"Where are you? How close to L.A.?"

"Arizona. I'm not getting any more specific."

"Arizona? You're just a couple old bats out of hell," said Amanda, laughing.

"Hush," Ina said.

"I'm ready for a change," Amanda said, her voice going low, as if into hiding. "I'm thinking of quitting my job, starting fresh. Maybe in L.A. I'll know people. I'll have family."

"Is he there?" asked Ina.

"He just left. We took the day off work," Amanda said. "You see? I do that for him—I don't even consider what's best for me. He goes home. I'm alone for the night and I can't even go to work. L.A. sounds very appealing right now."

"Wait until we get there," Ina said. "We'll scout it out for you—and then call you. Don't quit your job. And don't let that guy cause you to lose it, either."

A man began to speak, loud and insistent, on the walk in front of their room. Ina saw Helene turn toward the sound; her lenses threw off sparks.

"Let me call you back, sweetheart," said Ina. "Don't do anything rash."

She hurried outside, afraid for Helene, but Helene had hidden her blindness behind a vague air of detachment that had the man confused as to how to continue. He was a fat man in tight clothes and he set Ina's nerves on edge with intimations of discomfort. He balanced a hat like a cake plate on the tips of his chubby fingers.

"I'm Tom. I've come for the money to fix your headlight," he said.

"Will twenty dollars be enough?" asked Ina.

"The headlight was eleven dollars. My labor was fifteen. Call it twenty-five."

"Do you need the money now, or when you're finished?"

Tom put on his hat. "I finished two hours ago."

Ina, perplexed, stepped to the car and placed her fingers inside the mirrored cavity of the shattered headlight.

Tom said, "I can't vouch for what happened after I put in the new light. But I'm bound to be paid the money for the work I done."

"I'm appalled," said Ina.

"A terrible thing," Tom agreed. "A horrible welcome to Arizona."

"Do you have a receipt for the new headlight?" Helene asked from behind Ina.

"Sure do," Tom said. He produced a yellow receipt from his

shirt pocket. It was for $11.27, for a headlight. Ina put the receipt in Helene's grasp and she perused it at some length before handing it back.

"Where is the broken glass from the headlight?" Ina asked. The ground beneath the broken light looked nearly scrubbed.

"Maybe they cleaned it up," Tom suggested, causing the widows to laugh at him.

Ina went to her purse and took out money, which she handed over to Tom. "Use this to fix our headlight *again*," she said. "I'll pay you for the second light when you're finished."

"I'll get my tools," he said, departing.

"We had him," Helene complained.

"What did we have? He had to be paid at least once for doing the light," Ina said. "Now he's been paid. He'll fix the light— and if he insists on being paid again, perhaps then I'll let you at him."

"He sounded slimy," said Helene. "He smelled of close quarters. What if he comes back in four hours and says he fixed the headlight but vandals smashed it and cleaned up after themselves again?"

"He won't," said Ina. "He knows we had him this time."

Nevertheless, Helene sat like a sentry with a magazine in her lap while Tom repaired the headlight. Ina watched from the room, but soon lost interest and closed the shades against the sun. She drank a beer, wondering if the time had come to call ahead to her children. Her buzz left her feeling majestic and selfish for sleep. Having the headlight fixed reassured her; they could move on when they were ready. Through a gap in the door she heard Tom inform Helene that he was finished and that he wished to be paid. Ina admired his determination to play a scheme through to completion. Helene replied in an even, condescending tone that her sister handled the money, but she was asleep and in need of her rest and not to be disturbed, and would upon awakening leave the money with his girlfriend at the front desk. Tom seemed to hesitate at this arrangement; perhaps he had no ally in his girlfriend. But he was no match for Helene's obstinate, blank glare, and so he took his box of tools and went away.

They hit the road at midnight. Following a southern dip toward the California border to avoid mountains that Ina saw ahead on the map, they progressed at a decent clip through a night icy with stars. The beam of the new headlight was skewed up and out, as though they drove in search of something living in the air along the side of the road. Ina did not mention the cockeyed beam to Helene, who drove with loose-wristed aplomb, happy to be back on the road. At the end of the night's trip they were still in the desert and they remained there for three more nights of travel.

Late in their travels, Ina announced, "We've come to the Colorado River."

Beyond the river, at the California border, they were stopped at a checkpoint, as if passing into a foreign country.

A man in a California Department of Agriculture uniform asked them to get out of the car. He shined a light in their faces, not with any true malevolence, but sort of a benign curiosity.

Ina put a hand on Helene's arm, bidding her to stay where she was and keep her mouth shut.

"Turn off the engine, ma'am," the man said. "Hand me the keys. You oughtn't to be driving at night with sunglasses on."

Ina brought the keys around with her and unlocked the trunk. It was a beautiful night, a fragrant cool sparkle to the air.

The inspector leaned into the trunk with his poking beam.

"Do we look suspicious?" Ina asked.

The man straightened, wincing at some pain in his spine. He was a tall man with a pot belly and stooped shoulders.

"Fact is, you look so innocent you made me suspicious," he said. He began to pull out suitcases, lining them up at the side of the road. Then he took the cooler and overnight bags and blankets out of the backseat until a small mountain of stuff they probably didn't need in the first place had risen there.

"I have a little alarm in my head and you set if right off," he said. "Illinois plates, odd hour to be traveling for two elderly women. Plenty of places to hide contraband pests."

"Do we have to open all our bags?"

"We'll see," he said. "There are plenty of people who would

love to cripple California's agriculture. Illinois, for instance? Put
a dent in our society. People go hungry. Other countries—states,
like Illinois—pick up the slack. That's money out of our pockets.
Hell, governments have fallen for less. A little jar of medfly larvae
emptied here and there, this state would be on its knees. And not
just the medfly. Orangeworms. Scales. Buck bugs. Laser flies.
Chink beetles. And new ones being grown all the time. We've
got to be on our toes—all the time. Which bag do you want me
to inspect? I'll do one you choose, and one of my own choice,
OK?''

"I don't care. We aren't carrying bugs," Ina said.

"A shrewd answer. Put the pressure on me," he said. "By not
choosing, you rob me of the chance to try and read the hidden
meanings in your choice."

"There are no hidden meanings," Ina said. "Or bugs."

He picked out a small overnight bag and opened the latches.
The bag contained Ina's toiletries, her comb and brush, a stick
deodorant, a small pouch to hold what little makeup she wore.
He removed a Band-Aid box and emptied it in his palm: two
dozen Band-Aids, and beneath them a tight little roll of money
she had forgotten was hidden there.

The inspector looked up at her. She felt guilty, she didn't know
why.

"Traveling money," she explained.

He opened the bundle and counted, wetting his fingers, tenderly peeling the bills apart.

"Two hundred dollars," he said.

"I carry it that way to lessen the risk of losing it all at once,"
Ina said.

"What if you forget where you put it?"

"I know where every dollar is," Ina said.

He put the money back, packed the Band-Aids on top. The
next bag he opened belonged to Helene and in a side pocket he
discovered a supply of spare syringes.

"My sister is diabetic," Ina said. "She gives herself shots."

"I see. Where should I look next?"

"Look in this one," Ina said.

"Why there?"

"I'm trying to be helpful. You could have inspected them all in the time we've been standing here," she said, getting impatient to be moving. The sun was coming up; the air was full of bats going home and she feared one snagging in her hair.

He settled on one more bag, the biggest, a monster on wheels they had been stuffing with dirty clothes because Ina did not want to stop and do laundry, and because she envisioned presenting Ray with this bounty like treasure, a sign of abject devotion.

The clothes didn't smell too bad: stale, musty, old. But the inspector saw the dirty clothes as some manner of obscuring shield and he dug through them with gusto, as if the smell of old ladies' clothes was identical to the smell of some voracious herbivore. He dug deep. The air became snowy with slips, dresses, nylons, underpants, bobby socks, suspension garments. Ina caught what she could, gathered it all up in her arms; road dust, dark red and velvety to the touch, clung to the lacy edges. He emptied the bag and found no pests. In a pocket she had forgotten about he came across two more tubes of cash.

"Welcome to California," he said, and stepped around the mess he had made and went inside the station. She had to ask him to come back out and help repack the car. He sent out his partner, a sleepy young man half his age, who offered Ina a grape from the bunch he was eating.

"Can't get good fruit in California," he said. "They ship the best east. But these grapes, these are grade-A grapes."

"I'm sure. No thank you."

"Al there is paranoid about bugs," the young man said. He was intently pulling the skin off a grape with his teeth.

"My theory—they want in, they'll just fly across the border. Probably in broad daylight. What's stopping them?"

"He has a job to do," Ina said.

"I guess. We aren't even in season," he said. "But if you were carrying pests, I don't think I'd do anything but ask you to hand them over. Hand them over and be on your way. I could live with that. Al would want to prosecute. I'm not a fanatic about it."

"We aren't carrying any bugs," Ina said.

"I believe you. Deep down, Al believes you, too."

"I don't like having to pack this car twice in one night," Ina complained.

"I'm sorry." The young man helped until the job was completed.

"Back during the medfly era, Al's brother-in-law Dave, who works a station up on the Nevada border, he discovered a guy in a truck trying to sneak in a hundred crates of tainted oranges," the young man said. "They were going to leave them around the state, let them be discovered in places totally removed from the area of infestation and then California would have had to spend all that money and time to make sure the areas in between were clear. Dave was kind of a hero to the Ag Department and Al was jealous. He got Dave the job. He's been trying to catch up ever since."

"Are we free to go?" Ina asked.

"Al wants the syringes. They fall under the classification of transport vehicles," the young man said.

"My sister needs them. Her life depends on them," Ina said angrily.

"He wants at least three. You won't be reported," he said, "but Al can use them in his demonstrations when he talks to local schools about the perils to California's agricultural preeminence."

"I can spare one," Ina said.

"Three."

"One."

"Okay, two."

"One."

The young man went into the office. Ina saw him explaining the situation to Al. She opened her bag and removed a syringe.

"He'll take one," the young man said.

Ina handed it over. "Are we free to go?" she asked.

"You are free to go. Welcome to California."

They went on from there, the young inspector standing in the

road saluting as the widows pulled away. Sunlight was everywhere
and Ina had not looked ahead far enough on her maps.

They fell in behind a wagon being pulled by a tractor. The
pace was perfect. The wagon bed was loaded with farm workers,
men and women wrapped against the morning chill in blankets
and coats and torn caps. Those sitting on the left side of the
wagon, trying to be helpful, kept urging Helene to pass them
when no traffic approached. They gave directions with great enthusiasm and conviction, waving their arms and smiling to show
they could be trusted. They tried to get Helene to pass for several
minutes at a time, getting frustrated the longer their help was
ignored. Then a truck or a car would come from the opposite
direction and they would throw up their hands for the women to
stay where they were, nervous that perhaps the car behind them
was driven by an old woman confused about the rules, who
thought their waves to pass were warnings to stay put, and who
now would move out into the oncoming traffic as if they had
promised she was safe.

Traffic came up behind the Omega and was quick to go around,
the farm workers cheering as their help was accepted. But Ina
kept Helene a constant twenty yards behind the wagon. It was
the slowest they had traveled in a month. Ina had been spoiled
by the desert speeds and by traveling in the night. She doubted
the tractor and wagonload of people were going all the way to
L.A., but they were moving in that direction and she accepted
the pace.

"What are you looking forward to the most about arriving?"
Helene asked, bored.

"Arriving."

"Me, too. Why don't you call Annie and have her come and
get us?"

"Slow down. You're getting too close," Ina said. In her anticipation of arriving, Helene had accelerated slightly and cut the
distance between the Omega and the wagon in half. The people
sitting on the wagon's back lip pulled up their legs.

"I can't call Annie. You don't want me to, either."

"I don't?" Helene said.

"No. You want to finish what you started," Ina said.

"I'm willing to give myself up," Helene said. "I've proved to myself I can do this."

"If Annie comes and gets us," Ina said, "she can send us right back to Chicago on the next plane. Annie will be in control of us. But if we arrive on our own—"

"She can send us back on the next plane," Helene said.

"She could. But we'll be *there*. She'll have to kick us out of her own house."

The tractor and wagon turned down a wide lane lined with sheds.

"Slow. Slow," Ina said. "They're turning right."

"Wave to them."

"I will. I'll miss them."

Nobody on the wagon returned her salute. "They're angry with us," Ina said. "We refused their help and offended them."

"You're reading a lot into this," said Helene. "May I speed up now?"

"A smidge."

Ina had to get them off the road and out of sight. The wagon had been their protection, masking the strangeness of their traveling in daylight. Helene pushed their speed to twenty. She drove with activated emergency flashers. The road had a dangerous bend to it, with blind spaces around sandy bluffs and dips that took the road out of Ina's sight. Her imagination ran ahead faster than the car and she kept having Helene break at the tops of hills, only to encounter more mysteries down around the next curve. And once over the crest, she realized that they were out of sight of any vehicle approaching from behind, a vehicle surely moving faster than they were.

She liked the light, though. It provided more to look at, more information. It was the first time she had a sense of really seeing the country. The rest of the trip's scenery had been comprised of motel pockets, the buggy illumination above ice machines, and marvels glimpsed in the headlights. She had seen barely more of the U.S. than Helene.

A caravan of four red station wagons went by the other way.

Then a dump truck hauling a load of salt careened around the bend they were negotiating. A spray of pellets struck the car.

"Come right. Traffic is increasing," Ina said.

A motorcycle passed them, rider glaring back. Then there was another truck and a pair of cars, one skidding to avoid running into them. Ina would have pulled off and waited for nightfall, but there was no room at the side of the road, only gleaming aluminum guardrails to keep traffic from flying over the side. Ina kept Helene close to the rails, but that necessitated a slower speed. If they hit the rails they would throw off sparks. Turns kept coming, and traffic.

"Start a gradual turn to your left," Ina said. "A little more."

They were running downhill now. A distant town was revealed to them as they emerged from the bend. It was small and in their path, a collection of buildings grouped around a highway in the flatlands. The road they were on went through the town, but not any time soon. They followed the road around and the town went out of sight. Another salt truck, straining against the grade, went past.

"Town approaching," Ina said, to encourage her sister. "Get to the right. More. Right. Good."

"Does it have a motel?"

"I don't know, dear. We can hope."

They came through another turn, another descending curve, and Ina saw the town again, closer, from a lower elevation. Yellow water tower, buildings with the look of businesses close to the road, and residences spread out behind. There appeared to be no intersecting highway of any consequence.

"How's our gas?"

Ina looked. Half a tank.

"We might as well fill it up."

Around a last bend the road went down into the bottom of the valley, lost its uncertain nature, and headed straight west. The water tower was painted like a flower. Tulip was the name of the town.

They bought gas at the east end of the highway. Ina checked the oil, then poured in a quart from her stock in the trunk. She was relieved to be off the road. If she could have thought of enough things to do to the car she would have kept them there until nightfall.

She paid for her gas and asked the attendant, a middle-aged Indian, if there was a motel in Tulip. He looked up from putting her money in the cash register; it was about the only money in there.

Three other men were sitting in the gas station and her question gave them pause. They all smiled when the attendant said, "Closest thing to a motel is Queenie's. Go to Lawford and turn right. Look for a purple trailer on your left. She might give you a room."

She returned to the car with that news. The attendant followed and tapped on her window as Helene was starting the car.

"Fellas tell me you put in a quart of oil," he said.

"Yes. But it's our oil. We're carrying it in our trunk."

"We're carrying oil?" Helene asked.

"Yes," Ina said. She put up the window and directed Helene out onto the highway.

"Why are we carrying extra oil?" Helene asked.

"Just in case."

"We burned a quart? Since when?"

"I don't know. We go through it pretty fast," Ina said. "I don't feel like stopping to find the cause."

Tulip was hurting; many of the people were just sitting in front of businesses with nothing to do. The money they had paid for gas might be the only outside capital that came into town all day. An insurance agent's front window had been cracked and repaired with masking tape. Letters had fallen off the post office's sign.

"This is an expensive car," Helene complained. "If we're wrecking the engine, I want to know."

"You'll be the first to know," Ina said. "But Tulip isn't the place to check. Believe me."

Lawford appeared to be the main residential street. Quonset huts, trailers, houses raised on concrete blocks, their roof lines swooning, flanked the street. Skinny dogs barked. Round-faced children watched from windows. They crept through this neighborhood and out the other side without seeing a purple trailer. They were moving into the desert. The land was burned golden in the sunlight. Heat was rising. A mile out of town they found the purple trailer. No sign announcing Queenie's, but a soda pop machine out front seemed to be evidence of commerce.

The trailer was plum-colored, long and narrow, with power lines hooked on and leading back toward the main road, a monstrous TV antenna stuck like the feather of an arrow in the roof. Wash hung from a folding aluminum tree planted at the rim of the patio.

"It's just a trailer. Should we ask?"

"Maybe it's a bed-and-breakfast arrangement," Helene suggested.

"I'll see. You wait here."

"Check the oil again. That concerns me."

"We've only gone a hundred yards since I topped it off," Ina said. "If it was gushing out the bottom of the car, I'd do something about it. In my estimation, the problem isn't serious."

"And it won't be until you've reached your destination," Helene said.

"Exactly," said Ina.

She walked up chipped brick steps to the trailer door and knocked. Music was playing inside, banjo and snare.

A woman, impatient, kicked open the door. She was washing her hair, her hands locked in soap above her head, and she examined Ina with one eye squeezed shut, gray rivulets of water and suds dripping from her nose, her lips, her chin. She had her blouse unbuttoned and rolled off her shoulders.

"*What?*" she asked harshly.

"We were told we might find a room here for the night," Ina explained.

"Who told you that?" she asked, blowing water from her mouth in a mist that dampened the front of Ina's blouse.

"A man at the gas station?"

"Running Tooth," the woman said. She stepped back. "Come in a second. My eye is burning."

She had left a trail of water and soap from the sink to the

door, but she had put down a layer of newspapers, as if she were
accustomed to being called away from her duties and knew that
she dripped. The water was running in the sink and the woman
bent her head under the tap's meager stream.

"Sit," she ordered. "You're the victim of a Tulip joke. Sit."

The front of the trailer was surprisingly roomy: couch, coffee
table, two chairs, and a TV there on the edge of the kitchen area,
which the woman dominated with her enthusiastic efforts, water
flying everywhere, splashing the cupboards, the refrigerator, the
burners on the stove.

The hall leading to the rest of the trailer was blocked by a
fringed curtain. A hand-painted sign on the coffee table read:
DON'T PUT YOUR DAMN BOOTS ON MY FURNITURE!

This struck Ina as evidence of a public place and gave her hope.

Slowly the woman's hair began to emerge from the rinse. It
took so long Ina got up and looked out on Helene, who waited
in her implacable manner on the passenger's side.

The woman straightened up gradually from the sink, keeping
the water running on the unrinsed parts of her hair, and it looked
to Ina as if the woman was weaving clean, golden hair from the
mixed elements of soap and water. The hair grew longer, like she
was pulling it from a bowl in her hands.

Ina watched, amazed.

The woman's shoulders were wide and smooth. She had a thin
waist and no hips.

"Towel," she commanded, pointing to her right. Ina took the
towel off a chair and handed it to her. She stood up straight and
turned off the water with her elbow, like a surgeon. Her hair,
ropy, wet, and snarled, was nearly three feet long. Combed out,
flowing, it might reach her butt.

"So they sent you for a room, huh?" she said.

"My sister and I are traveling to Los Angeles," Ina said. "We
wanted a place to stay."

"You can make L.A. easy by this afternoon if you keep driving," the woman said. "Plenty of motels in L.A."

"We're tired. We've been on the road all night."

"Have her come in," the woman said. She turned away, rubbing her hair briskly with a towel.

Ina went out to get Helene.

"You should see the hair on this girl," she said.

"Hair?" said Helene. "What do I care about hair? Can we stay? I need a bathroom and a shot. And food. Hair I've got enough of."

The woman had brought a mirror on a stand and set it up on the coffee table. She was seated before the mirror, and with a big-toothed pink comb began to bring order to the nest of her hair.

"My name is Ina. This is my sister, Helene."

"I'm Queenie. Have a seat." She moved herself and her mirror all the way to the left of the couch.

"My sister would like to use your bathroom."

"All the way at the back. Don't flush it. Well takes a while to replenish after I do my hair."

Ina led Helene down the narrow hall. She counted four small bedrooms, two on each side, with a small sitting room off the back door, next to the bathroom. The bathroom had a toilet built inside a shower, with a sink just wide enough to put her face into and a minuscule vanity. Ina and Helene could not fit in the bathroom together. While Helene used the toilet, Ina prepared her shot on a table in the sitting room.

"You drug addicts?" Queenie asked, grinning in the doorway. She was like an electrical storm with all that hair and the effort of getting it dry.

"Helene is diabetic."

"You were sent here by a hateful, silly man—I'd guess it was Running Tooth, he works at the gas station—as a way to poke fun at me," Queenie said.

"We were just looking for a room."

"I've got three spares. You can stay for twenty-five a night, per person. Are you hungry?"

Before Ina could answer, Queenie went back down the hall, having to turn a bit sideways to get her elbows, raised and busy in her hair, through. She opened the refrigerator and took out a pitcher of ice water. Helene called to Ina and Ina stood in the bathroom door providing some privacy to her sister while Helene delivered the shot.

"We can stay," Ina said.

Queenie had poured three glasses of ice water. A table barely wider than an ironing board had been folded out from the side of the sink cabinet, a rod dropping down to support the table.

"Why are you going to Los Angeles?"

"To see my kids," Ina said.

"Most travelers don't find their way to Tulip," Queenie said. "Interstate is north of here."

"We wanted to go slow," Helene said. "See the sights."

"No sights in Tulip."

She sliced two potatoes into a plastic bowl. Her hair fountained all around her. She took care to swing it through the air like a blanket.

"I've never been to Los Angeles," she said. "Been to Phoenix. Dallas. Las Vegas. Closest I got to L.A. was Palm Springs, and that was fifteen years ago."

She was making potato salad. Helene and Ina watched from the couch.

"My ex is sheriff of this county," Queenie said. "He's not my ex by his choice, you see? So nobody in Tulip will give me work. Not that there's much work to be found. But he sees to it I get none of what's available. I literally have eight dollars to my name. I can put my hands on eight dollars. Who else in America is as poor as me? The most bad-off Indian on the reservation down the road has more than eight dollars put aside for emergencies. Seven singles and a dollar's change. That's all I've got."

She rinsed the knife, cleaning it with her fingers. "Well's slow coming around," she noted.

"You don't look poor," Ina said.

"You have beautiful hair," Helene said, an observation that befuddled Queenie, who seemed to have decided Helene was blind.

"Thank you. My hair is my glory. I wash it every day and spend most of my free time pampering it. More luxurious hair doesn't grow in California. My dream is to be a Breck girl. Ex brings me groceries and leaves them on the doorstep in the morning," she said. "He always knows what I'm short of. But he won't let me have a car. No credit. He has spies that know when I walk into town. He most surely knows about your car being parked here. He's already driven past, I'm positive. Your license plate will be checked out, but that will take a couple days. Ex has to do it by mail. Which is a big complaint of his."

A long, golden strand nearly thick as a wire came loose and she regarded it mournfully.

"That's a beauty," she said. "I'd replant her if I could."

"You don't miss them after a while," said Ina.

"Oh, I can't imagine that." She lowered the hair into a wastebasket under the sink. "To make a little money," Queenie said, "I hired three girls and put them up in my extra rooms. I didn't take part myself—I just collected their money. Sat out here and talked to the men and took their money. That lasted four days before ex shut me down and ran the girls off. But you'd think that was the only thing I've ever done in my life. That was over two years ago—for four days—and this place is still known as Queenie's. They're still poking fun at me by sending you over here. I go into Tulip for anything and I get nothing but snickers and evil looks. Where else am I going to show off this hair?"

The trailer got hot in the depths of the afternoon and Queenie turned on the window AC. Helene slept on the couch because the individual rooms were stifling. Ina watched a little TV, read some, drank two bottles of Mexican beer from Queenie's refrigerator, slept in a chair. Queenie was all energy, moving through the trailer just to be moving, brushing her hair until it pulsated with a golden health, and then repeating the long process fifteen minutes later. She nibbled constantly on fruit and cheese.

"This is not the life I'm cut out for," she lamented.

At sunset she made the widows come outside to watch the sun go down. They sat on lawn chairs, their faces turned toward the baking western light. Everything was flat and saltlike in that direction. Only Queenie didn't wear sunglasses. While they waited, a tulip-yellow sheriff's car drove slowly down Lawford. Queenie ignored it.

"He's about to bust from wanting to know what's going on here," she said. "Two elderly women—what could they be up to? Although I'm sure by now he's talked to Running Tooth. If you were two elderly men—he could make sense of that."

"We'll be leaving tonight," Ina told her.

"You'll be in L.A. in no time," Queenie promised.

"We'll leave about midnight."

"That's past my bedtime," she said. "Just be sure the door clicks when you go out."

Ina loaded the car in the light from the trailer windows. She put in more oil. At eleven o'clock, Queenie told them her hair needed its hundred strokes and said good-bye. She pulled the curtain shut behind her. They heard the TV go on in her room.

"Are you ready to proceed?" Ina asked.

"Where will we stay tonight?"

"I don't know, Helene. Someplace closer to our destination," Ina said.

"I'd just like to know we won't be on the road through most of the morning looking for a place to stop."

"I can't promise that," said Ina.

"I need to use the bathroom once more."

They pushed through the curtains and went down the hall. Queenie's door was closed. Ina waited for Helene in the sitting room.

"It will be nice not to go in a phone booth anymore," Helene said.

They drove back into the heart of Tulip. No one was out. The downtown was dark. They turned toward Los Angeles.

"Straighten it out," Ina said. "Let's try going thirty tonight. If we do that we'll end up in the heart of L.A. when the night's over. Queenie said there are plenty of motels in L.A."

They passed out the back end of Tulip, Ina happy to be traveling again.

"Come right a bit. You're getting into the oncoming lane," Ina said.

Muttering, followed by a commotion, came from the back seat.

"What is going on?" Helene asked.

"I might ask the same thing," Queenie said indignantly. She was digging her way clear of bags and blankets she had hidden under. "Can't you go any faster?" She glanced behind them. Hints of Tulip were clearly visible. "Ex is sheriff of the whole county and it's a big county."

Her hair was rolled up and hidden under a black hat, and she kept her head ducked down beneath the level of the windows.

"I would've bet money you were blind," Queenie said to Helene.

"Come right, dear. More," said Ina.

"You *are* blind!"

"Don't scream," Helene scolded. "It's a small car."

"You're blind. Do you travel like this all the time?"

"All the way from Chicago."

"You can't drive?" she asked of Ina.

"No."

"Want me to drive?" she asked, risking another look behind.

"What do you say?" Ina asked.

"Because pretty soon ex is going to hear your car is gone," said Queenie. "He'll call me to ask what you were up to. I won't answer and he'll stop by the trailer. He'll let himself in and see that I'm gone and he'll come after us with lights and siren. We'll only be five miles out of Tulip and that's still in the county."

"Nobody saw us leave," Ina said.

"Means nothing. Let me drive, *please.*"

"We wanted to finish the trip ourselves," said Helene.

"I won't tell. I'll drive you to Los Angeles and get out. You won't ever see me again. Please let me drive."

Ina guided Helene to the side of the road and almost before the car was stopped Queenie was out the door, running around to Ina's side to help her into the back seat, then guiding Helene over into the passenger's seat, always looking behind her at the dark road. Ina fit uncomfortably into the space Queenie had made in the back but she did not complain. They were going to avoid driving in Los Angeles.

Queenie took the wheel. She was laughing as they accelerated back onto the highway. She removed her black hat and flung it out the window.

"A clue," she said. She shook her hair loose, cascading it down over her shoulders, petting it like an animal that deserved an apology for being cooped up all day.

They were doing seventy.

"We'll go up and catch ten," Queenie said. "That will get us there directly."

So they entered Los Angeles like they had lived there all their lives, hurtling into the quandary of freeways so fast that Queenie and Ina, and in response, Helene, screamed. It was night, but who could tell? They hit traffic jams at 2:00 A.M., traffic jams with music and dancing. Everything was in pastels. Palm trees bent over the avenues. Cars stopped on the highways so people could cross. The air was warm and smelled of gasoline. They drove around lost, not minding.

"He'll never find me here," Queenie said.

They stopped to buy a map book. The store was crowded, mothers with babies doing the grocery shopping at three in the morning.

"Where are you going?" Queenie asked.

"Narrow Canyon Road," Ina said. She found the road in the index, then found the road on the map. It was near the ocean.

"Where are we?" she asked.

"Heaven," said Queenie. "Heaven on a fault line."

"Can you find this?" Ina passed the map book up to their driver. Helene did not complain about her job being taken; she saw the end as clearly as Ina.

"Wait." Queenie took the map book into the store. Ina saw her discussing the situation with the cashier. He pointed behind her, then to the west.

They were at the foot of Narrow Canyon Road within an hour. The road went up into darkness.

"I'll get out here," Queenie said.

Ina gave her two tubes of money and she put them in her pocket without counting them.

"If Helene can get you from Chicago to Tulip," Queenie said, "she can get you to the top of this hill."

PART SEVEN

◆ ———————————————————————

Heaven on
a Fault Line

NARROW Canyon Road spiraled up through jungle in the dark, no sign of habitation beyond parked cars and black arrows on golden diamonds that foretold the next coil in the road. At the top end was a cul-de-sac, hub of four driveways, three continuing skyward, the fourth leading over the edge to a house built in midair. The widows chomped sugarless gum for their ears. When the car nosed up onto the flat cul-de-sac Ina screamed for Helene to stop, certain that she had missed a turn, or a warning sign, and they were about to plunge into the sea of lights below.

A fine rain was falling, a mist. Helene, on the ascent, kept asking Ina if she could see the ocean. Ina could not be certain. She could not get her bearings. Through gaps in the foliage, or on the harrowing bends that leaped out into the air before snapping back by just the most offhanded adherence to gravity, Ina glimpsed dark pockets between the glittering hills that might have been the ocean.

In truth, she didn't care if she saw the ocean. She would be content getting them to the end of their journey; she was too exhausted for scenery. The road up to Annie's house was just one final challenge. Helene complained of the uneasy sensation of always rising, likening it to driving on her back. But no traffic passed them or came down the mountain toward them and they arrived at that frightening little tabletop cul-de-sac where Ina screamed at Helene to stop.

"This is better," said Helene, the car in Park on flat ground.

"We aren't there," Ina said. "We've only come to the end of the road."

"Do you have an address?"

Ina repeated the number she had memorized. "Forty-two twenty-four Narrow Canyon Road."

"Did we pass it?"

"I don't know," Ina said. Coming up, she had seen no numbers, no mailboxes. "There are four driveways here," she said. Peering through the rain, she saw no signs of identification. Even the house in midair had no number.

"Wait for me here," Ina said. "You're perfectly safe if you don't move."

The rain did not wet her, but made her skin feel oily, as if she would drop anything she touched. She felt something bounce in the road like three beats of a pulse beneath her feet, and then it stopped. Ina paused at the edge of the house's driveway, where the asphalt tipped from the cul-de-sac and ran down to a three-car garage. She had no way of knowing if Annie and Don could afford such a house; she had no gauge of what wealth was required to buy the stucco house hanging out over the sparkling canyon. She had no idea if Annie and Don possessed such wealth. Don was "doing well," Annie always made a point of reporting. But Annie never detailed what doing well amounted to. Was it so much that they could buy off the anxiety of dying in their sleep when their house fell from the sky? Who could afford such insurance? Who could sleep at night without fear of stumbling on the way to the bathroom out the wrong door and into the abyss?

The front door was double width, delicate filigree carved in the dark wood surface, but bearing no name or number. She pushed the bell and heard something like a hum in the canyon side of the house. Within seconds, a light came on over her head and muted music began to play. But no one came to the door. She pushed the button again, certain that she was at the wrong house. Meg was a light sleeper; on her visits to her grandparents she was up at all hours pacing the halls, getting into the refrigerator, reading at the kitchen table. She would have come to the door long before this.

There was a movement in the carving on the door and a small

circle of dark glass emerged to regard her. A sleepy, affronted voice asked over a speaker, "What do you want?"

"I'm sorry to bother you," Ina said, speaking to the glass circle. "I'm looking for the Bixler residence. Ann and Don Bixler. They live on Narrow Canyon Road."

"I don't know anyone by that name."

"What is your address here?"

"Why do you want to know?"

"Theirs is forty-two twenty-four. If I knew yours, I might know where to look next," Ina said.

"I can't tell you my number."

"We're really just hopelessly lost. We drove all the way from Chicago."

"Chicago? I'm from Detroit. Listen . . . what does this guy do for a living?"

Ina wasn't entirely sure. Like Vincent, Don seemed to go away for the day and return wealthier.

"He's a businessman of some sort. He solves problems for his company. I don't really know," Ina said.

The huge door swung open with an ease that belied its size. Heat escaped from the house, smelling of chlorine, smoke, and mildew. A very tall man absently shook her hand. He was dressed in a white silk robe that bore an incomprehensible snarl of mono-grammed letters at the breast. He stood barefoot on a slate floor, his toes curled back off the cold stone.

"My name isn't important," he said. "Nor is my house num-ber. But you look harmless, so I'll tell you this much. The next house over that way belongs to a guy in the music business. You'd recognize him. I'm not going to tell you any more than that. Aside from him, I don't know any of my neighbors. There are only seventeen houses on Narrow Canyon. I've narrowed it down to fifteen. Good night."

"Couldn't you just tell me your house number?" Ina pleaded.

"And what? Open myself to some scam?"

"It would make our night go so much easier."

"I'm not here for that," he said. "I've done more than most would. I turned off my alarm for you."

"Don't think I don't appreciate it," she said. "You have a beautiful house."

"Thank you. Now, good night."

He started to close the door, but Ina raised her hand and he retained enough gallantry to give her a few more moments of his attention.

"Don't tell me your number—I know that's too much to ask," Ina said. "But could you give me a clue in which direction I'd find forty-two twenty-four?"

"Try the next driveway that way," he said, pointing into the mist to his left. "If you don't find your party, try the next drive after that. Keep in mind, the fellow in the music business is zealously private. *He* has dogs."

Ina, with a devil-may-care curiosity, asked, "Do you worry your house is going to fall into the canyon?"

The man grimaced, looked behind him. "It's what I miss most about Detroit: freedom from that particular fear."

Helene had fallen asleep behind the wheel, lulled by the heater and the tap of rain. Ina rubbed her hands together down by the heater's warm wind. She felt unaccountably safe there in the middle of the road. She expected no traffic; the people of the neighborhood might never leave their homes, for fear of scams.

She shook Helene, who snapped awake with a machinelike clarity.

"Where to next, dear?"

"I talked to a man," said Ina. "He was as helpful as he felt safe being. Not very, as it happens. But he helped us narrow down the choices."

"Did you get the street number?"

"He wouldn't tell me his," Ina said. "Nor will he reveal where his house number is in relation to the other houses—the other sixteen houses on Narrow Canyon Road."

"That's being helpful?"

"Can you drive a little farther?" Ina asked. She was not personally willing to confront the other half of that question: Could Helene come down again, possibly in Reverse, if the first house they drove up to did not belong to Annie and Don?

"Why—I suppose so," said Helene.

"We have two driveways to choose from," Ina said. "They both go up rather steeply. I don't know what we'll find at the top."

"Pick one," Helene said brightly. "The one you pick will be the one we want. I have every confidence in you."

Ina sent them up a thread of track that doubled back on itself so that for the first part of the ascent she had wet vegetation close enough to touch at her right, and for the remainder of the ride she could look out at an emptiness whose beauty robbed it of its menace. Far below, the canyons were beginning to fill with light. The roads down there already looked clogged with traffic, the hour not yet five. Ina kept Helene tucked in so close against the side of the hill that hanging fronds whipped the windshield; if Don, in his desire to be at the office before sunup, came down now they all were dead. Around one last interminable bend, they reached the top. A Mercedes-Benz was parked in their path. Ina, talking fast, got Helene to miss the sedan by inches and then stop.

"We're at the top," whispered Ina.

The house was built of dark cedar, its occupants away or asleep. A topaz light burned on a pole near the corner of the house, illuminating a turn that led into shadow. A discreet little sign was tacked to the house: WESTEC, it read, and beneath that: ARMED RESPONSE.

"Is this the place?" Helene asked.

"I don't know," said Ina. She prayed that it was; her daughter might be happy in such a house, with such a vista, and Ina did not want to go back down the hill. A bird went off like an alarm in the trees.

"Go ask," Helene impatiently ordered. "If we have to keep driving, I want to know."

In back of the house was a swimming pool, built on a tiled turquoise ledge that looked no thicker than a mattress, with a bisecting float rope and a board that Ina imagined would propel any diver into the canyon at the slightest miscalculation. Walking near a corrugated plastic pool shed, she heard a scraping from

within, thought of dogs, and hurried on. She was desperate to
see a house number, but everyone wanted to keep their identity
to themselves. There was a fence, built of the same cedar as the
house, along the back line of the pool area, and in this fence was
a gate. Beyond the gate was a stairway leading down into the
green canyon, disappearing at the first bend with the promise of
further descent. And as Ina peered down this stairway a girl in a
hooded yellow slicker came into view, climbing up. She was tall,
her face obscured, her step tired, as if she had been on the stairway for a long time. In one hand, a cigarette smoked; in the other
she carried a glass of something that looked like orange juice. Five
steps down from the gate she stopped as if sensing Ina looming,
or smelling Ina's old lady odor after weeks on the road, her aura
of anxiety and beer. The girl raised her head and Ina cried out to
see her Meg, who had grown up without a word of warning to
her grandmother.

"Moomer!" Meg cried out.

"Baby!"

The girl leaped into Ina's arms, ditching the cigarette with
aplomb, spilling her drink and squeezing with both arms until
Ina felt her breath grow restricted, and realized the girl was sobbing.

Ina pushed back the hood and stroked Meg's hair. She was
wearing it short and red, the ends daubed with the last black
traces of an ancient dye job. She felt heavier beneath the slicker
than Ina remembered. The awkward preadolescent boniness was
gone.

"Baby," whispered Ina. "Don't cry. Don't cry now." But the
facts remained: Meg had come rising through the rain at dawn,
definitely smoking, possibly drinking something hidden in the orange juice. Was she returning home for the night or just unable
to sleep?

Meg sniffed, giggled, wiped her runny nose with the back of
her hand.

"There was a rumor you were coming," she said. Her eyes
had their old sparkle.

"We found you," Ina said. "Helene's with me."

"And she drove?"

"Is that the rumor?"

Meg let out another laugh, then smacked her forehead with the heel of her hand. "Too much," she said. "Let's go get her."

Helene, perhaps wondering who knew what, had slid over into the passenger's seat. She turned and smiled at the scuff of their approach. Meg pulled open the door.

"Auntie H!" she cried, taking Helene's hand and drawing her up out of the car, a hand held above Helene's head in protection.

"Hello, Meaghan," Helene said, presenting her cheek to be kissed.

"You drove all the way here?"

"Just about," said Ina.

"Too much," Meg repeated, looking from one old woman to the other.

"Where were you?" Ina asked.

Meg frowned, as if reminded of an earlier part of her morning. "My friend Katy lives downstairs," she said. "I couldn't sleep, so I went down to visit her."

"Was she awake?"

"No," Meg said, making a face. "Her father was passed out by the pool. He was soaked."

"Are your parents still in bed?" Helene asked. She had not moved since exiting the car; having transported them to their destination, she was helpless. She hadn't the slightest notion where to go, and so remained motionless.

"Dad's up and gone. Mom's asleep," Meg said. "Let's get in out of the rain."

Ina took Helene's hand and together they followed Meg into the house. She stopped in a mud room off the garage to hang her slicker on a peg, then moved on into the kitchen.

"Coffee? Grapefruit juice?" she asked back over her shoulder.

"Could I freshen a bit?" Helene asked, with a valiant attempt at offhandedness.

"Of course," Meg said.

She pushed open a door off the hallway into the kitchen and Ina steered her sister into the powder room. She got Helene positioned, the location of everything familiarized, before stepping outside and closing the door.

Meg was standing at a butcher block island in the center of the kitchen. She wore jeans and a linen blouse and had put on pink rabbit-head slippers. The room was chilly. Meg hugged herself, a cigarette going in one hand.

"Is she all right?"

"Helene? Sure. We're both just tired from the drive."

Meg came and gave Ina a quick hug. "It's so great—what you did," she said.

"Does your dad always leave this early?"

"He's at his desk by five-thirty A.M. Home around ten tonight."

"What does your mom think of that?"

Meg shrugged, smoked. "She thinks it sucks. She complains about never seeing him—but she doesn't bother to get up with him."

"Do you?"

"I see him off every morning. Or I'd *never* see him," Meg said. "After he left this morning, I went to visit Katy."

"You go to school with her?"

"She's very smart. Someday she's going to be a famous writer. All her stuff is about her mom," Meg said. "I would've gone in and got her up—but her dad depressed me, so I just came back up." She hugged Ina once more, nearly lunging for her, burying her face in Ina's shoulder for an instant. "And I'm glad I did," Meg said, "because I was able to be the first person to welcome you to California."

The toilet flushed in the powder room and Ina went to wait by the door so she could guide Helene into the kitchen. The rainy light, the relief of their arrival, the hour, all had infused Ina with an overwhelming exhaustion. She suspected the same of Helene. They would have to sleep soon.

"Are you cold?" Ina asked the others.

"It's always cold," Meg said. "Dad leaves the thermostat on sixty. He says this is California, we don't need heat."

"I could stand a sweater," Helene admitted.

Ina went to the car for one of their suitcases. At Queenie's she had cleaned out the accumulants of the journey. She would present a tidy, sober face to her children, though she had a warm half-case of beer left in a bag in the trunk. If while she slept her daughter came to sniff around in the car that a blind woman had driven from Chicago, there would be no cryptic empties rolling on the floor, no hint of senility in the crisp look of the vehicle.

"Meg says Amanda is here," Helene said upon Ina's return.

Ina draped a sweater over her sister's shoulders. Meg had made tea and laid out a tray of margarine, orange marmalade, and rice cakes. She tapped ashes into a Beverly Hills Hotel ashtray.

"Where?"

"Uncle Ray's."

Helene nervously rolled the edge of the sweater into a tubular bunching.

"I planned to call her," she said. "I don't understand . . . what's the rush?"

"She said she was just anxious to get out here," Meg said. "She said Chicago was cold and rainy—and L.A. would be sunny and warm."

"But it's cold and rainy," Ina said, and Meg laughed, but Helene had something fresh to worry about. They had made the trip with the sensation of drawing ever farther from Amanda and the frustrations Amanda's life visited on Helene, and it was disconcerting to have Amanda there when they arrived. Also, Ina had held Amanda in reserve as someone Helene could return to.

"Where's the thermostat?" Ina asked defiantly. "If Don complains, *I'll* pay. L.A. or not, I'm freezing."

She patted Helene's hand and was startled by its dead-cold feel, its slackness under her touch. She whirled to look in Helene's eyes, afraid she had missed something. Helene was smiling, cheered by the prospect of heat.

The thermostat was in an adjoining room, which had two glass walls looking into the canyon, a fireplace on another wall, a TV taller than any of the three women, and a sprawling arrangement of low, leather sofas and loveseats all pointed expectantly at the giant screen.

"Shall we risk seventy?" Meg asked in a whisper.

Ina had gone to the windows. The glass was water-green and smudged in spots at a height Ina guessed was caused by someone's nose or forehead as they gazed (longingly?) into the canyon.

"Seventy would be heavenly," Ina said, and as she spoke she heard the whir of the furnace turning on.

"Mom'll be up soon. She plays tennis every morning."

"We used to play," said Ina.

"She belongs to a club," said Meg. "Indoor. Outdoor. Dad bitches about the cost. An indoor court is seventy-five dollars a half hour. Can you imagine?"

"No," Ina said. "But if she enjoys it, and can afford it, what's the harm in it?"

"It's a waste," Meg said.

The kitchen was already warming up. Helene, as if melting, had let the sweater edges fall from her hands, and snuggled down into herself in the chair. She looked so contented that Ina envied her; there was nothing to keep Helene awake beyond sheer politeness, and even that could be abandoned under the proper inducements. Ina was the one with a daughter to wait for, to entertain when she awoke, to fill in, to take condemnations from. Worse, there was no place handy to sneak off and have a beer. No place even to keep some cold, unless she was willing to use Annie's refrigerator, and face all that that involved.

The door from the mud room opened and a tiny woman entered. She had maroon skin and jet black hair pulled into a stubby braid held in place with a pink thread of ribbon. The ribbon's color matched her uniform. She smiled at the people in the kitchen before dipping out of sight in the powder room and softly shutting the door.

"That's Jo," whispered Meg. "She lives in the pool shed."

"What?"

"She won't live anywhere else."

Ina looked and the shed door was ajar, with a curl of smoke rising from a gap in the roof.

"That's inhuman," said Ina.

"My Dad fixed up a nice room with a bathroom downstairs—

her own entrance and everything—but she won't use it. She's from Guatemala. Dad suspects the shed is a step up for her. He pays her more than he has to. Mom thinks it's too much. She spends more for a half-hour of tennis than Jo's husband made all last year."

Jo sounded happy enough behind the bathroom door, humming a song above the running water. When Ina looked again at the pool shed, a child had appeared. A boy, he had Jo's maroon skin and black hair, and he squatted barefoot on the wet pool tiles playing jacks.

Meg, laughing at Ina's stunned look, explained, "That's Ambrosio. Jo's son."

"A child, too?" Helene asked in bewilderment, even craning her head in a reflex effort to witness a curiosity.

"In the pool shed?"

"It's how they like it," Meg said.

"Who else is in there?"

"That's all. Mr. Jo is in Guatemala. Or San Diego. Jo isn't sure which, right now."

Ambrosio was chewing a biscuit the color of a golf ball, a small rain of crumbs falling at his feet. His hair was damp and carefully parted on the right.

A noise in the house sent Meg flying outside with her cigarette and ashtray. She doused the butt in the pool, dumped the ashes over the railing, and set the ashtray out of sight on the last step leading up from the canyon. She was back in her chair, with a wink for Ina, a bored expression in place, when Annie came into the kitchen.

For a moment, Annie actually came to a stop and Ina had time to examine her daughter. She looked tired, thin in the face, and older than she should. In the early morning shadows she wore sunglasses. Her hair was dishwater blonde, permed into a wave that broke upside down under the left side of her jaw. Her skin looked crispy brown in her white tennis culottes. She carried a pink tennis shoe in each hand.

"I don't believe it."

"It's true," said Meg. "They've been here an hour. Isn't it *fabulous?*"

Annie set down the shoes and in rising caught her mother in a hug, squeezing her with slim, dark arms that smelled of baby lotion, and then kissing her once perfunctorily on the cheek.

"We thought you'd have been arrested by now," Annie said.

"We were very sly," Ina said; the trip no longer seemed like any great accomplishment. Those first nights, before they were certain the trip could be made, that was when she and Helene had been proudest of themselves.

Annie leaned into a hug from Helene, and kissed her also in retreat.

"Helene—I thought you'd have had enough sense to waylay Mom," Annie said.

"Fortunately, I didn't," Helene said.

"You know Amanda is here?"

"Yes."

Annie tapped Meg's shoulder. "Make me a shake, would you, sweetie?" To Helene, she said, "Helene, Ray called three days ago—perplexed—and said Amanda had appeared at his door. He's called every day since, once in the morning and once at night, to see if you'd arrived."

"We'll go see her later," Ina said, patting Helene's hand.

Meg sliced a banana over a blender, into which she deposited juices, powders, and grains, a scoop of vanilla ice cream, an egg, an apple, wheat germ, and a flattened cigarette butt she found stuck like a bug to the bottom of her shoe. She didn't look around before putting in the cigarette, she didn't hesitate, and she didn't smile afterward.

"What's that?" Ina asked over the chug of the blender.

"My breakfast," Annie said. "Liquid health."

The drink was the color of dead shrubs and so thick Annie began to eat with a spoon straight from the blender, devouring each spoonful with a faint, grateful sucking of her lips, licking up every last bit. Ina saw no tobacco flakes suspended.

"Get me a straw, sweetie. Where's Jo?"

"In the john," Meg said.

"She's discovered makeup," Annie whispered, smiling. "I give her my free samples. She can't stop putting the stuff on her face."

"Next it will be tennis," Meg said. "Amor-quince. El double fault."

Annie gave her daughter a quieting scowl. Meg said nothing more, folded her arms, turned away.

"I smell cigarette smoke," Annie declared in a cool, threatening singsong voice.

"It might be me," Ina said. "The places we ate, people always smoked around us."

"Thank you, Mother. But Meg and I have had this conversation before."

"We've had *every* conversation before," Meg said to Ina.

"Listen to what I say—and we'll stop having the same talks over and over and *over* again," Annie said. "Are you ready for school?"

"Yes," Meg said sullenly.

"Can we take a nap?" Ina asked.

"Let them sleep in my room," Meg said excitedly. "I've got two beds—I can sleep in the guest room."

"Maybe one can take your room, and another the guest room," Annie said. "And *you* can sleep on the couch."

"Or in the pool shed," said Meg.

"Actually," Ina said. "Helene and I should be in the same room."

"Aren't you sick of each other by now?" Annie said.

"For mobility's sake, I should be nearby."

Annie blushed, which Ina found heartening, that she was still capable. "Of course," she said. "I'm sorry, Helene. I forget."

"Quite all right, dear."

"Well—*mi casa, su casa.* Jo can show you where everything is—if she ever comes out of the john," Annie said. "And I'm late for tennis."

She rushed out with her shoes untied, the laces clicking on the floor. The garage held another Mercedes, a long golden machine, parked next to a red Mustang convertible. To Ina's surprise, Annie got into the Mustang, fought against its damp reluctance to start, then disappeared down the hill with a wave. Minutes later, Meg kissed them good-bye and went out back for Ambrosio. He waited with an alien's smiling patience, his two textbooks and a small lunch bundle held carefully at his side. He wore red pants and a red and white striped shirt. He had put on a pair of Reeboks. Meg said something to him and he laughed. He came into the house and was allowed entrance to the bathroom where his mother still hummed the same little song. Then he emerged and joined Meg in the front seat of the gold Mercedes. She helped him with his seatbelt.

"Can you drive this?" Ina asked, standing at the car's side.

"Oh, sure. I've had my license a month already." The car, in starting, then idling, sounded silken.

"Who owns the one in the driveway?"

"That's Dad's. Jo drives it. Mom takes the Mustang because she's a lousy driver," Meg said. "The cost scares her."

"It scares me, too," said Ina.

"Dad says it's only money," Meg replied. "Gotta run, Moomer. Katy'll wonder about me." She stuck out her head and Ina kissed her. Meg backed out with a certain flair of nonchalance, showing off.

Jo, cheeks peached, lips pinked, eyes highlighted in lavender powder, emerged from the bathroom. The quiet seemed to have encouraged her. She might have thought the house was empty because she let out a musical scream when she saw Ina and Helene at the table.

"Hello—" said Ina, raising her hand. Helene was looking her way. Her eyes were weary, pleading. Fatigue hung on her like a fever.

"Meg's room?" Ina said.

Jo very briskly stepped past them, a scent of something expensive in a cloud around her. She had fine-boned hands and tiny feet and a nearly silent step even on the hardwood floors. She had perfected the glide of the domestic, the shadowy presence that did not exist upon closer inspection.

Meg's room was enormous, with yet another stunning canyon view, another wall of green glass that slid open onto a precarious airborne sliver of deck. Jo expertly stripped Meg's bed and with a single flick turned back the fresh linen of the bed next to it. She disappeared into the bathroom, leaving the sheets in a pile by the door. She emerged a moment later with an armload of damp towels. She took these and the sheets into the hall and shoved them down the laundry chute. Ina, smiling, imagined them exiting under the house, billowing open as they floated into the canyon. It's only money.

"Sit here, dear," Ina said, guiding Helene to the turned-down bed. A groan of relief escaped her. She nearly toppled back, willing to sleep in her clothes, but a last thread of resolve kept her upright for a few more minutes.

"We should run a test," she said. "I'll also have to use the bathroom."

"Jo is getting it ready," said Ina.

"Well, tell her to hurry. I'm exhausted."

"I know you are, dear."

Jo came back with fresh linen. Ina, retracing her steps through the house, found the kitchen, and went out to the car. The rain had stopped. The air carried a smell reminiscent of Jo's perfume. She unloaded their bags and set them side by side on the driveway. She took two tubes of cash from their hiding places and stuffed them into her handbag. She also took four lovely, heavy cans of Old Style and stowed them in her bag with the money. She locked all the car doors and carried everything inside.

The kitchen was empty, Jo still busy in Meg's room. Ina set down the bags, listened at the door for Jo's approaching ghostly step, then went out to peek at how two people could live in a pool shed. It was, not unexpectedly, cramped, but with a proud, tidy air. Ambrosio's clothes and Jo's uniforms were organized carefully on hangers on a rope stretched tight from one back corner to the other. A bench built against the wall held neat piles of underwear, hand towels, socks, Jo's brassieres, and an extra pair of Reeboks for mother and son. Against the opposite wall, looking out of place, was the pool equipment: a skimmer, two orange life vests, jugs of chemicals, and a ring buoy hanging from a hook. Balanced in this white foam circle was a small mirror, a tray of cosmetic samples, and a tiny painting of Jesus, hands clasped in prayer, eyes on the door. Jo and Ambrosio slept on two cots. In the space that remained a small stove had been built, with a flue of blue tin leading to a hole cut in the roof. The fire was out, but the room was warmer than the morning air. So this was a step up from Guatemala?

Annie's refrigerator was so full of jars, bottles, and foil-covered containers that Ina was confident she could surreptitiously chill her four cans of beer without eliciting comment from her daughter. "I *am* an adult," Ina murmured. She put the cans in different locations, so that if one were discovered the others might escape detection. She would, at the moment, kill for a cold one. But warm would have to do; in the quiet of Meg's room, perhaps on the deck, while Helene slept like a baby, their trip at an end.

Jo had made the bed. Helene had not moved. She might be disconcerting the maid with her impassive observation. The corners of the bed were crisp, the covers turned down. Ina stopped Jo when she made a motion to unpack their bags. The maid looked irritated, blocked in her role of helper by two old strangers. The woman was so tiny. Ina had seen little boys who were bigger. Her size suited the dimensions of the pool shed. Ambrosio would be the one to outgrow those accommodations.

"We will sleep now," Ina said, resting her cheek on her hands.

Jo nodded, let slip some utterance, backed out of the room and closed the door.

"Are we alone?" Helene asked.

"Yes."

"Do you need to get into the bathroom?"

"Of course."

Tiled in mauve, the bathroom was so spacious a couch fit between the double sinks and the tub, which by itself was larger than Ina's bathroom back home. Jo had supplied fresh towels, clean glasses, even toothbrushes in unopened plastic cases. The air was humid and perfumed.

"Your bag is here. I opened it for you," Ina said. "The taps are straight ahead."

"Still hot left, cold right?" Helene asked suspiciously.

"Yes, dear. This is L.A., but we're still north of the equator."

"That maid was going through my purse," Helene accused.

"Why do you say that?"

"She was always moving. I heard keys, money, like she was looking through it while she walked around the room."

"I don't think she knows you're blind," said Ina.

"She saw you lead me in here. She saw me sitting helplessly while you were out. Of course she knows I'm blind," Helene said.

Ina, to be supportive, examined her sister's bag, but she could not tell if anything was missing.

"I looked in the pool shed," Ina whispered.

"Where they live?"

"It was cramped and horrible, of course. But not bad, in a way."

"You could say that about where we've been living recently," Helene remarked.

"Cramped. Horrible. But not bad," Ina laughed. Helene washed her face. Ina took a seat on the couch. Hooked to the arm was a ring to hold a drink.

"What if they have a pool party?" Ina wondered.

"Jo serves. The kid lifeguards."

"They have a picture of Jesus. Their clothes were hung very neatly on a rope," Ina said. "They have a small stove."

"Everything she cooks has an odd, chlorine taste she can't get rid of," Helene said and grinned at herself in the mirror.

Ina stood up. She needed to get out of that soporific air. Helene, full of the luxury of knowing that sleep was only minutes away, had turned punchy and garrulous. Ina was determined to outlast her sister. She wanted to drink a beer alone, sit and savor the fact of their arrival.

Helene, with breathtaking precision, began to give herself a shot. She plunged the needle into a mound of blue-white skin wadded between her fingers.

"Blood in the syringe?" she asked.

Ina leaned close to be sure. Her sister smelled musty, sour, in need of a bath. Sadly, Ina recognized the smell as familiar, a generic decrepitude.

"No. No blood," she reported.

"Thank you, dear." She completed the injection.

"We should find you a doctor first thing."

"I have a doctor."

"A California doctor."

Helene, a ball of alcohol-sodden cotton held to the needle puncture, asked, "Do you really mean to stay forever?"

"My family is here, dear. Hell, so is yours."

"This isn't for us."

"I'm going to give it a try."

"I'm worried about Amanda. Why is she here?"

"She missed you," Ina said.

"She had a chance at a man with some prospects—and she let him slip away. Or, worse, she ran away from him."

Ina, for a moment, was at a loss. What man with prospects? Then Ina realized her sister had been holding in her mind an image of a man of substance, with two jobs, who wanted children; a figment planted by Amanda, who had dreamed up a wraith of pure convenience.

"Don't jump to conclusions," Ina said. "We'll go see her later. Maybe she was just worried about you."

Helene let her dress fall back into place. She held the empty syringe and ball of cotton, with a faint prick of pink where some blood had been stopped, out in the air for Ina to dispose of.

"May I have some privacy?"

"Certainly. Do you need anything before I leave?"

"I just want to change," Helene said.

"I'll be outside. The door is to your left. Holler if you need anything."

"Thank you, dear."

Under cover of running water, Ina risked the gasp of opening a warm can of beer. Foam gushed out the opening and she had to clamp her mouth over it; she nearly swooned at the taste.

She set the can on her night table. Something lazy and smooth had been released in her by just that small helping of beer foam.

She undressed and took out her nightgown. Snapping it out in front of her to rid it of any pests that might have made the journey, she launched a bundle of cash across the room. Unclear as to when she had packed it, the appearance of the money had a disquieting effect on her. They had arrived in California, yet she had no idea how much money she had spent along the way, how much had been stolen or lost, and therefore how much remained. She opened the bundle and counted the bills. Nine twenties, which troubled her further, for she did not recall taking one bill from a bundle without putting all the bills in her purse at one time. If that was the case, she had counted wrong at the outset, and that was worst of all. For in her memory of the planning stages she was nearly a young woman; a widow, true, but clear-headed, organized, and energetic. If she had not even counted correctly, what else might she have figured wrong?

She rapped on the bathroom door, irritated by Helene's leisurely pace.

"Can I get some time in there?"

"Just a moment, dear," said Helene.

If Helene could see the beer, Ina knew, she would blame it for the abrupt personality change. She would smell it, regardless. Ina retreated to the far edge of the bed, where her feet stood in sunlight, the remainder of her cool in the greenish shadows. She pulled shut the drapes on the deck windows. The dimness suited her. She slid across the open covers and sat against the headboard, holding her beer with two hands. Helene's ablutions dragged on. Ina took a short drink, then a longer one. She closed her eyes and for quite some time planned the next day's travel, when to start, how far to go, what to talk about to pass the time. She awoke in dark space, enveloped in a vaguely nauseating sensation of floating. The water ran on in the bathroom, its pitch changing when Helene held her hands in the water, took them out, formed a cup, drank with the slurping of a young child. Ina had more beer. Moments after closing her eyes again, she was talking to Vincent. He was dressed as he was always dressed. He was standing in their front room, a summer day, because the windows were open and breezy, the sun laying in rods and cones on the rug, the shadows surgically precise. He was scolding her about her drinking and when she looked down she was not holding a warm can of beer but the cold blue glass that she loved and relied upon. He was upset with her, she had embarrassed him, and his turning to leave the room in disgust made her cry out so loudly that Helene opened the bathroom door.

"Are you all right, dear?" she asked. The room spread open before her in all its perilous mystery.

"Ina? Are you all right?"

Admirably, Helene did not panic. She went back and turned off the water and closed the door behind her when she emerged. The bedroom felt faintly cooler. The first bed she reached was her own and she skirted it without interest, feeling at once its emptiness, smelling its fresh linen. At the corner of the mattress she took a seat and listened: Ina breathing, Ina asleep, Ina having moved through a bad dream. She followed the sound, shuffling through Ina's slippers, the damp heap of Ina's dress, until she reached the bed. Helene's hand found Ina's legs, drifted up to her waist, and there encountered a snag of confusion.

Ina was asleep sitting up.

Helene found her sister's cheek and gently cupped it.

"Ina?" Helene whispered.

Her sister did not stir.

"Ina, stretch out. You'll feel better when you awaken."

She explored the position of her sister's head and determined that she would not strike the headboard if Helene carefully pulled her legs down toward the foot of the bed. She could get Ina straightened out, get a pillow under her, take care of her for a change. But in pulling on Ina's ankles, Helene up-ended the can of beer Ina held loosely in her lap and the beer poured out startling as mercury. Ina awoke with a scream that caused Helene to stumble, falling backward with one hand groping out, upending a lamp, the bulb popping, her fingers sliding across a bureau's polished surface to crack the wall. Then she completed her fall.

"Oh—" Ina said, diving to help. She felt shot through her center with a cold lance. A stain soaked the mattress like the accident of an incontinent old woman.

She helped Helene to the edge of her sister's bed. Helene seemed merely befuddled, opening and closing her hand, making a fist to be certain everything remained connected.

"I'm sorry I frightened you. You were asleep sitting up."

"Are you hurt? Did you hit your head?"

"I'm fine. I smell beer, though."

"Do you?"

There was a knock at the door. Ina called out but no one answered. After a moment, there came another knock. Ina, feeling vulnerable in her daughter's house, opened the door to Jo, who smiled without judgment at the two old women who had produced a single scream.

"Jo," Ina said for Helene's benefit.

The dark little woman nodded. She waited as if summoned, patient for a command.

"There's been an accident," Ina said. "We'll need fresh linen."

"Accident?" Helene said.

Jo glanced at the wet spot on Ina's gown. She scanned the room with a rapid look, Helene on the bed with her back to the door, the drawn blinds, the broken lamp, the dim mysteries. In seconds she went away and returned with a crisp new set of sheets and a pillowcase. Ina switched on a light, an overhead fixture Meg had draped with green and gold pompoms. These hanging bundles threw a hairy light over everything and worried Ina with a specter of fire.

Jo, with the precision she had exhibited earlier, tore the wet sheets from the bed. She probed at the wet spot on the mattress as gently as if it were a wound, and with a ladylike grunt of effort flipped the mattress over.

In doing so her toe nudged Ina's beer can where she had hidden it beneath the bed. A foamy, warm stream pulsed out the opening. Jo knelt and put the can back exactly where she had found it without a glance at the widows.

"What kind of accident?" Helene asked.

"A small mistake," said Jo. "It is nothing."

She left them alone.

Helene slept like the dead. But Ina's nap ended too soon, disrupted by anxiety and the muffled, impatient sounds her daughter made as she moved around at the front of the house.

Annie had never been much of a sleeper. She had looked with derision on her mother's late risings. Her eye always went quickly but determinedly to the kitchen clock to mark the time when Ina got up in the morning. She was proud of having seen her father off, but Ina had been with Vincent late into the night and that was the time that mattered to her. The mornings were sharp, dangerous hours she preferred to avoid. One of her great disappointments in getting old was her decreasing need for sleep, as if she was being prodded to pay more attention to the time she had remaining.

She put on a clean, slightly wrinkled housedress and her slippers. She was worried about leaving Helene asleep. She might awaken, or rise sleepily to use the toilet and fall again in her disorientation. If she called, Ina might not hear at the far end of the house.

Annie was in the kitchen having a salad. She ate with one hand holding her hair up off her neck. Ina was struck by how young she looked from that perspective, with the back of her neck exposed, pale, somehow helpless, a girlishness in its thin fragility. The salad filled a large china bowl and Annie stabbed at the lettuce and cherry tomatoes and cucumber slices with savage accuracy. Her mouth full, chewing, she saw her mother and waved.

"How was tennis?" Ina took a seat at her daughter's right hand.

Annie raised her fork and nodded. She reattached the grip on her hair. Playing a hunch, Ina went to a storage closet off the hallway leading to the garage. On the inside knob hung garlands of rubber bands, the same place Ina kept hers. Seeing them there, Ina felt momentarily successful as a mother.

"I won four and two," Annie said when she could speak.

"Who did you play?"

"My friend April. My tennis love."

"Let's play again sometime—you and me," Ina said. She stood behind her daughter but could not bring herself to touch her. She had a rubber band stretched between her fingers; she strummed it with her thumbs.

"What are you doing?" Annie asked, looking up and back.

"Let me—" She closed her hands around her daughter's hair. It was damp, warm. She plucked up strands to thicken the clump, and as she worked Annie's head tilted back toward Ina and Ina was positive Annie's eyes were closed.

"There. Now you don't have to eat one-handed," Ina said, wrapping the rubber band three times; she would have gone around a fourth time, but was afraid that would make the rubber band hard to get off, and then Annie would forget the tender gesture later in her irritation at the difficulty in removing the band.

"Thanks, Mom," Annie said with a backhand touch. "I'm going to shower soon, anyway. Could I have Jo make you a salad?"

"Could she?"

"Don't be silly." She left the kitchen and was gone longer than Ina expected. Jo, looking sheepish, followed Annie when she returned.

"Jo tells me my salad used up the last of the salad ingredients," Annie said, jerking open the refrigerator door. Ina preferred she not inspect the contents too closely, lest she find her mother's beer.

"I'll have something else," Ina said, a forgiving wave for Jo standing motionless in the wind of her employer's anger.

"No," said Annie. "You wanted a salad. That was your first impulse." She took a twenty-dollar bill and a set of keys from her purse and handed them to Jo.

"Taco Bell," she said, and pointed to Ina. "Buy her a salad."

To Ina, she said, "You can pick out the hot stuff they put in— or would you rather Jo just goes to the market? She wasn't going until tomorrow, but this is kind of an emergency."

"She doesn't have to go anywhere," Ina said, embarrassed by the attention.

"Nonsense. You wanted a salad."

"It sounded good," Ina admitted.

"There you are, then. A salad is what you'll have. This is California, after all."

"I thought—if one was handy. It isn't necessary to send Jo on an expedition."

"It's just down the mountain," Annie said airily. "Receipt and change, too," she said, eyebrows raised. "Pronto."

Annie resumed eating. "Can I get you some iced tea? Decaf? Fruit juice?"

"No, thanks," Ina said. "Perhaps I'll have something when Jo gets back."

"Twenty minutes is all she'll be gone. I promise."

Ina excused herself and went to look in on Helene. Her sister was fast asleep. Ina was vaguely disappointed; were Helene awake she would require care, providing Ina with an excuse to delay her return to her daughter.

"How is she?"

"Asleep," Ina said, taking her seat.

"She's gained weight," Annie said. "Her skin looks unhealthy."

"For someone with diabetes she's in pretty good shape."

"Wasn't it foolish to bring her out here?"

"Once we got started, she was the force behind the trip."

"Believe that if you want," Annie said. She rinsed out her bowl in the sink. Ina ate a cherry tomato that had been hidden under the bowl's wide rim.

"What are your plans, Mom?"

Annie went to the refrigerator and peered inside as if regarding a puzzle of moderate complexity. She plucked out one of Ina's beers and wordlessly snapped it open. She set the can in front of her mother.

"I found them when I got home," Annie said, sitting again. "You don't have to hide them. It's no secret."

"It's a bit early, actually," Ina said, pushing the can away an inch, though its cold weight was electrifying, her desire for a long pull a lust. She feared the beer wasting away, having been opened too soon.

"Maybe when your salad arrives," Annie said. She put the can back in the refrigerator. Ina forced herself not to watch.

"Do you have any plans, Mom? I'm curious exactly why you're here."

Ina asked, "Is it L.A. that has made you rude? Or something else?"

"These are questions I have to ask," Annie said. "Out here, people say what's on their minds."

Ina put her hands flat on the table. "I've been here less than half a day."

"I realize that."

"Already you're plotting my return home."

"I'm just trying to get a fix on what the future holds," Annie said.

"I'm not going back to Chicago. I've told Helene as much." Ina sat very still and watched her daughter's face as she tried to phrase a question that would determine where Ina planned to live, if not in Chicago.

"What did she say?"

"Outwardly, she was unhappy," Ina recalled. "Secretly, I think she might feel relieved. There's nothing back there for either of us."

"What's here?"

"Ray is here. Meg is here. I thought you were here, too. Maybe not."

"I'm here," Annie said. "You just confuse me."

"Helene is here, too. She's a comfort to me."

"Don can help you find a place," Annie said, summoning some enthusiasm. "Prices are insane, but once you're on the elevator it just keeps rising."

"We have some money between us," Ina said.

Annie smiled ruefully. "You'll need it, believe me. I was always curious—how rich was Daddy?"

"We never had to worry. If that's what you mean," Ina said.

"Nobody *ever* has that much money," Annie said. "Don and I fight all the time about money. It's a war with us. About money. Meg. Whether to keep Jo, or send her away. But you'd think with what he makes we wouldn't have to fight about money. And it's me. I'm the one who worries."

Ina, embarrassed, stood. "You seem comfortably off. Your manner of spending could even be considered opulent. But I don't know your situation. Excuse me a minute."

She looked in on Helene, who slept in the same position, her mouth open perhaps a quarter-inch wider, one thin hand having fallen from under the covers. Ina took the cool, weightless appendage and tucked it back in. She wanted her sister to awaken. Helene's desires, moods, and needs were something she could rely upon.

"Still asleep?"

"Yes."

"You were gone a long time. Anything wrong?"

"No," said Ina. She had not expected to be questioned about her delay and therefore had prepared no excuse. "I was using the toilet."

"I didn't hear it flush."

"Where's Jo?"

"She'll be back soon."

"Good. I'm hungry."

"Can you excuse me?"

"Certainly, dear. Don was telling me you go to church."

"Sometimes," Annie said, looking uncomfortable. "It's nothing official. Just some time to myself." She hesitated, then said, "Without giving offense, what are your plans short-term? For this afternoon say?"

"Go to Ray's and see Amanda," Ina said. "Helene will want to."

"That sounds good. I know Ray is wondering where that situation is leading," Annie said.

Ina laughed. "The Chicago branch of the family arrives—and the L.A. branch just goes into a tizzy," she said. "What does the future hold? Where is the situation leading? Why are we here?"

Annie unzipped her culottes and stepped out of them. Her underpants had a hole the size of a dime near the waistband.

"Those are all valid questions," Annie declared. "You embark on an escapade—a dangerous one at that—and arrive here unannounced. Amanda does the same to Ray. We have lives to live, too, and we can't always absorb *escapaders* such as you, Helene, and Amanda."

Ina challenged, "Are you asking me to leave?"

Annie held her balled up culottes to her forehead, her eyes squeezed shut.

"No. Sit. Stay. When Jo comes back, enjoy your salad," Annie answered. "Forget what I said. I'm a bitch to everyone I love these days." She hurried out of the room before Ina could respond.

"Because if you want us to go, we'll go," Ina said softly to the empty kitchen. "I am *willing* to go."

Annie returned suddenly, as though she had been eavesdropping.

"Did you say something?"

"Muttering. A muttering old bat."

"Hush. But give me a half hour's notice before you go to Ray's—I'll get Don's driver up here to take you."

"Don has a driver?"

"Driver slash bodyguard," Annie boasted. "It's the latest."

"Don needs a bodyguard?"

"Everyone who can afford one has one," Annie said. "They're all afraid their wealth will make them targets."

Ina checked Helene; in her freedom now she urged her sister to sleep on. The beer was cold and golden going down. She took the open can out by the pool, where the air had warmed and turned a dirty red in the distance. Cars appeared and disappeared on the canyon bends. She unfolded a lawn chair and sat by the pool. She wished for Helene to remain asleep, for Annie to linger in her room, for Jo to take her time at Taco Bell.

She heard piano music, chimes, the growl of a sports car. A man spoke loudly. She smelled the ocean, her beer. She heard a rhythmic clicking on wood, then the piano again.

The clicking was coming from behind her; she turned, reluctant to be surprised. A golden retriever was coming up the canyon stairs, his nails clattering on the steps. He gave Ina one cursory glance, then dove into the pool. His big slicked head cut the water like a toy barge.

Ina wondered what she would do if the dog began to drown. She took a sip of her beer. He was swimming directly toward her.

"I'm not coming in after you," she said, and the dog ceased his paddling as if to hear what she had said.

"Don't stop. You'll sink. You're on your own."

The retriever evidently knew the pool, for he angled away to the ladder and clambered out. The spray he shook loose rained on Ina, who hid her face in her hands and laughed. The dog went back down the canyon steps.

Helene had rolled over, but slept on. No sign of Annie, no sound of a shower. Moments after Ina returned to her chair by the pool, Jo was back, a tiny made-up presence virtually lost behind the wheel of the Mercedes.

The paper bag Jo brought from the car was so heavy she had to carry it with both hands. With a smile, she set it like an offering at Ina's feet.

"Thank you, Jo."

Jo raised a finger, slipping inside the pool shed. She emerged with a TV tray that she expertly snapped into shape. The bag contained napkins, a plastic white fork, and a heaped salad cradled in stiff leaves of dough, which Jo, without asking, broke fragments from and ate.

The salad—full of too many bacon bits and shreds of cheese, and not enough simple, cold vegetables—was not what she would have ordered, but nonetheless delicious. The dough leaves were concocted of flour and air and seemed to dissolve with an effervescence of grease on her tongue. She ate looking out over the canyon. Jo stood at her side, reaching over and snapping off shards of dough without asking. Ina said nothing about this; she felt she lacked the worldliness to put a domestic in her place.

Annie came outside in a towel. Jo went inside; she had refined the technique of selective invisibility to such a degree that she could slip past Annie and into the house without being noticed. She counted on Annie's arrogance.

"Where's Jo?"

"I saw her around here."

"I see she got the salad. How is it?"

"Too spicy. But good."

"Now she'll play ghost all day in hopes I'll forget about the change and receipt," Annie said, with an unflattering poisonous squint in her voice. "How's the beer?"

"Sublime."

Annie went back into the house. She returned with a tray of makeup, a small mirror on a tripod, sunglasses.

"Would you like a swim, Mom?"

"I should tell you—a dog just went in there," said Ina.

"A dachshund?"

"Golden retriever."

"I don't know that one," Annie said.

She unknotted her towel and then, shy, dove out of it. The towel held her shape for an instant in midair, then collapsed to the tile just before Annie hit the water. She kicked over to the far wall without coming up for air. Her shape was undulant and boyish. She turned and came back, still underwater, and surfaced spitting like a seal at Ina's feet.

"Come on in," Annie coaxed.

"I couldn't."

"Just take off your dress."

"The two of us naked in a pool—in California—it is too much for me to imagine."

"Hand me my sunglasses then, please. And my towel."

She wiped moisture from her eyes with the heels of her hands. Ina offered to hold the towel for Annie, and she turned her back to her mother and hopped up onto the pool's edge, then pulled the towel down around her. She shook out her hair, and combed it back with her fingers.

"Jo!" she called suddenly.

The maid stopped on her way from the house to the pool shed.

"Do you have the change from the salad?" Annie asked, heartless as a teller.

"I will get it," Jo said.

"Bring it out here, please. The receipt, too." she said to Ina, "Now watch. She'll stall some more. She hopes I'll forget. Don lets her keep the change—but I don't have his guilt."

"Would you miss the money?" Ina asked.

Annie uncapped a bottle of pink polish and began to paint her toenails.

"Probably not. In fact, no," she said. "But I gave her a twenty— your salad was maybe four. The sixteen dollars, Don or Meg would tell me, is a year's pay for some people in Guatemala. It's a pittance in L.A. But we stay rich here by watching out for pittances."

"Maybe a tip for going?" Ina said.

"It's like raising a kid, Mom. You need to set limits."

"Maybe just to be generous?"

"Mom, I see early poverty for you out here."

"I'm going to check on Helene."

She stepped into the cool house, took a beer from the refrigerator, and opened it on the way to the bedroom. Helene was sleeping on her back. She had kicked off the covers. She looked so insubstantial, all sticks and paper, that she gave Ina a chill of premonition; her sister probably would not look much different dead. Yet there was perspiration like a gleam of health at her temples and in the hollow of her throat. Ina longed to wake her.

She was drinking the beer and reading a teen magazine on the bathroom couch when she heard a timid tapping from the bedroom, and hurried out thinking Helene was up and in need of her.

But Helene had not stirred.

The tapping was repeated, at the door. It was Jo.

"Please," she said, pointing into the room.

"Come in," Ina said.

They went into the bathroom.

"Smoke?" Jo asked.

"No, I haven't any," Ina said. "I don't."

Jo opened a cupboard under the sink. Hidden inside a tissue box was a pack of Marlboros and a book of matches. She took out two cigarettes and lit one, sucking with such greedy force that the ash grew half an inch.

"Meg," Jo said, grinning, then exhaling a thunderhead of smoke. She knocked the ash off over the rim of the sink.

A little slip of paper appeared in Jo's hand. It was the receipt for the salad.

"Annie's looking for that."

Jo nodded.

"Is there some problem?" Ina asked.

"Change."

"Where is the change?"

"I need it," Jo said.

"Have you spent it?"

Jo considered this question for a time, as if comparing the expected trajectories of several answers she had to choose from.

"No," she finally said.

"Then give it to her. That's the best course, believe me."

"I need it," Jo said. She added politely, "You don't need it."

"Pardon? What?"

"Money."

"Everyone needs money," Ina said, sounding to herself like Annie.

"No children. Rich daughter," Jo said. "No longer young. No worries. I am poor. Little boy. Husband gone. Many worries."

"It's stealing," Ina said, flustered by the woman's logic. "Whether from Annie—or me. Stealing, Jo."

Jo frowned. She produced a second receipt. This one was scratched with a shoe tread and water-stained; it reported a purchase of $18.86.

"Annie won't fall for it," Ina cautioned. "You'd only make her mad."

"No. You take back," Jo said. "Say food made family sick. Get money back."

Ina laughed. "They would never believe me. Where's the rest of the food? Where's proof my family is sick?"

"You are white," Jo said. "They are happy to see you."

"No, Jo. Give Annie her change. She likes you," Ina said. "If she catches you stealing—where would you and Ambrosio go?"

"Another pool house," Jo said. She had found a twenty-dollar bill somewhere on her person; the bill had a tendency to retain a tubular shape and Jo tried to flatten it on the skinny curve of her thigh.

"You give," Jo said, putting the bill and receipt in Ina's hand.

"She gave you a twenty. She shouldn't get a twenty back."

"I buy salad with my money," Jo said. With a quick, professional flourish she produced a cloth and wiped the mirror. "She owes me three and seventy-nine."

"Your money?"

"Easier that way."

"Than breaking the twenty?"

"Yes. Whites see Jo with twenty, they make bad change. I have to fight with them."

Ina took the twenty to Annie, who was putting on lipstick by the pool.

"Here's your money," Ina said, putting the twenty on the makeup tray. "You owe Jo three seventy-nine."

"What in the world is going on?" Her lips, pursed close to the mirror, looked plump, waxy with fruit color, lips a man would long to kiss only if there were a promise of something more to follow.

"She didn't want to break the twenty," Ina said. "She said whites cheat her."

"Jesus," Annie muttered. "It's in my purse. In the kitchen. Did you check *your* money?"

"For what?"

"For missing twenties."

Ina had considered this. But she had no desire to learn the truth; she liked Jo, her passive guile, the way she moved through a hostile world. Ina felt she could afford to be taken advantage of at least once.

THEY ventured down Narrow Canyon Road, two widows side by side in the back of a black limousine, the TV off, the ice bucket full, a beer in Ina's hand, Helene having refused the driver's offer of a beverage.

"Are you a bodyguard as well?" Ina asked.

"I'm a driver, ma'am. I'm in training to become a bodyguard."

"What if we're attacked?"

"I beg your pardon, ma'am?"

"What if we're attacked and we're protected only by a driver?"

"I can evade and flee, ma'am. In six months I'll be armed."

"Thank you," Ina said. "You may close the divider."

A polished shield rose up from the back of the front seat. Ina could see herself and her sister in it. Helene appeared uneasy. Ina said, "That's fine and dandy, in six months. What about this afternoon?"

"What's this about attacks?" Helene asked. "May I trouble you for a cup of ice chips?"

"Annie says the haves are busy protecting themselves from the have-nots."

"And none too soon," Helene said, sitting back. "It feels strange to be riding."

"He's very smooth."

"He *can* evade and flee, dear."

"I know. Here's your ice."

"Do we have far to go?"

"I'm not sure."

"I'm getting nervous," Helene said.

"It's only Amanda."

"I know. But this doesn't sit right with me—her being here. It's not a good sign for her relationship with Gordon."

Ina, nervous herself, said nothing. In the way of mothers she was looking forward more to a reunion with her own child.

Helene was dressed in the best clothes she had brought from Chicago. Her hair was freshly washed and set, her nails painted by Annie while Ina combed her lank hair into clusters and put them up in rollers. They fussed over her, complimented her every feature, while she sat like a queen. She spoke pensively of Amanda, who waited like a riddle at the end of their trip. Ina did not mention Ray.

He had called while Helene was in the shower. Annie came to Meg's room to report to Ina: "He says Amanda is still there. He says she's very jumpy. She hardly goes out at all. Frankly he'll be happy when she leaves. To where, is the mystery."

The driver took them along the ocean, up the California Avenue incline, then down Wilshire into Westwood. Ray's apartment was in a complex enclosed by high walls with white stucco towers poking above the tree line. The iron gate into the compound was made somewhat more inviting by a weaving of flowering ivy through the one-inch-diameter rods. A security camera, itself protected inside a Lucite box, looked them over. Ina found Ray's name on the directory and he buzzed them through after Ina identified herself over the intercom.

Once inside, she heard Ray calling her. He sounded far above them and out of sight. The place was preternaturally lush, with the apartment entrances and balconies and almost every other sign of human life hidden by electrically generated waterfalls and carefully sculpted canopies and drooping abundances of bougainvillea, ice plant, eucalyptus, and palm. The air was thick and cool, placid with the hum and gurgle of moving water.

A petite Oriental man swept grit and leaves off the walk and into a dustpan. A spray bottle of green liquid hung from a loop on his belt. He smiled at the women. Birds were singing, very pretty, somewhere above. The sunlight that reached the ground fell chipped and precious on the plants.

"Mom? Helene?" Ray called again.

Ina paused. "Yes, dear?"

"Are you lost?"

"Only marginally so. Where are you?"

"Follow the path around."

A man and woman, the man gorgeous, the woman a head taller than the man and on another plane of attractiveness above him, their air defiant and assured, passed Ina and Helene without a glance. They vanished like mists into the greenery.

"Something smells delicious," Helene said.

A second Oriental man materialized, a small basket of prunings hooked on his arm. He bowed, smiling, and pointed down the path.

"Yo, Mother! Where are you?"

"Here, dear. We are trying to arrive, but without success as yet."

"Keep coming."

They proceeded to a fork in the path. A sign nearly hidden in the growth told what apartments lay to the left and to the right.

"I see you!" Ray called out.

"Where?" Ina answered, annoyed, feeling choked by the plants.

"Up here."

"That way," Helene said, pointing unerringly to the source of Ray's voice.

He was up there. From the third floor, on a little parcel of balcony, Ray waved when he saw his mother catch his eye. Ina laughed. The sight of him did her in.

"About ten feet farther is a path to my door," he called, waving them on. "I'll let you in."

They found the walk; delineated by small orange lanterns, the path wound through still more cloying jungle until depositing them at a wide red door, a gold 22 hand-painted above the peephole. Amanda, to Ina's surprise and chagrin, was there to greet them.

Ina said hello, and spoke Amanda's name in warning, but Helene seemed to know. Her anticipation turned to wariness, set off by the imbedded codes of Amanda's perfume, the rhythm of her breathing, perhaps some tick of hesitation in opening any door that only Helene would recognize.

"Why are you crying?" Amanda asked, taking Ina in her arms, then setting her loose.

"You're crying?" Helene said, surprised.

"Just happy to see Ray," said Ina.

Amanda leaned around Ina (who craned the opposite way around Amanda, looking for her son) to take her mother by her shoulders and draw her reluctantly into her arms. Helene came forward, stubbed a toe on the threshold, and then enfolded her daughter. Amanda began to sob. Helene, thinking she knew why, joined her.

A small door slid open across the foyer and there was Ray, standing in a closet. He jumped out squealing and ran to his mother, swinging her up off her feet and setting her down carefully in a swirl of her cotton dress. As Ina hugged him she watched over her shoulder as the closet door slid shut and it dawned on her that her son had a private elevator.

Ray released her, and with a nod of his head at Helene and Amanda, whispered, "I was *afraid* this might be tearful."

He put his arm around her and steered her through a dining room where the table was a sheet of glass balanced on four stone spheres, then into a sunlit kitchen.

"God, I can't believe you're here," he said. "For weeks we wondered where you were. I was certain you were going to crash somewhere and never be found. It was *madness*, what you did."

"Well, here I am. All in one piece."

"You know, it sounds very exciting in retrospect. Crazy enough to be fun. But you must promise me: never again."

"I promise," Ina said, smiling.

"Sure you do. I don't believe you, but I'll just have to settle for it. Do you still drink beer?" he asked, a stern eye on her.

"Of course."

"Want one now?"

"I'll wait," she said, wanting to make him happy.

"We'll give them a minute alone." He set out four cups and saucers, then poured tea into each from a china pot warming on the stove.

"You take sugar—" he said and dropped one cube into her cup. "Amanda does, too. I know Helene can't." He removed a pitcher of cream and a plate of sliced date-nut bread from the refrigerator.

"I don't know what is going on, Mom," he admitted in a low voice. "I've never felt particularly close to Amanda—but she appeared here and I offered her a place to stay. She keeps to herself. I heard her crying in her room. I don't feel any closer to her.

Frankly, she's overstayed the welcome I extended her. But I don't want to kick her out."

"It's the end of a romance," Ina said. "Or so we surmise."

Ray shrugged. He was setting the table, moving from place to place and getting each setting just right. Ina watched him, gorged with love for him; she almost felt the love would split her apart. But he reminded her so much of Vincent, his enthusiasm, the lightness of his step, the set of his face in repose, his attention to detail, his self-absorption, that he inflicted a measure of pain with his presence.

"I can't believe it's only that," Ray said.

Amanda led Helene in. Helene's eyes were dried, but scoured red by her tears. Ray jumped to get her chair out, her coat off, make her comfortable.

"Tea, straight," he said crisp as a waiter. "Directly in front." He swung out a chair to Helene's right. "Amanda, you're here."

She sat without a word. Above her head, Ray rolled his eyes and grimaced. She combed her hair with a nervous rake of her fingers. That sensual heft of her body was missing. She no longer exhibited that forthright impatience to get to the resolution of a desire that Ina had always admired about Amanda. She had lost weight. She needed to get some rest, get out in the sun and cook that cold, sad look out of her eyes. She brought the tea to her mouth with both hands, blew on it, and drank.

"Here, Mom," Ray said, gesturing to a chair by the window. The window looked to the back of the apartment, onto a small patio and garden fenced high enough to discourage the curious; fences within fences. The door in the fence led to a garage.

"Amanda's in the top bedroom," Ray said, sitting on the very edge of his chair.

"How many floors to you have?"

"Four," Ray said. "It's basically a square silo built off the elevator shaft. Kitchen and dining room here. Living room on the second floor. Then my bedroom on three, Amanda on four. And bathrooms on every floor, of course." He winked at Ina. "Maybe you can come help me do some business—while Amanda and Helene visit."

"That sounds great," Ina said. She wanted her son to herself and she wanted an hour or two when Helene was in the care of someone else. Amanda drank her tea without a word. She didn't touch the date-nut bread. Abruptly she reached over and touched her mother's face, smoothing a strand of hair back behind her ear. Helene, startled at first, smiled and leaned shyly into the pressure of her daughter's hand. She seemed so stunned by an accumulation of circumstances and emotions that she had forgotten it was her habit with Amanda to nag.

"I can't believe you're here," Helene said.

Amanda turned her attention elsewhere and kept silent.

"I can't believe *you're* here," Ray said, jumping into the awkward silence like the perfect host.

"It really was no trouble," Ina said. The trip seemed like it had taken place years ago, something they had once experienced.

"For you, maybe," said Ray.

"It was stupid and dangerous," Amanda declared, sudden anger giving her some color.

"But you made it safely," Ray countered, "and that's what's important."

"And what have you accomplished?" Amanda asked heatedly.

"It's obvious, isn't it?" Ina said. "We got to California."

Ray, nervous, took his cup and saucer to the sink.

"Now that you're here," Ray said, "I'm going to take my mother to some of my stores while you two catch up."

He whirled Ina out of the kitchen and into the elevator. It rose with a muffled hum of machinery.

"We'll go to the top," he said. "Show you Amanda's room. *Your* room if you say the word."

The room was generously sized, octagonal, and Amanda's bags were open on the floor, clothes flung about. From the balcony Ina looked down on the roof of the jungle and was surprised to see a pattern to the walks, the waterfalls, the other apartments. A family of pink birds preened each other's feathers at the top of a eucalyptus almost close enough to touch.

"In here," Ray called from the bathroom, "a small refrigerator for who knows what. Fresh fruit. Your own bath. Air-conditioning.

At night, a breeze from heaven.'' He patted her arm. ''Think about it.''

In Ray's room, Ina waited on the balcony while he changed. He had a wicker chair and a cordless phone out there, a small spider plant in the corner. His room was very stark, no wasted surfaces. A twin-sized bed, a boy's bed, against the wall. The walls were colored cream, the carpet gray. There was an air of loneliness, to Ina's mind. It needed a touch of something. His desk was polished black wood, fastidiously organized, the phone white with red buttons, four lines, the handset so streamlined Ina was confused how it would fit in her hand. He had a computer terminal on a stand of matching wood arranged perpendicular to the desk. The cursor blinked, a rectangular calling.

''I feel something good is about to happen,'' Ray announced, taking a billfold and set of keys from the desk drawer. ''For so long I've tried to get you out here—and now I've got you.'' He squeezed her shoulders.

''So much depends on Helene,'' Ina said.

''Amanda is here. If they need money to get a place—I'll help,'' said Ray.

''Amanda doesn't have the patience. Or the interest.''

They looked in on them before leaving. Neither Amanda nor Helene appeared to have moved or spoken.

''Will you be all right?'' Ina asked.

''Fine, dear,'' Helene said.

''We'll be back—when?'' Ina asked of Ray.

''As soon as we can. Amanda knows where everything is. They'll be fine.''

''We'll leave the driver for you,'' Ina said. Still, a reluctance to leave pulled at her. Amanda stared off into the distance, and Helene seemed to be staring at the opposite horizon. Could they save each other in an emergency?

''Come,'' Ray said.

Out in the jungle coolness, Ray took Ina's arm and pulled her merrily along. Damp, waxy fronds brushed her cheek. The driver sat reading in his idling limousine, all the windows up, a mist on the inside of the glass.

He saw Ina and stepped out.

"Have you somewhere else to go?" she asked.

"I'd like to make a pit stop, fill the tank, get a bite to eat," he replied. "Otherwise, I'm yours until you send me back."

"By all means, dear, take a break. My son and I are going out for a while—but I told my sister you'd be waiting if she needed you."

The driver saluted and departed.

"Nice touch," said Ray. "Don's?"

"His company. Our driver is merely a driver in training to be a driver slash bodyguard."

"Don has a bodyguard?" Ray said. "Why would anyone hurt innocuous old Don?"

"Annie says it's not Don—it's wealth. The wealthy are the targets now."

"Don should drive a Pinto then. He'd be perfectly safe," Ray said.

"I'll bring that up with him."

"Me, I can walk to my first stop. Care to accompany me?"

They linked arms and set off toward UCLA. As they neared the campus there were students everywhere, on skateboards, bicycles, in cars. Beautiful boys and girls walked only until they encountered someone they knew, and then their progress was halted to exchange the news of the day. This ritual held in the streets, as well, and traffic, for that reason, was slow and piecemeal. Yet no one seemed to mind; they were in college.

"This place is loaded," Ray confided. "Rich, *rich* kids. They routinely soil their clothes, then they pay me to get them clean. I'm an institution here—but nobody knows me."

"Like an undertaker," Ina said.

"Like Dad."

"No," Ina said. "He was in the public eye. He was a member of the community."

"He told me himself," said Ray.

"Told you what?"

"That the secret was to discover the enduring service—and provide it better than anyone else," Ray said.

"We had an occasional lean season," Ina said, though she could not remember one.

"Dad could always move a piece of property," Ray said. "That was his vanity."

"He came home discouraged more than once."

"I don't remember that," Ray said, disappointed he might have missed something about his father.

"Oh, yes. The long face. The twinkle absent from his eye," Ina said. "He would lose faith in his ability."

They arrived at Ray's Laundromat. The establishment took up an entire block, the front all glass, the UCLA football schedule and results painted to fill one entire pane, the basketball schedule waiting on another. Music roared through the room from speakers like black refrigerators suspended in each corner. A young man with spiked blue hair sat in a booth at the rear playing records. He did not wave to Ray, but rather raised his eyebrows with such nonchalance that it barely qualified as a greeting. Mirrors covered the walls; everyone in the place was busy looking at himself, or at someone he was sure he was looking at him when he wasn't looking. There were pay phones by the door, video games, and machines dispensing laundry soap, bleach, soda pop, candy, and condoms at the back.

Every washer and dryer was in use. Boys and girls in blue and gold Ray's Laundromat shirts danced around giving change, dispensing advice about stains, moving wash to the dryers for the students too busy to stay and see their laundry through to completion.

"This is quite a sight, Ray," Ina hollered in his ear.

"Eighty-eight washers. Seventy-five dryers," he answered. "Usually someone has to wait for a dryer. Or share. My people bring people together. They fall in love, marry, have kids, all because of me. Having to wait for something creates the impression of value—of *rarity*. As long as they don't have to wait too long, it gives the place a sense of panache, like a hot new club."

"It's certainly busy."

"This is my showplace, Mom," Ray said. "I've got ten others

around town. They all have their moments, but this is the one that hums day and night. This is the one I'd bring Dad to."

"He'd be very proud," Ina said.

"You think so? I like to think so."

"He would just want you to be happy."

"Secondarily," Ray said. "But I think he'd first of all want me to show a profit."

Ray met with the laundromat's manager (a beautiful woman with a gold ring in her nose) for a half-hour while Ina sat on a chair outside the office, reading the student newspaper and wishing she had a beer. The music was painfully loud; she missed the silence of her world with Helene. Just at the moment she had worked up the courage to ask Ray to turn down the music, he emerged from his meeting and took her away from there.

They were gone about two hours, long enough to visit four laundromats. None were as busy as the UCLA location, and in two near the airport an aura of sullen danger was palpable. The clientele in these was mostly black or Hispanic women with plump, shaded babies tucked like bundles on the benches or propped against a bag of folded whites. Interspersed among these women were young men who went to the front window to examine Ray's car and then turned to examine the car's occupants. Ina felt she was being weighed as the potential object of a crime. What sort of resistance would she offer? These young men had narrow, feral faces, mustaches fine as two lines of mascara, and scars like strokes of pale paint on their caramel skin.

Ray spoke Spanish where it was called for. The manager (in his Ray's Laundromat shirt) was always Hispanic or black, and they discussed business in general terms out where everyone could see them. Ray dipped into the office for the receipts and records only toward the end of the visit, and only for a moment. He kept Ina by the office door where he could see her. He parked his car where he could watch it at all times.

They arrived home late in the afternoon. There was a threat in the jungle shadows despite the engineered waterfalls and piped music and fractured illumination of hidden lights. The coiled sensations of the neighborhoods they had visited worked at Ina's uneasiness. Ray pulled her along as if he felt the same thing.

Broken glass crunched under Ray's foot in the foyer. His first thought was to have his mother wait outside, but she pushed him ahead like a shield.

The glass was from a vase, which had held an iris now lying on the floor in a little corona of moisture and cracked petals. Ray was looking for something in the valise he had carried on his business calls, then out came a pistol.

"Put that away," said Ina.

She could not wait, and skirted her son's protection and his refraining reach.

"Helene!"

Helene called back, "Thank God!" It carried out from the kitchen. "Where on earth have you been?"

Helene sat where they had left her and she stood immediately and thrust out a hand and commanded Ina, "Take me to the bathroom at once."

"Where's Amanda?"

"First the bathroom. Please steady me, my foot is asleep."

When they came back to the kitchen, Helene told them she had been alone for most of the time they were gone.

"I'd say within twenty minutes of your departure, Amanda and I had had a fight," Helene said. "Out she stormed. I assumed she would settle down and come back. But she never did. I tried to find the bathroom myself—but I got all turned around. I broke something. I'm sorry. I started to cry"—and she started again—"and got scared that nobody would ever come back. I found my way back to the chair and I've been sitting here with my legs tightly crossed for the last hour."

Ina squeezed her sister's shoulder. Ray put a cup of tea before Helene and opened a bottle of beer for Ina.

"You poor dear," Ina said. "I will never forgive that girl."

"She's crushed. Worse than I've ever seen her," Helene said. "She had a romance—a legitimate chance at a husband and a family—and now it's over. She let it slip away."

"And that's what caused the fight?"

"That is the root of it," Helene said. "The end of the romance devastated her, and I was upset that she'd let Gordon get away. I said some things I probably ought not to have said."

"Don't tell me," said Ina. "You're terrible with her. Treating her like she's thirteen years old."

"I had hopes for this one," Helene admitted. "How many men do you meet who want children?"

Ray returned from the foyer, the pieces of vase swept into a dustpan. He listened politely to Helene go on about Amanda's lost love, and Ina made a face at him before she realized he did not know the truth. In fact, she and Amanda were the only two people who knew the real story of Gordon. Ina actually was surprised Amanda had kept the truth from her mother; in the heat of their argument the facts about her relationship with this man would have slid like needles through Helene's heart. Yet Amanda had let the story stand. Gordon remained eligible, employed, a lover of children.

And what *was* the truth? Had he rediscovered what he had loved about his wife? Had he grown tired of Amanda and found someone else? Or would Amanda return to him when her vacation was at an end?

"I wonder where she could have gone," Ray said.

"She didn't stop to pack," Helene said. "She stormed right out."

"I wonder if she took our driver," Ina said.

"Is it dark out?"

"No."

"I'll send the guy home," Ray said. "I can drive you to Annie's."

He left by the front door and while he was gone they heard the elevator begin to run. Ina took her beer into the foyer, Helene perched anxiously on her arm. The elevator arrived, the door opened, and out stepped Amanda.

"Hello, everyone," she said, a wary look at her mother, a questioning glance at Ina: *Now* what have I missed?

"You've been upstairs all this time?" Helene asked incredulously.

"Yes. Where did you think?"

"You left! The door slammed! Didn't you hear me crying? Didn't you hear the glass break?"

Amanda had on a bathrobe and she hugged the neck shut tight and swept into the kitchen. Her hair was tousled, her face scrubbed blank by sleep.

"I went up to my room," she explained, examining the contents of the refrigerator, settling on a small basket of blueberries. She sat down to dip them with her fingers into the sugar bowl.

"I was here all alone," Helene cried. "I practically exploded waiting for someone to help me to the bathroom."

"I don't hear a thing up there," Amanda said. "I laid down to relax—and I fell asleep."

Appalled, Ina asked, "Didn't you think she might need some looking after? In a strange house? You the only one who could help?"

"I'm sorry. Okay?"

"I'm blind," Helene shouted.

"I *know*. What do you want me to do about it?" her daughter answered, leaning forward, spraying sugar.

Ray returned then. He saw Amanda and said, "You were upstairs?"

"Yes. I *was* upstairs. I *did* fall asleep. I *am* a worthless child."

ALL together now, Ina thought, we are a family again. They were sitting around the pool at Annie and Don's while Jo grilled steaks. Ambrosio played jacks on the tile. Meg knelt beside him and watched; she was dying for a cigarette and paused frequently at the head of the stairs where Katy might appear and rescue her with a summons to go for a walk. She could be back in ten minutes and smoke two in that time.

Amanda was not there, although Helene had assured her it would be rude to refuse the invitation. Don was home but he hadn't come outside. Annie sat between Ina and Ray. Ina sat with one hand on the arm of Helene's chair. She kept being fooled by the perspective when she turned to look at her sister, who appeared to teeter on the edge of the canyon. The air was coppery with approaching night. She wished she were back at Ray's, where she could have a beer like an adult. Annie went inside to look for her husband.

Someone was coming up the canyon stairs. Meg stood hopefully. Helene turned her head to listen. The tread was heavier than a young girl's, more deliberate, ponderous: a man advancing with a purpose.

He came into view. He was slim, handsome, dressed in linen slacks and a pale peach sport coat, no socks, tan ankles. He searched their party for a familiar face and something like shyness bloomed in his eyes before he finally came to Meg, who could not hide her disappointment that it was not Katy, but Katy's father.

"Hi, Meaghan," he said.

She made rapid, semirude introductions Each time she called him Mr. Mendel, he cheerfully corrected, "Call me Boyce."

"Boyce it is," Ray said, standing and shaking hands.

"Is your dad home, Meaghan?" he asked.

"Mom just went looking for him. He's probably working."

"That's why he lives up here," Boyce said.

"I'll tell him you're here."

"Can I fix you a drink?" Ray asked, waving like the host at a cart Jo had wheeled to the edge of the pool.

"A Perrier? Ice?"

"Ice water? Lemon?"

"That would be fine."

"You got it."

Ina perked up. "Beer?" she asked.

Don, Annie, and Meg came out the back door. Boyce approached them, hand extended, and in that moment Ray dipped the glass into the pool, added ice and a twist of lemon, and presented the drink to Boyce with a swell of bonhomie and a patted shoulder.

Boyce took a sip and winced. He glanced at Ray, who was nonchalantly opening Ina's beer.

Boyce addressed Don: "I've come to speak to you about the stairway."

Don, half listening, went among his guests shaking hands and kissing cheeks. He had a few words with Ina and Helene, holding their hands. Then he moved on to Ray, then a fleeting inspection of the meat Jo was tending, and finally a quick ruffle of Ambrosio's hair.

"What about the stairway, Boyce?" he said, taking a seat on the diving board. He was wearing shorts. His legs were pale and muscular, a man too hard at work to tan.

"You heard about the Tylers?" Boyce said.

"I haven't," Annie said. She had fixed her husband a drink and handed it to him. But she didn't sit beside him.

"They were at the Lakers game," Boyce said, "Someone came up the back stairway and cleaned them out."

"How do you know they came up the stairs?" Meg asked suspiciously.

"The front door wasn't touched. Their patio door—they just threw the chaise longue through it," Boyce said. "That's three break-ins in four months. I've had enough, Don."

Meg said, "Maybe they went to the front, found out nobody was home, then went around back."

"I know you and Katy like the stairway, Meaghan," Boyce said. "When it was first put in it was a nice idea. Neighbors could visit without having to walk on the road. And for you and Katy— that's what it still represents." He hesitated, sighed. "But for a lot of us—speaking for myself now and a significant percentage of the other homeowners on this side of Narrow Canyon—the stairway has become an invitation to trouble. Anyone can climb them. Thieves. Vandals. Low-lifes. They're full of dark areas where the owners haven't kept the bushes trimmed back—places any sort of creep could hide, they can go up and down virtually unobserved. They scare me, Don. I think it's time we took them out."

"No!" Meg shouted.

"You mention a 'significant percentage,' Boyce. Who else have you talked to?" Don asked. Ina watched him draw up his legs, clasp his knees to his chest. He was so contained; an absence of slippage. Ina was often at a loss to understand what Vincent had found so likable about him.

"You're the first—officially," Boyce said. "Unofficially—just testing the waters—a half dozen. I wanted to have the weight of your support for the plan before I went to the others."

"It seems awfully *radical,*" Annie said.

With a flicker of annoyance, Don took Boyce's side against his wife, almost out of curiosity.

"What Boyce proposes *is* radical," Don said. "But this is a radical problem. The Tylers are only two houses down. What's to stop them from coming all the way up?"

"Nothing," Boyce said fervently, believing he had won his point.

"But those stairs have been there for years," Don said. "And this is the first *real* problem."

"Hardly the first, Don. I see my insurance bill. And who's to say the problem won't just continue to *intensify?*" Boyce said.

"The late '80s syndrome, Boyce?"

"It's the times, Don. My point is: Why provide them with a runway to launch their crimes? Why provide access?"

Don smiled evenly. "Nice images, Boyce."

"Can I count on you?"

"Who will take out the stairs?" Don asked.

"My company can do it for cost," said Boyce.

Don laughed appreciatively. "Mendel—I like your style. Your company will do it at cost."

"Don't laugh, Don. You get estimates, they see the neighborhood, the price goes through the roof," Boyce said. "My cost would be half your low bid, I guarantee it."

"And who pays?" Don asked.

"The residents would have to pay, of course."

"And how would you divide the cost?"

"A for-instance: You've got nine houses with access to the stairs," Boyce said. "You take the price and divide it by nine. Simple. Or, say someone bitches that they have fewer stairs on their property than someone else, they shouldn't have to pay as much. Okay. Measure the length of the stairs on each piece of property, divide everyone up according to their percentage of the total. When there's a dispute over whose property a chunk of stairs is on, I'll take that out for nothing. Or, say that grump down at the bottom—Morton—he says he only walks from his house down, he never goes up, so he doesn't use the stairs as much as you or me or the Tylers, so why should he have to pay as much as someone who walks farther on them? Don't let on, Don, but I'd pick up that guy's share because he's a schmuck and I could feel superior to him."

Don, Ina, even Helene laughed. Boyce was startled, then pleased with himself.

"You've got it figured," Don said. "I should've expected no less. What do you see as a price?"

"A rough estimate: seventy-five hundred. Eight hundred, roughly, per house. The total could reach eighty-five, but no way do I see the individual shares exceeding one thousand."

"What do you say to the people who just refuse to take part?" Don asked. "To pay. To even give permission to remove the stairs on their property?"

"Moneywise," Boyce said, "I don't see where the amounts I'm talking about would be any problem at all in this neighborhood. You could cover the whole tab with what you've got in your billfold, if my estimate is on target—and I think it is. Me—I'm in a similar boat. So I don't see anyone being turned off by the price. If they are, I'm willing to carry a certain percentage of dead wood because I believe this project needs to be completed. As for the other thing, that's why I came to you first. I need you to get the ball rolling, so to speak. If I can go to the others with word that Don Bixler at the top of the mountain is on board, then that puts a very solid, subtle pressure on everyone below you. It's kind of like a dam breaking. You're the force. The others feel it. Do they resist—or do they go with the flow? That's why I need you, Don. Are you with me?"

"Not yet, Boyce," said Don. "Let me think it over. Talk to my wife and Meg."

Boyce, crestfallen, put aside his drink. At the head of the stairs he made a final pitch.

"They've got to go, Don. I see complete strangers on those

stairs every day," he said. "They pass within ten feet of everything I hold dear—and they could be *anybody.*"

"I'll be in touch," Don said, shaking Boyce's hand, sending
him away.

Don smiled politely at his guests, all of whom were in some
way family. Meg went and hugged him; Ina was certain Meg
thought she had won her father's support, but Ina knew better.

"He makes sense," Don said, stroking his daughter's hair.

Meg pushed away from him. "He's just paranoid," she declared. "Katy says the same thing. He's afraid of everything. He
keeps her and her mom practically prisoners."

Ina said, "He must read the papers."

"Those strangers he talks about are just friends of kids who
live up here," Meg said. "What's the big deal?"

"Ask your father about his bodyguard," said Ina.

Don had gone to the grill to inspect the steaks. Jo handed over
her long fork and Don turned each dripping cut, studying it, then
setting it back in place.

"Mr. Mendel is just nervous," he said. "Everyone is nervous."
To Jo he said, "These are done."

Jo stuck the fork into the meat and hoisted each steak onto
the platter. Ambrosio sat back on his heels. He held a silver jack
between his lips and it sparkled like a gem he was ready to eat.
His mother had an accident carrying the meat to the house. A
steak, one of the larger ones, slipped off the platter and fell on
the tile. Ina liked the sound it made: the heavy, wet slap of boun-
teousness. Clucking, Jo stabbed the meat with a distaste usually
reserved for a dog's mess on the carpet, and set it on a tray beside
the grill.

"That's perfectly good," Annie said, a declaration to no one
in particular.

"No. Dirty," Jo said. "Germs."

"Let her dispose of it," Don said. "We have plenty."

To Ina, Annie said, "She drops one every time."

Don, going through the door into the kitchen, playfully
punched her arm.

"*Don't* hit me," Annie said sharply.

"I was trying to get you to lighten up," Don said.

Jo danced ahead. She had the table set, flowers in vases, candles burning in white glass cups. She pulled out chairs for Helene, then Ina, then Meg. By then, Annie was seated, and it was too late to help her.

They questioned Ina and Helene through most of the meal. It was a glancing, polite sort of interrogation about their journey, full of exclamations of disbelief over mundane events, with no interest expressed in motives, desires, or plans for the future. Toward the end of the meal Don excused himself, shook Ray's hand, kissed the women, and went to bed.

"He'll work now for two hours," Annie said, half incredulous, half exasperated.

"Is that such a terrible thing?" Meg asked.

"Why not stay and talk?" Annie said. "Jo?" she called.

The door to the pool shed opened. Ina saw Ambrosio, a small shadow hunched protectively over a plate. Jo came inside, but with no sense of hurrying.

"You enjoy that steak?" Annie asked.

"Goodness, Ann," scolded Ina. "You ought to be ashamed."

"But I'm not."

"Mom, you're so rude," Meg said.

"Thank you," Annie replied. She helped Jo clear the table. Her spirits seemed to have been lightened by that minute secretion of poison.

"What will you do tomorrow?" she asked her mother.

"I don't know," Ina said. "Buy a house. Get a job."

"You can work for Ray."

"You can be my assistant," Ray said. "You and Helene both."

"How about Meg? Can you give her a job? Something in management," Annie said.

"Mom! I don't want a job," Meg said.

"Don't I know that."

"Meg will always have a job with Ray's," he said. He turned to Ina. "Where are you girls staying your first night in L.A.?"

Ina longed to go home with her son. She could sit and drink

and talk. But she could not leave Helene and Helene would not want to see any more of Amanda that night.

"We'll stay here," Ina said, covering Helene's hand.

"Good," said Meg.

"Maybe we'll visit you tomorrow," Ina said.

"Consider it a date." Ray was standing, shaking his keys. He said his good-byes, then took his mother's arm and had her walk him to his car.

He put his arm around her. "I'm worried about Amanda," he admitted.

"She's just heartbroken."

"That will pass," Ray said. "But I was hoping for some resolution of her living situation. Frankly, I'm getting tired of having her around."

"I know you are, dear."

"I'm being a boorish host, aren't I?"

"Understandably so."

"Let's get her and Helene set up in a little place in the canyon," he suggested enthusiastically. "And you can live with me in Westwood."

Ina frowned. "I don't think you're going to split us up, sweetheart," she said. "None of the parties involved would stand for it."

He hugged her, then kissed her cheek. "Let's work on it, okay?" he said.

"It isn't going to happen."

"Don't say 'isn't.' Don't say 'can't.' Don't say 'n't' at all."

WHEN her body felt the hour arrive to be on the road, Ina awoke from a fitful, irritating sleep to find Meg in the room. Helene was asleep, a whistle to her breathing. Meg was quietly looking for something in her dressing table. She was all shadows, something you could put your hand through.

"Should I turn on a light?" Ina whispered.

Meg floated over to her. "Did I wake you up?"

"No. Keep your voice down. What are you looking for?"

"Nothing."

"Why do you have a jacket on?"

"I'm meeting Katy."

"Can I come?"

Meg resumed her search. Operating by touch, she removed items, inspected them, cataloged them with her fingers, then set them out of the way. At last she put everything back and returned to Ina.

"I'm just going downstairs. You'll be bored," she said.

"You don't want me to go. Say so."

"You'll catch cold. We just sit outside and smoke. It's boring."

"You don't want me. Tell me. I can take it."

Meg made an impatient sound. *"Get dressed,"* she said.

Ina did not hesitate. She was willing to force herself on Meg for the opportunity to get out in the night. She carried her clothes into the bathroom, shut the door, and turned on the light. She undressed with her eyes squeezed shut. Her skin felt cool and electric.

A tap on the door.

Ina shut off the light and let Meg slide into the bathroom.

"Close your eyes."

"Closed."

Ina turned the light back on.

"What about Auntie Helene?" Meg asked, a hand over her eyes.

"She won't wake up."

"But what if she does?"

"You couldn't talk me out of going. Now you're trying guilt?"

Meg lowered her hand. Her eyes still closed, she was smiling. Her teeth were turning dingy from cigarettes. She wore a leather flight jacket with the collar turned up, a red beret folded in an epaulet. Her jeans had tears in the knees. She was gorgeous, Ina thought, and stank of cigarettes.

"It's my time with Katy," she said.

"This is my time with you," Ina said. "My time away from Helene."

They turned out the light, then Ina had them stand in the dark until they could see well enough to proceed. After the pitch of the bathroom, the bedroom seemed almost garishly illuminated by the moon and the canyon glow. Ina paused at Helene's bed to gauge the pulse of her sister's sleep; she judged it to be deep and enduring.

In the kitchen, she stopped to put a can of beer in the pocket of her windbreaker.

"Ready?" Meg asked. "Remember Jo. We don't want to wake them up."

The moon was flying over the hills. Ina felt a strumming beneath the stillness, a subtle and insistent hum. Light ran up the canyon, moved on the roads, poured out in all directions with the heedless abundance of sand. Light glowed inside Jo's shed. Below, in the canyon, she could see swimming pools floating like turquoise beans.

Meg went down a dozen steps to a small landing couched in shadow. A bench had been built there in a little alcove, a place to tarry, a place out of sight. Meg did not sit down, but paused to light a cigarette.

"How do you know Katy will be out?"

"She knows I'm coming."

"Did you call her?"

Meg peered at Ina as if she had come to the sudden realization that her grandmother was incredibly dense.

"We're *friends*," she said.

"How far do we have to go?"

"Come on." Meg drew on her cigarette and continued down. She was no longer as careful about the noise she made. She went ahead. Ina took her time. She was reminded rather distressingly of her age and the fact that a fall here would be serious. The space between one step and the next possessed an unwelcome mystery. In the darkness, in the shadows, her foot might come to rest on anything before attaining the solid comfort of the stair.

Meg waited for her at the next landing. She sat on the outside of the railing drumming on her knees and smoking.

"What if you fell?" Ina asked.

Meg looked curiously below, as if the prospect had never occurred to her.

"Am I holding you up?" Ina asked.

"A little, but that's okay."

"Wait until we're going back up," Ina said like a threat.

"I don't want you to hurt yourself," Meg said.

"Me neither. Who lives here?"

They were at the back of a patio much like their own, except the pool was empty and lawn furniture was stacked against the house.

"They moved," Meg said. "I don't remember their name. They had a boy younger than me named Greg. Or Gary. Or something like that. Katy will know. She absorbs details like that."

"It looks sad," Ina said.

Meg turned to view the empty house. She merely shrugged.

"It's just a house," Meg said, swinging her legs over and hopping down. "The next house, the Tylers? The ones who got robbed? When we're behind them I'd be kind of quiet. Katy's dad said they bought a gun or some kind of killer dog."

The Tylers' section of the stairs was painted white, and small wooden plant holders crowned four of the posts. Ina appreciated this effort to make that portion of the trip up or down memorable, and she wondered if that attempt had drawn the burglars' attention, and irritated them. The rear of the house was lavishly illuminated. Meg led them past briskly, crouching.

Katy awaited them farther down, or rather she awaited Meg, for she accepted Meg's introduction of Ina with a cool, rude look, and not a word. She was sitting on a bench in an alcove outside her family's back gate. A cigarette burned in her lips. The knees in her jeans were gone and when she pulled her legs up under her chin, small luminescent green faces smiled out of the rips.

"Neat," Meg said, laughing and leaning forward to inspect them. She touched one of the faces with a fingertip. A speck of paint came off and Meg touched it to the tip of Katy's nose, leaving a gleam like a pinprick. Katy tried to lick the dot off, but her tongue wouldn't reach, and Meg laughed, and leaned down and kissed her friend very firmly on the mouth.

"Just a moment, young lady," Ina scolded, mortified.

"We're just friends," Meg said, hunching her head down between her shoulders.

"Friends do kiss," Katy said.

"Not like that," said Ina.

"How then?" Katy challenged.

"On the cheek. On the forehead."

"Let's try it," Katy teased. She kissed Meg on the cheek, then on the forehead. "Is that better?"

"Don't make fun of me. Girls do not kiss on the mouth in public."

"Did Meg invite you down here with her?" Katy asked.

"Katy . . ." Meg said. "Don't."

"Because this was to be a private function until you arrived," Katy said.

"Ignore her, Moomer," Meg said. "She got this way from her mother."

Ina was sitting on the bench perpendicular to the girls, positioned where she could watch down the stairway and also look out into the canyon. She took the beer out of her pocket and opened it.

"Oo, beer," Katy said.

"Would you like a sip?"

"Meaghan said you drink a lot of that stuff."

"I didn't say 'a lot,' " Meg protested.

"Yes you did." Katy drew on her cigarette. "And no, I don't want any. That stuff is poisonous."

Ina took a long drink. It gave her such a glorious chill. "I love it," she said.

"I'll have a sip," Meg said. She took the edge off this small rebuke of her friend by leaning against Katy as she drank.

"Hold out your hand," Katy ordered.

Meg did so. Katy produced a nail-polish bottle of luminescent paint. She uncapped it and worked at Meg's palm with the brush. She painted a long straight line diagonally across Meg's hand, then a semicircle whose two ends touched the line, and from the semicircle long rays of glowing paint radiating up each of Meg's fingers. Meg smiled as she saw what it was, but she didn't make a sound. Katy, as she worked, very lightly ran her free fingers up and down the back of Meg's hand. Meg's eyes fell closed. She looked to Ina too languorous for her age. Ina felt herself go hot in the face remembering her willingness to force herself on Meg's little escapade, certain it was to be nothing more than two girls sneaking away to giggle and talk.

"Sunrise," Meg said in a low, thickened voice, admiring her hand.

Katy asked Ina, "Would you like me to do yours?"

"How about a flower on your thumbnail?" Meg suggested. She blew on her hand to dry it.

"All right," said Ina.

Katy painted a small, five-petal flower with the impersonal expertise of a carnival artist, and then she moved back beside Meg and lit both of them a cigarette.

"Now you do me," she said to Meg.

"I can't paint."

"Come on!" Katy teased. The hand she plopped in Meg's lap was long and narrow. She held the paint in her other hand.

"What should I paint?" Meg asked shyly.

"Anything you want."

Meg lifted the hand in her own hands. She turned it over and ran a finger along the skin from wrist to fingertip, as if seeking the smoothest surface. Then she pushed up the sleeve of Katy's sweater, exposing to the cool night that place where the pulse bubbled, where white skin was nearly like ice. She reached across and took the brush from the bottle, wiping the excess off on the rim. Katy giggled when Meg began to paint.

"Hold still!" Meg scolded, glancing at Ina, who had looked away.

A movement in the darkness down the stairs had caught her eye. When she looked closer, nothing was there. But when she looked back at Meg's painting, the movement returned, and she ignored it to give it a chance to stop by itself.

But the movement continued.

A man was coming up the stairs. He progressed three or four steps at a time, and then stopped to crouch, listen, and look all around. Ina didn't think he had seen them, because he paid as much attention to the darkness he had just come through as that yet ahead. Rather he seemed a man whose natural state was suspicion, who would walk down a street in daylight with the same careful scrutiny of everything around him.

Katy whispered, "M."

The man was dressed in dark clothes. His skin was a shade lighter than the night, but his hair was a perfect match. He seemed young, capable of prodigious leaps, and though he exuded a danger by his presence and his suspicious air, he was also an intriguing figure, a romantic figure, so that when he hopped up onto the landing and into the presence of the three women, he did not unduly frighten Ina.

They all stared at each other. The man was embarrassed. His clothes were old and in need of washing; a veil of dust seemed to permeate the air he stood in. He clutched a paper bag with a fervency that betrayed this bag held everything he owned. Clearly he did not belong in that neighborhood, on those stairs, whereas the three women (one with the word ME glowing on her wrist) clearly did.

Yet the man chose to break the spell. Rather than admitting that he was out of place, that he had been discovered in his criminal intent, and running back down the stairs, he jumped three steps up, then three more, and then he was out of sight.

"We should tell someone," said Ina.

The girls didn't seem concerned. Katy was admiring her wrist; Meg was preparing the brush to continue.

"He was a wetback," Katy said.

"So? We should call the police."

"They'll never catch him," Katy said with grave patience. "He'll get to the top and realize he's wasted his time climbing all the way up there. Then he'll either come back down or go down the road—or disappear into the canyon."

"What about the Tylers?"

Katy said to Meg, "He didn't look like the type—did he?"

"I really didn't get a good look at him."

"He was definitely on the run," Katy said with an air of pronouncement. "He wasn't looking for TVs or VCRs, just a place to stay. The people who did the Tylers—they needed a place to take all that stuff. Our friend, he didn't have anyplace like that."

She displayed her wrist proudly, as if a diamond bracelet had materialized there.

"MEG," Meg read. She leaned and kissed her friend on the cheek, glancing at Ina.

"You've marked me for all time."

"At least until you wash."

"No. I'll never wash this spot." Katy swept her arm back and forth to dry the word, her other hand on her sleeve to keep it from falling.

"I think it's time we went back," Ina said.

"Moomer! Don't worry."

"I'm sorry—but I *am* worried."

Katy said, "She's right. You should go home."

Meg gave her a disbelieving look. Katy pointed to her wrist and smiled.

"Your grandmother won't feel better until she knows that everything is okay," Katy said.

Meg started angrily up the stairs. Ina went after her, but Meg gave no sign of waiting. On the Tylers' landing there was no evidence of life. The lights at the rear of the house had an interrogatory feel, but Ina welcomed them, for in that stark, bright patch there was no question about the stranger's presence. Out of the light, he might be anywhere.

Halfway between the Tylers' and the empty house, Ina heard someone running up the stairs behind her. She didn't have the energy to flee. She moved to the side of the stairs, a thick green frond falling over her shoulder like an arm.

Katy moved through the light behind the Tylers', then into the darkness again. She stopped just below Ina.

"You okay?" she asked.

"A little nervous."

"Where's Meaghan?"

"I've annoyed her. As punishment, she's making me find my way home alone," Ina said.

"You should spank her," Katy suggested.

"Maybe I will," Ina said. Although Meg seemed too old for that, perhaps Katy had had some success with that measure in the past.

"Come on," Katy said. "I'll walk you the rest of the way up."

They paused when Ina was short of breath and they progressed slowly when she felt able. Katy did not convey the least impatience. When Ina rested, Katy smoked.

"Meg says you're going to be a writer."

"I am already. I write every day—poems, sketches, stories."

"What do you write about?"

"How I'm feeling. I'm planning a big novel about my mom."

"Will she like it?"

Katy scoffed. "She won't even read it. I gave her some poems to read. Nothing. I gave her some stories. Nothing."

"I can't believe she didn't read them," Ina said.

"I couldn't believe it, either. She was like a cliché bad mother," Katy said. "So I gave her a story—page one on top, ten blank pages inside."

Ina smiled sadly, feeling for the girl, finally seeing something of what Meg might like about her.

"And she claimed to have read it?"

"She said it ended too abruptly for her taste," Katy said. She laughed, waited. She touched Ina's arm and revealed, "That's a joke. An old writer's joke."

"Oh," said Ina.

"I'm going to fry her in my novel. People on the street will look at her like she's dirt—and she won't know why," Katy said. She threw her cigarette away.

They had come to the head of the stairs. Meg was not around. The light was out in the pool shed. No sign of the stranger.

"If my daughter wrote a book about me," Ina said, "I'd be so proud. Even if she didn't write all wonderful things—at least I'd know she was thinking about me."

Katy shrugged. "Oh, I think about her all right. No question about that."

The back door had been left unlocked for Ina.

"Tell Meg good night," Katy said. She headed back downstairs.

The house felt warm and safe as Ina stepped inside. She pushed the door shut, locked it, and fastened the chains. The stranger might be in the house with them, she realized without particular dread. Meg might never have made it home; she might have left the door unlocked so she wouldn't have to bother taking a key. She might have been grabbed and tossed into the canyon.

Ina yawned. She didn't care. She was tired and disappointed, unaccustomed to being abandoned in the dark.

Meg came into the kitchen.

"I wanted to make sure you were okay," she said.

"I'm very angry with you."

"I know. I'm sorry. But now I'm going back to see Katy."

"She walked me home," said Ina. "I like her more than I like you."

"I said I was sorry."

"So?"

"So why did we have to come home?" she demanded in a furious whisper.

"A stranger passed us, heading this way," Ina said. "In Chicago, that's reason for concern."

"He disappeared, just like we said," Meg countered.

"Take a key. I'm locking the door."

Ina ended the night as it began, leaning over Helene to examine her sleep. There was no evidence that she had awakened. Ina took a fresh beer to bed and drank in the moonlight. She did not hear Meg come home. She was awakened early in the morning by Annie, who was frantic with a crazy story of Ray calling to report the police had come to his home and arrested Amanda in connection with the death of a man in Chicago.

PART EIGHT

◆ ─────────────────────────────

The Man
Who Wanted
Children

THEY were in the kitchen waiting for Ray when the stranger Ina had seen on the stairs ducked out of the pool shed. In the sunshine he was quite handsome, with a clean white shirt making his maroon skin gleam, his black hair combed wet, his eyes lively after a night's sleep.

Jo, making breakfast, announced to Annie, "My Octavio come last night. Don say okay."

"Don?" Annie said, flummoxed.

"Saw this morning. He say Octavio stay."

"In the pool shed?"

Jo nodded. "Very roomy."

Octavio approached the back door, carrying a toothbrush. Jo filled a glass with tap water and handed it out to him. He took the water to the edge of the pool and squatted to brush his teeth, but Jo snapped a phrase of Spanish at him and he returned immediately to the pool shed.

"Where's Ray?" Helene asked, a question she had been asking all morning, the question that had to be answered before she could begin to ask all her other questions.

"He's on his way," Ina said.

Annie had awakened them from deep sleep with news of Amanda's arrest, and the shock had rendered Helene clumsy and incontinent. She had stumbled into Ina's arms, then had to be helped into the bathroom, leaking like an infant.

"What did she mean?" Helene demanded.

"I'm sure it was a misunderstanding," Ina said. She pulled her sister's wet nightgown over her head, removed her sodden underpants, and steered her to the toilet. "Sit," Ina said. "Relax."

"She said she's been arrested," cried Helene.

"True," Ina said. "But it's nothing that can't wait until you've gone to the bathroom." She arranged Helene on the toilet, then draped Meg's robe over Helene's sloped shoulders to fight a chill.

"Call me when you're finished," Ina said. "I'm going outside."

Annie was waiting. Ina, furious, pushed her back against the balcony doors, as far from Helene as the room allowed.

"You had to barge in like that?" Ina scolded in a harsh whisper.

"I thought you'd want to know."

"We did. But you don't wake her from a deep sleep shouting her daughter has been arrested. For God's sake, Annie!"

Annie stepped clear of her mother. She would never say she was sorry; later she might make a gesture of amends to Helene, out of her mother's sight.

"Ray is on his way," she said airily. "I've told you everything I know."

When Ina returned, Helene asked, "What did she say?"

"Nothing more."

Helene stood up. She held out her hand like a queen.

"Dress me. I'm freezing."

Ina gave Helene a quick bath with a warm washcloth, helped her step into clean underpants and bra, then dropped a slip and a dress down over her head.

"Shot?"

Helene sighed. "I suppose."

She said nothing while Ina prepared the injection and administered the shot. Her eyes followed her sister, though, as if she knew where everything went, where Ina should be and what she should be doing at each moment. She gave a small exhalation of pain when the needle stabbed into her bunched flesh.

"Sorry," said Ina.

"I'm just a baby."

"You're a stalwart."

"Amanda arrested," Helene said speculatively. "For killing a man?"

"It sounds too preposterous to even consider," Ina said, remembering the man perched on the counter. "We don't know anything, really," she said. "Wait for Ray."

"It has to be Gordon."

"You don't know that," Ina said. She massaged her sister's shoulders. "Have a seat on the bed while I use the bathroom," she said. "We'll talk to Ray when he gets here."

Helene looked up and behind. Her useless eyes were full of tears.

"None of that," Ina warned good-naturedly. "You've got nothing to cry about."

"My *daughter* is in jail!"

"I'll bet she's had breakfast," Ina countered. "Which is more than we can say."

MEG would not meet Ina's look and then it was time to leave for school. She begged to stay and hear Ray's report. But Annie refused to call her in sick.

Dressed for tennis, her health drink consumed, Annie said, "Nothing in the paper."

"Would this be in the paper?" Helene asked.

"Who could say what interests the media anymore?"

"Where's Ray?" Helene said.

"Morning traffic. He might not get here until noon," Annie predicted.

"Maybe I should be at the jail," Helene said, even beginning to stand.

"We'll go to the jail. But what jail? We don't know enough," Ina said. "Just relax, dear."

"Could you relax if I was in jail?" Helene demanded.

"For what? Tell me your crime," Ina said.

Annie checked her wristwatch against the clock above the sink and the clock on the microwave; evidently they all agreed. She was torn between playing tennis and hearing the details of her cousin's arrest.

"Ray. Ray," she muttered. "Where *is* he?"

Octavio had unfolded a lawn chair and was sitting with his feet up on the deck railing, enjoying the canyon view with a mug of coffee and a cigar. Jo stood like a waitress at his right, wringing a dishtowel in her hands.

"All the way from Guatemala," Annie said, watching. She checked the time once more. "I can give Ray four minutes."

He arrived as she spoke, his car rising over the crest of the driveway so fast he nearly hit Helene's car, parked where they had come to the end of their journey. He glanced at Octavio, smiled, and came inside. He hugged his aunt. This gesture of solace seemed to confirm Helene's worst fears and she began to sob.

Ray said, "Don't now, Helene. Don't cry. Listen to what I have to say. It's not hopeless by any means."

"Would you like a Danish?" Annie said. "Raisin toast? A granola wedge?"

Ray pondered this offer, stirring his coffee. "Some raisin toast sounds good," he said. "Just a little margarine? All this started so early—I never got a chance to eat." He glanced at Helene, then touched her arm. "How barbaric of me, Helene. Your daughter arrested and me discussing my appetite."

"What happened?" Helene said.

Ray crossed his legs. His demeanor was scrubbed, serious, but with a light in his eyes and his voice that revealed the fact he found all this very exciting; he had always loved being the center of attention.

"When I got home from here last night, Amanda was waiting for me," Ray began. "She was in the kitchen having a glass of sherry. Some of my better vintage. She gave me some money—a ten—and said she needed to make a long distance call and the money would cover it. She also told me she realized she had overstayed her welcome and—despite my protests—she would be leaving soon. I was quite embarrassed. My house is hers"—he glanced at Ina, winked—"but she insisted. We took the elevator up together. I got off at my room and she continued up. That was the last time I saw her last night. It was about midnight. She made one call. The light went on on my desk phone. She was on pretty long. Maybe a half hour. I read and fell asleep."

Annie gave him his toast. He took a bite and a sip of coffee. Helene did not move; her gaze was directed at Ray and it seemed to disconcert him, for he put the toast down and continued.

"At seven this morning," Ray said, "my doorbell rings. And rings and rings. *Very* insistent. My inclination is to ignore it, but whoever it is just won't give up. I chew them out over the intercom. Of course, it's the police." He spread out his hands. "Two in suits. Two in uniform. One of those a woman. The two in suits show me their ID. They are homicide detectives. They ask me if I am Raymond Lockwood, do I live at the address I'm at. I'm *wide* awake now. My first thought was someone got killed at one of my stores. One of my managers. No, they ask if Amanda Bolton is staying with me."

"They asked for her by name?" Helene said.

"Yes."

"I thought maybe there had been a mistake," she said.

"They were pretty sure of themselves," Ray said. "I tell them Amanda is my cousin, and she is upstairs. One of the detectives then tells me very politely that they have a warrant from Chicago to arrest Amanda for the murder of a man they found in her apartment. Walter Gordon was his name."

"My Lord," said Ina.

Ray nodded at his mother. He gestured with an open hand for her to keep silent, and what followed in his story seemed sanitized for Helene's benefit, to get the facts across, but to withhold the gruesome color.

"I looked at their paperwork. They said if Amanda agrees to return to Illinois there won't be a problem. If she fights extradition, she'll go back eventually, it will just take a little longer. It would look bad, they said. They were very polite, Helene. I went up in the elevator with the detectives and the woman in uniform. Amanda was awake and dressed. She was brushing her teeth when we got there. She listened to them read her her rights with her mouth full of toothpaste. Then they thanked me and took her away."

"Where is she?" Annie asked.

"Sybil Brand."

"She'll need a lawyer. I'll have Don call one."

"I already sent over a guy I know," Ray said. "She seemed prepared to just go back. My friend can watch her rights until she gets out of California—then I can line up a good defense lawyer in Chicago."

"Tell us the rest," Helene said, irritated by the talk of legal strategy.

"That's all," said Ray.

"How did they know she was staying with you? How was he killed? Who found him? Amanda's been out here almost a week— maybe she has an alibi," Helene said.

Ray sighed. "He'd been dead a while, Helene. He'd been shot. The Chicago police got a tip. He'd been absent from work and his family hadn't seen him. Everyone assumed he ran away. He evidently was pretty irresponsible."

Helene said, "He wanted children. That doesn't sound irresponsible to me."

Ray glanced at Ina, who shrugged; she was relieved, however, that Ray was about to fill Helene in and absolve Ina of the responsibility to do so.

"He *must* have wanted children," Ray said. "He had four of them. And a wife."

"No," said Helene.

"It's the truth."

"No wonder she killed him," Helene said bluntly. "She must have just found out."

"I don't know, Helene. My address was on a piece of paper next to the body."

"That's why she was so antsy here," Helene said. "What a thing to carry around with you. Ina, we're going to see her immediately. And we're returning to Chicago to be with her."

Ina said, "We can discuss that."

"She'll need me," Helene said. "She has no one back there."

"We can talk about that," said Ina.

◆ ◆ ◆

RAY drove them downtown, where they sat in the front row of a small courtroom and listened attentively as Amanda was ordered returned to Illinois within seventy-two hours.

"How does she look?" Helene asked.

"Surprisingly good," Ina remarked. "She's got some color in her face. Her hair looks freshly brushed. She smiled at us when they brought her out."

"Is she handcuffed?"

"Yes. But not blatantly so," Ina said. "She's wearing a jail smock sort of thing that—as you'd imagine—isn't very flattering. And rubber thongs."

"Like the beach?"

"Yes, dear. They're taking her out now."

Amanda brought her hands to her mouth and blew a kiss, which Ina dutifully reported, and Helene returned, but Amanda had already been taken away.

"When will I be able to talk to her?"

"Let's wait until she gets back home," Ina said. "We'll fly to Chicago, get her a good lawyer, let her get settled, tie up some loose ends of our own. She knows you know."

Ina held her sister's arm at the curb. Ray had gone for the car. They would be returning to Chicago sooner than Ina had wanted. But they had been gone a long time in the small scheme of things. A trail of curiosities had sprung up behind them. They might be celebrities. She wanted to take a good look at her house; she had sorting to do, a thinning out, deciding what meant enough to her to transplant it in California.

"I'm selling the house when I go back," Ina announced, giving her sister's arm a squeeze.

"Don't do anything rash."

"I'm staying here, Helene. I'll go back this time. And if Amanda goes to prison, I'll go back to visit. But I'm from California now."

Helene did not respond. She fixed her gaze forward. Traffic rushed past like a chain and from some unseen break in it Ray's car dodged free and came to the curb.

"Here he is," Ina said.

"Don't put your life in Ray's hands," Helene warned, holding Ina back when she dipped to get the door.

"He's my son. He's made a place for me—"

"Stay with *me,*" Helene said, "He'll resent you—elevator and all. He'll hate the sound of you moving around above him."

Ray's door opened. His face came up smiling over the roof of the car. "Everything okay?" he asked.

"Just discussing the future," Ina said. "Come, dear. In the car."

Helene asked to go to her room to rest. The beds had been made, little wafers of green chocolate on each pillow. Ina unwrapped one and set it in Helene's palm.

"Like the finest hotels," Ina said.

Helene smelled the candy and gave it back.

"Are you trying to poison me?" she said. "We're just guests here. We'll wear out our welcome."

"Not with Ray."

"With any of them. It's all gesture. It's just manners," Helene said. "Once the gesture has been made, they're content."

"Not Ray."

"You haven't accepted his offer, have you?"

"Not in so many words. But I think he knows I'm staying. You have been my only stumbling block."

"Stumbling block. Thank you, dear."

"To my accepting his invitation," Ina said. "Our concern was for you—what would become of you?"

"And what *will* become of me?"

"You'll be with me," said Ina. "And we'll be with Ray."

"And Amanda will be in prison," Helene said, her voice catching.

"Perhaps. Let's proceed on the assumption she will be," Ina said. "I said we'll visit her. You visited her once a month or so when she lived three blocks away. Okay. Every month we'll fly out and visit her in prison. Her killing someone doesn't mean you have to restructure your life around her prison sentence. Are you going to take an apartment outside the prison walls? Don't be silly. *She* killed him, if she did. Not you. We get her a good lawyer, let her know we're behind her—that's all we can do."

"She needs me, though," Helene said. "Look at your children. They don't need you. That's why you'll become a burden, even to Ray. I want to cast my lot with someone who needs me."

She placed her hand firmly on Helene's shoulder, to leave no doubt when she said, "This is a question of *my* needs, dear. I need Ray. I need to be near him—and Annie, too. I just want to be near my children now. If you feel you need to be near Amanda—or she needs you—then that's a decision you'll have to make. But I won't stay in Chicago. You'll be on your own, if you decide to stay."

"You'd leave me there?" said Helene.

"Yes."

"I don't believe you."

"Believe me," Ina said. "Come back here. Live in the sun with me. What would you do without me? How would you get around? Who would you rely on? Your daughter in prison?"

Helene took a breath deep and ragged with sobs. She whispered, "You shit."

So back they went.

Ray turned into Ina's driveway at dusk of a cold day and just sat there in answer to Ina's unspoken request. She did not want to move; she did not want to go inside the house. The yard was tidy, leaves raked into piles at the Strodes' property line. Hector had kept his promise to watch over the place. A light was on in an upstairs window and another in the kitchen. The mail would be heaped on the kitchen table. Vincent would be in there. She would never be able to thin this life down so that it was sufficiently light to carry to California. She should have remained in L.A. and let Po and Hector keep the house. She didn't need the money, and anyone who bought the house would never meet the Strodes' requirements for a neighbor.

Drawn by the strange car in Ina's driveway, Hector emerged from his house, came across his gardens and through the leaves, his hands in his coat pockets in a neighborly attitude of defenselessness. He had lost weight, a great deal of weight. A flesh-colored oval of bandage was affixed like a tire patch to the right side of his face, giving him a swollen, off-center appearance. Stopping within ten feet of the car, he projected a wary patience.

Ina stepped out, giving Hector a smile, worried why Po had not accompanied her husband on this mission of danger.

"Are you carrying your gun, Hector?"

"Ina," he murmured, then attempted to smile. The bandage, or whatever the bandage covered, made smiling difficult and painful, for the effort was abandoned with a shocked look almost of recognition. He took from his coat pocket the gun he had long ago offered to the widows.

She went to him without hesitation and crushed him in her arms. He cried for as long as she would allow, until she released him and stepped back. She gave him time to compose himself by speaking of unimportant matters.

"The place looks good, Hector," she said. "I should have just stayed away and left you to it."

"Thanks. No. It's too much," he said, speaking each word with great care.

"Don't give it another thought. How's Po?"

"She's home," he said. He pointed across the familiar space. "I've been hard on her."

"What happened to you, Hector?"

"Cancer of the jaw," he said. He bent to look inside the rental car.

"Helene?"

"Helene and Ray. You remember my son," Ina said. She pulled the door open. Ray stepped out, eyes on Hector's gun. Helene called a greeting but she did not get out. Ray and Hector shook hands.

"Heard about Amanda," Hector said.

"We're back to see she gets taken care of," Ina said. "I'm putting my house up for sale, too, Hector."

He fixed her with his pained, tired eyes.

"Nice in California?"

"Beautiful," Ray butted in like a salesman. "The best."

"It's nice here, too," Ina said.

"Po will be shocked. Said you'd never come back."

They helped Helene out of the car and went to the back door, where Ina fumbled with her keys, looking for the right one. Hector had taken it upon himself to close over the milkbox hole. He had matched the wood and the paint perfectly and refused Ina's offer of payment, instead leaving to get Po.

"She won't believe me," he said.

Her house was cool, musty-smelling. Hector had the furnace set at fifty-five degrees. The mail was on the table, as she had guessed, and the Strodes had taken the time to divide it into classifications: mail addressed to Ina Lockwood in one pile, mail addressed to Vincent Lockwood in the other. After all this time, Vincent's pile was still larger, all his correspondents refusing to believe in his death. Hector also had set aside the receipts and canceled checks of the bills he had paid for her. The checkbook she had left with them was right on the counter, along with a pen from Vincent's office, every penny accounted for.

There was no food in the house. She would have loved a beer just then, and a long sleep. She walked absently from room to room in fear of Po Strode's arrival. Disease had been hard on Hector, who in turn had been hard on Po, and Ina did not want to see what those trials had done to her. Ina had come back from L.A. with the hope of finding everything untouched and unchanged, providing for an effortless passage through.

"This will sell easily," Ray said. For some reason, his assessment annoyed her; the tone of his voice, the glib passing of judgment on something that occupied her with an ensnaring complexity of emotions.

"Just like that, huh?" she said.

The snap of her fingers under his nose startled him.

"And stop shilling for California," she warned.

"What? When—?"

"He's sick. He doesn't need to be told there are better places than here. 'Beautiful. The best,'" Ina said derisively.

"He *asked*," said Ray.

"He asked *me*."

They heard the backdoor slap. Po's voice, nervous and excited, came to them. "Is it true? Ina's back?"

"Ina's back," Hector avowed.

Ina intercepted them in the hall. "I'm back," she said and caught Po Strode as she fell into her arms.

Hector had not been so hard on Po that it showed. She had put on a pound or two. Her condemnatory squint was gone. Smelling of perfume, in a dress that felt new, she wore a little makeup. Disease had worked its coarse magic on her husband, but Po Strode had taken on a burgeoning health as if to mock whatever had a hold of Hector. Watching the two women hug, he looked in danger of snapping in half. Ina guided them all to her kitchen, to get them off their feet.

"I didn't think we'd ever see you again," Po said. "I was telling Roger—Roger Hawkins, do you remember him? From down the block? He's a widower?—and I was telling him that you were gone for good."

"I know you'd be back," Hector said.

Po Strode nodded. "Hector believed," she said. "How are you, Helene? We heard about Amanda."

Helene, startled at being included, replied, "I am doing as well as can be expected."

"I knew," Hector said, "that Vincent . . . Lockwood's wife would not . . . leave property just . . . sitting."

They all laughed, made nervous by the effort Hector expended in uttering that sentence. Ina went from cupboard to cupboard in search of something to offer in her role as hostess, but Po had cleaned them out.

"It's all in boxes next door," she said. "I hope you don't mind— I didn't want to risk you getting pests.'

"You do whatever you want with it," Ina said. "It actually serves my purpose."

"She's selling," Hector said.

"Is that true?"

"We're just here to get some things straightened out," Ina said. "And to see Amanda."

Po turned to Helene, raised her voice and said, "She couldn't have done such a thing. I just know it."

"Did you ever meet Amanda?" Helene asked.

"Meet Amanda? Of course we met Amanda," Po said. She looked to her husband for corroboration, but Hector said nothing.

Ina cast about for a graceful reason to depart. Ray, sensing his mother's desire, but holding a grudge, sat without moving.

Hector stood up. "Welcome back, Ina. Helene. Time for my medicine."

Po Strode encircled her husband's wrist with her fingers and gave a shake.

"I'll be a minute," she said. "I want to catch up with Ina."

He bent and hugged Ina briefly around the shoulders, the smooth nap of his bandage brushing warm across her cheek, the weight of the gun in his pocket clunking against the table.

"He'll kill us all," Po Strode said when he was gone. "That gun will go off. He carries it everywhere."

"What does the doctor say?"

"He has a hole in his face," she said. "There's some talk of trying to rebuild the jaw—but right now he prefers to just live with it rather than drain our savings."

"Is he in pain?" Helene asked.

"Just now, I could tell it was getting worse. They give him medication," Po said. "It makes him feel better—light-headed, he tells me. And frisky," she whispered, blushing, glancing at Ray. "He gets very persistent—but the hole in his face, I try not to pay any attention to it—but I just can't ignore it. It has a smell." She sighed. "The whole thing has been terrible for him."

Ray cut them loose with a reminder that they needed to find a place to stay for the night.

"Why not here?" Po asked.

Ina looked around: The notion had never occurred to her. She was visiting. The house felt uninhabitable, no food, or beer, the air stale, every room tripped out with memories.

"Two houses in the city—and we're going to stay in a hotel," Helene said.

"On me," Ray said. "Two rooms somewhere overlooking the lake."

"Walk me home, Ina," said Po.

She kicked up leaves from the pile they had to traverse to reach her gardens. She clung to Ina's arm, pulled on it like a weight to keep her from getting home too quickly.

"You remember Roger Hawkins, don't you?" she asked, her voice tentative.

"Chubby. Balding. His wife died of a stroke," Ina said, taking a guess at the man, but recalling clearly the woman's face.

"Every day that Hector was in the hospital," Po said, "Roger gave me a ride over, then he picked me up after visiting hours. He was so *caring*. He'd do small things around the yard—he cut your lawn a couple times, as a matter of fact." Po had reduced her pace to a step every half-dozen words, a standstill, virtually. Ina sensed a revelation trying to find the best way out of her neighbor, a revelation Ina had no desire to hear.

"He sounds like a good friend," Ina said.

"More than a friend," Po said. She looked toward Ina, who avoided her eye; Ina, who Po Strode, for almost a lifetime, feared was plotting to steal her husband.

"I really don't care to know the details about you and Roger Hawkins," Ina said, shaking loose from Po's grip. "Give my love to Hector," she said, and left Po there in her gardens.

They drove past Helene's house in the dark. The place looked derelict, haunted, no lights, no shine of glass in the windows, a raggedness about the shadows.

The house next door, Katherine Grunwald's house, was for sale, as was the house on the other side of Helene.

"How does it look?" Helene asked. "Can we go inside?"

"Tomorrow. It's late," said Ina.

"Is it a dump?"

"It's too dark to tell, dear."

"Who's been taking in your mail?" Ray asked.

"Her neighbor," Ina said.

Helene said, "Amanda couldn't promise to get it every day."

"Shall we pick it up?"

"I'm frightened," said Helene.

She was a presence between Ina and her son; she was abruptly something approaching a burden, with a whiny trace in her voice.

"Stop the car," Ina said. "I'll go to the door."

Ray had to go around the block to find a place to park, but there was no space to be had.

"Double park," Ina said. "How long can it take?"

"If we're not here when you come out, we'll be circling," said Ray.

"Be here," Ina said, warning him with a look.

A light came on when she pushed the doorbell and a large man approached from the far end of the hall. His wide frame plugged up the light trying to get past. Two children accompanied him, boiling at his feet so that he had to dance his way toward her, careful where he stepped. His face was suspicious filling the window to inspect her, and then he opened the door.

"I've come for Helene Bolton's mail," Ina said. She came up to the man's heart; it was an effort to elevate her line of sight up above his stubbled jaw, his overbite, into calm blue eyes.

"Is she back?" he asked.

"She's in town briefly," Ina said.

"Invite her in, Tom," said a voice behind him.

Tom stepped back against the children pressing forward to see. Katherine, immensely pregnant, gave Ina an exhausted smile, leaning against the hallway wall. One hand was on her hip, the other hoisting the weight of her belly.

"My goodness," Ina said. "You were big when we met in August."

"I'm overdue," she said. "I have large, late babies."

Tom carried a cardboard box from another room and handed it to Ina.

"This is it," he said. "Not much here. But we gave up trying to get her mail. It's too dangerous over there."

Ina glanced at the contents of the box: occupant, misspelled name, Bolten, Bloton, the folks at, junk.

"You're moving?" Ina asked.

"We'd like to," Tom said. "If we can ever sell the house."

"We need more room," Katherine said.

"The neighborhood's kinda shot."

"We're putting Helene's on the market."

Tom winced. "It's been pretty badly vandalized," he said.

"They know no one's home, so it's become their clubhouse. A fort. I called the police, but they figured out who called and broke a couple of my windows. The people on the other side are *really* angry. They blame you—your sister." He smoothed hair back from Mickey's face. "They think your sister leaving gave them a toehold in this neighborhood—a reason to come to this block."

"Do you believe that?" Ina asked.

"I know my asking price on this house is four thousand dollars below what I paid for it," he said. "And nobody has even come *close* to that. We got one bid twenty-five thousand dollars below what we paid."

"Tom," Katherine said.

"You think having that place next door helps?" he asked angrily. "No windows. Weeds up to your ass. Obscenities on the walls. Punks smoking on the front porch and playing their radios at all hours. Yeah, I'd say that guy has a point."

"She's blind. She's alone," Ina said.

"She'd better not go in there," Tom said. "They'll throw her out on the street. They like her house too much."

"I'm taking her to California."

"Good. Burn it down," Tom said. "You'll never sell it."

"Tom," Katherine warned.

"And we'll never sell until something is done about her house," Tom said.

"Thank you for getting her mail," Ina said.

"My kids are afraid to play outside," Tom continued. "They make lewd remarks to my wife."

"I'm sorry," said Ina. To Katherine, she said, "Good luck with your new baby."

"You want me to burn it down?" Tom asked, a kind of madness in his voice, in his eyes.

Ina put the box under her arm and tried to leave. Tom ordered his wife and children into the kitchen. Ina made it out onto the front porch. No sign of Ray.

"Wait," Tom said. He filled the doorway; he looked behind them to be certain they were alone.

"I'm serious," he said. "They'll blame the punks. Your sister will get insurance. Pay someone to clear the ruins. Then you can go to California—and I can sell my house."

"Good night," Ina said.

Down the stairs, out onto the sidewalk, Tom followed her. He was not threatening, only imploring. And in the cold emptiness away from the house, he proved a comfort to Ina. A young man's howl, arrogant as a wolf, rose up from Helene's.

"Hear that?" Tom asked. "It goes on constantly. This is not a special night."

Ina moved toward Helene's to clear her line of vision. In the kitchen window she saw a flicker of low light, as if someone had set a small campfire on the floor.

"They can't just take over another person's house," Ina said.

"If they're allowed to, they will."

"Where do they go during the day?"

Tom shrugged. "To school? Maybe some have jobs? Maybe they stay in there."

A car turned down the block. Ina prayed that it was Ray, and it was.

"Thank you again," Ina said.

"A thousand dollars," Tom said. He hopped from foot to foot, out in the cold without shoes or socks. "A bargain," he promised.

THEY returned the next day in brilliant sunshine. They planned to visit Helene's house, then go on to see Amanda. Ray looked too refined, too prosperous for his role as protector of the widows. Ina wished they could bring Tom along. He possessed the size and requisite motivation.

She had told Ray what Tom had said. With Helene squared away in the hotel bathroom, Ina filled in her son on what they faced.

"They aren't there during the day?"

"He wasn't sure."

"Maybe we should just not go," Ray said. "Hire a realtor, give them a big commission—triple their commission—and let them worry about it."

"She'll never agree to that," said Ina. "She'll demand to go back."

Ray said, "In the morning, I'll make some calls. We'll tour the house, get what she wants, then put it on the market."

Now they were parked across from Helene's. Ray made them wait. The house was a wreck. Cracked Styrofoam coolers floated like chunks of ice in the high grass. The fence lovingly erected by Rudy Bolton in the year they bought the house now contained a sea of bottles, dented beer kegs, and fast-food litter. Every window was broken. Condoms pendulous with dark liquids were strung festively from one upstairs window to another. From another window a long brown stain ran down the wall, as if something fecal and disgusting had been emptied out in a halfhearted attempt at housekeeping. Bewildering symbols and straightforward obscenities had been spray-painted in tall red letters boastful as a billboard on the side of the house.

The front door was gone.

"How does it look in daylight?" Helene asked.

"Not good, dear."

"Not good? What does 'not good' mean?" Helene said, her voice tremulous.

"It means vandals have been busy."

"Helene," Ray said, turning toward her, "there is nothing that says you have to go inside. You've already got your clothes out and some of your other things. If there's anything else, tell us and we'll get it for you."

"I want to go in."

"It's not the same house, dear," said Ina.

"It's *my* house," Helene said.

"Which brings us to my next point," Ray said, a glance at his mother. "I've hired a realtor to handle the sale of your house. I had to offer him significant incentives even to take the property on. He'll be going through with us."

"I don't recall telling you I wanted to sell," Helene said.

"It's best, dear. Our home is L.A. now."

"With me," said Ray, touching Helene's arm.

"I could have been consulted," she protested.

"We're consulting you now," Ray said.

"But I have no choice?"

"You'll have to sign everything," Ray assured her. "You have that power. We only think this is the best course for you."

"What about what *I* think is best?" Helene demanded.

"All right," Ray said with artificial patience. "What do you want to do?"

Helene said nothing. She swiveled her head toward the house, her expression pained behind her lemon-framed sunglasses. Ina was dying to tell her sister the best way to proceed; she did not feel they had the time for Helene to come to the decision herself. They had so much left to do.

"Helene?" Ina said softly. "Tell me the things you remember most clearly about the house. We'll try to salvage those for you."

Helene straightened in her seat. "Amanda's box of schoolwork in the upstairs closet," she said, relieved to have something definite to concentrate upon. "The picture albums in the hutch. Rudy kept the important papers in a strongbox in our bedroom closet."

"Good," Ina said, touching her sister. "We'll look for those things."

"Here they are," Ray said.

A long bronze Cadillac double-parked in front of the house. Two men emerged, one small and natty in a dark blue suit and overcoat, the other man large and identically dressed. The large man carried a briefcase. The small man was named Mr. Patkin, the large man was named Mr. Green. They shook hands with Ray and the widows on the sidewalk, and then Mr. Green led them through the fence gate, up the stairs and into the house.

The door was gone, but a smell like a door hung there. Ina felt herself gag, a taste of copper and beer. Helene gave a tiny moan of sadness and found a handkerchief to hold over her mouth.

"We're lucky it's chilly today," Mr. Patkin said cheerfully. He had fallen back in line to take Helene's arm and lead her along.

"Watch your step, Mrs. Bolton. Broken glass underfoot," he said.

They were entering the lair of animals. Ina did not recognize it as Helene's house, and for long moments felt like a stranger touring the home of creatures not sufficiently evolved to feel embarrassment.

Every piece of furniture had been slashed open or hacked with an ax or in some other manner offhandedly damaged. Stuffing, puffs of fiber rolled on the floor like dirty clouds. Drawers had been torn out with bored abandon, their contents scattered. Ina made no mention of any of this, and there was among all those with vision an unspoken compact that Helene did not require a detailed account of the devastation they were passing through.

"I can tell that you kept a lovely home, Mrs. Bolton," Mr. Patkin said.

"What have they done to my house?" Helene sobbed.

"My sister has some things she wanted to get out," Ina said.

"Let's finish here," Mr. Patkin said. "Mr. Green will look for whatever you want."

Mr. Green had advanced into the kitchen. He had inspected each room they encountered before allowing the others to enter. The kitchen walls were splashed with paint and spaghetti sauce and motor oil. Precise handprints had been pressed against Helene's flowered wallpaper, then wiped downward until they disappeared in a kind of cleanliness.

The kitchen had been used to burn the photo albums. They had set the fire on the floor, using chopped-up chairs and stacks of family pictures. The tile was black and rippled from the heat. Ina saw bits of people she knew, curled at the edges, a torn leg, Rudy looking to one side with a question, Vincent's smile, her sister's pretty young face, when her eyesight was perfect, never imagining. Ina did not stop for any of this. She hurried toward the bathroom, trusting Mr. Green to clear the way, the awful stink and the beer she had drunk at the hotel filling her like a cavity with nausea.

But the toilet had been blasted from its moorings by some unimaginable disregard, and she stumbled in a field of porcelain chunks, looking down the dark pipe, her hand over her mouth and nose. The sink was gone, too, pulverized like another facet of the job.

She went out the backdoor into the clean sunshine and was

sick with a ladylike dribble of beer-tinted spittle into the trampled flowerbed. Her son held her upright.

"Let's take her away from here," Ray said, giving his mother a handkerchief.

"I'm so glad she can't see this," Ina said. "She can smell it. Hear it. But that's nothing compared to the way it looks."

Mr. Patkin brought Helene to the backdoor and helped her outside.

"Get them out of there!" she shouted ferociously. "I want them out of my house!"

"We will," Mr. Patkin said. He snapped his fingers at Mr. Green, and he came to his side. "Mrs. Bolton wants you to look for some things inside the house."

"A strongbox in an upstairs bedroom closet," Ina said. "A box of her daughter's schoolwork, also in an upstairs closet."

"And the photo albums," Helene prompted.

Ina raised a finger to Mr. Green and Mr. Patkin; they had seen the picture remains on the kitchen floor.

"The photo albums have been burned, dear."

Helene asked to be shown to the backyard bench. She sat with Ina in the chilled, delicious air while Mr. Green went back inside the house. She pushed up the frames of her sunglasses to blot at her eyes.

"Burned?" she whispered.

"I'm afraid so, yes," Ina said.

"I wanted you to describe them to me," Helene said.

"I know, dear."

A young man, skinny, scared, recently awakened, was shoved out the backdoor by Mr. Green. The kid was trying to get his pants up. His expression was at once stupefied and arrogant.

"I found him asleep upstairs," said Mr. Green.

"Beat it," he told the boy.

"My chews," he said, pointing into the house. "I don' leave wit'out my chews."

"Yes you do," Mr. Patkin said. "And tell your friends—they don't come here anymore. Understand? No more." He introduced Mr. Green. "Or he deals with you, okay?"

"This our place now," the kid said, retreating.

"No," Mr. Patkin said.

From a distance the boy called out an almost jovial obscenity and then departed down the alley.

"We've put the word out, then," Mr. Patkin said, seeming cheered by the development. "Tonight Mr. Green and I will come through and remove anyone who didn't get the message. Can I speak with you a moment, Ray?"

The two men went off down the walk beside the house. Mr. Green carried the strongbox and a cardboard box to where the widows sat. The vandals had been unable to open the strongbox lock. Its steel face was gashed from an ax, but the lock had remained shut. They hadn't touched Amanda's schoolwork. Helene put the box on her lap and removed the top. She picked up the first item, a book covered in pastel construction paper and bound with knotted lengths of pink yarn.

"Amanda had her moments as a student," Helene said.

"She's still a smart cookie," Ina said. Helene's fingers picked down through the box's contents: drawings, report cards, perfect attendance certificates, love notes from home, valentines marked with the penciled scrawls of other children's names, beads glued to cardboard in the shape of a tree. Later she might ask Ina to go over everything with her in detail, but for the moment she was content just to have something from her past safe and in her hands.

"Be honest with me, dear. It's ruined, isn't it?"

"Pretty much," said Ina.

"It made you sick."

"A little."

"All this trouble because I wanted to go for a drive again," Helene said.

THEY visited Amanda, sitting on the opposite side of a high counter from her, in a room lit like the basement of a church. At the doors and in the corners stood women the size of Mr. Green, keeping watch. Other women in the room talked in low voices with their lawyers, or strained with fingertips across the table to touch their kids' hands.

Amanda looked good. She had cut her hair boyishly short and wore a blue jumpsuit that brought out her eyes. She was sharing a cell with a woman named Doris, who was charged with murdering her husband.

"Did she?" Helene asked.

"We don't talk about that. She tells me what he was like. We don't talk about what came next," Amanda said.

She looked away from her mother, toward Ray.

"The new lawyer was here," she said. "He walked me through the bond hearing. I like him. The PD they assigned me was this little, overworked *weasel.* He told me to plead guilty and hope for the best."

"*Are* you guilty?" Helene asked, affronted by not knowing, by having to ask.

"I told you—we don't talk about that here," Amanda said.

"But *are* you?"

"I cut my hair so people couldn't yank it," Amanda revealed, ignoring her mother's question.

"What is your bond?" Ray asked.

"Fifty thousand. Bail is five."

"You told me this man wanted children," Helene said.

"Did I?"

"Now they tell me he had a wife and kids," Helene complained. "Why did you lie?"

Amanda gave Ina a tired smile. Her hair did indeed look slippery and hard to grab.

"You're getting my boyfriends mixed up," Amanda said. "I've got so many. I can see how it would be hard to keep them straight."

"Don't make fun of me," Helene warned.

"I'm not. Gordon was a guy I met a while back. We got together for drinks, dancing, a movie now and then. Arnold Davies is who you're thinking of. He wants to settle down, have kids. At least two, maybe three, if my biological clock allows.

362   Charles Dickinson

Then there's Fred Duke. He's a computer nut. He helped me with my taxes—and just kept calling. He's a million laughs. Harmless."

"Which one did you murder?" Helene asked.

Amanda wiped her eye.

"Gordon is the one who is dead."

"Do you miss him?"

"In a way."

"Maybe one of your other boyfriends killed him," Helene said. "Jealousy? A jealous rage?"

"Arnold and Fred know nothing about Gordon," Amanda said. "They aren't the killer type."

"What type was Gordon?" Helene asked.

"He was handsome, sexy," Amanda said, glancing at Ina, smiling just a little. "He had a bad side, too."

"Did he hit you?" Helene asked abruptly.

Amanda seemed not to be surprised by the question. "He could get carried away."

"Tell them that," said Helene.

"My lawyer knows. We'll be pursuing that line of defense," Amanda said.

"How often did he hit you?"

"Enough."

" 'How often?' What am I saying? Once! Once is enough," Helene said.

A buzzer went off and they all jumped.

"Sixty seconds," announced the guard by the door.

"I'm selling the house," Helene said. "Ina is taking me with her to California."

"I loved California," Amanda exclaimed. She smiled at Ray. "It was my big vacation."

"You're welcome any time," Ina said.

Ina was drinking beer alone in the hotel when she heard the phone ring next door in Ray's room. He answered immediately but Ina could hear only a murmur, though she was bored and pressed her ear to the wall in an effort to put some spice in the evening. She would have liked to go next door and visit with her son, but it was after midnight and she was a little abuzz.

He came to her instead, tapping with a fingernail on the hollow steel door between their rooms. She set her glass down and carefully slid open the deadbolt.

"Come in, come in," he whispered, agitated. She stepped into his room. The TV was on, the sound turned down.

"Is she asleep?"

"For the last hour," Ina said, looking for a seat, a place of calm and balance that would not fail her.

"That was Mr. Patkin," Ray said. "Those punks set fire to Helene's house."

"How bad?"

"Bad. It's still burning."

"Oh, Lord," Ina said. She took a seat on the edge of the bed. A piece of chocolate floated on the pillow. Ray scratched at the stubble on his cheeks.

"Not an entirely bad turn of events, actually," he mused. "Was her insurance up to date?"

"I suppose so. I don't know."

"With Rudy gone—and her blind—I didn't know if she had let it slip," Ray said.

"She isn't senile."

"I know. But if he had handled that part of their lives—and I assume he did, since she was blind—she might not have ever been aware insurance existed."

"She isn't stupid, either."

"Forget it," Ray said, peeved. "Let's assume her insurance is paid up."

"She did everything for *him*," Ina said. "Even after she went blind. Cooked, cleaned, stayed out of his way."

"Did Uncle Rudy hit her?" Ray asked suddenly. "That exchange with Amanda today, I got the feeling she was saying if this Gordon hit Amanda, it was all right for her to kill him."

"Rudy was a rather traditional husband," Ina said. "Her diabetes frustrated him. But I'm certain he didn't beat her. She couldn't keep such a secret from me."

"Patkin told me this afternoon the house was going to be a very tough sell," said Ray. "It needed forty thousand dollars in repairs right up front. A total rehab. They had even taken an ax to the furnace and the hot-water heater in the basement. A fire— well, it clears up some things. She'll get some insurance money, though with an arson they take forever. Patkin can move the lot. He might even buy it from her himself."

"What about my house? Should I set it on fire, too?"

Ray looked affronted. "Don't be silly. Yours will be easy. It's on a corner lot, good neighborhood, across from a nature area—"

"The river?"

Ray smiled. "Water frontage. Almost a beach property," he said. "The house is old but solid." He chucked her lightly on the arm. "Like you."

"Thanks," Ina said, steeped in indignation. "You left all your charm in California."

Ray blushed, befuddled. He did seem out of place, unsure where he fit in.

"Are you in a hurry to get back?" she asked.

Ray avoided her eyes, shrugged. "I have businesses to run," he said. "Amanda has to go before the grand jury and she has to be arraigned. She won't go on trial for months."

"Could you pay her bail?"

"I don't have it in my checking account. But, yes, I could. Then what?"

"Then she'd be out," Ina said. "She could work."

"And date? Freddie and Archie and whomever?"

"She says those things to keep her mother at bay," Ina said. "To buy herself a little space."

"Where would she stay?"

"At her apartment? Or, if she can't go back there, at my place— until it's sold," Ina said.

"Will she run?"

Ina was ready to go to bed. The dribbling TV light in Ray's room had exhausted her, given her a headache.

"I don't think so. Where would she go?"

"I just need to know she won't run," Ray said. "It's not the money. I would just need some sort of commitment."

They took Helene by her house the next morning and everything seemed to Ina identical to the day before, only the house was missing. It had fallen in on itself, a blank succumbing to the fire. One fire truck remained. Water was being poured on a hot spot near the kitchen. A yellow rope had been strung around the property and it seemed an irritation to the firefighters who remained; they had to fling it up out of the way each time they wanted to pass.

"I can smell it from here," Helene said. She had taken the news of the fire almost stoically; a couple more tears. But when Ray explained to her the possible benefits, the lightening of her responsibilities, she started to cheer up again.

Ray lowered the window. Now Ina could smell the smoke and wet ashes. She held her sister's hand.

"Rudy would have liked to see this," Helene said. "He always hated that house. He resented having to buy it from Vincent— when you and Vincent got yours free."

"I know," Ina said, unwilling to fight. She glanced up the street and there was Katherine sweeping leaves on her front walk. Her belly remained ludicrously round, a caricature of pregnancy, and at her feet two children gleefully kicked apart the pile of leaves she had assembled. Ina watched her a long time, waiting for the woman to lose her patience. Vincent, Rudy, Katherine's Tom, each would have snapped by then, scolding the children, complaining about having to do the job more than once. But the woman kept raking the leaves into an inviting pile and the shrieking kids kept scattering them, and Katherine just laughed and began again. She was infinitely patient, Ina decided, or a touch mad.

Later the same day, Ray brought Amanda to Ina's house.

"Thank you, Ina," Amanda said, hugging her. She looked all around, as if stunned by the size of the room.

"It was Ray," said Ina.

"Ray's money," Helene said. She was seated at the kitchen

table, fidgety, lacking the confidence to move even slightly, though she knew the house nearly as well as her own.

Amanda kissed Ray on the cheek.

"I don't want you to worry," she said. "I'm not going anywhere—though I wish I was going back to California with you."

Ray, dressed for travel, eager to be gone, said, "When this is all over, you can come out."

"It will have fallen into the ocean by then," Helene said.

"No doubt," said Ray.

He gravitated toward the door, pulled by the rental car, the airline tickets in his briefcase. Ina listened to her house come back to life; the furnace was drying the damp air, the wood and ducts making soft snaps that would continue all winter like sensors monitoring every function of the structure.

Ina touched Amanda's cheek.

"Take good care of my sister," she said.

Amanda stared at her mother.

"We'd better go," Ina said. She kissed Helene. "I'll be back for you."

"Do you think she'll kill her?" Ina asked on the way to the airport.

"The question is," said Ray, "who will kill whom first?"

"They'll never last until the trial. I give it two weeks."

"She wanted to try. She had no real interest in my plan until I told her Helene wanted to stay with her," Ray said.

AMANDA's trial was scheduled for the twentieth of May. Ray and Ina caught a plane back to Chicago. L.A.'s weather when they took off was warm and wet. The plane headed west, out over the ocean, as if the pilot were confused. But gradually they turned east and headed back, ascending, Ray pointing through the mist at the hills where Annie lived, the location of his stores (they had visited the one near USC on their way to the airport, Ray wanting to surprise the manager, whom he suspected of not doing his job).

Ina was excited about seeing Helene. They had talked to each other on the phone every day of their separation. Ina was alert to any indication that Amanda wasn't taking care of her mother.

But Helene remained enthusiastic about the arrangement; she reported that Amanda was staying home, being of help. She was available to help Helene to the bathroom at any hour. They slept together in Ina's bed. Helene said they were even talking to each other.

"What do you talk about?" Ina asked, a little jealous, out of touch in California.

"Girl stuff," Helene said. "Slumber party stuff. She's had this entire life that I was totally unaware of. It's mind-boggling."

"Has she talked about Gordon?" Ina asked.

"Oh, yes," Helene said. "I ask her questions and she answers them. I can sense her hesitating, wondering if she should tell me something. Then she does. And if I'm shocked by what she tells me, I try not to show it. I'm afraid she'll stop talking."

"Tell me something shocking," Ina said.

"Oh, I couldn't. It's between Amanda and me."

"We've never had secrets from each other," Ina said, hurt.

"Yes, we have."

"We have?"

"Oh, yes. You don't know the half of it, dear."

Amanda's trial was postponed. Her bail remained in force, and Ina had to return to California without her sister. She cried at her backdoor when Ray tried to lead her away. Helene promised she would stay in touch, like someone she had met at a party, someone she would never see again.

"Come back with me," Ina said to Helene.

"I can't," Helene said. "Amanda needs me."

"I need you, too. I miss you in Los Angeles."

Helene grinned smugly. "I'll be out there soon," she said. "This is a good chance to get to know your children."

"I know my children. They have lives to lead," Ina said.

"Are you a burden to them?" Helene asked innocently.

"No. But they're busy," Ina said. "I don't have their capacity to stay busy. I need someone as slow and easily amused as me. I need you."

"And you'll have me, dear. Just be patient."

The trial of Amanda Bolton was held in the dead late heat of

August. A jury of seven women and five men was impaneled. Enclosed in a dank, high-ceilinged room where the marble walls were moist to the touch, a judge who kept a fan running under his bench dispatched with all the testimony before lunch. The deceased's wife was summoned for the defense. She was a spidery, disgruntled woman with a carefully rehearsed tale of woe and regular physical abuse at the hands of her husband. She already had plans to remarry.

Amanda was next.

"I met Walter Gordon in front of my apartment," she testified. "I had parked in the street after going shopping and I had too many bags to carry in one trip. I closed my trunk, but not all the way, and I carried one load upstairs. When I came back down he was standing by my car. He said I shouldn't leave my trunk unlocked in that neighborhood, especially with it full of groceries. I thanked him. He offered to carry my groceries upstairs for me. I said I could manage. He said he understood my reluctance. So I lugged the rest of my groceries upstairs and I figured I'd never see him again. I knew he was handsome. He didn't wear a wedding ring. He had potential. He was about my age, a little older. There was just something about him I liked. He was sexy. I remember wishing he had asked me to go somewhere. For dinner. Or a drink. But I wasn't stupid enough to let some strange guy carry my groceries into my apartment. So I just forgot about him. A week or so later, I saw him again. I was getting out of my car. He started to talk to me like we were old friends. This was in the afternoon. I asked him if he lived around there and he said no. He said he was just in the neighborhood and wondered if he could find me again. So he came to my apartment building and waited. He offered me a drink from his thermos bottle. It was lemonade. We sat on the grass in the front yard and drank lemonade. Then he said he was hungry and I waited for him to ask me to dinner. But he didn't. Finally I went upstairs and made us a couple of sandwiches and brought them down. He was very honest about being married. We talked all afternoon and he seemed genuinely interested in me. I was waiting for him to put a move on me, because I was disappointed he was married and I wanted the satisfaction of cutting him down. But he never did. He just kept talking and then late in the afternoon he asked if he could use my bathroom. I said I didn't think so. We talked another ten minutes and finally he said if he couldn't use my bathroom he would have to go find another one. So I was faced with a decision and the decision I made was not to let him leave. I allowed him into my apartment. That turned out to be the last time we were out together in public. He used the bathroom. Then he walked around complimenting me on where I lived. His attitude was subtly changed. He was slightly more confident. Just a tad cocky. He had worked his way into my apartment. The rest, as it turned out, was easy.

"He began to come over regularly in the afternoon, three and four times a week. And for the first two or three months this arrangement was what I lived for. I changed my hours at work to be available. I waited for him to appear. He had a job that allowed him to come and go as he pleased. We had lunch, something to drink. Sex. In the beginning he was very attentive and sweet. But that changed as the novelty of me wore off. He turned out to be the type of man who demanded that all his needs be taken care of pretty much chop chop. He'd come in: Right away we'd eat if he was hungry. Or have a drink if he wanted a drink. Or have sex if he wanted sex. He didn't go in much for idle conversation. After his needs were taken care of he started to complain about his life. How he didn't make enough money. How he was trapped by his wife and kids. How he never had any time during the day to do what he felt like doing. How his life was one aggravation after another. He went on like this. He would bring a bottle of something. As he talked and drank, he got angrier and angrier. He turned mean. He'd start to pick on me a little. Tell me I had trapped him, too, just like his wife and kids. He said everything I did for him was all part of my trap. Food, sex, drink, someone to talk to. All a trap. He accused me of trying to get him away from his wife. Which was not the case—*ever.* I told him I didn't force him to come back to me. He was free to go. He hated that. He hated when I stood up to him. When I had an answer for him. He knew I didn't buy what he was saying. I called it his 'trap crap' to his face and he laughed. He said that was the first funny thing I'd ever said to him. He said women didn't have a sense of humor. They laughed, but they couldn't make men laugh. He said that to get me mad. He was happier when he could make me mad, or scared, or just unhappy. We couldn't just have a normal afternoon together—where he told me things and I told him things and we were just together, like at the start. Where we could have sex because we both wanted to. We couldn't just take a nap or eat in front of the TV. Just be together. We always had to take care of *him*. One day he came over with a new pool cue. It was in two pieces, in a leather case like a musical instrument. He had paid over a thousand dollars for it. And he complained about money. I didn't even know he played pool. One thing led to another, we were in bed, and he told me he wanted to put his cue inside me. I drew the line at that. He kept coaxing me, rubbing that cold stick along my leg. I kept refusing. He went into a sulk like he always did when he didn't get his way. He laid there with his back to me. Holding his cue. I was not finished, personally, I just wasn't interested in a pool cue. So I started rubbing his back, talking to him. I could tell he was warming up again. He rolled over and started to kiss me a little, then he tried to force that damn cue inside me. I screamed and he freaked and started to jab me in my thighs and my breasts with the blunt end of that thing. He left bruises. Black and blue circles.

"He always hit me. I hated that and I tried to avoid it, but he didn't really follow any pattern. If I knew that he would hit me only after he got to a certain level of frustration or anger, I could keep him from reaching that level. But some days he would be just enraged about something and not touch me. And some days he'd seem to be in a pretty good mood and then out of the blue he would pop me. I always made a point of getting in one good punch myself, because I thought if he had a bruise or a cut to explain to his wife he might think twice about hitting me. So I raised a mouse on his lip once. And after things had calmed down with the pool cue, he was in the bathroom and I waited for him and when he came out I bashed him good in the neck with it. Left a mark like a long hicky. I wanted him to go home and have his wife say, 'Honey, how did you lose your front teeth? How did you break your nose?' But evidently she never did, because he kept hitting me.

"There was a lot of crime in my neighborhood. Break-ins. Assaults. Rumors of women being dragged into alleys by gangs of men. I worked at night and got home late and I was nervous. I had trouble sleeping. I talked to him about this—he said not to worry, he would protect me. Sometime later, a week or so, I mentioned it again to him. He said not to worry—I said I *was* worried. He almost popped me again. I could see it in his eyes. The *frustration.* The way he got when demands were made on him. The next time he was over he handed me this cigar box. Inside was a gun—a twenty-two. And a box of bullets. He said he had paid a hundred and fifty dollars for it, but it was his gift to me because I was such a sweetheart. I didn't really want a gun. It frightened me. A big dog would have been more my style. But he insisted I keep it and I put the thing high up in my closet where it would do me no good at all if someone broke into my apartment.

"I had been planning to go to Los Angeles. My mother and aunt were going out there—I was looking forward to visiting them. I needed a vacation. I needed time away from Gordon. I was going to get my things together, then fly out. In the back of my mind I was hoping to start fresh out west. But I made the mistake of telling him. I tried to be decent. I should have just left. He hit the roof immediately. No gradually getting angrier. One second he was in a pretty good mood because we'd just had sex. The next he's in a rage. He told me I couldn't go. He refused to let me go. I got out of bed because I could see where all this was leading—to me getting slugged. I got out of bed and put my clothes on. I told him he had no power over me. I realized then I just wanted him to leave. I wanted to be rid of him. So I told him to get out. I was scared of him. It was like my eyes opened for the first time since I'd met him. I wanted him gone. But I also understood that he would never leave without hurting me. And he would never stay away. I could kick him out and tell him we were finished—and he might punch me, then leave—but he would come back. He would get horny and come back—and I would probably let him in. But right at that moment, I just wanted him to leave. So I told him to get out. He got up and got dressed. He didn't say anything. I went into the kitchen and put on some coffee. He went into the bathroom and brushed his teeth. He had a complete set of toiletries at my place. I wanted to tell him to take them but I decided not to press my luck. That would be one more thing to hold him there a little longer. I'd throw them away later. He came into the kitchen and said he wanted a cup of coffee. I said no. He told me he would come and see me the next day. I said no, I was going to L.A. He didn't say anything to that. I was scared to death. This was a new strategy he was using, being somewhat reasonable. I'd never seen it before and that's why it frightened me so badly. I didn't know at what point he would flip out. He sat at the table to put on his shoes and socks. He was very handsome. And he smelled so good. He'd put on after-shave and brushed his teeth. He knew what I liked. He was a charmer. A snake. I went into the bathroom hoping he'd leave while I was in there. He was still at the table when I came out. I stood by the door. I remember thinking I had almost gotten rid of him. He was two steps from being outside. But then he started patting his pockets. His keys were missing. He went into the bedroom—there they were. On his way back I let him get too close and that's when he hit me—the hardest yet—one punch right under my right breast. My feet came up off the floor.

"I was on the floor in the hall when I woke up. He was gone. He'd left the door open. I closed it, locked it up tight, then crawled back to bed. I got up later and made myself some dinner. My chest hurt so much. I slept off and on, then at four A.M. I finally got up for good and started to pack. At eight A.M. I phoned the airlines and booked a flight to Los Angeles. At nine I called work and gave notice. They were stunned, to say the least. I had vacation coming—they offered to let me take it right away. But I wanted to quit. He would keep after me if I stayed. He would find me there. I wanted to leave no trace.

"I fell asleep again and slept until early in the afternoon. When I woke up I knew he was there. Not in the apartment, but in the building, or the street outside, coming to see me. I got up and went to the door. I looked through the peephole and there he was. He knocked. He had brought flowers and a big bottle of champagne. And carry-out pasta. Open up, he said. He wanted to apologize. He offered to pay for my ticket to L.A. He kept knocking and finally I just let him in. I knew I was never going to be rid of this guy. He was very friendly. Sweet. We ate the food and drank champagne. He did the dishes. A first. He wanted to call the airline and put my ticket on his credit card, but I said that wasn't necessary. I didn't mention L.A. I was going to play along, do as he wished, let him go home when he was ready. Then I would just leave. He'd come over again and I'd be gone. He'd get the hint then, maybe.

"We went to bed. It was very nice. He talked and laughed. He took my desires into consideration. Also a first. I started to feel so sad, because it could have been that way all the time. He was capable of decency. If he kept it up—if he didn't *play* at it to get something—I would have followed him to the ends of the earth. When he was through he even held on to me. This was a new man. We took a nap. When we woke up I wanted to have sex again, but he wasn't interested. His mood had changed. This black look was in his eyes. I remember thinking he had almost fooled me. That little bit of tenderness and affection had already started to melt me—but when I saw that look in his eyes, I knew he was the same old Gordon.

"I got up and got dressed. I went into the kitchen. He came in and started complaining about his wife—something along those lines. I was only half listening. I wanted him to leave so I could get on with my packing. Out of nowhere he starts telling me about plans he has for us. He would leave his wife and kids, he'd marry me. We'd be happy forever. He said I couldn't go to L.A. because that would ruin our plans. He said we had a future together.

"I said nothing. I stayed busy. A moving target. He accused me of not listening and I said I *was* listening. He asked me to repeat what he'd just said and I did, word for word. He came up to try to hug me and I let him, but when he let me go and stepped back he slapped me across the side of the head—then he hit me with his fist right where he'd hit me before, and I threw up pasta and champagne on him. I disgusted him. He called me a pig. I remember very clearly deciding I had had enough. He went to the bathroom to wash his face and wet a rag to wipe his shirt—and while he was gone I took the gun out of the closet.

"He opened the bathroom door and I was waiting there and I shot him between the eyes and he fell dead at my feet and that was that. I didn't look at him again. I wrote down the address of where I'd be in Los Angeles, then I called a cab to take me to O'Hare. I didn't worry if anyone had heard the shot. Anywhere along the line I could be arrested—and I didn't care. As it was I made it to L.A., where I had a wonderful time. When I was ready I called the police in Chicago and told them where they could find me and where they could find Gordon's body. Not surprisingly, he hadn't been missed."

An aura of rectitude and inevitability enveloped Amanda as she stepped down from the witness stand. The jury was given the case in the afternoon and they filed out of the room, the last woman in line glancing back at the defendant, which Ina took as a good sign. But they weren't gone long. They returned the next morning with a guilty verdict and Amanda was taken back into custody. She was allowed to hug her mother across a railing. A bailiff waited. Helene whispered something to her daughter. They both were crying. She was to be sentenced a month later and Ray, Ina, and Helene flew in from California for the hearing. The judge admitted he was moved by Amanda's testimony, but he could not overlook the sheer weight of her having killed a man, deficient as he may have been in some respects. He also was troubled by the sense that Amanda had seemed to come to a decision to kill Walter Gordon, and even allowing for the brutality of his actions there existed the impression of premeditated murder, and for that he sentenced Amanda to twenty years in Dwight Correctional Center. Her lawyer was delighted with that length of time; he was confident she could be out in ten.

His cheerful assurances enraged Helene.

"Ten years?" she screamed, batting with her handbag at the

spot where she gauged the man to be, but missing by plenty, for the lawyer had already begun to move on to his next case.

"Ten years," he repeated, coming back a step. "Each day she serves and stays out of trouble—two days are taken off her sentence. Time moves twice as fast as in the real world. She killed a man who had a wife and kids. The head of a household. I went into this expecting her to get forty years, out in twenty. So a twenty-spot, out in ten? Hey, ten years is nothing. That Amanda is a terrific storyteller."

The lawyer went away with his shoulders squared, his step brisk.

Ina steered Helene to a bench along the hall.

"What did he mean, she's a terrific storyteller?" Helene asked.

"He means she sold her story to the judge," Ina said. "She was convincing."

"He thinks she's lying."

"No, he doesn't," Ina said.

"He doesn't believe her."

"What does it matter if he believes her or not? It's over now."

Helene said, "He might have tried harder if he believed her. He might have kept her out of prison."

"She admitted killing him," Ina said. "The only argument was over why."

"She had her reasons," Helene said. "With better planning—and I told her this—she could have avoided being caught."

EPILOGUE

◆ ────────────────────────────────────

Ina

Helene comes to me now in the evenings to tell me she is bored with our life here in Los Angeles. She has been hinting at travel. In her idle hours she makes plans to get the Omega and curl back down the mountain from Annie's house. She tries to tantalize me with visions of the world we haven't seen.

I will admit it is an intriguing possibility. We have slipped away before; we could do it again.

But circumstances hold me here.

I am not a burden to my children. It is something I take pride in. They moved away from me years ago, almost at my urging. I don't think it would be fair now to expect them to return. So I have encouraged Ray to keep his life as it was, and he assures me that is the case. But all he does is work. I try to account for his time out of my sight, hoping to find an illicit portion of the day when I couldn't reach him in an emergency, when he might be with someone or enjoying a pastime he wanted to keep secret, but every minute is taken up with work or traveling between stores. He calls me frequently and these calls become bothersome, I must admit. He means well, but I don't need such careful looking after. If he calls with news or something to laugh about, fine. But I suspect he is only making sure I haven't hurt myself or his home.

We have settled into Amanda's room. Helene knows her way around already. All her medicine, her testing kits, our clothes, our belongings, they are precisely arranged in our room on the top floor. It isn't a large room, but we share the space without problems. After countless discussions about the impossibility of living together in Chicago, where we had two empty houses to choose from, we now find ourselves getting along just fine in one room shaped like a stop sign.

Ray had Braille pads installed on the elevator buttons and then learned Helene didn't know Braille. Now he is paying for her to learn. The excursions into the center of the city to attend the class and the confidence she developed learning the language got her thinking about traveling again. She always wants to go to the library to read books and old newspapers in her new language. She is proud of the toughened skin at the ends of her fingers. I read her the paper at home; headlines first, and if her interest is caught, the rest of the story. We don't concern ourselves with the outside world. Helene always wants a story that will make her laugh. She likes to hear the weather forecasts, but only if they do not predict conditions that will lead to cataclysmic fires or the washing away of the earth under her feet.

The only time she had a sip of beer was after a tremor in the earth, when the little porcelain boy holding her rings began to dance on her dresser top. The picture on the TV went off; a moment later it returned, sharper than before, but upside down. The refrigerator door opened and a can of beer fell out on the bathroom floor and rolled toward us.

"It's a sign," I said.

"What's happening?" Helene asked. She was flat on her bed, her hands gripping the mattress.

"A tiny earthquake," I said.

I opened the can and caught the fizz with my mouth and poured the beer into two glasses. She sat up and drank.

"A sign of what?" Helene asked, her lips frothy.

"Nothing. Just relax."

But it was difficult to relax. We spent the rest of the day waiting for the big roll that would crumple our tower. We were reluctant to get into the elevator, but not scared enough to take the stairs down. Ray phoned from his car on the Santa Ana Freeway and reported feeling nothing.

We have been back once to visit Amanda. Helene wanted to

drive but Ray couldn't spare the time. We drove a rented car from O'Hare to Dwight and that was nice. Helene pestered Ray to let her take the wheel for a mile or so and he glanced over at her nervously, afraid she was losing her mind right before his eyes. Amanda showed us around the prison as much as she was allowed. She looked tired. They had put her in the laundry room because she was new, and now her focus was on getting transferred from there to the infirmary. She explained the challenge of getting the job she wanted with an intense, hard-lighted look in her eyes. She had taken up smoking and jogging. No questions about California; she didn't seem to want to hear. Helene cried most of the time, seeing her daughter caught there in the grim fact of the place. She had been able to forget, or deceive herself, in Los Angeles. Forgetting again was difficult, something I had to start working on the instant we stepped back out through the gates. I promised Helene that we would return often, but I thought it unlikely. Once a year. Maybe twice. Amanda could write. She could phone. But there was no point in putting my sister through that trip more often than was necessary.

The insurance company gave Helene problems after the fire at her house. Because the fire had been set, they pestered her for details about her whereabouts when the fire started. When they learned she was blind, they questioned me and Ray, her alibis, thoroughly. They wanted a detailed accounting of everything that burned inside the house and Helene was unable to provide much of a list. I was of some help, but in truth I hadn't paid that much attention. Possessions have never held that large a spot in my heart. I liked the people in a house and those things that gave me comfort.

Ray suggested we sit down and imagine the house a room at a time. Don't leave that room until we had remembered every inch of it and what it held. This was of some benefit, although I kept seeing the rooms in their vandalized state. Helene was living in my house with Amanda then and we spent hours on the phone thinking about her house. Often my mind wandered and I would step out of her kitchen into a room in my own house. These little excursions turned up memories and we would begin to reminisce and lose the point. Amanda was of little help. She had a clear image of her childhood home, of the feelings it stirred, but the details were lost. We came up with a list of possessions. The insurance agent saw the list, read it carefully, then said they would also need photographs of the items in their burned condition.

"I can't do that," Helene told me on the phone. "I don't even have a camera."

She decided to take what the insurance company offered, a substantial amount of money, but less than the property was worth. It was the option I suggested. The effort and heartache were not worth a few extra thousand dollars. In addition to the insurance money, she was paid $37,500 by Mr. Patkin for her land, and all that added up to a nice deposit in a California bank.

"But what if you die before I do?" she asked fearfully. "What if Ray moves me out after you're gone? He's only letting me live there because you'll be with me. What if I suddenly have to pay for housing? Food? That money will be gone in two years."

"He'd never throw you out," I said. But it was a new worry. My plan had always been to outlive Helene, as it had been to outlive Vincent. Everything was easier if I was left behind to take care of things.

I went to Ray and said, "Promise you won't evict Helene if I die before she does."

His look was spooked. This talk of death, it bothered him. But he agreed and asked if I was withholding some health information from him. I said the promise was only to ease my mind and Helene's. She was skeptical of his resolve when I reported Ray's promise to her.

Once Amanda and Helene no longer required it, my house sold quickly to a young couple with children. An attraction for them was the fact that all my furniture, cutlery, dishes, linen, drapes, lawn mower, a garage full of tools, and everything else was included in the sale price. It was like moving into a pre-owned life; they only had to provide the personalities. While in town to visit Amanda, Helene, Ray, and I went through my house the day before the closing and I removed the things that meant the most to me. Photographs, primarily. And things that reminded me of Vincent. Ray was valuable because he kept reminding me of the limited room awaiting us in Westwood. Helene kept exclaiming, "You can't leave that behind!" And each time she said that, I tended to agree. But Ray, the grump, the rational ogre, talked sense to me. Nothing existed in my old house that I needed in my new home. So I thinned my life down until it fit into one large cardboard box. The rest I left for the new owners.

I closed on the sale and walked out of the lawyer's office with a fresh-cut check for $144,800. From there, Ray drove us to my bank and I emptied my accounts. My first impulse was to take it in cash, in twenties rolled into tubes, but the amount was too large. I had lost my daring. It was all the money I had in the world; there was no more to go back for. So they totaled up the amount and to that figure I added the check for my house. They wired all of it to Ray's bank in California. At home again I drew up a new will, giving it all to Helene, should I die first; upon Helene's death my fortune will go into a trust for Meaghan Bixler, whom I don't see much of anymore.

Meg spends all of her time downstairs with Katy. Below Katy's, the stairs are gone. They have been closed off, torn down, the gate at the bottom bricked shut.

Early on a Sunday morning, before Ray awoke, Annie came to our door to take us to church.

Annie was dressed more appropriately for tennis, her sunglasses pushed up into her hair because the light there in Ray's jungle was faint and fragrant. She had on blue shorts and a Dodgers shirt and yellow beach clogs.

"This joint gives me the creeps," she whispered to us as we went outside. "Too much like a monastery. All those towers and the silence and the gurgling streams."

She had brought the Mustang. The top was cranked back. Helene took the front seat and I sat in the middle of the back seat, my elbows propped behind them, where I could rub my sister's neck to calm her. Annie pulled the sunglasses over her eyes and we were off.

"What church are we going to?" Helene asked. She had chosen for the occasion her best summer dress, with a bow at her breast and a hat and handbag to match.

Annie glanced at me in the mirror. I was curious myself.

"It's my church," she said, almost defiantly. "I should've told you not to get dressed up."

We followed the route we always took from Ray's house to Annie's house. At the bottom of the California Avenue incline she turned right and we drove along the ocean for two miles. Helene held her hat in place. I had a beer headache and kept my face hidden from the wind behind Helene's seat. We passed the turnoff we would take to get up to Narrow Canyon Road. I guessed we were going to a church in Malibu, someplace unstructured and relaxed, where you could attend in your bathing suit and walk around during the sermon.

But then Annie put on her signal and turned across the oncoming lanes into a beach parking lot. She followed the blacktop to the point farthest from the entrance and stopped.

"My church," she said.

"The beach?" I said.

"The ocean," she said. "The perfect place to be alone."

Helene sat bewildered and expectant while Annie and I got out of the car. Helene took my arm and we followed Annie down a flight of wooden steps to the sand.

"This might make a nice church," she whispered to me, but loud enough for Annie, who was one step down, to hear.

Annie turned to me and smiled. I shrugged.

"It might," I said, more for my daughter than Helene.

"I just stay an hour," Annie said. She walked half tiptoe through the loose sand, her legs crossing back and forth over each other. She was making a line toward the darker, firmer sand near the water. Helene and I struggled to keep up. There was nothing to push against as we tried to walk.

"Then I go back home and make breakfast for Don and Meg,"

she said. "This calms me down. All week long I'm being left behind by those two—especially Don. Rush out before the sun's up. Come home after dark. Is it necessary to be at work before six A.M.? I wonder. I get tired of being left behind. This is my chance to make them wonder about me for a while." She had gained a strip of firm sand and kicked off each of her clogs in succession, catching them in the air and slapping them together angrily. "My coming here," she said, "doesn't reflect too well on my marriage—I understand that. But I don't care. Does Don care what his being gone seventeen hours a day says about our marriage? Obviously not."

"He loves you," I said, but having no proof.

"What about the fact my daughter loves another girl?" Annie asked. Helene turned her attention to this. She had been staring at the ocean.

"I don't know. A phase?" I offered. Her question made me anxious to help, to not waste an opportunity. So much time had passed since my children had come to me for answers.

"My tennis friends? Their daughters are boy-crazy. I have nothing to contribute," Annie said.

"No chance of teen pregnancy," Helene chimed in.

Annie laughed, aghast.

"Can I taste the salt water?" my sister asked. She took one unerring step toward the Pacific. "Listen to that," she said. "It's like breathing."

We removed our shoes, and then, there in the open, I reached up under my sister's skirt to unhook her nylons and roll them down her legs. Then I removed my own. The ocean was cold, the dying edge of each wave fanning up across the sand before heading back out. Helene clutched my arm, laughing like she was six years old, as I led her into the water. A wave broke around our feet, and the next one wet our knees. She put her finger down and touched the water, then put the finger in her mouth.

"We're farther west than anybody else we know," Helene said.

"What about someone in Hawaii?" I asked.

"Who do we know in Hawaii?"

"I don't know. But someone might have moved there. It's possible."

"All right, then," said Helene. "We are farther west than anyone we know from our shrinking circle of acquaintances."

Avon Trade Books—
The Best in Fiction

THE WIDOWS' ADVENTURES
Charles Dickinson
70847-7/$8.95 US/$10.95 Can

THE FOOL'S PROGRESS:
AN HONEST NOVEL
Edward Abbey
70856-6/$9.95 US/$11.95 Can

SPARTINA
John Casey
71104-4/$8.95 US/$10.95 Can

THE LAST TO GO
Rand Richards Cooper
70862-0/$7.95 US/$9.95 Can

THE TWENTY-SEVENTH CITY
Jonathan Franzen
70840-X/$8.95 US/$10.95 Can

NIGHT OVER DAY OVER NIGHT
Paul Watkins
70737-3/$7.95 US/$9.95 Can

THE EYE OF THE HEART
edited by Barbara Howes
70942-2/$10.95 US/$12.95 Can

Muriel Spark

A FAR CRY FROM KENSINGTON
70786-1/$7.95 US

THE GIRLS OF SLENDER MEANS
70937-6/$7.95 US

LOITERING WITH INTENT
70935-X/$7.95 US

Alison Lurie

THE TRUTH ABOUT LORIN JONES
70807-8/$7.95 US

ONLY CHILDREN
70875-2/$7.95 US/$9.95 Can

FOREIGN AFFAIRS
70990-2/$7.95 US/$9.95 Can